HE SMELLED SOMETHING SUSPICIOUS . . .

Jackie smiled brightly at the manager of the dog-training academy. "Tell me—if I were to sign Jake up for a class here, I think I would really have to see the grounds. Could you show me around?"

"We do our obedience training right out front there." He gestured toward the large field that separated the kennel operation from the house.

"Oh." Jackie bit her lip. "But what if Jake needs to spend the night? I'll have to inspect the dogs' living quarters, I think, before—"

"Look, Mrs. Walsh. *If* that's your name." Tom Mann had risen suddenly from his chair, and he stood glowering at Jackie. He raised his voice and pointed an accusing finger at her. "I don't want to be rude, but we've had an awful lot of reporters snooping around out here. Some of them pretended they wanted to have their dogs trained. They were a *little* bit better at it than you are—because at least they brought their own dogs with them, not some rent-a-dog from the nearest kennel." He gestured sharply at Jake.

Jake looked solemnly at Mann. . . .

Diamond Books by Melissa Cleary

DOG COLLAR CRIME

MELISSA CLEARY

DIAMOND BOOKS, NEW YORK

This book is a Diamond original edition, and has never
been previously published.

DOG COLLAR CRIME

A Diamond Book / published by arrangement with
the author

PRINTING HISTORY
Diamond edition / May 1993

ISBN: 1-55773-896-3

Diamond Books are published by The Berkley Publishing Group,
200 Madison Avenue, New York, New York 10016.
The name "DIAMOND" and its logo are trademarks
belonging to Charter Communications, Inc.

PRINTED IN THE UNITED STATES OF AMERICA

10 9 8 7 6 5 4 3 2 1

DOG COLLAR CRIME

CHAPTER 1

Among the members of the executive committee of the Greater Palmer Dog Fanciers Association, all was not well. Angry retorts flew fast and furious between the former friends who made up the small group. Committee meetings were often contentious affairs, and when the object of the committee's interest was a subject close to everyone's heart—as it was among the Palmer Dog Fanciers—feelings were often hurt. The monthly committee meetings had never been particularly pleasurable.

But no other meeting had approached this March debacle for sheer venom. In all the thirteen years that the executive committee had assembled, never had the members of the small group exhibited such animosity toward one another.

A stout woman of a certain age was speaking in a low, throaty voice that was accustomed to command. Her figure amply filled the large armchair from which, for the last half hour, she had been launching rockets of recrimination and missiles of disgust.

"You did it *deliberately,* Melvin. Don't try to hide it. You played a dirty trick on me, to humiliate me and embarrass me."

"Thalia, for the last time, just shut your trap." The man

accused of playing a dirty trick was standing near a portable
bar in the corner. From a ceramic pitcher in the shape of a
basset hound, he added a touch of water to a stiff Scotch on
the rocks. His name was Melvin Sweeten, and he was widely known to breed the finest championship basset hounds in
the country. He was also the owner of Mel Sweeten's Dog
Academy, a training school and kennel that he operated
here on his own property. He had made quite a lot of
money off of other people's dogs, but his heart belonged
to bassets.

The decor of his living room was a testament to his
devotion to the breed: the room was lit by basset-hound
lamps and decorated with portraits of bassets. On the tables
were ashtrays and coasters that had been painted with the
likenesses of bassets, and before the fireplace was a large
ottoman whose needlepointed cover showed a basset curled
up, asleep.

Mel Sweeten bore a certain resemblance to a basset
hound himself: his ears had long, dangling lobes covered
with a fine peach fuzz, and his lower eyelids seemed to
droop in the middle. His belly protruded, and his legs
were a bit too short for his torso. His feet were enormous and rather thick. Most of the time his face had a
worried look. He looked even more worried than usual
tonight.

He wheeled on Thalia Gilmore, the stout woman who
had accused him. "I'm sick and tired of listening to you
nag. Just give it up. There is absolutely nothing wrong with
the hound you bought from me. There is everything wrong
with the way you have handled him, from the beginning.
You totally ruined him for anything serious, and he was the
best pup in the litter."

"Pah!" spat Thalia Gilmore. "Best pup you could find at
the Humane Society, you mean."

Mel Sweeten shook his head. He and Thalia Gilmore had been having this argument for nearly two years now. Somehow she always managed to bring the subject up. She had bought a puppy from Sweeten, one of a litter born to Ch. Nightingale of the Forest, otherwise known as Karen. Karen was now snoozing outside in her kennel with her friend and sometime consort, Ch. Dartagnan's Finest Hour, known familiarly as Fred.

Karen had been carefully bred three or four times, and her pups had always met with great success—all but the one that had been sold to Thalia Gilmore, which had somehow turned out badly. Thalia Gilmore claimed that Mel had swindled her, substituting a dog-pound refugee for a champion pup. Sweeten claimed that Thalia Gilmore had ruined the dog by not knowing how to handle him properly. It was the old Nature *versus* Nurture controversy, in microcosm.

"I warned you that bassets are difficult. They are not a breed for amateurs," Sweeten said condescendingly.

"Did you hear that, Dick?" bellowed Thalia Gilmore. She was appealing to the third member of the executive committee, Dick Buzone, a lanky, red-haired man of middle age who was lounging on the sofa. His pale skin seemed to shine in the light cast by the basset-hound lamp at his elbow, and his yellowish eyes glittered strangely. He had heard this argument many, many times.

"Both of you are just tiresome," he said in his reedy voice. "Just forget it, Thalia. Move on."

"Move on? Did you hear that insult? How dare he call me an amateur?" By now the stout woman was quivering with rage.

"Probably no worse than a lot of other things one might say about you, Thalia," said Mel Sweeten. He took a stiff swallow of Scotch.

"You *humiliated* me, in front of all my friends, with your

dirty trick. Trying to pass that mongrel off as a purebred dog. You will pay for humiliating me, Melvin. And you will pay for what you did to poor Clematis in Philadelphia."

"Oh, lay off, Thalia. I never touched Clematis. She was sick from the chicken livers you fed her the night before. You should know better than that."

"We have a lot to talk about tonight," Buzone reminded them, glancing at his watch, "and I have to leave in half an hour. So I suggest you stop your childish squabbling and let us get on with the business at hand. Mel, you've had enough to drink. You always get nasty when you drink, and you've heaped more than enough abuse on Thalia. So knock it off. Let's get to work."

Buzone reached for a clipboard on the coffee table and harangued them with the points that needed to be covered. The first big dog show of the spring season was right around the corner, and as judges and organizers of the event they had a great many important tasks yet to perform—setting up the ticket booth, designating volunteers to the clean-up crew, and, most important of all, discussing the sponsorship of the Palmer Dog Fanciers cup. There were two dog-food companies in hot competition for the honor, but Buzone was in favor of giving the sponsorship this year to a pharmaceutical company that had developed a new heartworm pill. He didn't mention to the other two members of the committee that he had just bought a large block of shares in the drug company, but pushed for his position on other grounds.

The argument had gone on for a good twenty-five minutes when a baying noise erupted outside. Something or someone had aroused Fred and Karen from their slumber. Stiffly, Sweeten got up to find out what had caused the disturbance, leaving Thalia Gilmore alone with Dick Buzone. She instantly turned on him.

"If you don't back me up on this, Dick, I might have to go to Am-DOG and tell them what I know."

Am-DOG was the American Dog Owners Group, the watchdog organization that established all the guidelines for breeders, show judges, and competitors in the dog-show circuit. Dick Buzone was president of the Palmer chapter of Am-DOG, but he was known to be in bad standing with the national president, who wanted him out. Nobody was certain about the reasons for the animosity between the two, but it was widely known to exist.

"Shut up, Thalia," said Buzone mildly. "You talk too much."

"He poisoned Clematis in Philadelphia. You know it as well as I do. He put something in her carry crate."

"Thalia, that's water over the dam. That was seven months ago."

"Seven months. That's right. Perhaps I should charge you interest on the two thousand dollars you owe me."

"I don't owe you a nickel, Thalia."

"You *promised* me, absolutely promised. And first Clematis was poisoned by that man, and then he sold me a dog with forged papers."

"I never promised you anything, Thalia." He turned on her. "And I suggest that if you want to play with the big boys in this game, you learn to keep your mouth shut."

She appeared to digest this advice, which had sounded more like a threat than anything Buzone had uttered so far. The two sat a few moments longer in uneasy silence. Finally, Sweeten came back in the room.

Fred and Karen had stopped their baying, but Sweeten looked shaken and pale.

"Got a prowler?" Buzone asked, his tone bored.

"Something like that," replied Sweeten.

The three uneasy allies went on with their meeting.

In another fifteen minutes Buzone had prevailed, the heartworm-pill company had been awarded the sponsorship, and the meeting broke up on a note of boredom, with enmity all around.

CHAPTER 2

"Oh, yeah? Well, *I* heard your dog was afraid," said Eric Persil contentiously. "I heard that when it happened, he just ran away and left his owner there to die, because he was a *coward.*"

Peter Walsh didn't bother to respond to the insult. He merely reached over and scratched Jake behind the left ear. Jake stirred but did not open his eyes. Apparently he would ignore the affront too.

Peter's friend Isaac Cook, however, was not one to take such matters lightly. Besides, he had himself once been skeptical of Jake, but Isaac had learned to admire and respect him. As Isaac's practiced fingers flew skillfully over the buttons controlling the Nintendo game, he pried his glance away from the television screen for an instant— just long enough to give Eric Persil a withering look.

Ordinarily, that look of Isaac's was enough to send his classmates running for cover. But it didn't seem to be working on this cold and rainy March afternoon.

"Well, look at him," persisted Eric defiantly. "He just *sleeps* all day."

"I wouldn't be too sure about it, Eric," replied Peter. "Could be that Jake's just resting up so he can take a bite out of you later."

Some people.

While speculation about his mettle raged around him, Jake was drowsily dreaming on the floor, stretched out lengthwise with his back along the length of the sofa in Peter's den. Peter was seated on the floor next to him, also with his back against the sofa. He ran his fingers up through the long, thick fur on the back of Jake's broad shoulders. Jake moved his left front paw in sleepy response, resting it on Peter's outstretched leg.

Jake was a German shepherd—or, if you took Isaac Cook as your authority, an Alsatian shepherd—a veteran of impressive years, with an interesting but incomplete personal history. He had turned up one morning on Peter's doorstep with a bullet wound in one leg and in need of a friend.

That was some months ago. Since the day of his arrival, the dog, whom Peter had christened Jake, had shown no interest in wandering off again. A dog in need of a home is clever indeed if he manages to find a boy in need of a dog.

Jake's cleverness was not under discussion, however; it was his reputation for courage that Eric Persil was determined to savage.

"He doesn't look very brave to me."

Isaac glowered. "You don't know anything, Eric, so why don't you just shut up?"

Peter thumbed through a pile of old comic books on the floor, selected one, and began to read. Peter's collection of old Superman and Spiderman adventures was legendary— the comic books had belonged to his mother when she was a little girl. Nobody was allowed to touch them but Peter and Isaac—so having them out today was kind of rubbing Eric's nose in it.

Eric Persil had never been one to take a hint, however. He had been there for four hours, and showed no interest in leaving until he had got some information. Like everyone else in the fifth-grade class, he was intensely curious about Peter's dog. He had heard rumors.

For starters, Eric had heard that Peter's dog had once belonged to an ex-cop named Matt Dugan. He had also heard that Dugan had been murdered in the seediest neighborhood in Palmer, right behind a nightclub called Leanna's Piano Parlor, and that the dog had been there. Now Eric was trying to pry some inside facts out of Peter.

He had tried the direct approach earlier in the afternoon, but he had been swiftly rebuffed. Now, in his frustrated desire to force from Peter the particulars about Jake, he had resorted to casting aspersions on Jake's character. Even Eric Persil, clumsy and bullying as he was, should have known that this was the wrong procedure.

Peter and Isaac, when they discovered that Jake had once belonged to a murder victim, had embarked on a clandestine bus ride across town one day to take a chilling look at the scene of the crime. There had still been faint chalk marks on the asphalt, indicating the spot where Dugan had fallen, and ominous-looking dark stains that could *easily* have been bloodstains. Probably were bloodstains, the boys had later concurred.

This was the sort of information that Peter and Isaac would never grant to Eric Persil, whom they tolerated but did not actually like. Eric was at Peter's house today through one of those arrangements that mothers make for everyone to have fun together. Peter and Isaac, by tacit consent, were being polite without giving an inch. Eric, they agreed, was sort of a pain. There had been no need to discuss tactics.

"Well?" Eric persisted. "If he's such a great dog, how come the guy that owned him is dead?"

Peter replied without raising his eyes from the page. "Because he was murdered," he said in a reasonable voice.

He might have been discussing fractions or geography, for all the interest that he permitted himself to show. Peter liked to keep things to himself.

"Yeah," agreed Isaac, with passion. "And you'd be dead too if somebody pulled a Magnum on you." He made a pistol with his right hand, aimed at Eric, and fired, making a noise like a gun. Then he turned his attention back to the game in progress, Super Mario Brothers.

"Unh-unh," protested Eric. "Not if I had a really *good* guard dog. A *really* good one, not some dog that the police didn't want anymore."

"Shut up, Eric," said Isaac again, his eyes glued to the television screen.

From Peter's and Isaac's point of view, the subject of Jake's bravery wasn't even debatable; still, it was a fascinating subject, one that merited constant discussions between the two friends, and other people as well.

"So?" Eric's voice had become a whine. "Why didn't he attack the guy?"

"Look. Maybe he did," said Peter. "We weren't there, so how do we know? Maybe he bit the guy. Took off his right arm, all the way up to the elbow."

"He looks too old."

In truth Jake did look as though he might be past his prime. His brown and black coat was tinged with gray, and there were a few pale whitish hairs around his muzzle. But Peter and Isaac knew that Jake could be ferocious—they had put him through his paces one day, and had been amazed at the results. That had been just shortly after they learned that Jake had once been a member of the Palmer K-9 squad. Retired, with distinction, Peter had later been told. Upon his retirement from the K-9 squad, Jake had gone to live with Matt Dugan—who was also retired from the Palmer police, but not with distinction.

"Jake's not too old," Peter replied. He carefully turned the page of the Superman adventure. The story involved Mr. Mxylptlx, one of Peter's favorite villains.

Eric persisted, switching to a logical approach. He leaned forward earnestly.

"Look—if he *bit* the guy, then the police should be able to find him. Like at the hospital, getting his arm sewed back on or something. But my dad told me that they never caught the guy. So your dog *didn't* bite him. He just ran away, probably because he's too old."

"He's not too old," Peter repeated in a tone of certainty. Jake's bullet wound had been proof enough, for Peter, that the dog had fought bravely. But he didn't go into it with Eric. What was more, Jake had recently been called upon to use his skills right here in Peter's own house—he had saved Peter's mother from the frenzied attack of an intruder. Inevitably, this tale too had gotten around a little bit, but Peter didn't like to talk about it. That had been serious stuff, and Peter had been frightened. Of course, Isaac knew the whole story, but Isaac and Peter weren't about to let a nerd like Eric in on the details.

"You don't know if Jake even defended the guy," said Eric. "You weren't even there."

Isaac, nearing the end of his Nintendo game, was also reaching the limit of his patience. He turned to stare at Eric. "Listen," he commanded, pointing an imperious finger at Eric Persil. "What the police know and don't know, *maybe* we know and maybe we don't. But if you don't shut up we'll sic Jake on you, and he'll rip you to shreds. And then we'll go and scatter the pieces out in the country, and nobody will ever know what happened to you."

"Hey, Isaac, is that a promise or a threat?" Eric did his best to sound sarcastic. "I don't believe this old mutt's got

what it takes." He glanced nervously toward the sleeping
dog. He didn't sound convinced. "Gimme that." He grabbed
the Nintendo controls from Isaac.

Peter and Isaac exchanged a look. Eric Persil was a
colossal pain.

Peter sighed and turned a page of the comic book. "Hey,
Eric. What time is your mother coming to pick you up?"

Not far away from Peter Walsh's house, at the Central
Precinct of the Palmer police department, Jake was a subject
of another, equally considered debate.

Cosmo Gordon was easing his large frame back into the
well-worn wooden armchair opposite Lieutenant Michael
McGowan's desk. Gordon dropped a manila envelope on
the floor. The envelope landed with a loud slap. In it
was a postmortem report for McGowan. "So, Mike, what's
eating you?"

"Hi, Cosmo." He was leaning comfortably back in his
swivel chair, his long fingers toying idly with a rubber band.
He looked relaxed; but Cosmo Gordon, who knew him well,
could sense the worry. The senior medical examiner in
Palmer, Gordon had worked with McGowan on hundreds
of homicides, and the two were close friends despite the
twenty-year difference in their ages. "Brought the report?"
asked McGowan.

Gordon nodded.

McGowan, his dark blue eyes in shadow, scowled up at
the medical examiner. "Cosmo, I've been thinking about it,
and I have to tell you I'm still kind of worried. I'm not sure
it's safe for her to keep that animal."

Gordon knew instantly who the "her" was—Jackie Walsh,
the woman who, with her young son, had adopted Matt
Dugan's dog. The dog had been present at the time of
Dugan's murder, and there had been some talk in police

circles that the animal might be useful, when and if the murderer was caught.

"We've been over all this, Mike," answered Gordon. "She didn't seem to me to be likely to change her mind about it. They're both too attached, both she and the boy. Besides, she's probably better off with a guard dog."

Gordon had remarked to his wife Nancy, just the other day, that McGowan had obviously fallen for Jackie Walsh.

Gordon didn't blame the younger man. Jackie Walsh was a very attractive woman, with energy and brains to match. An instructor in the film department at Rodgers University, she had recently been involved in a homicide case. Involved, hell, thought Gordon. She had helped them nail the murderer, and without her the Palmer police would have been nowhere on the case. A spunky woman.

But she was also recently divorced, and gave every indication of wanting to keep her distance—not just from McGowan, it was nothing personal—from men in general. In Gordon's book, being gun-shy was understandable—but it looked like McGowan was declining to understand.

"A watchdog, sure," said McGowan, opening a palm, conceding a point. "But Dugan's dog? That animal's not a pet, it's a police dog. Not a family friend."

"You forget that Dugan and the dog retired at about the same time," said Gordon. "The dog's had four or five years to adapt to retirement. Besides, if anyone is a friend to that family, it's the dog. Don't forget what happened to Philip Barger's murderer, right there in Jackie Walsh's kitchen."

"Yeah." McGowan considered it. The dog had saved Jackie's life. "I wish we could get the guy who killed Dugan, though. I'd feel better about the whole thing."

"Well, now you're talking. That's what you should really be worrying about, Mike. Not about Jackie. Any leads?"

"No." McGowan shook his head. "It's been more than two months now, and the trail's pretty cold."

"What about the weapon?"

"It hasn't turned up yet—but you know the way with that kind of thing. Either the gun got tossed somewhere, and it'll turn up eventually, or the guy's still got it, and he'll use it again, and then it will still turn up eventually. Ballistics has the info, and when that gun shows we'll get the shooter. It's a waiting game."

"I wish I had paid closer attention to him that night," said Gordon, for perhaps the hundredth time. Shortly before his murder, Dugan had visited Gordon, an old friend from his days on the force. Since his dismissal from the Palmer police, Dugan had gone sadly downhill, drinking heavily and gambling more heavily. There had been talk that some of his bets had been bankrolled by dangerous sources, the kind of people it wasn't smart to borrow from. He had been sensitive enough about people not to ask much of his old friends, especially his cop buddies—nor had most of them sought him out. Gordon, however, had made sure to stay in touch, albeit erratically. He and Matt had been close friends, once.

The night of his visit to Gordon, Matt Dugan had talked, not very coherently, about some kind of conspiracy of corruption in the upper echelons of Palmer politics. He had also mentioned his fear that someone was out to get him.

For once, that night, Cosmo Gordon's judgment had been clouded—not by recalcitrance so much as by pity. Full of sorrow for his old friend's trembling hands and hesitant manner, Gordon hadn't really paid much attention to Dugan's ramblings. He had dismissed them as the talk of a man done in by his own weaknesses.

Three days later Dugan had been shot.

"You're right, Cosmo," said McGowan, breaking a long silence. "I have to get the shooter. Then nobody'll come after Jackie's dog."

"Mike, the dog is okay. Nobody's going to come after him. And whatever you do, skip the advice-giving. Don't try to tell her what to do—you'll only give her a reason to tell you to get lost."

"Yeah." He shot the rubber band across the room and leaned forward. "So. Speaking of dogs, I think I can guess what you've brought me. You've got the results of the postmortem on that dog man that turned up dead today. Melvin Sweeten."

CHAPTER 3

Cosmo Gordon leaned down and picked up the manila envelope from the floor, and tossed it onto McGowan's desk. In it were the contents of his postmortem examination of Melvin Sweeten, Palmer's leading dog trainer and breeder.

"Cause of death, like you thought. And the choke collar looks like it."

"Hmm," said McGowan, pulling out a sheaf of papers. He skimmed it quickly.

Most of the information merely corroborated the conclusions he had reached yesterday, when he had been summoned to examine the body of Mel Sweeten. Sweeten was fairly well known in Palmer as a dog trainer, and he ran the best boarding kennel in the city (charging correspondingly high prices). Sweeten's passion for basset hounds was also well known among those who cared about such things. Mel Sweeten's basset puppies sold for large sums, and when they grew old enough to keep from stepping on their own ears they were entered in dog shows, where they won plenty of ribbons, just for being themselves.

On Wednesday, March 23, Mel Sweeten's body had been found inside one of the dog runs at his establishment. There was a choke collar about his neck—the type used in training dogs to sit and heel. So far, the police had no leads, although the widow, naturally, was being carefully looked over as the suspect of choice.

McGowan put the report down. "And?"

"And nothing. Well, you can read it for yourself, I don't need to spoon-feed you. Time of death, between nine and midnight, give or take the usual. Don't even know why we bother with the time of death in these cases—we almost always have to include a fudge factor of an hour or so. Cause of death, asphyxiation of the glottal apparatus— oh, hell. He was strangled, Mike. Or maybe we should say choked."

"Tell me, Cosmo," said McGowan, leaning back in his chair to shoot a rubber band up at the ceiling, "what kind of guy just sits there while a murderer slips a dog collar around his neck?"

"Kinky, maybe."

"Maybe, but that's not what I've got from witnesses."

"What did they give you?"

McGowan picked up a small notebook and leaned back in his chair. He flipped through the pages, looking down now and then while he gave Gordon the known facts about Sweeten.

"Thirty-nine, married, no kids. Wife is much younger, twenty-six, called Amy. She's a researcher in the art history department at Rodgers. He was kind of a dull guy, if you ask me. Totally into his dogs, his basset hounds—but he made a nice living running a boarding school for dogs, with a staff of one. Charged top dollar."

"What did you make on the wife?"

"I talked to her yesterday afternoon. She was visiting her sister in Wardville, she says, and came home yesterday morning, just in time to find his body. We're waiting for corroboration from the sister—but why would she lie when we can easily check?"

"Huh," agreed Gordon. He stretched out his legs and contemplated his feet.

"Her late husband was widely regarded as the owner of the best strain of bassets in the country. She likes dogs all right, but she's not a fanatic. She says she isn't especially fond of basset hounds"—he consulted his notebook—"because they're 'fussy and stubborn.' Doesn't know who would want to murder him or why, thinks it must have been an accident." McGowan raised his brows. "She actually said that."

"An accident. He accidentally slipped a choke collar around his neck? And then gave it a yank?"

McGowan shrugged. "Who knows? I think she's lying, but I have Felix Cruz checking her whereabouts. Until he pokes a hole in her alibi, that's all we have."

"What time did she get in from her sister's place?"

McGowan looked at his notes. "Early. Nine-thirty, give or take. She unpacked, fixed herself a cup of coffee, and read the newspaper."

"The newspaper is delivered?"

McGowan nodded. "She says she thought that was odd, that Mel hadn't taken in the paper, or that he'd gone out before it came, she wasn't sure which."

"And then what?"

"Then she went into this little study, where she does a lot of reading, and typed up some notes she'd made at the museum in Wardville. Finally at about eleven o'clock she thought the dogs were barking too loud, or something, so she got exasperated and went out to look at them to tell them to shut up."

"Hush Puppies."

"Huh?"

"That's what those dogs are, those basset hounds. They're the Hush Puppies dogs."

"Oh." McGowan laughed. "So they are. Right. So Amy Sweeten goes out to the kennels, which are about a hundred yards from the house, to tell the puppies to hush, but before she actually gets there she sees her husband lying facedown in one of the dog runs. So she turns around and runs inside to the phone to call the doctor."

"She knew he was dead?"

"She thought he'd had a heart attack or something. But, get this, she says she didn't get close enough to him to find out whether or not he was dead." He turned a page of his notebook. "She says, 'I thought it would be more useful to solicit professional help.' " McGowan raised a brow again. "Then she waited inside for the doctor, and when he came they went to the kennel together."

Gordon was frowning. "You think?"

McGowan shrugged. "Yeah—I see it. The problem is, we've got to make it stick."

"Wife comes home from a trip and finds her husband prostrate. She doesn't bother to check if he's breathing, she just calls the old GP up the hill."

"I agree."

"Well, there's your answer. How'd she get the collar on him, though? Some kinky stuff, maybe?"

"You think?"

"Could be." Cosmo Gordon rose to leave.

"Thanks, Cosmo," said McGowan, tapping the report.

"Sure. Keep me posted. Sounds kind of interesting."

"It will be." McGowan permitted himself a smile. "I'm going to talk to all my sources at Rodgers. See what I can dig up about Amy Sweeten from her fellow faculty members."

"Uh-oh," said Gordon. The fellow faculty member in question was Jackie Walsh, of course. "You'd better handle her carefully, Mike. And for God's sake don't try to tell her how to run her life. She probably ran away from her husband because he got too bossy."

"Right," said McGowan. "I'll remember that. Thanks for telling me how to run my life. Now you run away."

Gordon left and McGowan reached for the phone. He didn't need to look up Jackie Walsh's telephone number. Inside of a minute, he had secured himself an invitation to dine tonight with Jackie and Peter. Meat loaf at seven. He smiled and hung up the phone.

CHAPTER 4

At seven thirty-five, when Michael McGowan still hadn't arrived at her newly renovated loft on Isabella Lane, Jackie Walsh found herself torn between irritation and relief.

On the one hand, McGowan had invited himself—and by this time, Peter was getting hungry and was ready for dinner. He was cranky too—probably because he'd spent a long, rainy afternoon inside with that tiresome boy, Eric Persil. Jackie told herself that she just had to learn to say no to Rosemary Persil, the boy's mother. She liked Rosemary well enough, but her son was a nuisance—a "dweeb," according to Peter and his friend Isaac. It wasn't fair to inflict the dweeb on them.

What was more, if Peter were to eat now, then it would just be Jackie and Michael having supper together later on, which was strictly not what Jackie had in mind when McGowan called. Irritating—especially since both Jackie and Peter were looking forward to seeing him. It had been several months since they'd last seen him. Jackie kind of missed him.

On the other hand, Michael's being half an hour late—more, really—meant that maybe the pressure was off. You couldn't be thirty-five minutes late—no, forty minutes late (she glanced again at her watch to make sure)—if you were trying to impress someone. Since he hadn't managed to get there on time, or even close to it, there would be no question of the lieutenant's staying too late, or wanting anything from her but information about Amy Sweeten.

That was where the relief came in, or so Jackie told herself.

Michael McGowan hadn't said so, but of course Amy Sweeten was the reason that he had called. That was fine with Jackie. The murder of Amy's husband was front-page news in Palmer, and it had caused quite a stir at Rodgers University, where Amy was well regarded by the faculty. She wasn't one of them, exactly, being only a teaching assistant and researcher; Jackie suspected that if ever Amy tried to pass herself off as being right up there with the art-history bigwigs, her colleagues would give her the cold shoulder pretty fast.

But where the outside world met the university, in that small union of the two disparate universes, it was clear who was in and who was out. In the faculty cafeteria today, at lunchtime, there had been a lot of discussion about what should and shouldn't be said by the faculty, with a great deal of accompanying talk about solidarity.

Jackie Walsh thought all of that had been nothing but claptrap and posturing. As far as she was concerned, if it was murder, then the police could have everything and welcome to it. She wasn't romantic about murderers.

Besides, Jackie liked Michael McGowan, and wouldn't have thought twice about telling him anything and everything she knew to help him with one of his cases. Last fall, when one of Jackie's colleagues in the film department had died a sudden, violent death, Jackie had found herself not only in the midst of the police investigation, but also in the thick of the university's official response to the murder. Jackie hadn't enjoyed all the politicking, but she had enjoyed—well, not *enjoyed,* but found stimulating—her involvement in catching the criminal.

Those events had struck frighteningly close to home, but over time, the memory of that fear had diminished. She had to admit to herself that she wouldn't mind being in on another murder investigation with Michael McGowan.

How far she had come in the past months! Jackie and Peter had moved to Palmer fairly recently—on the heels of Jackie's divorce from Cooper Walsh, her husband of over a decade—and Jackie had gone back to work at her old job, as an instructor in the film department at Rodgers University. She found it invigorating, to say the least, to be once more a child of the city, after her long suburban exile in Kingswood, which was a good forty minutes from downtown. It was wonderful to be working for herself again, after all those years of dancing to Cooper's tune. Of course, there was a good reason for her harsh opinion of those days.

She didn't think of those married years as wasted, exactly; but when she fled the suburbs she had also fled, with her whole heart, the life of a suburban housewife. She just hadn't been cut out for it—she had simply been the wrong wife for Cooper. She had, unfortunately, too many ideas of her own.

Cooper thought that suburban life was perfect, and, moreover, that suburban wives should just sit back and enjoy what came their way. He had been a good provider, and had thrilled to barbecues and golf on the weekends. Jackie, on the other hand, hated golf, and wasn't even really keen on barbecues. She failed to see the romance, especially since Cooper had insisted on buying one of those fancy propane grills. The propane had killed Jackie's enthusiasm for barbecues altogether.

Yet she had been content to follow Cooper's lead, to
answer his needs. She had considered that her part of the
bargain; after all, he devoted himself to providing for them,
right? So she had spent the prime of her life taking his
shirts to the laundry, picking up his socks off the floor,
cooking his favorite meals, and rearing their child. All
of which might have been fine—but Cooper had repaid
Jackie's devotion by falling in love with someone else. So
Jackie had promptly decamped, taking Peter with her. She
had no regrets, and surprisingly little bitterness. Nor would
she ever go back.

It had been less than a year since her return to Palmer, but
already Jackie felt whole again. She had worried that she
might be lonely, but with Peter around she never felt alone.
What was more, the job of renovating and decorating their
loft on Isabella Lane had filled many of her long evenings
at first; and of course as a Palmer native Jackie had ties
to the place. Her mother lived only about twenty minutes
away, and there were still a few friends from high school
around. Even an old boyfriend or two—but from them
Jackie kept her distance. She wanted no part of romantic
entanglements.

On the other hand, there was Michael McGowan, who
was certainly an interesting specimen.

When McGowan finally showed, at a quarter to eight,
Jackie had forgotten her irritation with him for being late.
It was good to see him again, and Peter was delighted;
even Jake seemed to remember him, greeting him with a
welcoming bark and a vigorous session of tail-wagging.
McGowan quickly enlivened their little dinner circle with
hilarious stories about the fat, slow-witted sergeant in Missing Persons, who was known as the Meatball. Jackie was
soon very glad McGowan had come.

When dinner was over, and Peter had sped away to his

room to finish up his homework, McGowan rose and began to help out with the dishes.

"Sorry I was so late," he said, pouring soap into the sink. He grinned at Jackie.

"It's all right," she answered. "I suppose you want to ask me about Amy Sweeten."

"Is it that obvious?"

"Well—of course. And why not?" Jackie brushed back a curl of her lustrous dark hair and smiled at him. "It's not as though her husband's murder isn't all over the news. And art historians *do* sometimes get to know film instructors." She filled two mugs full of steaming hot coffee for them, brought a plate of homemade ginger cookies to the kitchen table, and sat. "Forget the dishes. Come and have some coffee and ginger cookies. Then you can go ahead and grill me."

"All right." McGowan dried his hands and joined Jackie at the table. He reached for his coffee mug. "Tell me what you know about her."

"Not much, really—but I hated to disappoint you, so I've been thinking long and hard about her all afternoon. I've met her, of course, and seen her at various functions around school—meetings, faculty teas, that sort of thing. Socially our paths don't really cross all that often, but she was at a baby shower I went to about ten days ago. For one of the members of the English department."

"And?"

Jackie leaned back in her chair and crossed her arms. "Off the record, of course."

"Of course. This is unofficial. If anyone wants to know why I came here tonight, you can tell them it was just for the pleasure of your company. Yours and Peter's."

"And Jake's."

"Of course. I thought that went without saying."

"Okay. My impression of her—have you seen her?"

"You bet. I spent most of yesterday afternoon with her."

"Then you know what she looks like—really pale, really thin, with that pale golden hair. Not naturally thin, but as though she doesn't eat right."

"I'd agree with that. Although I wasn't sure if it was just the shock of her husband's death."

"No." Jackie shook her head. "It may be more noticeable now, but that's the way she generally looks." McGowan waited patiently, his blue eyes sparkling. Finally Jackie went on. "Rodgers is a pretty big place, but you get to hear things about people. I've heard that Amy Sweeten is a little bit strange."

"Why?"

Jackie shrugged her shoulders. "That I can't tell you. But she always seems kind of preoccupied, and unhappy, with that pale face that never sees the sun."

"So you saw her at this party. Did she have fun there, at least?"

"No. She was absolutely miserable, and paler than usual. Much paler."

"Why?"

"Well, I did try to guess, that night, but I sort of figured it was for the obvious reason—the subject, babies. She doesn't have a baby, no children. And I know that to be at a party like that, if you don't have a baby and desperately want one, can be really tough. Wishing the new mother well, and wanting so much to be a mother yourself."

McGowan eyed Jackie thoughtfully. Peter was ten years old; he had put Jackie, at a guess, somewhere between thirty-six and thirty-nine. So perhaps there had been a time when she had wanted a baby, like that.

Jackie knew what McGowan was thinking, and she

ignored him. Her comment had invited speculation, but she hoped he would keep his distance. "I sat next to her the whole night, and I had the impression that there were difficulties."

"Marital difficulties, or physical?"

"I couldn't tell you for sure, but here's something you should know. Just a general fact. When women get together for an occasion like that, they tend to be rather free with information about their physical states. I prefer not to join in, and frankly I hate it when a roomful of women who are comparative strangers to each other just go ahead and spill the beans about how hard *they* had to try to get pregnant, or they compare the embarrassing personal medical details about their deliveries. They like to talk about centimeters, and that kind of thing."

"Not your bag," affirmed McGowan. He looked gratified. He wasn't sure what the centimeters were all about, but he was pretty sure he didn't want to know.

"Right. Not my bag. But there's something about the chemistry at a baby shower that makes people spill that sort of thing. It's like an encounter group, or group therapy, with gifts. God, how I hate showers."

"Me too."

Jackie flashed him a smile. "Well, Amy Sweeten just sat there on the sofa all night and hardly said a word. She wouldn't touch the food, which was terrific, and she wouldn't drink anything but tap water with a little slice of lemon in it. She just sat there, listening to everyone's stories and, it seemed to me, trying not to cry. She left as soon as she could. So that was how I got the impression that she was upset by the occasion."

"Hmm."

"I know—it's not much. But I thought maybe it was a sign of some kind of trouble, one way or another."

"What's the dope on her at Rodgers? Is she well thought of?"

Jackie nodded. "She has a reputation for being a real workhorse. Long, long hours, assembling the slides for all the art-history lectures, taking photographs of paintings and developing them, getting down details for the professors, who are either too busy or too lazy to do the work for themselves. The joke that goes around is that they hope she'll never finish her dissertation. They need her too much."

"Right." He reached for a cookie. "Did you make these?"

"Of course."

"Not 'of course.' Plenty of very accomplished people can't make ginger cookies. I'm glad you can. Now, what about her husband?"

"Don't know. I never met him—he didn't come to the baby shower."

"No, I guess not." McGowan reached for his coffee cup and sipped at it thoughtfully. "It's kind of strange, don't you think, that a woman with her nose in the library would marry a man whose interests are all outdoorsy? A dog trainer."

"Maybe, maybe not."

McGowan sighed and asked Jackie a few more routine questions about her colleague. There really wasn't much more Jackie could offer, but she promised McGowan that she would keep her eyes and ears open. He told her—in the strictest confidence, and totally unofficially—about some of the information in the postmortem report, and about Amy's discovery of the body as she had related it. These details weren't exactly secrets, but they weren't going to be given to just anyone.

Jackie agreed with McGowan—it was extremely odd that

Amy had called the doctor before checking to see if Mel was all right. But, then again, Amy was sort of a matter-of-fact person. Either she had behaved very sensibly, or she had been suffering from shock.

Peter, finished with his homework, came downstairs to say good night. Jackie went up with him—*not,* as they told McGowan plainly, to tuck him in or anything, but just to be sure he turned off his light.

When she returned to the kitchen McGowan had finished the dishes.

What a man, thought Jackie, although she didn't say it aloud. It could be that he was only trying to impress her, and that the dish-doing wasn't part of his regular repertoire. There were men who had been known to put on saintlike performances in that area, only to reveal their true natures later on.

But in spite of herself Jackie was sufficiently impressed to allow the conversation to shift to more general things; and it was nearly midnight before McGowan, looking very pleased with himself, headed home.

Jackie Walsh, as she bade good night to Jake and head-ed upstairs to bed, was full of curiosity. McGowan had given her some of the details of Mel Sweeten's death—which had been fairly grisly. Just on the face of it Jackie doubted that Amy would have the strength to strangle a man to death, even with a choke collar. And then there was the question of their relative heights. McGowan told Jackie that Mel Sweeten had been about six feet tall. Amy was a little thing—probably at least nine inches shorter, and weighing about a hundred ten pounds. To Jackie's knowledge, Amy had never been seen at any of the faculty aerobics classes, or playing squash at the gym. She wasn't the athletic type.

As Jackie dropped off to sleep, she tried to imagine it, and couldn't. Dimly she wondered if perhaps Amy had stood on a milking stool or a crate or something to yank the choke collar tight. Otherwise, she'd never have gotten the leverage she needed to kill her husband.

CHAPTER 5

Jackie Walsh wasn't really sure why she did what she did on the Saturday following Michael McGowan's visit. In the days to come she would wonder about it again and again, speculating that she might be growing nosy, or obsessed with murder, or maybe just losing her marbles.

But on that Saturday morning, with Peter out of town visiting his father, and with no real program in mind, she took Jake over to Mel Sweeten's Dog Academy to sign him up for a refresher course in obedience training.

Not that Jake needed training—he was far and away the most obedient dog that Jackie had ever known. He seemed to be able to tell by the look on your face what you wanted him to do next; and he responded to oral commands with an alacrity that belied his years. So as they drove the two miles to the Dog Academy, which was on the far side of the university, near the Palmer city limits, Jackie offered Jake a brief apology.

"I hope you won't feel like a pawn," she said to him.

Jake, in the backseat, drooped his head over and rested his chin on Jackie's right shoulder.

"Or a toy, a trifle, a cat's paw," she went on.

Jake let out a low growl.

"It's just that you're the best excuse in the world to go out there. So I will *have* to use you." She reached her hand back and scratched Jake gently on the furry middle part of his nose. "I hope you won't feel it's all too undignified to be borne."

Jake emitted a low *woof,* and he and Jackie drove the rest of the way in silence.

She had supposed that other people besides herself would be curious about the scene of the crime. She thought that all the dog owners in Palmer would turn up, asking for boarding room for the night for Fido. Jackie thought she might have to stand in line, buy a ticket to look at the sights—*step right up!* But as she pulled her gray-and-red Jeep into the parking lot, she noted that there was only one other car there.

She and Jake climbed out and presented themselves at a small, ramshackle clapboard shed, with a sign saying OFFICE over the door. She and Jake stepped in out of the freezing cold March air, drawing only vague looks from the three other people present.

A large, red-faced man with fat, freckled arms and beefy fists sat behind a desk; a little plastic plaque riding in a brass-rimmed holder identified him as Tom Mann, Manager. Jackie could tell at a glance that the two overcoated visitors on her side of the desk—big, square-jawed, square-shouldered men with closely cropped hair and well-polished, square-toed shoes—were city employees. She would have bet even money that they were undercover detectives. She would have taken odds that they worked for Michael McGowan.

Trying to look as though she never thought about anything but dogs, Jackie plopped down on a chair to wait her turn. Jake sat down quietly at her feet, lifting his chin a bit in a way that gave him an unquestionably noble aspect. Jackie noticed that he gave the detectives a tolerant, almost respectful glance. There must be something about the way they carry themselves, she reflected, or maybe there was a particular scent at the precinct house.

The detectives, for their part, had obviously not recognized Jake as one of their own. They didn't give him a second look. That was just as well, Jackie thought. It wouldn't do for Michael McGowan to hear that she'd been snooping around at the Dog Academy. Michael would know in a minute that she wasn't interested in furthering Jake's education.

Apparently the detectives were winding up their business. One of them was busily putting away his notebook, while the other dropped a card on Tom Mann's desk.

"Anything else you think of, anything at all, and you let us hear from you," he said, sliding the card toward Mann. "All right?"

"Sure thing," responded Mann, in a kind of hearty-squeaky voice that reminded Jackie of Keenan Wynn. Or maybe it was Ed Wynn. She never could remember which was which, and always had to check the film credits carefully—which was embarrassing for a film instructor, to say the least. Mann's voice had that same high, breezy quality, almost a laryngitic squeal. Jackie always distrusted people with voices like that.

Tom Mann rose from behind the desk and shook the officers' hands. "Sure thing. I'm glad you fellows are on the job. I mean to write the police commissioner and tell him so."

"No need for that," responded the talkative one. Jackie wondered if the other one ever opened his mouth. "Just doing our job," the detective added. He turned smartly on his heel and nodded to the silent partner, and the two men strode out. He ought to have touched the brim of his fedora, thought Jackie—except he wasn't wearing a fedora. The hat would have completed the impersonation of Robert Stack as Eliot Ness. Even without the hat, it wasn't a bad performance. Much as there was to admire about Kevin Costner, she really thought Robert Stack had been the perfect Ness, capturing the stern-jawed rectitude of the man week after week on the old television series.

"Help you, ma'am?" came Tom Mann's squeak.

"Oh, yes please." She rose and turned to Jake. "You *stay,* boy. *Stay,*" she said in the pleading voice of one accustomed to disobedience. The little charade wasn't fair to Jake, but he didn't look as though his feelings had been hurt. He blinked at her and stayed. Jackie went to the desk.

"My son and I have recently adopted this dog, from— from a friend," she lied, "who couldn't keep him anymore, who was, um, moving. Moving to New York. And since we've never *had* a dog before, and since he's not really *our* dog, and he's kind of old, I thought it would be a good idea to bring him by." She glanced nervously over her shoulder at Jake, who was still staying. "I would think that he could be kind of ferocious, and I want to make sure he knows that he has to do what we tell him to do. And a friend of mine mentioned that you have short courses in obedience training, so we thought—"

"Whoa, now, whoa," said Tom Mann. "First, let's have some information." He indicated the chair just in front of the desk, and Jackie obediently sat in it. Then, just as swiftly, she took a moment to marvel at her instantaneous response to his gesture. It must have something to do with all those years of teaching dogs to sit, she thought, amazed.

Tom Mann pulled out a small white file card from his

top drawer and grabbed a pen from a holder. "Name?"

"Jackie Walsh."

"No—I mean his name." Mann nodded to indicate Jake.

"Oh—he's called Jake."

"Just 'Jake'?"

"Sure. He doesn't need a last name, does he? If he needs one, he can use ours."

"No, he doesn't need one," said Mann, printing carefully. J-A-K-E. "No, he doesn't. On the other hand, he looks like a fine purebred shepherd to me, Mrs., um—"

"Walsh. Ms."

"*Miz* Walsh," said Mann, drawing the syllable out. Evidently Tom Mann, Manager, didn't approve of "Ms." "He looks like a dog with papers. And a dog that comes with papers generally comes with more than just 'Jake' for a name. You know—like a big white standard poodle might be called 'Champion Ferdinand's Boules de Neige,' on its papers, and just be called 'Frenchie' by his owner. But if its owner tells us we're training 'Boules de Neige' you can be pretty sure we'll ask the owner a question or two about the dog's parentage, see what kind of stock he comes from, and so forth. That way, we get a deeper understanding of the individual animal."

"Oh." Jackie glanced over her shoulder at Jake, who was still staying. "Well, if he's got some kind of fancy background, we don't know anything about it."

"Uh-huh." Mann didn't look as though he believed her, for some reason. Jackie tried to look nonchalant.

"Age?" asked Tom Mann.

"Um, we're not certain. About ten, I think."

"What about your friends? Didn't the people who gave him to you know how old their own dog was?"

"I don't think so," said Jackie. "As far as I know, they got him from the pound."

"Uh-huh," said Mann, his squeak even more skeptical than before.

He got up from behind his desk and crossed to where Jake was sitting. "Good boy," he said, extending the back of his right hand for Jake to sniff.

With a glance for Jackie, Jake leaned forward and duly sniffed. He didn't look impressed, but neither was he evidently annoyed.

"Good *boy,* Jake," said Jackie in an artificially bright voice. Jake gave her a look.

Mann squatted down, duck-walked forward about a foot, and put a hand up toward Jake's mouth. Very gingerly, he lifted one of Jake's lips to take a look at the dog's teeth; then he rose to his full height.

Jake stayed.

At least six feet two, thought Jackie, studying Tom Mann. He could have done it easily, without needing to stand on a crate or anything.

"I'd say about ten is right," said Mann. He circled back to his chair behind the desk and took up his pen once more. "Okay. What you'd probably like, *Miz* Walsh, is to let us give the dog a series of basic tests to evaluate his obedience skills. When that's done, we'll enroll him at whatever level seems most appropriate. I don't imagine you want to show him?"

"You mean, in a dog show?"

"Not a horse show." Mann chuckled at his little joke.

"Well, do you know it hadn't entered my mind," said Jackie, voice full of rising interest. "I've never even been to a dog show."

"Well, showing is a lot of fun if you have the stamina and the interest, but it's not something that appeals to everyone. If you don't mind my saying so, Mrs. Walsh, you don't seem the type for it somehow."

So they were back to "Mrs." Jackie let it go—she wanted information. "Probably not," she agreed, looking thoughtful. "But tell me, Mr. Mann—"

"Call me Tom. Everyone does."

"Okay." Jackie smiled brightly. "Tell me—if I were to sign Jake up for a class here, I think I would really have to see the grounds. Could you show me around?"

"We do our obedience training right out front there." He gestured toward the large field that separated the kennel operation from the house.

"Oh." Jackie bit her lip. "But what if Jake needs to spend the night? I'll have to inspect the dogs' living quarters, I think, before—"

"Look, Mrs. Walsh. *If* that's your name." Tom Mann had risen suddenly from his chair, and he stood glowering at Jackie. He raised his voice and pointed an accusing finger at her. "I don't want to be rude, but we've had an awful lot of reporters snooping around out here. Some of them showed their credentials, nice and polite and professional. Some of them pretended they wanted to have their dogs trained. They were a *little* bit better at it than you are— because at least they brought their own dogs with them, not some rent-a-dog from the nearest kennel." He gestured sharply toward Jake.

Jake looked solemnly at Mann.

"Stay, Jake," said Jackie calmly, her voice full of authority. "Good boy. Just stay."

Mann resumed his tirade. "I think we've had enough to deal with here at the Dog Academy, without this kind of nonsense. It's rude, nosy people like you who make things like this intolerable. So I suggest that you get out, and quit wasting my time—"

He stopped abruptly and looked up toward the office door, which had suddenly opened, letting in the cold, wet

March air. Amy Sweeten stepped in quietly and closed the door behind her.

"Something wrong, Tom?" she asked.

Amy must have heard him bellowing, thought Jackie.

"No, Amy. Nothing wrong." He glared at Jackie. "Just getting rid of a snoopy reporter, that's all."

Amy Sweeten allowed her glance to fall on the client seated at the desk.

"Jackie?"

"Um, hi, Amy," Jackie replied, working hard to hide her embarrassment. "I was awfully sorry to hear about Mel. Are you all right?"

"I'm fine. Thanks." Amy Sweeten looked back at Tom. "That's not a reporter, Tom. That's Jackie Walsh. She teaches at Rodgers."

"Well, what's she doing here, Mrs. Sweeten?" asked Mann in a complaining voice. He glowered at Jake. "With that animal?"

Amy glanced at Jake. "Well, Tom, if I had to guess, I'd say that's her dog, a stray that she took in last fall. She told me all about him at a party we went to two weeks ago. His name is Jake." She transferred her glance back to Mann, who was still standing behind the desk. "Since he *was* a stray probably Jackie has come here to ask about an obedience course for him. Fix her up, please. And give her a discount. Twenty percent. She's a colleague."

"Oh, Amy, that's—" Jackie began.

Amy waved her interruption away. "Jackie, when Tom is through maybe you wouldn't mind coming up to the house for a cup of tea? You're exactly the person I wanted to see."

CHAPTER 6

It had taken Jackie less than a minute to get over her embarrassment from the encounter with Amy. For Tom Mann, Manager, it hadn't been so easy. He had begun with profuse apologies, but Jackie had waved them away. Then he had graciously proposed a tour of the Academy's grounds. This suggestion Jackie declined—she had decided, while Mann was talking, that she would prefer to poke around without Tom Mann for company. It would be more expedient simply to ask Mel Sweeten's widow for permission to take a look around the Dog Academy.

Jackie did accept Mann's offer to give Jake a free and immediate "obedience evaluation." She would take advantage of the interval to go on up to the Sweeten house and hear what Amy had to say. After all, a chance encounter with the widow and an opportunity to inspect the scene of the crime were really what she had come for. Michael McGowan hadn't *exactly* invited her to join his team of crack investigators; neither had he warned her off. Jackie decided that silence does indeed give consent. She left Jake with Mann and went to the Jeep to get a loaf of homemade zucchini bread, which she had brought with her as a small offering for Amy.

On her way up to the house, Jackie passed a small group of eight or nine fairly large enclosures, with a low, long shed running along the back. The dog runs, where Mel Sweeten had died. On one of the gates there was a yellow tape seal, bearing the legend CITY OF PALMER DO NOT BREAK in huge letters. The tape was all too familiar in its aspect. Jackie had last seen the seal of the Palmer police force on Philip Barger's office door, last fall. Seeing it here gave her a chill.

The last enclosure, the one nearest the house, was far grander than the rest. As Jackie got close she could see the reason why. Within, sleeping comfortably on bean-bag dog beds, were two large basset hounds, their foreheads a mass of heavy wrinkles, their ears spread like silky blankets over their front paws. These, she knew, were Mel Sweeten's pride and joy. One of the dogs looked up and sniffed the air as Jackie walked by; then it rested its massive head once more on its paws. Basset hounds really were cute, thought Jackie. They always looked to her as though they'd been designed by an upstart apprentice on the master artist's day off—all feet and ears and wrinkles and spots.

"I don't know what I'm supposed to do with them," said a voice. Jackie started. Amy had come up behind her very quietly.

"Let sleeping dogs lie," offered Jackie, feeling that it was a rather lame response. Even as she said it, the dogs awakened. They took one look at her and let out with an enormous, alarming noise, kind of a combination of a howl and a bark, deep and plaintive and somehow frightening. Jackie knew that bassets were fond of raising the alarm around strangers, but she hadn't counted on the deafening effects of a chorus of two.

Amy raised her voice to be heard. "They're supposed to be in a dog show today and tomorrow. Right here in Palmer, for a change, at the armory. Usually they have to travel."

"Well," replied Jackie, shouting over the noise of the bassets, "they look kind of tired. Maybe they need the day off."

"Yeah," said Amy Sweeten with a laugh. She began to lead the way across the lawn that separated the house from the Dog Academy. The dogs, watching the stranger retreat with the mistress of the house, quieted down. "Their fans will be clamoring for them," said Amy. "I suppose I have to figure out what to do with them. I don't know whether I should keep them. I would think that, technically, they will count as part of Mel's estate."

Yikes! thought Jackie. She had never contemplated dogs as constituting part of someone's estate. "Well, they *are* kind of cute," she ventured. One of the dogs had opened an eye halfway—just enough to give Jackie a heavy stare.

Amy shrugged. "Depends on your point of view, I suppose. I imagine that Mel thought they were cute too. Mostly, he thought they were worth a potful of cash. Fred's stud fee is something like a thousand dollars." On this strange note, she opened the kitchen door and ushered Jackie inside.

Jackie settled herself in the living room while Amy went off to the kitchen to make a pot of tea. She looked about her at the furnishings, which were for the most part well worn, in good taste, nothing special. But here and there a few items testified to Mel Sweeten's fondness for basset hounds. On the end tables on each side of the sofa were two lamps shaped like basset hounds standing up on their hind legs, their fat front paws playfully reaching up toward the light bulbs. Before the fireplace was a cushioned bench bearing a large sleeping basset on its needlepointed cover. There were ashtrays and nut dishes and other suchlike items scattered about, all bearing the likeness of basset hounds. And over a handsome table against a far wall was an enormous watercolor portrait, skillfully executed, of two bassets sleeping, their blue ribbons dangling carelessly about their fleshy necks.

Jackie, having taken in the basset touches of the decor, began to study the house. After a look at the front door and the hall beams she decided it was of the same vintage as the clapboard "office" out back—probably just over a hundred years old. It wasn't quite a farmhouse, and it wasn't really a residence, either. It was an anomaly.

Something of her puzzlement must have shown on her face, for as Amy came in with the tray and sat down, Amy said, "Don't mind the dog lamps. And if you're wondering about the house, it used to be a dormitory."

"Oh—of course. The James Lincoln Academy." Jackie nodded. "I should have realized."

"When Mel's father bought up the old school property— in the Depression, naturally, and for about three dollars— he thought about doing a lot of different things with it. Had all kinds of grand ideas, but according to Mel he was one of those people who always have pipe dreams. In the end, of course, he just sold most of it off, to developers. But he kept the hockey field—that field where the training takes place, where Tom is working with your dog now—and the Briar Patch. That was what the girls at James Lincoln called this dormitory. Because it was on the main road, and it was so easy for the boys from Rumson Hill School to sneak over in the night and kiss the sleeping beauties." Amy giggled.

Jackie didn't wonder at Amy's apparent high spirits. She supposed that in four days the shock of finding her husband murdered—or maybe it was the shock of having murdered her husband—had not entirely worn off. Jackie knew that it was often useful, in times of stress, to fix one's mind on trivialities. If one could. So they made small conversation, about the James Lincoln Academy, and Mel's father's grand schemes, and the school's final transformation into

Mel Sweeten's Dog Academy. At last, Jackie came to the point.

"I suppose the police have been here badgering you," she said.

"I would hardly call it 'badgering,' " replied Amy with a look of relief on her face. Perhaps she had been waiting for Jackie to broach the subject. "After all, he *was* murdered. But of course I can't tell them anything at all that's useful." She brushed back a languid hank of red-gold hair. "I wasn't here." She looked carefully at Jackie. "I know— well, everybody knows—that you were involved in the police investigation into Philip Barger's murder. That's why I wanted to talk to you. I was hoping you could tell me what to do next."

"Um—" Jackie began, but Amy held up a hand.

"You see, this is all foreign territory to me, and I don't have anything to judge it by. I've never been *in* a murder before. But you have. So I was hoping you could tell me how the police think, so I know how to respond. I don't have any references for this kind of thing."

There was something precise and scholarly about the way Amy Sweeten asked Jackie for advice. She might have been talking about evaluating a work by an unknown artist. In a way, thought Jackie, that was appropriate—her mind would probably take a scholarly approach to the problem, with her husband's death by violence as her primary resource material.

"I don't think I should try to advise you, Amy," Jackie replied. "Besides, other people's advice is never really much good. I never follow advice. The only good it ever does me is to help me see different sides of a question."

"All I can see is that I'll probably be arrested."

"Why do you think that?"

"Oh—lots of reasons. To start with, I don't really have a whatsit—an ironclad alibi for the time. I'd been over to Wardville for a couple of days, to visit my sister and look at one or two things in the museum there. They have a wonderful Eakins that I was hoping to photograph for our slide collection, but it was out being cleaned and so I couldn't get near it. So instead of staying until Thursday, as I planned, I came back here early on Wednesday. There were other things I needed to do. And that's why I found Mel."

Jackie gave what she hoped was a sympathetic nod, and Amy went on with her tale.

"The police think he died shortly after a meeting he had here with his doggy friends. I've heard that the meeting broke up around eight-thirty or so. They have those meetings every month, which was one of the reasons I went to my sister's house. I can't stand those dog people."

"No?"

"No. All they do is argue. So, anyway, the problem is that I went out on Wednesday night—I went out to supper, by myself, in Wardville."

"Somewhere nice?"

Amy Sweeten shook her head. "Denny's. My sister's kids were making so much noise that I couldn't concentrate on the notes I wanted to make. And the library was closed. So I thought if I just went somewhere by myself for a couple of hours, I could get some work done."

Jackie sympathized. It was difficult to concentrate with other people's children clamoring for your attention.

"But probably the people at Denny's will remember you, Amy," she reassured her colleague. "The person who took your order will remember you."

"I hope so."

"Besides, why would the police suspect you?"

"They think my behavior was . . . not right. The next day, when I came home, I mean."

"What happened?"

"Well, I was home by nine-thirty the next morning. By that time, I guess he'd been dead about twelve hours. But I didn't go out to the kennels, didn't find him until about eleven. I think that delay has made me a suspect. The police don't think it's reasonable."

Jackie considered this point. She knew some of the details already, thanks to her conversation with McGowan—and she knew that the time of death had been fixed for anywhere between nine and midnight. But Jackie also figured that such estimates generally included a margin of error of an hour or so. If Mel Sweeten had been killed at nine, Amy would have had time to drive the half hour from Wardville to the Dog Academy, kill her husband, and then drive back to her sister's house. But why would Amy want to kill her husband? She wondered if there was something that Amy was holding back.

"No," she said at last. "The police probably won't clear you entirely with that timetable working against you, until they have witnesses who can prove you were at Denny's." She looked Amy straight in the eye. "Did you kill him?"

Amy Sweeten looked scornful. "Of course not. If I'd wanted to kill him, I'd have done it long ago—with a little strychnine, or maybe Drāno, so he'd have suffered nicely."

"Oh." Jackie swallowed hard. This was hardly what she'd expected to hear.

"He had many characteristics that made him a really bad husband," said Amy, her voice strictly matter-of-fact. She might have been discussing a subject in a portrait—Henry the Eighth or someone. "He was fat, self-involved, boring, and adulterous."

"Oh!" said Jackie again, this time with more emphasis. She doubted that Henry the Eighth had been boring.

CHAPTER 7

"So, you see," Amy Sweeten was going on, in her matter-of-fact voice, "that's the other reason that the police might have thought I would want to kill him. Except they don't know about it, yet. Of course, they'll find out. And when they find out, and realize that I was holding out on them, then they'll come and arrest me. And, speaking frankly, I really don't have time for that. I have so much to do, and already I'm falling behind on my work, because I don't seem able to concentrate."

Good heavens! thought Jackie. Aloud she said, "Of course you can't concentrate. I would think that your best course right now would be to ask Dr. Westfall for a leave of absence for a few weeks, until things get straightened out." Dr. Westfall was B. Crowder Westfall, the dean of faculty at Rodgers University. "If you like, I can speak to him for you—he and I are on very good terms these days, even if I am only a rather mature instructor, and not a full professor."

Amy smiled thinly at this little academic jest, and then shook her head. "No, I really want to do my work. It's the only thing that's sustained me through the worst years of my life. I think it would be consoling now, if only I could pay attention."

Jackie took a deep breath and bit the bullet. "All right. So you haven't told the police, but you *have* told me, what kind of a husband Mel was to you. Want to tell me more?"

"Oh, sure. Now that he's dead I don't feel bad about telling it. Before, the whole thing made me feel kind of ridiculous. Inept. I didn't want people to think me inept."

She sighed and reached for another slice of zucchini bread. Mel's death had clearly improved Amy's appetite.

"We got married about two years ago. I was fresh out of graduate school—I had just gotten my master's degree—and Mel seemed sort of exciting, and different, to me. Well, you can imagine that he *was* pretty different from the kind of man I met in graduate school in art history. He was totally involved in outdoorsy kinds of things—in his dogs, and in dog shows, and everything to do with dogs. Not dogs—not just any dogs. Basset hounds. Those smelly, droopy ones out back that you think are so cute."

Jackie nodded. She really *did* think so, and found no reason to be ashamed of her feelings. In general, bassets were pretty adorable, and the ones out back were especially so.

"They've got fancy names, that they came with, but Mel called them Fred and Karen. As basset hounds go they're pretty important. Super deluxe champions or something ridiculous like that. Mel doted on them, and I suppose he loved them as much as he was capable of loving anything or anybody. He'd had a few others, before, that had been important too. In the dog world." Amy spoke contemptuously. "Mel's bassets have always been champions. They won all kinds of awards at dog shows, and he bred them and sold their puppies for a small fortune. Bassets have big litters. I would say Mel made quite a lot of money, over the years, thanks to Fred and Karen and others like them." Amy looked up at Jackie expectantly.

"So they were kind of the focus of his life," said Jackie. She didn't know what else to say. Mel Sweeten didn't sound like much of a prize. Jackie did her best to remember that this was his disillusioned young wife talking. Probably he hadn't been quite such a creep as Amy seemed to think. "I see."

"Do you?" Amy sounded skeptical. "Maybe. It was so strange, I tell you, to find that I had married a man who was totally consumed with basset hounds. I think they're sort of absurd dogs, anyway."

"I could see how you might want him to have at least one other interest." Jackie could sympathize a bit with Amy, who had married a man who seemed exciting and outdoorsy, but turned out to be a monomaniac. *Marriage always has surprises in store like that,* thought Jackie. *You marry the greatest man in the whole world, and then he turns out to be only, human, just a so-so kind of guy. If you were lucky, he wouldn't burn you and leave you scarred for life.*

But Jackie felt strongly that in fairness to Fred and Karen, someone ought to say something nice about them. Besides, they had just lost their master—and no matter what kind of a person Mel Sweeten had been, undoubtedly he had loved his dogs, and probably he had been very good to them. Today they had looked sort of sad to Jackie. But of course they were bassets, and bassets generally look a little forlorn. How would you ever know how they felt? Maybe they hated Mel, much as Amy seemed to have hated him.

In Jackie's mind, however, they deserved a strong defense. "But it's not their fault that Mel had a mania. I think they're sweet," she said firmly.

Amy nodded vaguely. "Well, most people do. I suppose I would too, if I hadn't had to live with Mel's obsession. Every weekend of the year, he was off at a dog event of one kind or another—either showing these dogs, or being a judge, or selling his puppies, or checking up on his puppies, or just hanging around looking at somebody else's. After a while, it really began to get to me."

Jackie could imagine that it might. Still, a man's hobbies, even if they bordered on mania, didn't usually provide people with an impulse to murder. Adultery, on the other hand, had been known to provoke.

"Um, Amy? You mentioned that Mel was, um—"

"Yeah." Amy nodded. "You wouldn't think he'd have time to look at women, not with so much energy devoted to breeding Fred and Karen to the right bassets, and with having to make so many trips all over. It never occurred to me, really, that he would. Or when I thought maybe he was, that she would be the one. I was surprised, frankly, that she could stand Mel. *That* way."

"Um, who's 'she'?"

"Sylvia. Sylvia Brown. She's an aerobics instructor, part-time, at a gym on the west side. And to pick up a few extra dollars, she hires herself out on weekends as a handler for dog shows."

"A handler?"

"You know—the people who take the dogs around in a circle in front of the judges at the dog show. On a leash."

"Oh. A handler. Huh—I thought the owners were the ones who did that."

"Sometimes they do. The real amateurs, usually, or the professionals who want to be seen or who don't trust anyone but themselves. But half the time at a dog show, especially a big one, the owners are really tense, worrying about their dog's performance, and they know things will go more smoothly with a handler. Or they don't have time to travel every weekend, and would rather not go to every dog show. Or if they're like Mel, really disgustingly competitive, then they spend their time trying to butter up the judges. Dog shows aren't really very nice, if you're one of those people. People like Mel. For them, a dog show's full of backbiting and intrigue."

"I had no idea," responded Jackie, who really was surprised. She had assumed that everyone—including the dogs—went to dog shows because they were somehow fun. She shook her head. It didn't sound like much fun at all. "So this woman, Sylvia, knew Mel through dog shows?"

Amy nodded. "She worked for him sometimes, showing Fred and Karen. Apparently she was just great with them, and they love her. Mel told me once that she seemed to get the best out of them."

"Do you know her?"

"Oh, sure. She used to come around here a lot—I guess until her guilty conscience got the better of her."

"Are you sure she was having an affair with Mel?"

"No. Well, I should say that I'm sure somebody was. Whether she was the only one or whether he had a whole string of them, I couldn't say. I think it was Sylvia Brown. You could say I'm convinced, but not actually certain."

"Why?"

"She seems like the logical person. She was just like Mel, about the dogs, I mean. Really into them, into their prizes. Every time she and Mel showed his basset hounds, or went to some dog thing, the animals seemed to come home with another ribbon or award or championship point. I don't know about you, but I can't stand the idea of giving dogs ribbons and awards and points. Even before I married Mel, I thought it was weird. Now I *know* it's weird."

"Well." Jackie wasn't quite sure how to respond. Surely the people at dog shows weren't all like Mel Sweeten— weren't all "disgustingly competitive," as Amy had put it. Jackie wasn't at all certain that Amy's idea of what was weird and what was normal was something that the rest of the world would understand. Amy seemed pretty weird herself, if you asked Jackie.

But Jackie wanted to know more about Mel's supposed affair with the aerobics teacher cum dog handler. Now, *that* seemed like a situation with all kinds of possibilities. So she forged ahead. "It sounds just like a working relationship. Amy, why are you so sure that she and Mel—"

"I just knew it. It had gone on for at least eight months."

"If you don't mind my asking, how did you know?"

"Well, first of all, there were the overnight stays after the dog shows—perfectly unnecessary, most of the time, but Mel would always say that he just had been too tired, after two days of showing, to drive home on Sunday night. Ridiculous. Then he'd turn up Monday morning, with new ribbons and medals and photographs of those dogs to hang in the office. Naturally I assumed something was going on, but I didn't want to think about it, so I didn't. And then, of course, I got the proof in the mail."

"The *what*?"

"Oh, some motel where Mel had stayed during a show. They sent a package addressed to me—that is, to Mrs. Melvin Sweeten—containing a black-lace nightie that was definitely not mine, saying that we, that *I*, Mrs. Sweeten, had left it behind in *our* room."

"Oh, dear."

"I suppose, in a way, they had done me a service. Before, I had always looked at the situation from a totally personal perspective—from the point of view of the person being cheated on. It was offensive, but since I was the only one seeing it, so to speak, I didn't think of it as an event, or a series of events, taking place in the public view. I thought of it as something having to do with *me*. That was a pretty selfish viewpoint. The nightgown made me see the situation more objectively."

"What did you do?" Jackie asked, trying to keep her voice level. Clearly, "weird" was just the first in a string of adjectives that might be used to describe Amy Sweeten. She was either a deluded saint or martyr of some type, or a murderess. Or maybe some wacky combination of good and evil, like something out of a movie. Bette Davis and Paul Henreid in *Now Voyager*. Except Sylvia Brown would have to be cast in the Davis role. "When you got the nightgown, what did you do?"

"Well, of course I wrote back and thanked them, because returning it really showed it was a well-run motel. I thought they deserved a note. But the nightgown was too big for me. I would have been swimming in it—ridiculous. So I gave it to the St. Vincent de Paul thrift shop."

"No, I meant—well, never mind what I meant." Jackie was amazed. She couldn't really believe it—but on the other hand, she had never heard rumors that Amy Sweeten was crazy. Plus, from what little Jackie knew of the woman, she couldn't see her being happily married to a guy like Mel. It just didn't seem to fit. So it was possible that Amy had been just as cold-blooded about it as she sounded.

Or maybe it was a question of religious principles. The St. Vincent de Paul Society was a Roman Catholic charity, Jackie knew. Maybe Amy was Catholic.

But murder was at least as big a sin as divorce, so why murder him if you could condemn your soul forever by the simple expedient of paperwork?

Maybe murder would be appealing for reasons of economy, Jackie reasoned. Divorce lawyers cost money, as she well knew. Murder was cheap—at least do-it-yourself murder was. Almost free, in this case. The choke collar probably belonged to the Dog Academy.

Amy was going on. "As long as I didn't have to think about it too much, I could just pretend to myself that it was a passing thing. That he would get over it."

"Did you want him to get over it?"

Amy Sweeten considered the question for a moment. "Not really. Not at all. I think what I really wanted was to come home from the university some evening and find a completely different man here. A new husband, I mean. Someone thin and handsome, with eyeglasses, and an appreciation of what I think are the important things in life. Somebody who might go to a concert or museum with me, who knew something about things. Preferably someone who liked cats, rather than dogs. But I knew that it wasn't right to think that way."

Her voice had taken on a dreamy quality, and she paused, evidently imagining this prince charming, who sounded kind of dreary to Jackie. On the whole, Jackie thought she herself might have preferred Mel—if she'd had to choose.

Amy became businesslike as she picked up the tale once more. "I didn't like to be the one suggesting that we go back on our vows. That would have put *me* in the wrong, at least in my own mind. I was really just biding my time, waiting for him to tell me he wanted a divorce. Then it would be his idea, not mine, and the onus of breaking our vows would have been on him."

"Well, I don't want to split hairs with you, but hadn't he already broken those vows?"

"Sure. But he hadn't admitted it to me. Maybe the point was academic, but then so am I." She smiled sadly to herself.

Jackie decided that the best course, for the present, was to take Amy Sweeten at her word. The young widow hadn't mentioned her suspicions of Mel's affair to the police, but certainly, if Mel had been carrying on, they would find out.

If it was true, probably everyone on the dog-show circuit knew about it, or suspected it.

True or not, those suspicions now gave Amy a clear-cut reason to have hated her husband enough to kill him. If the affair had gone on for some time, the police would still consider those suspicions a good motive for murder.

"When did you get the nightgown in the mail, Amy?"

"What? Oh." She sat back in her chair and thought. "About two weeks ago."

Uh-oh, thought Jackie.

"I know—perfect timing," said Amy. "But, Jackie—I want you to believe me. I didn't kill him. Well, just *look* at me." She held out her spindly little arms, which seemed composed of bone and near-transparent flesh, and nothing else. Not a muscle anywhere. "I *couldn't* have. Not that way. For that kind of thing, you need to be in good shape. You'd have to be an aerobics instructor or something."

Jackie listened a little bit more to what Amy had to say. Amy had known next to nothing about Mel's business—after the first few months of marriage, she had realized that she would never be interested, so she had even stopped asking the barest polite and pro forma questions. All that Amy knew was that Mel made a lot of money, both from the Dog Academy and from his breeding. Tom Mann, Amy told Jackie, had been with Mel for at least ten years, maybe more. She filled Jackie in on some of Mel's friends and associates, but she really didn't know much more. Jackie had very little respect for women who lived in cocoons like that. At least Cooper, for all of his faults, had talked to her about the important things in his life.

Jackie soon made her escape, after first securing the widow's permission to take a look at the scene of the crime. Of course the dog run where Mel Sweeten had died—the one closest to the little office building—was still sealed off with police department tape. But Jackie wasn't interested in stepping in, and through the chain-link fence she was able to see as much as she needed to.

There wasn't actually all that much to look at; nonetheless Jackie stood contemplating the adjoining enclosures and the long, low shed running behind them for some minutes. The shed evidently was sort of a long doghouse with partitions; there were little doorways out of it giving on to each of the runs. The enclosures were about thirty feet long and ten or fifteen feet wide, with a gate at the end opposite the doghouse. There were eight enclosures, not counting the grander one where Fred and Karen still slept. A pretty small operation, the Dog Academy. And all of the dog runs were empty, except for the one with the bassets. Jackie wondered if business had been slacking off. Times were tough; in a recession, your dog's obedience-training budget has to be one of the first things to go.

Jackie looked up as Tom Mann approached, with Jake on his lead. The manager eyed her carefully as he turned over the end of the lead.

"Mighty nice animal, *Miz* Walsh."

"Oh!" responded Jackie. She had almost forgotten about Jake's evaluation. "You think so?"

"Yup. If I didn't know better, I'd think he'd had some pretty serious training somewhere."

"Was he good?"

Mann nodded. "Real good. Almost like he'd been trained by an expert." He gazed steadily at Jackie, who did her best to look proud and surprised. "He don't need a refresher course, *Miz* Walsh. He don't need anything. I wonder who taught him what he knows?"

"So do *I*," enthused Jackie. "Good boy, Jake." She patted him lightly on the head, and he gave her a bored look.

"See," Tom Mann went on, "I know he's never been here with us before. I'd remember him. But there aren't very many places around here where a dog gets a good training like that. And I'd remember him, if he'd been one of ours."

"Oh, well—"

"Because I have a memory for dogs. Like some people remember other people, I always remember dogs. Their names, and where they come from, who they belong to, things like that. Good for business."

"Yes, I guess it must be." Jackie kept her voice light. "But I'm pretty sure you're right, that Jake hasn't been here before."

"Nope. I'd have recognized him. Dogs like that don't come by every day." He stared at the dog. "Whoever trained him did a good job of it." He returned his gaze to Jackie. "If you find out where he got his training, you let me know, okay? I may be looking for a job, one of these days."

"Sure," said Jackie, trying to sound grateful and obliging. "Good boy, Jake," she said again, and took her leave.

She was glad to be getting away from Mel Sweeten's Dog Academy. As weird as Amy was, she at least had seemed manageable. Tom Mann, on the other hand, was an unknown quantity.

Squeaky voice or no squeaky voice, he was a big, beefy fellow. It would have been quite simple for him to pull hard enough on the choke collar to kill Mel Sweeten.

CHAPTER 8

Early on Sunday morning, sipping coffee quietly in the den, with Jake asleep at her feet, Jackie was still puzzling over her outlandish conversation with Amy Sweeten. It was almost impossible to believe that anyone could be so untouched by suspicions of her husband's infidelity. Yet precisely because Amy's attitude was so very odd, Jackie found herself wanting to believe in it.

Moreover, Jackie had no reason to doubt Amy's word that she hadn't murdered Mel. And she was of the firm opinion that Amy would not have had the strength, or the height, or whatever it might have taken, to slip a dog collar over Mel's head and about his throat and pull it tight. No— the crime had to have been committed by someone taller and stronger than Amy. Surely that much would be apparent to the police.

Jackie wondered how tall Sylvia Brown was. Amy had said the nightgown was far too big—the black lace number that Sylvia had left behind at the motel. Had Amy actually *tried it* on? Jackie shivered. A wife who could do such a thing was evidently superhuman in some way, or maybe subhuman. And they did say that people could develop superhuman strength to meet the challenges of extraordinary occasions.

58

Jackie roused herself from her thoughts, finished the coffee in her cup, and reached for the sports section of the *Chronicle*. Amy Sweeten had said that there was a dog show at the armory today. She looked up the schedule. The dog show started at eleven. The hounds were scheduled for noon, right after the sporting dogs. Presumably basset hounds went with the hounds, although they seemed sort of like sporting dogs, in a way, to Jackie, who had really no idea what was meant by "sporting dog," except probably a dog that you could take with you outside when you went out to have some fun. In that case, almost any dog would be a sporting dog, so probably that wasn't the criterion. Jackie looked at her watch. Plenty of time.

With a sigh, Jackie admitted to herself that she was behaving in a really nosy fashion. Yesterday's foray into police territory, unbidden, might be excused, although on very shaky grounds. But a trip to the dog show? That was sheer nosiness, and there was no way around it. She wanted to have a look at the mysterious woman whom Amy suspected of adultery.

Besides, the dog show *was* a public event.

What was more, Jackie could console herself with what she felt was a right to be nosy. After all, Amy Sweeten had confided in her, and was trusting Jackie to help her prove her innocence. Either that, or Amy Sweeten was a homicidal genius determined to make use of Jackie to clear herself. One way or the other, Jackie felt she was *directly* involved, and no apology would be needed for being seen to be intrusive.

Thus Jackie resolved to take a look around at the dog show. She rushed upstairs to her bedroom and threw on a pair of comfortable but respectable blue jeans, a soft maroon turtleneck, and a warm, knobbly, gray hand-knit sweater, which her mother had made for her. A visit to the

dog show wouldn't hurt, Jackie reflected as she brushed
her long, thick, dark hair and tied it back in a ponytail,
a style that she thought might be right for a dog show. She
put on a pair of earrings, to dress up the outfit somewhat.
If she caught a glimpse of Sylvia Brown, then she might
want to call Michael McGowan and fill him in a little bit
on her ideas.

As she stepped out into the brisk March air to walk the
fifteen blocks across town from Isabella Lane to Morrell
Street, Jackie gave some serious thought to her approach.
She realized that if she wanted to be any good at surrep-
titiously learning things about murderers, or about people
who could be murderers, she would definitely have to practice her technique. It had been very dismaying, yesterday,
the way the manager at the Dog Academy had seen through
her ruse. Of course, that had been partly Jake's fault—because he really was far too well trained to need any kind of
refresher course. Anyone but a perfect idiot could see that
at a glance.

Jackie, to slake her curiosity, didn't mind appearing like a
perfect idiot. But she had no illusions that such an approach
would work more than once. She would just have to play it
by ear.

If the Sunday morning traffic jam on Morrell Street was
any indication, the dog show apparently was a popular
event. The crowd of dog lovers who had turned up today
looked like a relaxed and fun-loving bunch. As she made
her way through the press of people gathered near the huge
arched front door of the armory, Jackie was on a careful
lookout for bared fangs, sneers, frostiness, and other signs
of the nightmarish competitiveness that Amy had described.
But all that Jackie saw was a healthy crowd of ordinary-
looking people, many of whom seemed to know each other

well. They greeted one another with hearty "hellos" and heavy back-thumping; they inquired after one another's animals, and they discussed the dogs that were going to compete today.

The armory was a huge building, dating from the very early part of the century. It was not only massive-looking, from the outside, but also startlingly capacious, once you got inside. It had once been the headquarters of the Fifth Regiment, but that crack unit had been combined with another regiment from nearby Wardville, shortly after the First World War. Ever since, the armory had been an invaluable part of Palmer life. Its doorways were large enough to permit the passage not only of tanks, but also of elephants; hence the circus had always been held at the armory. High schools had dances here, and groups of traveling acrobats swung from the ceiling here. There were auctions and flower shows and political rallies; and Jackie remembered significantly loud rock concerts being held here, in her high school days. The red brick must have intensified the sound of amplified electric guitars by another two or three hundred decibels— it was astonishing, really, that Jackie and her high school friends had any hearing left at all.

By the standards of those days, the crowd that had turned out for the dog show seemed small, quiet, and well mannered. Jackie entered through the main doorways on the Morrell Street side. Straight in front of her, occupying about one third of the floor space, was a large ring, in which the dogs would evidently be performing. On the right, covering about half the ring, were the grandstands— Jackie recognized the old, splintery, green wooden benches. They had been here forever. To the left of the ring was an area that was evidently reserved for dogs and their owners; it was separated from the entranceway by a large picket fence, in white wood, that might have come out of someone's backyard. At the far end of the huge room was a reviewing stand, evidently for the judges.

After about ten minutes of sizing up the layout and watching the crowd, Jackie decided on her technique. She would wander about in the crowd, selecting small clusters of people at random; then she would eavesdrop on their conversations, hoping to hear something about either Mel Sweeten or Sylvia Brown. If someone seemed to notice, she would just flash an innocent smile and simply drift away to the next cluster of dog lovers, trying hard not to be obvious.

Edging in this manner from one cluster to another, Jackie finally drew close to the ring, where the dogs being showed would shortly be called upon to exhibit their best qualities. Over to the left was the white picket fence separating the spectators' section from the area where the dogs and their owners awaited their big moments. From where she stood, Jackie could see what seemed like hundreds of carry crates and temporary cages. As she neared the gate in the fence, Jackie could sense the heightened tensions on the other side. Evidently the good-fellow feeling that prevailed among the spectators dissolved amid the anxiety of actually competing.

Jackie saw an argument shaping up right in front of her. Just on the other side of the fence stood a man of about fifty, with a toothbrush mustache and thick gray hair, and a stagily handsome face, as though he might once have been an actor. In one hand was a quivering mass of brilliant white, which looked to Jackie at first glance like some extraordinary small rat or weasel that had been held by its hindquarters and dipped in marshmallow fluff. On taking a second look, Jackie recognized the white mass as a poodle, with one of those decorative, pom-pommy haircuts that people seemed always to give them. The poodle's owner was scolding a red-haired, earnest-looking, firm-jawed woman of fifty or so. Evidently, the man felt that her beagle had strayed too close to the poodle's carry crate.

"*Some* people think they own a dog show. *Some* people think they can just *ignore* the rules, and *flaunt* the mandates of common courtesy," the man was saying passionately. Then he spoke gently to the little thing quivering in his arms. "Hush, Serena, my little flower, hush," he said to the dog.

The lady with the beagle reminded Jackie of Maggie Smith in *The Prime of Miss Jean Brodie*. The woman inhaled deeply and gave her dog's lead a stern tug. "Clematis wasn't in your way, sir," said the lady. "This is a public concourse." She nodded toward the poodle's crate. "Your box is over the yellow line. I certainly hope you won't attempt to make any foolishness over such a small incident. If you do, I shall see to it that your silly little dog never competes in this town again. The whole episode was in your imagination, anyway."

Clematis, the beagle who had been thus fiercely championed, tossed her nose into the air and sniffed merrily. Who could say, it might be her lucky day—there might be a convention of rabbits going on somewhere at the other end of the huge hall. She let out a short, sharp baying noise, a kind of a *brooop!* and was led away by her stomping mistress.

"Honestly," said the man with the poodle. He looked toward Jackie for sympathy. "She should *know* better. She does know better." He gave his poodle a comical look. "Feeling okay now, baby girl?" He smiled at Jackie. "Serena here isn't afraid of anything. But she knows how to lay it on thick at a show. Plus, her nerves are naturally just the tiniest

bit on edge, because the competition promises to be fierce."
He leaned across the fence to say in a low voice, "Believe it
or not, there's a woman here with the most *flea*-bitten bichon
frise. And she actually expects to win best in show." He was
deeply contemptuous.

"Oh," said Jackie, wondering what a bichon frise might
be. "Is that a kind of dog?"

"Well, of *course*, my dear." The man looked at Jackie
more carefully. "I take it you're not an aficionado of our
all-consuming diversion?"

"I really don't know anything about it—this is my first
dog show."

"Not really?" The man was scandalized.

"Afraid so. But I have a new dog, a very nice one, and
I was wondering what it would be like to show a dog—"

"What kind?"

"A shepherd. German shepherd."

"Oh, I think they're so nice, for working dogs. Don't you
agree?"

"I like ours," replied Jackie, trying to sound enthusiastic.
Working dogs, sporting dogs—to her, they were all just
dogs, and should do as they pleased. But she knew that
that attitude wouldn't get her far at a dog show.

"And he must be handsome," the poodle's owner went
on, "if you're thinking of showing him. Or is it a bitch?"

"A bitch? Um—no, no, he's a boy. A—a male dog."

"Good. They tend to be better in that group, I don't know
why. At least, so I think. But you were telling me—you've
never shown, and you came here today to see *what* this
madness is all about. Am I right?"

"That's right," Jackie lied.

"Well, then." Balancing the white poodle in one hand, he
fished in a pocket of his jacket and emerged, in a moment,
with a badge that said COMPETITOR/DAY 2. "Here." He held

it out. "I didn't bring a handler with me, and I don't have any cheering section here today, so it's extra. You can have it if you promise to cheer for us when we face our moment of truth. Put that on, my dear, and then you can come right on backstage here and see for yourself exactly who and what a bichon frise is, and anything else that might strike your fancy. Just be careful not to go too close to the carry crates, unless you like to make enemies fast."

Jackie grinned. "Thank you so much," she said, pinning the badge on her sweater.

"Unfortunately, you can't come in this way—you'll have to go all the way around to the other side, the Beadleston Street entrance, where they make you sign in and everything. But that's just as well, because this little thing"—he cuddled the dog—"and I have work to do. Just tell the dragons at the gate that you're with me—Phil Watts. Oh, Serena," he added, talking to the dog, "your hair is just a wreck." Serena was still, as far as Jackie could tell, a quivering mass of nerves. Hardly living up to her name.

Phil Watts smiled at Jackie. "We'll be on at about one-thirty. Wish us luck!"

"Of course," replied Jackie. "Thank you so very much!"

She made her way hastily through the growing crowd, around the back of the horseshoe-shaped grandstands, out one door onto Beadleston Street, and back in at the competitors' entrance. Doing her best to look like a professional of some sort, she flashed her badge and scribbled her name hastily in the logbook, then passed through to the competitors' side.

Preoccupied as she was, Jackie didn't notice that she was being observed. Across the way, almost hidden by the grandstands, Michael McGowan was watching her. On his face was an expression of mingled amusement and irritation.

It was only natural that an inherently curious and intrepid person like Jackie Walsh might turn up at the dog show today. But Michael McGowan was investigating a homicide—and so, clearly, was Jackie. Or at least she probably thought she was. Cosmo Gordon had warned him against trying to boss Jackie around, so McGowan was content, for the moment, to observe.

Nevertheless, he wasn't entirely happy that she had turned up here today. It had been one thing for Jackie to go around talking to suspects when the head of her department had been murdered. It was another thing altogether for her to be exposing herself to the dangers of a murder investigation in which she had no conceivable role. He wondered what on earth she was doing here.

McGowan moved out from under the shadow of the grandstands and followed Jackie out through the back entrance of the armory onto Beadleston Street.

He had better keep an eye on her, for her own sake.

CHAPTER 9

Once she had crossed through the competitors' gate, Jackie was immediately aware that the atmosphere had changed. There were about fifty or sixty dogs competing today, she guessed—if the number of people and carry crates was anything to judge by. There were dogs of all colors, dogs of all shapes and sizes, being fretted over and cajoled by their owners. Some of the owners and their animals appeared to be taking it all in stride; others were clearly more nervous.

The large waiting area was broken up into six or seven large zones, in which dogs of a certain affinity were grouped together. Jackie stopped briefly near the front desk to look at a hand-lettered chart that indicated the layout. It seemed to her that the most logical place to start was with the hounds.

It seemed to Jackie, as she passed along the aisle where the dogs and their owners waited, that this crowd was really not all that friendly. She noticed that people tended to stare at her in a suspicious manner—those people who weren't all caught up in the anxiety of preparing their dogs, grooming them, and giving them last-minute words of encouragement or advice. There wasn't much bonhomie on this side of the white picket fence. Jackie tended to associate dogs with lightheartedness, but there was nothing lighthearted about the people here today. They were all in deadly earnest.

She made her way past the terriers, who were all keyed up, some barking incessantly, others merely giving off palpable quantities of nervous energy. Then she wandered slowly through the sporting dogs, who looked to Jackie to be having more fun than anyone she'd seen so far. A Labrador retriever was lying happily on the ground outside of his carry crate, chewing on a sodden mass. Closer inspection revealed it to be an old tennis ball. Across the aisle from the Labrador, two vizslas, obviously old friends, were curled up asleep next to each other, making an indeterminate, soft-looking pile of velvety reddish fur. Next to them, a golden retriever was being groomed, its head proudly erect, its long fluffy tail a plume of feathered sunshine. On the dog's face was the breed's customary look of obliging cheerfulness. They made wonderful pets, Jackie reflected. But then, so did Jake.

As Jackie looked up from the golden retriever, a movement on the other side of the aisle caught her eye. There was a striking-looking blond woman about thirty yards away, on the left. She seemed to be a familiar of the dog-show world; as she walked by, people greeted her, and she nodded at them and returned their salutations.

Jackie watched with interest as the woman left the main aisle of dog crates and opened a large wooden door. This door led into a back hallway that ran the length of the armory's main floor; in Jackie's high school, rock-concert days, the passageway had been notorious as a place where you could find a little privacy with your date. According to the layout map that Jackie had studied earlier this morning, the dog-show judges had been given a room off the passageway in which they could relax between rounds.

Jackie thought fast. She had a feeling that this woman was Sylvia Brown, Mel Sweeten's handler. She could follow the woman innocently enough—the door apparently wasn't locked. The only difficulty was in figuring out how to sneak through the door without causing suspicion—undoubtedly, the judges' room would be off-limits to casual visitors.

Jackie soon found the perfect excuse. It was a large black dog, looking like an overgrown black poodle without a haircut, and it was waiting impassively in a large crate just in front of the door, at a considerable distance from the other dogs in the group. There didn't seem to be anyone around. It would be easy enough to pretend to admire this poodlelike dog, and then slip through the door after her quarry.

But she had no sooner crossed the aisle and approached the carry crate when she was stopped by a voice.

"Ma'am, if you please."

"Oh, sorry." Jackie stopped short and turned to face the man, embarrassed. She supposed it was the dog's owner; a short, round, middle-aged man with spectacles and a face that was all spherical lumps—a lump of a chin, lumps for cheeks, and a round lump of a nose. He looked as though he had been assembled from parts. "I just wondered what kind he is," she lied.

The man gave her an odd look, and Jackie was suddenly conscious of her badge. Competitors ought to know these things, she reasoned. "I'm strictly an observer here. Helping out a friend. In one of the other groups."

The man raised an eyebrow. "Well, if you're an observer, then maybe you don't know the rules. But the first rule of a dog show is you never, ever go near anybody's dog without being invited."

"I should have known," said Jackie, feeling truly embarrassed. She *should* have known. She would give herself away, and be expelled from the dog show, and never find out anything about Sylvia Brown, if she wasn't more careful about the regulations.

Jackie's ruefulness did the trick—the man seemed to relax a bit. "And the fact is, there's been a little trouble lately," he added, unbending.

"Is that so?" Jackie felt her nerves tingle. "What kind of trouble? Dogfights?"

"Oh, no. That happens, of course, but those little scuffles are easy enough to deal with. No, we had a tragedy a while back at a show near Philadelphia. One of the dogs competing was poisoned."

"How *terrible!*" Jackie was deeply shocked. "Did the dog die?"

"No"—the man shook his head—"but it was out of the show, and that was really upsetting to its owner."

"Maybe it was just sick, then," said Jackie. "After all, who would poison—"

"Oh, people go to all kinds of lengths to be sure they win their championship points." The round man shook his head.

"It wasn't *your* dog, was it?"

"Nope. A beagle. One of Thalia Gilmore's." He added this last bit of information in a voice edged with respect.

"Oh." The man seemed to expect Jackie to know who Thalia Gilmore was. It seemed that the criminal nature of the offense was heightened because the poisoned dog had belonged to Thalia Gilmore. Whoever she was.

"Now, this dog over here"—he gestured toward the poodlelike animal—"she wouldn't let anybody near her long enough to slip her poisoned food."

"What kind of dog is that?"

"An Irish water spaniel."

"She looks kind of cute."

"She may look cute, but she's pretty aggressive, especially with strangers, and especially on show days. That's why she's way over here."

"Are you her owner?" Jackie was now making conversation just to be polite. She couldn't very well sneak through the door to the judges' room with this man watching. But a glance at her watch showed that it was nearly eleven-thirty. She was suddenly impatient to reach the hounds, but she managed to keep her impatience under wraps.

"No, I'm her handler," the man answered. "Her owner's off on some yacht in the Caribbean right about now."

"Hmm. Listen," said Jackie eagerly. "I wonder—oh, you must be really busy."

"Not just now, no, I have a minute or two to spare." He gave her a curious look and folded his arms.

"Well, a friend of mine had suggested that I show my dog. But I don't know anything about it—about dog shows, that is. Then someone else told me about dog handlers, and I thought maybe that would be the way to go about it. Do you think I should try to find someone to help me show my dog?"

"What kind is it?"

"A German shepherd."

"Does your dog have papers?"

"Um, yes, of course." Jackie supposed that Jake had some kind of papers, somewhere. At least a diploma from the K-9 school, and probably something telling who he was and so forth. His records would be on file at the Palmer police. "He couldn't very well be in a dog show without papers, could he?" She flashed the man one of her working smiles.

"Well, not in this kind of dog show, at least," said the man, showing the first faint hint of a smile. He had begun to sound more agreeable. "So you'd like to find yourself a handler, you think?"

"That's right."

"Well, I tell you what you do." He reached in his back pocket and came up with a small folded pamphlet. "Get yourself a copy of this little publication." He held it out. *The Canine Chronicle* proclaimed the title. "It comes out once a month—it's on sale out in the front there, next to the grandstands, for a couple of dollars. Dog handlers looking for work tend to advertise."

"Oh," said Jackie. "You don't happen to know of anybody, just off the top of your head, who might be free?"

The man scratched his head. "Well, not really. Not for a shepherd. Except, now, wait a second . . . of course! I had forgotten. Terrible, just terrible. But you might want to try Sylvia Brown. The guy she used to do regular work for died, and she may be looking for new clients. I think she's probably here today."

Jackie took a small notebook out of her handbag and scribbled the name. "Is she good?"

"They say she's very good," replied the man with an odd chuckle. "She's been on the circuit a long time. You should look for her over in the hounds. You can't miss her. Blond, six feet tall, built like an athlete. Tell her Ralph Stevens sent you."

Aha! thought Jackie. But she merely smiled upon the man, thanked him for his time, and headed off toward the hounds.

Michael McGowan had prevailed upon the guard at the gate to allow him passage to the competitors' area, and he had spent the last half hour following in Jackie's footsteps, amused by her erratic progress. It was easy enough to see which dogs she liked and which she didn't. The non-sporting dogs didn't rate much of a look, except for a rambunctious dalmatian that was straining at his lead, and a very cute pair of Tibetan terriers, one golden and one black-and-white, both looking as though they'd do anything for anybody. McGowan had a cousin who raised Tibetan terriers. They were wonderful dogs, no question about it, although McGowan's cousin, who had a dozen of the boisterous little things, was a little overboard about them. People got that way about their dogs, though.

From next to the Tibetan terriers he had watched as Jackie made her way through the sporting dogs. Predictably, she had sped past the pointers but stopped to linger over the retrievers. Pointers, springer spaniels, and other tightly wound outdoor dogs were breeds that required deeper acquaintance to be appreciated; whereas the retrievers were everybody's pals, pretty much from the start.

Now McGowan himself was among the sporting dogs. He stood in a small group that had gathered around a phlegmatic-looking lump of a dog—someone had mentioned that it was a clumber spaniel—and watched Jackie's conversation with the Irish water spaniel man with interest. As Jackie ended her conversation and headed off at a brisk pace down the long aisle, McGowan detached himself from the clumber spaniel's admirers and began to follow. She looked to be heading straight for the hounds; evidently the man with the Irish water spaniel had told her something of interest. As he trailed her down the long aisle, McGowan made a mental note to tell Jackie to work on her poker face.

When Jackie reached the hounds area, there was no sign of anyone who might be Sylvia Brown. Jackie determined that her best strategy, for the moment, would be to try to pick up what information she could, before tipping her hand, by listening to the conversations about her.

She looked around, trying to locate a spot that seemed promising.

In the first carry crate there was an enormous bloodhound, sound asleep and snoring loudly, looking like a huge brown blanket of wrinkles. On a chair next to him was a man who—except that he was a man and not a dog—might have been a bloodhound himself. There were the same pendulous jowls, the same long, loppy ears, the same look of thoughtful assessment that you might see on the face of a working bloodhound. The man looked, too, like he might drop off to sleep at any moment. Then the resemblance between him and his dog would be complete.

Nothing doing here, thought Jackie.

The next spot was occupied by the beagle lady, whom Jackie had already seen engaged in a heated exchange with Phil Watts, owner of Serena, the poodle. The beagle lady looked like a more promising source of information—she was even now calling out to one woman across the aisle, while physically detaining another.

"I tell you it's just not right," the woman was complaining as Jackie moved close enough to hear. "Yooo-hooo! Virginia!" She beckoned to the woman from across the aisle. Then she turned back to her audience. "And I don't *care* if it was only a letter to the editor. Then it's the *editor's* responsibility as well. Dick Buzone ought to be disqualified from judging, just for having printed something so inflammatory, and so unfair. He positively maligns poor Clematis, and all of her sisters and brothers. He never knew a thing about beagles anyway."

"Oh, now, Thalia," said the woman whose wrist the beagle lady was holding. "Don't fly off the handle, will you? You *know* that if you lodge a complaint against Dick Buzone you'll only get his back up and make it worse for yourself." She patted the beagle lady's wrist and gently extricated herself from her grasp. "I must go, really. They're calling the non-sporting dogs, and just look at the time."

The woman addressed as Virginia arrived just as the other woman escaped. "Oh, Virginia. There you are," said the beagle lady. "Here, have you *seen* this outrage?" She waved a copy of *The Canine Chronicle* under Virginia's nose. "Have you *seen* what that man said about my dogs?"

"I *did* see it, Thalia," said Virginia, her voice warm and full of sympathy. "But if I were you I wouldn't let it worry you. After all, the man is dead."

Jackie perked up her ears.

"Yes. He's dead, but he lives on. An utter nuisance, in death as he was in life."

"Now, Thalia—"

"Besides which, I do *not* see the purpose that it serves to print such garbage. Dick Buzone should know better. I am going to circulate a petition to have him disqualified, Virginia, and I will expect you to sign it." Thalia Gilmore—for Jackie had concluded that this was she, the awe-inspiring woman whose dog had been poisoned in Philadelphia—folded her arms across her impressive front and glowered at Virginia.

Virginia, however, was apparently used to the beagle lady's tirades, for she neither acceded nor promised even to think about it. She merely changed the subject.

"Have the police been to see you yet, Thalia?"

Jackie, pretending to admire a saluki tied up across the aisle, moved in a little closer.

"Why on earth would the police want to see me?" retorted Thalia Gilmore.

"Well, after all, Mel *was* murdered. And you did see him that very evening, didn't you? At the meeting."

"He was alive when I left. They can't possibly think I had anything to do with that," sniffed Thalia Gilmore. "I wouldn't stoop to it. Wouldn't stoop. I'm surprised at you, Virginia, I really am."

"Well, you must admit that you and Mel had a quarrel brewing."

"Well, dear heavens, yes! He was such a provocative man. The way he treated my poor Clematis, the last time she stayed at that idiotic Dog Academy, was something else indeed. But I wouldn't murder him, when I could simply shun him. Far more effective." She lowered her voice to impart confidential information; Jackie could still easily hear every word. "He was banned, you know, from the Greater Palmer Bassets and Beagles Association, on *my* recommendation. That's why he wrote this tripe." She waved *The Canine Chronicle* again. "But Dick Buzone—he's another matter altogether. Printing this nonsense—especially after my tragedy in Philadelphia. Oh, the two of them were thick as thieves, but I am surprised that the murderer was so clumsy. Only did half of his job. To think, Virginia, that I'm a *subscriber*."

"You know that never makes any difference to Dick. Now, just calm down. Look at poor Clematis—she's all ready to go, Thalia, and you're a wreck. Comb your hair and put on some lipstick. They're ready for the hounds. You'll be on in five minutes."

Clematis, the beagle, did indeed look as though she was impatient to show off for an audience. She wagged her tail merrily and sniffed the air with a cheerful readiness. Thalia Gilmore, with a sniff of her own, withdrew an old powder compact from her pocket and began to powder her nose. The scent of the powder reached Jackie, reminding her powerfully of her childhood, of waiting for her mother to get ready. Jackie hadn't known they still made that kind of face powder.

Evidently Virginia's pep talk had worked. Thalia Gilmore,

in another minute, took a deep breath, squared her shoulders, gave Clematis's lead a sharp tug, and strode off toward the show ring.

Jackie looked at her program of the day's events. The judge for today's competition in the hounds was a man called Richard Buzone. Apparently, he was not very popular with the hound owners—if Thalia and Virginia's conversation was anything to go by. Jackie wondered how she might be able to approach him. But that would have to wait. First she must see if she could find and size up Sylvia Brown.

Finding her, now that the hounds and their owners were all concentrated near the show ring, proved to be a much simpler matter. Jackie soon saw her leaning up against a dog crate, her elegant arms folded, her pale thin hair cascading down her back. She seemed to sense Jackie's presence, for she turned around and gave her an inquiring look, then turned her attention once more to the ring.

She was indeed unmistakable, as the water spaniel's handler had said—six feet tall, at least, with long blond hair, a fresh-looking face, and a graceful way of moving. If Amy's suspicions were true, it wouldn't take much to imagine Mel Sweeten falling for her. Or any other man, for that matter.

Suddenly there floated into Jackie's mind an image of little Amy Sweeten trying on this Amazon's black-lace nightie—Jackie had to stifle a laugh, not of amusement but of horror. *Poor Amy!*

Now that she was face-to-face with the woman, Jackie was utterly at a loss. It was one thing to pretend to want to hire a dog handler; it was quite another thing to boldly march right up to the woman and make conversation. Especially in a setting like this, where everyone seemed preoccupied, with their minds very much on the events of the afternoon. What could Jackie hope to say? "Oh, by the way I wanted to know if you were having an affair with Mel Sweeten"? No, hardly. That wouldn't do.

There was another possible approach, however. Amy Sweeten had mentioned that Sylvia taught aerobics at a gym on the west side. It would be easy enough to sign up for a class, and then strike up a conversation afterward. That approach would be much more natural, Jackie reflected.

As these thoughts fluttered through her mind, Jackie was startled to hear a pleasant, familiar voice behind her.

"Miss Brown?"

Jackie turned around hastily. There was Michael McGowan. He gave Jackie a quick look that plainly said, "Play it cool." Jackie took the hint and kept silent, shrinking back a little way as McGowan dug out his identification. "I'm Lieutenant McGowan of the Palmer police department. I wondered if I might have a word with you?"

Sylvia Brown sized McGowan up with a quick glance. Then she lifted one side of her mouth in a smile. "You sure took your time about it." She gave her long hair a toss and moved closer to the detective. "Your place or mine?" she asked in a soft voice.

Jackie felt an unreasoning rush of something that felt suspiciously like jealousy. She stifled it, and managed to don an amused smile for McGowan's benefit.

"Oh, my place, I think. The view is spectacular." He smirked at Jackie and headed off, guiding Sylvia Brown gently by the elbow.

"That little worm," muttered Jackie to herself.

CHAPTER 10

"An apology?" said Jackie coolly into the telephone. "What on earth for?" She furiously stirred a potful of spaghetti sauce on the stove. She was still pretty annoyed with the way her afternoon's sleuthing had turned out.

"Oh, come on, Jackie," said McGowan. "I was just doing my job. Don't be that way."

"I'm not being any 'way,' Michael."

"Yes, you are. I called to apologize for acting like a schoolboy, or something, today."

"It's quite all right. You don't owe it to me to act like a grown-up." Jackie knew that probably stung, but it was true. Still, she really ought to come down off her high horse a bit. She genuinely liked Michael McGowan. "Oh, okay. You acted like a schoolboy, but I forgive you. Is that better?"

"Much. Don't you want to tell me why you were sneaking up on that woman today?"

"Of course I do." Jackie caught herself. "But I wasn't sneaking up on her."

"You were too. I followed you all morning, Jackie, and you were *definitely* sneaking. Hey, I snuck up on her too—it's nothing to be ashamed of, take it from me. So. When would it be convenient for me to come over and grill you?"

Jackie looked at the clock. Nearly suppertime. "How about now? But only if you promise that you'll bring a bottle of red wine for us and some ice cream for Peter. That is, if you want any spaghetti."

"Of course I do." McGowan sounded pleased with himself. "What flavor?"

"Hold on a minute." She covered the receiver and called to Peter, who was in the den with Jake. Chocolate, the answer came back, and was duly relayed.

"Is he your boyfriend, Mom?" asked Peter predictably when Jackie told him that McGowan was coming for supper.

"No, baby, he's not my boyfriend. He's just a friend. He's working on a case, and he thought maybe I could help him."

Peter looked suitably impressed. "Like before."

"Well, kind of. Not quite as much in our own backyard, but a man was killed last week, and I happen to know his wife. She works at Rodgers. So—that's all there is to it, really. Did you have an okay time with your dad this weekend?"

"Uh-huh." Peter clammed up.

Just as well, thought Jackie. It was infinitely preferable to her not to know anything about her ex-husband's activities, or to know as little as she could get away with.

Thus Peter and Jackie turned their attention to the spaghetti sauce, and then to making garlic bread and a salad. So that by the time McGowan got there, around seven o'clock, everything was ready. Peter was rather proud of the garlic bread, which he considered to be his specialty.

● ● ●

When supper was finished, and the chocolate ice cream was gone, Peter absented himself from the kitchen table to finish his homework (fractions), leaving his mother and McGowan to talk about the events of the day.

"Listen, Jackie," McGowan began in a solemn voice, "I don't want to be telling you what to do. But how was it that you turned up at the dog show in the first place? And why were you sneaking up on Sylvia Brown?"

Jackie smiled. It was kind of fun to mystify her detective. And she was curious to find out if the police suspected that Mel was having an affair. "I wasn't sneaking. And a dog show is, after all, a public event. I bought a ticket, just like everyone else."

He shook his head. "Jackie, really. You ought to trust me, you know. After all, it's not just a coincidence, is it, that you were spying on the woman who handled Mel Sweeten's dogs?"

"There's no law against going to a dog show, is there? Why did you come to grill me?"

"Because it's my job." Sometimes the simple truth was the best course. "Besides—you could get hurt. And I think that would be my fault."

Jackie pondered this. After a moment's thought, she nodded. "I appreciate that. Okay. I suppose, in a way, I got a little curious."

"A little curious?" McGowan laughed. "Any more curiosity and I'd have to swear you in as a deputy. Now—spill it."

Jackie took a deep breath and told him about her visit to Mel Sweeten's Dog Academy. He was vastly amused by her cover—the attempt to sign Jake up for a refresher course in obedience training.

"I tell you, Michael, I didn't really have a comfortable feeling about that manager, Tom Mann. He gave me the creeps. Have you checked him out?"

"We have. He was away on vacation all last week, in Florida."

"Oh." Jackie was disappointed. "Maybe he came back early?"

"Nope. Well, we're double-checking, of course. But I imagine his story will hold up. You can't fudge that kind of thing for long. At least, you can't lie to the police about it."

"Oh. No, I guess that would be pretty stupid. But frankly, Michael, I don't think Amy Sweeten could have done it. For one thing, she told me that she didn't."

He grinned. "Did you expect her to say that she had?"

"No—but you never know. She's kind of an odd person. She—well, since you were sneaking around at the dog show, I guess that means you know, um, something about Sylvia Brown?"

"Oh, yes." McGowan teased her with a grin. "Not that I wouldn't like to know more. But we're working on the relationship between Sylvia Brown and Mel Sweeten, if that's what you mean."

"I guess maybe that's what I mean." Jackie felt great relief. She hadn't wanted to violate a confidence. But Amy hadn't actually asked her to keep anything confidential—in fact, that was sort of odd, when you thought about it. Jackie was suddenly overcome with the certainty that Amy had wanted to use her as a conduit to the police. For embarrassing information that it would have been too difficult to pass along on her own initiative. She furrowed her brow.

"What?" asked McGowan.

"I wonder if I'm being used," replied Jackie.

"Of course you are. I'm using you right now, as a sounding board and a source of information. If that man's widow talked to you—and I think she probably bent your ear—then it's a sure bet she wanted you to talk to us."

"How do you know?"

"Because." He leaned forward and rested his arms on the kitchen table. "When I turned up there to talk to her last Thursday, she said she knew that you and I were friends."

"Oh!" Jackie sat back in her chair.

"So—forget all about the seal of the confessional, and tell me what you think."

"Okay." Jackie took a breath and related to him most of her interview with Amy Sweeten. She omitted any mention of the nightgown, out of a desire to protect Amy's weirdness from the bald scrutiny of the police. Nor did she say that Amy suspected Mel of cheating on her, but McGowan had already drawn that conclusion.

"Did she mention anything about a nightgown?" he asked.

"Umm—" Jackie hesitated. "A nightgown?"

"Yeah—a little lace number from Victoria's Secret," he told her as Jackie hesitated. "We know all about it. The motel manager called us Friday morning, after reading about the murder in the paper. Seems someone calling herself Mrs. Sweeten, who had booked a room at his place for one night, left a nightgown behind. So he mailed it back to her. Then about a week ago he gets a thank-you note in the mail. Very punctilious, you might say. But he thought the note was kind of odd, because Mrs. Sweeten asked the manager to write back and confirm the date on which she had stayed at the motel."

"Yikes," said Jackie.

McGowan grinned. "I agree. The manager thought that was pretty weird, and when he read about the murder he thought he ought to tell us. Wanted to be a good citizen. Which just goes to show that cheating husbands never seem to learn."

Jackie ignored the jest and McGowan seemed to sense that he had stepped on a sore point, because his expression quickly grew somber again.

"So, Jackie, here's what I think. Off the record, of course. I think Mel Sweeten was having an affair. Maybe with Sylvia Brown, maybe with someone else. From the police point of view, you know, that's a pretty strong motive for murder. Tried and true, anyway."

"I suppose so," agreed Jackie reluctantly. "Okay, suppose Amy did have an idea about it. She still probably wouldn't kill him. She wanted him to divorce her." She told McGowan briefly about Amy's waiting game. "I admit that her logic about sticking around seems thin, but then people do cling to straws. Besides, I don't see how Amy could have done it. She's not nearly tall enough to sneak up behind a six-foot man and throw a choke collar over his head. But Sylvia Brown is plenty tall enough."

"Tall, yes." McGowan grinned again. "Okay. Personally, based on my interview with the victim's wife, I'd have to say that she doesn't look like she's strong enough to swat a fly. But we have to look at a few other things too, like opportunity and motive. The motive is big as all outdoors."

Jackie shook her head. "No, I disagree. She told me plainly that she might have wanted to murder him, but if she had she would have made sure he suffered. She was quite remarkably matter-of-fact about the whole idea."

"Most murderers are."

"Yes, but, Michael—if she had done it, why kill him right there at home? Why not do him in on one of his road trips? Besides, she says she was at a Denny's in Wardville, having dinner." Jackie rolled her eyes. "Now, if you were dreaming up an alibi, would you come up with something as dweeby as that?"

"Yeah, you have a point," McGowan conceded. "Okay, here's the story as far as we know it." He filled Jackie in a little bit on the meeting of the executive committee of the Greater Palmer Dog Fanciers Association. "At about a quarter to eight, there was some kind of racket outside—the dogs were barking their heads off, I guess. Sweeten went outside to check it out, and came back in again about ten minutes later. This guy Buzone thinks he was upset about something. Figures maybe there was a prowler trying to steal the dogs. And that Sweeten went out again later, after the meeting was over, and caught the guy red-handed. So the guy killed him."

"Strangling him with a dog collar but leaving the dogs behind? Come on, Michael."

"It's not *my* theory," he said defensively.

"Then what happened?"

"The meeting broke up at about eight-fifteen. Apparently it wasn't a friendly meeting—they had been arguing about something, but according to Dick Buzone, the president, the monthly meetings were always like that."

"I hate meetings," put in Jackie. "What were they arguing about?"

"Who should be the sponsor of the blue ribbon at the dog show. Not the sort of thing you ordinarily would kill somebody over."

"These people are anything but ordinary, Michael. Did you get a load of the decor out at Mel Sweeten's place?"

McGowan chuckled. "The dog lamps and dog ashtrays? Yeah, nice touches, eh? But I still don't think that passions about a dog-show sponsor lead to murder. And as far as we can tell, that's all that was discussed at the meeting."

"Do you believe that?"

"I don't know, really. No, I'm sure they talked about other things. But Buzone says they had a pitched argument about who the sponsor should be. The company that won out is McKean Pharmaceuticals."

"Doesn't sound very promising," agreed Jackie.

"Besides, let's look at the wife's motive again. She's off in Wardville, but that's only half an hour from here. She says she went to Denny's—but what if Amy Sweeten came home a day early and surprised Mel in the embrace of Sylvia Brown?"

Jackie shook her head. "Nope. If she came home and surprised them in an adulterous embrace, your blond bombshell would be a witness."

"She's *not* 'my' bombshell." McGowan fidgeted in his chair. "Okay, let's say for the sake of argument that Mel Sweeten was having an affair. With whoever. Doesn't matter. Say Amy comes home a day early, sees them, but they don't see her. Then the other woman leaves, Amy kills the husband, and then drives back to Wardville. Nobody, by the way, can vouch for her at Denny's."

"That's hardly surprising. The woman is practically invisible, she's so little and pale and skinny. No." Jackie was firm.

"You have to admit the thing about the nightgown is weird," said Michael. "Right? You admit she's weird."

"Look." She leaned across the table, intent. "I admit she's a weirdo. But this is what I think. She's trying to cope with the shock of being actually *glad* that her husband is dead. She's thrilled, like the Munchkins, you know, when Dorothy's house lands on the Wicked Witch of the East."

McGowan scowled.

"Well, then, like—like—" Jackie fished around.

"Like the wife in *Double Indemnity*."

"Right," said Jackie. "Like Barbara Stanwyck. She's delighted. She feels absolutely no regret at his death—and she's ashamed of her reaction, maybe, because it's not how she'd imagined it would be. Not how she'd always expected her marriage to turn out." Jackie colored slightly, but McGowan didn't appear to notice it. "You know, you have these ideals, and then the guy's a bum and you're— you're glad he died. But naturally if you have any sense of what's right and wrong, you're ashamed of that."

McGowan conceded that Jackie's logic had some strength to it.

"The way I see it," she went on, "there are some other possibilities. You wouldn't believe all that I saw and heard today at the dog show. Those people are worse than university faculty members for sheer internecine nastiness."

McGowan nodded. "So I gathered from my interview with Sylvia Brown. She told me it's a nest of vipers, the dog-show circuit. Of course, they close ranks like crazy when confronted with an outsider. You gotta have a dog to belong. Which is one of the reasons I wanted to talk to you. I want you to do me a favor."

"Oh?" Jackie smiled, interested. Evidently McGowan's territoriality didn't extend to things he couldn't easily do for himself. She would teach *him* to stroll off smugly with tall blond suspects.

He shrugged. "Well, I have to admit you gave me the idea. What would you think about sending Jake back to work?"

"Aha." Jackie frowned. "You mean that the Palmer police want him back?"

"More or less." McGowan could see that the idea wasn't going over very well. "Just for a little while, so that we can use him to get next to some of those dog people when they don't have their guard up."

Jackie glared at him. "I can't believe what I'm hearing."

"Why not? He's used to police work, you know. It's not

as though it would be hard for him."

"Maybe not for him—but how about for us? Haven't you got some other dog you could use?"

McGowan shook his head. "I tried that already. Spoke to Cornelius Mitchell about it—he's the guy in charge of our K-9 outfit. But no—remember the shipment of cocaine that came into the airport last week?"

Jackie nodded. "They're busy on that, I suppose," she said. "Noses to the grindstone."

McGowan chuckled. "A shortage of dogpower, that's all." He gave her a pleading look. "It would only be for a little while, Jackie."

"No."

"No?"

"No. What if something happened to him? Besides, they're sure to smell a rat, those dog-show people, if you send some of your big fat flatfoots around. So it would be a pointless exercise. They'd be on to you in two minutes."

"No way," protested McGowan.

"Yes, they will too. There were two of those guys at the Dog Academy on Saturday, and I knew at a glance they were yours. They stick out, Michael."

"Oh." He sounded disappointed. Jackie realized that she might have hurt his feelings—detectives were supposed to be good at undercover work.

Jackie grew thoughtful. "Here's a compromise," she said at last. "You can have the services of the finest ex-police dog in Palmer if you agree to let me be the one to handle him."

"Oh, come on, Jackie—"

"No, Michael. Either that, or forget it."

"But, Jackie, he's kind of not yours. I mean—is he?"

"Fine." She glared at him. "Go ahead, take him away right now, for good." Her eyes filled with tears. "Because either he's our dog or he belongs to the police. If he's ours, Peter's and mine, we'll be glad to help you on our own terms. If he's your dog, then go ahead and take him away, but don't you dare come back again. Anything else wouldn't be fair to me, or to Peter, or to Jake."

McGowan didn't have to think about it very long. "A deal," he said, "under one condition. And that is that if things get rough, or if you learn something important, that you tell me right away, and that you do what I say."

"Fair enough," said Jackie, who had no illusions about her own native ability to cope with murderers. She would leave that to the professionals—to McGowan, or to Jake, as the case might be. She stuck out her hand, and they shook.

"Now." Jackie rubbed her palms together. "Where do you think we should start?"

McGowan considered her question for a moment. "Now that people have seen you at one dog show, maybe the thing to do would be to go to the next one in the area."

"That's not for another month, Michael." She wrinkled her brow at him. "The schedule was right in the program. Honestly, don't you detectives detect anything?"

"I guess not." He grinned, trying hard to look humble.

Jackie tossed her long, dark hair. "If you hadn't been so busy sneaking around—"

"I was too busy," he admitted, contrite. "Sneaking is very hard work sometimes."

"But I have another idea." Jackie sat forward, alert. "Why don't I just pretend to be interested in signing up for a dog show, and kind of interview some of the leading competitors from the area. How about that?"

"Great," he said sarcastically. "Or maybe you should just tell them you're writing an article for your high school paper."

"It's not *such* a dumb idea," she retorted.

"Of course it's a dumb idea."

"Oh. Well, maybe it is dumb. Have a better suggestion?"

"No."

"Okay. Then we'll go with my dumb idea. And I think I know where to start."

"Yeah?"

"Yes. With one of the judges in the dog show. Dick Buzone. From what I could gather, everyone hates him. Did you hate him when you interviewed him?"

"I didn't exactly warm up to him. He's sort of like a flounder or something. Cold and pale."

"Well." Jackie grew enthusiastic. "I heard some old battle-ax saying that he and Sweeten were thick as thieves—but she just had a bee in her bonnet. She hates Mel Sweeten. Hated."

"If she's so full of ill feeling, why don't you start with her?"

"Nope. She hates Dick Buzone too. So, if I start with him, then I can move on to her, and we can both hate him together."

"Perfect."

CHAPTER 11

At a glance, Jackie guessed that it might be extremely easy to hate Dick Buzone. She disagreed with Michael's description, however; he was more like a long, thin eel than a flounder. He was cold and pale, definitely, and thin, with the kind of ascetic thinness that seemed to be a reprimand to people who like to eat. In his presence, Jackie was instantly conscious of the french fries she'd had for lunch. His lips were thin too—pale little lines of flesh that nearly disappeared when he closed his mouth. His eyes were pale amber, half-hidden by lids that reminded Jackie of the chameleons she'd had as a child. His hair was the only part of him that wasn't thin; it was dense, wavy, and the color of wheat. Jackie thought the hair was unjust. There were lots of agreeable and deserving men his age who would have given a potful of cash for a head of hair like that. It sat upon his head like some outlandish trophy. He was an eel with hair.

It was lunchtime on Tuesday, and Jackie had prevailed upon Dick Buzone to give her some advice about showing dogs. This much had been easy. Amy Sweeten had told her that Buzone was the president of the local dog fanciers club, and that he had been at the executive committee meeting at her house the night that Mel was killed.

Amy had also told her that if you wanted to break in to Palmer's dog world, you had to talk to Buzone. Mel used to laugh about it, Amy told her. It was almost as though Buzone thought he should interview people before allowing them to join his little circle. Amy, however, had never heard of anyone's being turned away. The membership dues, Jackie soon discovered, were thirty dollars a year, payable by check made out to Richard P. Buzone.

Now as Jackie sat conversing with him in the small office adjacent to his house, where he worked as an advertising consultant, and where *The Canine Chronicle* was published every month, she wrestled with the feeling that he was on to her. She had handed over her check and duly registered herself as a member of the Greater Palmer Dog Fanciers Association; in exchange, she had been given a bumper sticker for her car ("Show Dog On Board!") and a membership card. All that remained was to try to sound him out about Mel Sweeten.

"Well, I imagine that our chances are slim," she said, her voice sounding artificially bright in her own ears, "because I'm a novice, and our dog *is* getting on in years. But even if he doesn't win any prizes, I thought it would be nice to join. For my son's sake as well."

"Yes, indeed," said Buzone, studying her check carefully before tucking it away in a small safe behind his desk.

"But you're experienced," Jackie went on, "so probably you can tell me. Do you think a dog of advanced years has any chance of becoming a champion?"

"Depends on the dog," was Buzone's reasonable reply; somehow he managed to make it sound like a put-down.

Jackie controlled her defensive impulses and forged ahead. "He's very well trained, and he's beautiful to look at."

"Yes, I'm sure." Buzone shifted restlessly. "Look, Mrs., um—"

"Walsh. But please, call me Jackie. Everyone does."

Buzone looked at her. Clearly, he was not "everyone." He cleared his throat and continued. "Dog shows aren't for the fainthearted. It takes a great deal of dedication, and a great deal of time; even given the application of hard work, earning championship points also requires an outstanding dog. If you are only casually interested, I would suggest that you begin with obedience competition for your dog. You said he was a German shepherd?"

Jackie nodded. "What's an obedience competition?"

"It's a growing field," he replied, dismissive. "A less exacting type of competition, in a certain way. Obedience trials test a dog's readiness to perform certain tasks, and his ability to carry through with his job. Not more than that."

To Jackie, these sounded like things that might be more important, after all, than mere appearance. But she bit her lip as Buzone continued.

"An obedience competition does not test a dog's conformity to the breed's standard—and that, after all, is what we look for when awarding championship points to a dog. So if your dog is in any way short of the mark—which he probably is, most dogs are—you can still enjoy participating in a group event, get to know some people hereabouts—you said you were new to Palmer?"

Jackie nodded again. Another white lie for the scoreboard; she had grown up here, after all, even though she and Peter had only recently come back.

"Yes." Buzone was brisk. "Well, you'll find that at obedience competitions there are plenty of interesting people who attend. You will find it an easy matter to break the ice. It's not quite such a tense affair as a standard dog show. More of an outing."

"That sounds like fun," said Jackie, lying again. If there was anything that didn't sound like fun, it was a group outing with a bunch of dog nuts, watching their pets fetch and sit and jump and heel. "But I wouldn't know where to begin, really, with something like that. It doesn't sound much like an amateur's event. Do you think I need to hire someone to help me?"

"Ah, you mean a handler." Buzone considered this question, folding his lips inward until they became invisible, and his mouth was just a seam between his nose and his chin. He gave the freckled tip of his nose a businesslike tug and looked at Jackie with his pale eyes.

"I don't see why not, if you would feel more comfortable. As it happens, I know a very able young woman, about your age, who might be free to help you. She was regularly employed as a handler by one of the finest breeders in the area, but unfortunately their working relationship has come to an untimely end."

"I see," said Jackie, racking her brain desperately for a follow-up. "I think maybe I heard something about that, at the show on Sunday."

"Oh? You were there?"

"Didn't I mention that? That was how I found out about the Dog Fanciers Association. I spent most of Sunday at the show, because I wanted to see what one was like."

"I see." He stirred in his chair and tugged at a shirt cuff. "Yes, we observed a moment of silence at the start of the hound class in memory of Melvin Sweeten, one of the most outstanding men in our field."

Jackie nodded soberly. A moment of silence. Well, she hadn't noticed it, but then perhaps nobody had told the dogs that they had to stop barking and yapping. "He—he was *murdered,* wasn't he? And the police think his wife did it."

"Oh?" Buzone's pale amber eyes lit up. "I didn't know they had a suspect."

"Well, at least that's what I heard. But maybe it's just a rumor."

"The newspaper indicated that she was out of town at the time."

"Oh? I didn't know that."

"Yes. Out of town." Buzone shifted in his chair and tugged again at the tip of his nose. It must be a sign of interest, thought Jackie. He really was a repellent man, although she couldn't have said exactly why she disliked him so. But she was now eager to be gone.

"May I ask where you heard this information about the police interest in Mrs. Sweeten?" he inquired, sounding casual. "Her husband and I were longtime friends, and I'd like to be helpful to her if I can. Who told you the police suspected her?"

"Oh—I don't really know, actually," said Jackie evasively. "I think maybe I heard some people talking about it at the dog show."

"I'm surprised I didn't hear the rumor myself." He crossed his long, skinny legs and regarded her thoughtfully. "Are you certain?"

"I don't know how *I* could be certain of anything about it," replied Jackie reasonably. She was certain, however, of one thing—that Dick Buzone was displaying a great deal of interest in the matter. "I didn't even know the guy."

"No." He sniffed and raised an eyebrow. "No, so you didn't." He rubbed his dry palms together, making a chuffing noise, and reached into a drawer of his desk. "Well, then. Thank you for your interest." He regarded a small white card that Jackie had filled out. "Would you rather have your home number listed in our little directory? Or your office number?"

"Oh, the home phone, I think."

"But you do work?"

"Yes. Yes, I'm teaching film history at the university."

"Ah. Mrs. Sweeten is one of your colleagues, then."

"I know. There's been some talk on campus—but she's an art historian, and I deal with popular culture. You know that those are two very different worlds." *Lies number three and four,* thought Jackie.

"Yes, I suppose they are different. Ahem. Well, now. Why don't I give you this form to fill out"—he handed her the paper—"and you can submit it next weekend, for entry to our first obedience trials of the season. It's good fun."

Jackie sincerely doubted that anything with Dick Buzone could be good fun, but she dutifully folded the paper away into her pocketbook and thanked him. "About the woman?"

"What woman?" snapped Buzone.

"The one that you said might want to be a handler for me. For my dog."

"Oh, yes of course. Forgive me." He drew a single large sheet of blank paper toward him and picked up an expensive-looking fountain pen from a tray on his desk. "Her name is Sylvia Brown, and although I don't have her home telephone number, I'm sure she's listed. During the week, she teaches some sort of class at a gymnasium. This is the address. You will probably find her there, most evenings."

Jackie thanked him again and rose to leave. "Oh, one more thing," she said. "I almost forgot. You probably need my address. For the newsletter."

"The newsletter?" He didn't look pleased.

"Well, yes. I mean, isn't a subscription part of the membership?"

"Oh, no. *The Canine Chronicle* is quite a separate operation, Mrs., um—"

"Walsh." Jackie tried not to sound impatient.

"Yes. We don't sell subscriptions to the *Chronicle*—just single issues. Haven't got the manpower to mail it out—or the revenues, I'm afraid. But you'll find it on sale at the important shows, of course."

"Oh." Jackie let disappointment register on her face. Better that than puzzlement.

"Although," said Buzone in an expansive tone, "maybe we should give a thought to including the first copy free with paid membership. That's not a bad idea. Here you go." He reached around behind his desk and grabbed the most recent issue. "Gratis. For giving me the idea."

"Thank you," said Jackie, looking over the little magazine. "I appreciate your time."

"You're most welcome." Buzone was ready for her to go.

Jackie, for her part, was glad to be leaving.

CHAPTER 12

"Michael, why is it that every time you call me you apologize?" Jackie was in her office, between classes, looking over her standard lecture notes on the comic films of Harold Lloyd and their significance in the sociocultural setting of the twenties and thirties. The class would see *The Freshman* today. Jackie was pretty tired of *The Freshman*—one way and another, she had seen it about thirty times. She was aware, however, that very few comedies stood the test of time so well. So she resigned herself, and flipped through the note cards, and chattered away to McGowan.

"I don't expect you to be at home every time I call," she said. "And you certainly don't have to apologize to me for being out. That's what answering machines are for."

"Okay," said McGowan, sounding relieved.

Perversely, McGowan's eagerness to put things right with Jackie made her curious. For the first time, she felt that she *might* like to know where Michael McGowan had been last night, and with whom. But it wouldn't do to have that kind of feeling—that sort of thing would deliver her right into his hands. She dismissed her curiosity and grew businesslike.

"I only wanted to report on my conversation with Dick Buzone—the one you think is a flounder."

"Oh, yeah. Did you talk to him?"

"Yup. He's creepy. I think he probably did it. He's got yellow eyes. Icky."

"I agree that he's icky," McGowan said lightly. "Probably I should arrest him just for his ickiness."

"Well, you probably think I should go fly a kite, but I feel strongly that it's my duty as a citizen to tell you something about him."

"Like what?" McGowan sounded bored.

"Like this. He puts out a little monthly magazine that's on sale at all the dog shows. It's mostly ads, and then a few stories about things like dog hairstyles, or a new kind of chewy bone, or something." Jackie was fishing desperately in her bookbag for her copy of *The Canine Chronicle*; at last she found it and hastily flipped it open. "Here's one, in this month's issue, called 'Puppy Cuts for Older Poodles.' "

"Terrific. And?"

"Well, and this. At the dog show on Sunday I heard some old bat with a beagle say she was a subscriber. But Dick Buzone told me they didn't sell subscriptions."

"Jackie, that's hardly a clue."

"Oh." Jackie was stung. "Well, you don't have to sound so superior about it."

"I'm not being superior," McGowan protested.

"I thought it was kind of suspicious. I mean, there I was with my checkbook in my hand, all ready to fork over significant dough for a newsletter about *dogs,* for Pete's sake. And Dick Buzone says no, he's terribly sorry, but they don't take subscriptions."

"I don't see what's so strange."

"It's strange because I *know* that this lady with the beagle had a subscription. I heard her say it. Plus, I wondered how Mel Sweeten had gotten himself involved in the magazine. He had an article in it that the beagle lady was complaining about. The beagle lady, for your information, was very angry with both Mel Sweeten and Dick Buzone. And I think she's a very important person in the dog world. Her name is Thalia Gilmore." Jackie was rather proud of this bit of information, but McGowan's response took the wind out of her sails.

"Ah, yes—the one that's like a great tank."

"You know her?"

"She was one of the people there at the executive committee meeting. But Buzone saw her leave, and she has an alibi for later on that evening."

Jackie hid her disappointment. "Oh, well. How's the investigation going on your end?"

"Uh—not nearly as well. While you've been befriending suspects, all of my people have been coming up empty-handed."

"No evidence who the nightgown belonged to?"

"Not so far. We're tracing it, but it will take a few days. It came from Victoria's Secret, we know that. But it could have been a mail-order number. It will take a while."

"You still think Amy did it, don't you?"

"I never said I thought that Amy did it."

"Oh, Michael. You didn't have to say what you thought."

"Oh."

"Hey, listen. When you were at the dog show on Sunday, did you happen to watch any of the competition?"

"A little bit, when I wasn't hunting for suspects or sneaking around with Sylvia. Why?"

"Well, it just occurs to me that you and Bathsheba— I mean Sylvia—sneaked off right about the time that the hounds were competing."

"Yeah, I was really sorry to have to miss the big sniff-off in the center ring. So?"

"Well, so—be sensible, Michael. Bassets hounds are *hounds*."

"No, really?"

"Boy, you are being snide today. What's gotten into you?"

"Nothing. I just don't get the excitement about the hounds, that's all."

"Well, you and I are not dog nuts. Thank heavens. But those people are really serious about this stuff, Michael. I think you ought to talk to somebody called Frank Dill."

"Who's he?"

"He's the guy that won the hounds. Or his dog did. You should have seen his dog—looked kind of like an old Brillo pad. But a cute Brillo pad. It was something called an otter hound."

"And I should talk to the owner of the Brillo pad?"

"Yes. Because, after you snuck away with that woman, I heard someone say that if Mel Sweeten's dogs had been there, the Brillo pad never would have won."

"Aha. You think maybe this guy Dill killed Mel Sweeten so his Brillo pad could win the hound group at the dog show."

"It's a possibility. Isn't it?"

"Right. Okay, Jackie, I have to get back to work now. Listen, let me know if you make any more earth-shattering discoveries."

"Sure thing."

They hung up.

" 'Sylvia,' " muttered Jackie aloud, as she thumbed impatiently through her note cards on Harold Lloyd. "He calls her 'Sylvia.' "

At his desk at Palmer Central, Michael McGowan doodled on a note pad.

Last night he had interviewed Sylvia Brown at length. He was still trying to piece together his impressions. One thing you could be sure of, Sylvia Brown wasn't shy about trying to make an impression.

"And *eight, seven, six, five, four, three, two, one,*" said Sylvia Brown. "Remember to breathe," she coached. "Now, take it down and *stretch* it out, good! *Eight, seven, six, five, four, three, two, one.*"

Jackie, sweating and groaning her way through forty-five minutes of vigorous aerobics, wondered vaguely what "it" was. Whenever someone taught an exercise class, they told you to take *it* down, and stretch *it* out, or do a variety of other things to "it." In her experience, every aerobics and calisthenics teacher in the world talked about "it."

It was well that Jackie's mind was thus occupied, for the class was a strain. She realized with chagrin that it had been many months since she'd had any kind of serious exercise. This time, she vowed half seriously, she would stick with it. Sylvia Brown's was an early evening class—five-thirty— and the gym was just two blocks from home. It would be easy to get there two, three times a week, she fantasized— she could drop Peter over at Isaac Cook's house for an hour. Soon, Jackie vowed, she would be in really magnificent shape.

There was no question that Sylvia Brown gave you something to aim for. Her height alone would have made her impressive; but in her Day-Glo spandex suit, she looked less like Bathsheba than she did like some fierce Amazon, or a goddess out of Greek mythology. Like Diana the huntress, chaste and fair. Well, Sylvia was fair, anyway, reflected Jackie. There was no way Diana would have fallen for a guy like Mel Sweeten, not with Apollo around.

"Time for everyone's favorite: ab*dom*inals," Sylvia

Brown called to the class. The women dutifully hauled out mats and began a punishing round of sit-ups. "And *crunch,* and *up* and *up* and *up!* Come on, you can do it," Sylvia urged, smiling at the class as she crunched. Apparently Sylvia had muscles of steel. Like those steel fibers that they made radial tires from. "Just sixteen more!"

Jackie's stomach muscles protested fearsomely. This was probably the punishment she deserved for sticking her nose where it didn't belong. Also for those french fries, which she had repented of already in Dick Buzone's office. *Never again, never again,* she said to herself, crunching up. *No more fries, ever again.*

When class was over, Jackie lay exhausted on her mat and watched wearily to see what Sylvia Brown would do. As Jackie had hoped, she headed for the women's locker room. As soon as she recovered her strength, Jackie followed. She had come equipped with shampoo and towel, for the sake of verisimilitude, but Sylvia apparently hadn't worked out hard enough to need a shower. She had barely raised a glimmer of perspiration. Jackie, feeling her age, groaned inwardly.

"Great class," Jackie said brightly, hoping that nobody would keep score of the lies she was telling. All in a good cause.

"Thanks," replied Sylvia, somewhat vacantly. "You're new to my class, aren't you?"

Jackie nodded. "Actually, my son and I just moved to Palmer about six months ago. So we're sort of new to everything around here."

"It's not a bad city. Working?" She spun the combination of her locker.

"I teach film history at Rodgers." Jackie pulled off her limp T-shirt and quickly donned an old turtleneck.

"Oh. Right around the corner." Sylvia slipped a pair of warm-up sweats over her spandex suit. "Like it?"

"Pretty much. I taught there a while ago, actually—then I got married and moved away. Now—well, I'm back again."

"Back in the saddle."

"More or less." Jackie struggled into her baggiest jeans. Honestly, it was terrible the way you could just let yourself go. Women built like Sylvia Brown didn't have this kind of problem. It wasn't fair—it was like Dick Buzone's hair. Jackie sucked in her stomach, trying not to be obvious. She would have to do something about it. Well, she *was* doing something about it, sort of. At least tonight.

"Listen," she began hopefully, when she had her blue jeans zipped up. "Um, I was talking to someone the other day who thought you might be able to help me."

Sylvia Brown looked at her swiftly. "Thought I could? Help you?"

"Yes—you see, my son Peter and I thought it might be kind of fun to enter our dog in a dog show—except that we don't know anything about it. Then someone told me that you do that professionally—take dogs to dog shows, that is. And I thought, 'What a coincidence!' because I had already decided to sign up for your aerobics class."

As Sylvia Brown listened, her expression changed from interest to wariness. "Who told you?"

"Huh?"

"I said, who told you about me?"

Jackie thought fast. For some reason, she was impelled to avoid the mention of Dick Buzone. "Just somebody I met on Sunday. I went down to the dog show at the armory. Some guy with a big black dog, who looked sort of like a poodle. The dog, I mean, not the guy."

Sylvia Brown swung her gym bag over her shoulder and

gave Jackie a long, thoughtful look. "Ralph Stevens?" she asked finally.

"*That's* the guy," Jackie exclaimed, stuffing her gym clothes into a tote bag. "I couldn't think of his name for the life of me."

"Huh." Sylvia Brown led the way out of the locker room and down a ramshackle staircase to the ground floor. "What kind of a dog do you have?"

"A German shepherd."

"A puppy?" They had reached the street and paused in front of the gym door. The early dark of the March night had settled in around them like a blanket. It was cold, and damp, and the street lamp in front of the entrance to the gym seemed to have something wrong with it. It hissed and buzzed, and flickered into a pale yellowish-gray life, only to die again, every few seconds.

Jackie was suddenly conscious of the sleeping strength of the other woman—of her height, and the power she had displayed in class. With a chill, Jackie wondered if she had made an enormous error in judgment.

Nobody knew she was here. Peter was at Isaac's house, but he had made that plan ages ago—the two were working on a history project together. Jake was at home, guarding the house. And Jackie hadn't been smart enough, or humble enough, to tell McGowan of her plan to see Sylvia Brown tonight.

Yet she knew that this woman could easily have pulled that collar tight around Mel Sweeten's neck. What was more, she knew a little bit about what kind of a woman she was—fairly ruthless, at a guess. The best that could be said was that she bad allowed herself to become involved with a married man. Nor had her approach to Michael McGowan, on Sunday at the armory, been lost on Jackie.

Jackie's blood ran cold. Did Sylvia Brown remember

seeing her at the armory on Sunday? Had she noticed the conspiratorial look that had passed between herself and Lieutenant McGowan?

Jackie forced herself to continue the conversation as normally as possible.

"A puppy? Oh—no. He's grown-up, all trained and very well behaved. He's ten, we think. More or less. Which way are you going?"

"Over to Chestnut Street." She looked at her watch. "Going to meet a friend. How about you?"

"Home—just a few blocks from here."

They began to walk together toward a working street-light. Jackie began to wonder if it was reasonable to be so suspicious of this woman. There could be another, more prosaic reason why Jackie wasn't taking a shine to Sylvia Brown. If she got home in one piece tonight, she'd have to examine her motives very carefully.

"For a show dog, you know, ten's kind of past it," said Sylvia Brown, her tone dismissive.

On the other hand, Jackie reflected, maybe the woman was just really and truly a jerk.

"Well, we don't expect him to win very many prizes, but I kind of thought it might be a good hobby for Peter."

"Your son?"

"Yep."

"How little is he?" Sylvia Brown's tone was not that of a woman with a fondness for children.

"He's ten too." Jackie took a deep breath. The air was freezing. She dug her hands deeper into her pockets and hunched up her shoulders. "I thought it might take his mind off of things, a little bit. There have been a lot of changes for him lately."

They had reached the corner, and stood there talking for a few more moments. "Thank you for asking, but I really don't know if I'll be keeping up the dog handling," said Sylvia. "I had a bad experience." She looked at Jackie sharply. "A good friend of mine, the person whose dogs I used to work with, was recently killed."

Jackie was taken aback. She hadn't anticipated that Sylvia Brown would open up to her in this way. "That must be very hard for you," she said lamely.

"Maybe you've heard about it," Sylvia went on, giving Jackie a sharp look.

"Um, could be. If you mean the man who was murdered at the Dog Academy, yes, I did read about it."

"He was a very good friend of mine," Sylvia said, as though to make sure Jackie understood. She looked at Jackie with something like appeal in her eyes. "I had worked with his dogs for a long time, so we knew each other very well. We talked to each other a lot, told each other things. And he was murdered, and I don't know why he was murdered, or who would want to kill him. I'm terrified."

Jackie was impressed. If this confidence was a put-on, it was excellently contrived. Of course she was scared—the mistress of the murdered man, to whom he had confided all his secrets, would naturally be frightened. Unless she knew herself, for some reason, to be safe. Unless, perhaps, she had done the murder herself.

"I don't blame you for being shocked and worried," said Jackie. "Last fall, someone in my department was murdered. I was shaken up for weeks afterward. I think I can understand how you feel."

"Can you?" Sylvia Brown lifted a well-kept eyebrow. "Maybe." She shrugged. "I think I'd better say no for now. But maybe I'll change my mind. Okay?"

"Sure," said Jackie. "Thanks a lot."

They parted.

Jackie, as she headed for Isaac Cook's house to collect

Peter, wondered if all of her speculation was foolish. Sylvia Brown seemed perfectly nice, for an adulteress. If she even was an adulteress. Amy, after all, had no proof that this was the person Mel had been involved with. And even if it had been Sylvia Brown, he had probably been a bum husband to start with. Amy was certainly better off with him gone.

For just a moment, thinking about marriages and mistresses, Jackie was swept with an unaccustomed bitterness over the failure of her own marriage. For an instant, Jackie felt that she would give anything to be once more in the happy first years of her marriage to Cooper, before his selfish indulgence had poisoned everything that the two of them had built together.

The sensation lasted only a moment, however. Jackie was a practical woman, and she knew that dwelling on such idle wishes would be the road to collapse. So she firmly redirected her thoughts. She and Peter had much to be grateful for in their new life—she especially, now that she was freed from the confines of a life that had not suited her. The bitterness passed, and Jackie was left feeling merely a sort of mild contempt for Sylvia Brown, whom she had privately labeled a home-wrecker.

But that was idiotic, she realized, shaking her head. Amy Sweeten hadn't made a home for herself and her husband. She had merely lodged at the Dog Academy, just another domestic animal, like the boarder dogs or the champion basset hounds, Fred and Karen. Except that, unlike Fred and Karen, Amy hadn't even loved Mel—on the contrary, she was glad that he was dead.

Jackie decided that Amy's was a funny attitude, no matter how you looked at it.

On the other hand, what on earth had Sylvia Brown seen in Mel Sweeten? By all accounts, he had thought about nothing but dogs, dog shows, breeding and selling dogs, training dogs, and just being around dogs. Whereas Jackie was pretty certain that Sylvia Brown had other interests.

CHAPTER 13

On Thursday morning, in his office at Palmer Central, Michael McGowan was refining the target of the police investigation into the murder of Mel Sweeten. He had been unconvinced by Jackie's talk of the high pitch of emotions among the dog-show crowd, and he had done some serious spadework on a more prosaic level. Finally, this morning, he had unearthed something that looked like a lead. The information was contained in a stack of impenetrable money-market investment reports, now piled high on his desk.

He looked again at the trades, and made careful notes. Mel Sweeten had a nephew, a young man of about twenty-six, by the name of Ned Whiting. He had recently gone to work at Nash Brothers, the most respected investment firm in Palmer. The young stockbroker had been mentioned in Sweeten's will as one of the principal beneficiaries of the victim's estate, which turned out to have been quite large. At least it seemed large to McGowan, who didn't really understand how it was possible to make a million dollars running a dog kennel and going to dog shows. But such was life. And there it was—Mel Sweeten had been a millionaire.

The term "millionaire" nowadays was rather discounted;

there were plenty of millionaires who bore little resemblance to the top-hatted tycoon on the Monopoly box. But you couldn't argue with inheritance as a motive to murder. What was more, Ned Whiting had managed his uncle's investment portfolio, which Nash Brothers had valued on the last day of December at about three hundred thousand dollars. It was a nice chunk of change for a young man to be managing on his own.

At last, McGowan and his forces had something a little more solid to go on. He had never wanted to believe that the mysterious other woman and her displaced nightgown were all that important to the murder investigation.

Two days earlier, McGowan had met briefly with Whiting to talk about the inheritance. Now, after looking quickly through the money-market records, he decided it was time to interview the young broker again. But first he needed some background. He picked up the phone and called an old classmate from high school days, Johnny Shaw, who was now a managing partner at Nash Brothers.

When the two old friends had finished discussing the bleak hopes of the Palmer basketball team for the present season, McGowan came to the point. "You have a young man there by the name of Whiting," he said finally.

"I didn't really think you were calling to talk basketball," said Shaw, relief in his tone. "I'm glad you called. I'd been wondering if I ought to call you, in view of the large amount of money we were managing for that Sweeten character."

McGowan's interest stirred. "Has anyone there looked over the portfolio?"

"I did. Shortly after the trading for it was suspended."

"And?"

"And I didn't like what I saw."

"Glad to hear that. Now, explain. This stuff is gibberish to me, you know."

"Right. Well, the file is incomplete, for one thing. There appear to be confirmation slips missing for certain trades; their absence may or may not indicate some sort of malfeasance. The numbers for the account don't really add up, either. But it's more than likely to be just sloppiness. He's a sloppy kid, that Whiting. And the account was losing money. Ned Whiting was picking bad buys."

Shaw went on, enumerating some of the transactions recorded in the file. More than half of them had been substantial losses. McGowan listened in silence as Shaw went over some of the trades.

"Does the record mean anything?" the detective asked at last.

"To me, yes, of course. It means that Whiting doesn't have any investment sense."

"Anything besides that?"

"Not technically, no. But I don't understand why the numbers don't add up. It almost looks as though there were some extra funds coming in, which is not the way it usually works in cases of embezzlement. If that's what you're thinking about."

"We have to consider every angle," said McGowan.

"Well, one thing you can be sure of. If this is more than just sloppiness, we would have caught it quickly enough—we have an internal system in place, just in case. He would have been found out by the end of the month, at the latest. Which is why I'm inclined to think he was just being lazy, not following through with the paperwork."

"On the other hand," said McGowan, his voice heavy with satisfaction, "maybe he was robbing his uncle blind."

"I suppose there's always that possibility," Shaw agreed. "And if so, Nash Brothers will have to face it squarely. Let me know if there's anything else you need."

"Will do," said McGowan.

An hour later, Ned Whiting sat smoothly in one of the two hard wooden chairs in McGowan's office. He had come quickly from his office when McGowan phoned, professing himself happy to be of service to the police; he had maintained his cool as McGowan questioned him closely about Mel Sweeten's portfolio.

Now he leaned his lanky body easily back in the chair and regarded McGowan with a challenging stare. The smooth planes of his face seemed to gleam in the fluorescent light; his dark hair, which was on the long side, had an almost indigo cast to it. His eyebrows were heavy and thick, a dark line dividing his face. He looked every inch a successful young stockbroker—with his boldly striped but still conservative shirt, bright red suspenders, and four-hundred-dollar shoes. He had arrived in a bright red Porsche convertible, which was now parked outside in the lot, next to McGowan's ten-year-old Dodge station wagon. Straight or bent, Ned Whiting was doing all right for himself.

"Look, Lieutenant," the young man said, "I agree that my uncle's portfolio might have been better managed. But I don't see why that's any of your business, frankly."

"Anything and everything is my business, if I want it to be," said McGowan. "I understand that there are confirmation slips missing from the file. Which either signifies that you were neglecting your fiduciary duty, or that you were acting without your uncle's approval."

"Uncle Mel didn't know the first thing about investing. He only knew about dogs. So his approval wouldn't have been meaningful, for my purposes."

"That's not relevant. I've been through some records that he kept at his house and compared those records to the file." He tapped the large stack of computer printouts. "There were trades that he apparently asked you to make, for which there are no confirmation slips." Johnny Shaw had explained that the confirmation slips were the firm's way of making certain that a client knew exactly what was happening to his money. The absence of such records could mean that Whiting had been pocketing the investment money that came in to his account at Nash. "That suggests to me the possibility that you were playing fast and loose with his money."

"No way," protested Whiting. "There's just no way I would have tried something like that. I would have been caught within the week. At Nash Brothers we have all kinds of systems in place to detect that kind of thing."

"Suppose you tell me, then, about the missing confirmation slips."

"They're not 'missing'—I just never got around to sorting through things and getting the hard-copy file up-to-date. The computer records will show the trades, and that's all that counts, really."

"Except for the fact that you didn't tell your uncle what you were doing with his money."

"We've been through this, Lieutenant." A supercilious smile flitted across Whiting's pudgy lips, and he leaned forward with a patient look on his face. "There is absolutely no way for you to demonstrate that my uncle didn't know, so I suggest you abandon this line. Either that, or take my word for it."

"And then," McGowan went on, "there's always the possibility that your uncle discovered that you had been defying him. He called you, I imagine, to talk about the situation. You made an appointment to see him after the meeting that was already scheduled to take place at his house that night. At about nine o'clock, you headed over to the Dog Academy and solved the problem. It didn't take long at all, really. You solved your problem, and you got the cash you wanted. Maybe you even needed the cash."

"That's ridiculous."

"I'm not so sure. Let's hear where you were the night that your uncle was killed."

"We have been through this a hundred times. Right after work, I went to Charlie's Place with some of the other brokers. We hung out there for a few hours, drank a lot of beer, and then about nine-thirty I left. I didn't feel like going home, so I decided to go to the movies. The Senator Theater is on my way home, so I stopped in for the ten o'clock show of *Thelma and Louise*. By myself."

"Do you often go to movies alone?"

"Hardly ever," said Whiting with a grin. "But that's not the kind of movie you take your girlfriend to, Lieutenant. Not unless you want to give her a bad idea about men."

"All right. What did you do after the movie was over?"

"I went home. You can ask the doorman in my apartment building."

They went over and over the same ground. Finally, McGowan decided that he would do better if he gave the suspect a rest. Ned Whiting was an extremely cocky young man; if he thought he had the police fooled, he might trip himself up.

McGowan kept Whiting for another half an hour or so, then finally dismissed him. He was pretty sure he had his man. And now that he had someone in his sights, McGowan was prepared to play a patient waiting game. Experience had taught him that this was the soundest approach.

CHAPTER 14

At six o'clock that evening, having accepted Cosmo Gordon's invitation to meet for a beer at the Juniper Tavern, Michael McGowan was feeling satisfied. He was busy filling his colleague in on the details of his interview with Ned Whiting and his conversation with Johnny Shaw.

The Juniper Tavern was the kind of spot where you could be sure of cold beer and cold beer mugs, of hamburgers and french fries done to your liking, and of waitresses and bartenders who remembered your name. The Juniper was cozy, and usually full in the evenings. The tables and booths were made of solid wood, and the long bar that ran half the length of the main room was a century old, made of dark mahogany with well-shined brass detailing and a long mirror behind it, against the wall, framed in the same dark mahogany, but intricately carved. Gordon and McGowan were seated far in the back, in the last booth on the right, which was their usual spot when they could get it. It afforded the privacy that their conversations often demanded.

"Nephew," said McGowan, reaching for a french fry and dunking it in ketchup. "It's perfect. He's twenty-six, living it up, a broker at Nash Brothers. According to a credit check we ran this afternoon, he's pretty deeply in debt. Got a car worth about fifty grand, and a half-paid-for condo, and shoes that would cost me a week's pay, and zippo in the bank."

"So he's like the rest of his generation," said Gordon. "That doesn't make him a killer."

"He had a big-time motive," replied McGowan.

"You think?" asked Gordon. "Did he stand to inherit?"

"A big chunk of cash—close to half a million."

Gordon whistled. "There's your motive, anyway."

"Not only that. He was managing the portfolio for Nash Brothers, but the records appear to indicate that he was stealing from his uncle. John Shaw says the internal system would have caught him by the end of the month."

"Doesn't sound like a bright fellow."

"Top of his class, obviously," concurred McGowan. "So the beer's on me. We're well on our way to wrapping that one up. What's new on your end?"

Gordon looked uncomfortable. "Something has happened. I feel kind of silly, but I thought I'd talk to you about it. If it's nothing to worry about, tell me, and I'll just forget all about it."

"What on earth are you talking about?"

"This." Gordon reached for his briefcase, which was sitting on the bench beside him, and opened it. Carefully, he withdrew a clear plastic envelope, which he laid on the table.

Inside was another envelope, ordinary letter size, with Gordon's name and address typed on the front.

McGowan carefully turned the plastic envelope over. The other side of the inner envelope was blank.

"Nice," said McGowan. "Got a sweetheart you haven't told Nancy about?"

"Right," said Gordon, evidently in no mood to joke. He reached into the briefcase and brought out a larger plastic envelope. This one contained a letter, typewritten, on ordinary bond. McGowan could see at a glance that it would be hopeless to try to trace the paper and the typewriter. He reached for the plastic envelope and held it carefully.

> Dear Dr. Gordon,
>   We know that you had a meeting with an old friend of yours. It's important to us to know what your friend said to you. We can't ask him, so we'll have to ask you, at a time and place of our choosing.
>   Be sure to keep yourself available.

"Nice one," said McGowan, putting it down gently on the table.

"You think it's for real?" Gordon sounded relieved. Better to face actual danger than to make yourself ridiculous by falling for some schoolboy hoax.

"Got to be." McGowan shook his head. "I guess old Matt knew what he was talking about."

"You think they're talking about Dugan? About the night he came to see us, just before he was killed."

"Got to be," replied McGowan. "Somebody wants to meet with you, find out what you know."

Gordon looked abashed. "I could kill myself, really, for not listening to Matt more carefully that night. But he was rambling. You don't know the way he had begun to just go on and on and on. He'd come up real close to you, and look at you with these sad blue eyes of his that could hardly focus, and all I could ever think about was how sad it all was. He used to be a great cop. Great."

Gordon downed his beer and signaled the waitress for two more. "We've gotta get to the bottom of this, Mike. I owe it to my old buddy."

"Right you are." McGowan looked at the anonymous letter again. "You'd better let forensics take a look."

"Oh, I will, don't worry. I'll drop it by the lab on my way home tonight. I just didn't want to make a fool of myself."

"Nope. God forbid you should make a fool of yourself."

Not far from the Juniper Tavern, in an up-scale bistro that was the habitual hangout of Palmer's advertising professionals, designers, and graphic artists, another tête-à-tête was taking place.

"I told you, Dick, I'm sick and tired of all of this," said Sylvia Brown. She ran a hand through her long blond hair. Her face, reflected in a long mirror behind a chrome-and-marble bar, looked haggard. She was not a very good advertisement, at this moment, for the virtues of aerobic exercise. But perhaps that was because she hadn't slept peacefully in over a week.

Dick Buzone snickered and lifted his glass, glancing casually at his reflection in the mirror as he sipped at a very dry martini. "And I told you, my dear, that you will do what I say."

His voice, ordinarily thin and reedy, held an unaccustomed hint of a threat this afternoon.

"Why?" asked Sylvia defiantly. "I went out on a limb for you. In a big way. And so far, there's nothing to show for it." She stared at him defiantly.

Buzone smirked, his thin lips wriggling like little flesh-toned caterpillars. "Patience, my dear. Anything worth having is worth waiting for. That's what I tell all those silly women who want me to give their dogs blue ribbons. Patience will bring you rewards." He sipped gently at his drink.

"You and your famous patience." She took a hearty swig of her club soda. "If you ask me, I think that detective is on to something."

"Why?"

"He keeps calling me in to police headquarters for these long interviews." She rolled her eyes. "I'm not sure exactly what he's after, what he wants. But he's definitely after something."

"Maybe he just wants to date you." Buzone smiled faintly, as though he had made a joke. He apparently thought that the idea of anyone's wanting to date Sylvia Brown was absurd.

"I think I know the difference, Dick," said Sylvia with venom. "God knows I've had enough experience."

"Get next to him. Figure out if he knows anything. Or talk to that nosy broad, his girlfriend." It was an order. Buzone smacked his thin little lips together and gave his reflection an approving glance. He enjoyed giving orders.

"What girlfriend?" Sylvia Brown sounded annoyed.

"The one I sent to see you. Dark hair, teaches film history at Rodgers."

"Jackie Walsh? You sent her to see me?"

Buzone shrugged. "She came to me with some cock-and-bull story about her dog, or her son's dog. I took her money and told her to hire you. Find out why she came to see me."

"Forget it."

Buzone looked sharply at Sylvia. "What do you mean by that?"

"I mean forget it. From now on you can count me out. My classes at the gym are doing really well, and I don't want to hang around dog shows for the rest of my life. So let's just call it quits. We're about even."

"No, my dear. You don't quit until I tell you to." Buzone

had reached out and grabbed one of Sylvia's wrists. He began to twist.

"Let go of me, you creep," said Sylvia. She caught the bartender's eye. He came striding swiftly over.

"Everything okay, ma'am?" he asked with a practiced look at Buzone.

"No. Everything is not okay. This man is trying to molest me, and it's not the first time. I'd like you to call the police."

The color drained from Buzone's face. "You little—"

"I think you'd better leave, sir," said the bartender, who had seen this kind of thing before.

"Don't pay the slightest attention to her," said Buzone, recovering his icy composure. "She's crazy. Just got out of treatment for severe paranoia."

"Right, and you're Doctor Jekyll," retorted Sylvia. "If you come near me again, I swear I'll call the cops." She gathered up her gym bag and her pocketbook and put on her coat. Then, without pausing even to look at Buzone, she stormed out into the cold March air.

Buzone gave the bartender a knowing look. "She can't help herself," said Buzone, man-to-man. "She's in love."

CHAPTER 15

On Thursday afternoon at lunchtime, Jackie ran into Amy
Sweeten in the faculty cafeteria. She hadn't seen the young
widow since the day they'd talked at Amy's house, almost a
week ago; Amy looked better, more lively, but she was still
as pale as ashes. She asked Jackie to share a table with her
in the corner.

"Are you all right?" asked Jackie, sure this was a necessary question. Amy Sweeten looked anything but all right.

"I'm fine," came the response. Amy's voice was surprisingly clear and strong. "Just tired of talking to policemen
all the time."

"I can imagine," responded Jackie sympathetically. "Have
you heard about any progress on the case?"

Amy Sweeten shrugged her thin little shoulders. "I guess
they're trying everything they can think of. One of them
came out to the house last night and got all of our financial
records for the last six months." Amy grinned slightly.
"Including Mel's credit-card slips, and all of his motel
bills."

"Oh." Jackie took a thoughtful bite of her tuna-fish sand-
wich. "You think they're looking at that angle still?"

"How should I know?" Amy sounded as though she
didn't care. "All I know is that they never seem to leave

me alone. I wish they would. I'm ready to get on with my life."

Amy's way of talking unnerved Jackie. Mel Sweeten had been dead less than two weeks, and already his widow was bored with the murder investigation. How would she feel if they kept it up for months? Jackie shook her head. Art historians were supposed to understand that the process of inquiry could be lengthy. Maybe Amy didn't have the patience for scholarship.

"At least," said Amy, sounding just a bit affronted, "they could investigate that woman."

"Which woman?" asked Jackie, sure of the answer.

"The one he was having the affair with. The one who left her nightgown in the hotel."

"Amy, are you *sure* that Mel was having an affair with her?"

"Of course I am. He went away almost every weekend with her, to one of those stupid dog shows. I think she's the one that did it. Don't you?"

"How should I know?"

"Have you seen her?"

Jackie considered briefly whether or not to lie. This conversation was getting on her nerves; Amy Sweeten had a dull, childlike flatness to her voice that was most annoying. On the other hand, there wasn't really any reason to hold back the whole truth.

"I did see her, actually. I went to the dog show last Sunday, and she was there."

"You *did*? You went to the dog show to look at her, didn't you? Isn't she awful?"

"I wouldn't call her awful." Jackie felt a sudden urge to rush to Sylvia Brown's defense. She wasn't close enough to Amy to feel otherwise.

"She *is* awful. All you have to do is look at her."

Jackie wanted to change the subject. "What about the business?"

"Huh?"

"The Dog Academy. What's going to happen to it?"

Amy Sweeten shrugged her tiny shoulders. "Tom Mann resigned. There weren't any dogs there, anyway. Not much business. Now all I have to do is figure out about Fred and Karen. You want some basset hounds?"

Jackie shook her head. She had thought Fred and Karen were very lovable-looking, but she was sure there were plenty of professionals who might be interested in them. She expressed the idea to Amy.

"Oh, there are. My phone never stops ringing, and they're all calling about the dogs. They all ask me, 'How are they coping?' As if I could possibly know how a basset hound feels. It's idiotic. They don't give a damn about how *I* feel. They're just like Mel."

"Oh!" said Jackie. She hadn't thought about it, but it must be galling to have your dead husband's friends all inquiring about the emotional state of the dogs. "Is there anyone in particular they might go to?"

"Well, there's a woman who wants them, but she and Mel hated each other, so I don't know."

"She's a dog-show type?" asked Jackie, feeling a prickle of curiosity.

"Yeah. She raises beagles, but that's almost the same."

"The beagle lady," murmured Jackie. "I think I saw her at the dog show. Her name is Thalia Gilmore."

"That's the one," replied Amy, nodding. "Thalia Gilmore. Mel couldn't stand her. She banned him from some club or something. They had one of those feuds about nothing that go on and on for years."

"I'm surprised she wants Mel's dogs," said Jackie.

"I'm not. Everyone knows they're the best bassets. In

fact, that Gilmore woman bought one of Karen's puppies, a couple of years ago, but it turned out to be a dud, never won any ribbons."

"But she's willing to try again?"

"I guess so. She offered me a thousand dollars for the two of them. What should I do? Should I take it?"

Jackie thought that Amy should do anything that would keep the poor bassets from languishing any longer in their kennel, so she was on the verge of urging Amy to accept the offer. A thousand dollars seemed like a lot of money for two dogs; and the feud obviously didn't extend to the dogs.

On the other hand, perhaps Thalia Gilmore was pulling a fast one on Amy—to get back at Mel, or to exact some other kind of weird satisfaction. Or just to get champion dogs at bargain-basement prices. It might be smart to ask around.

"I'll tell you what," she responded at last. "Why don't I look into the question for you? I'll talk to some of these dog people that I've met and find out what the going price would be for two champions like Fred and Karen. Okay?"

"That would be great," replied Amy flatly.

Jackie turned the conversation to other topics—Rodgers University was going to the regional championships in basketball, and everyone, even art historians and other-worldly professors of astrophysics, were breathless with anticipation. So the lunch ended on an upbeat note, but when Jackie returned to her office she thought long and hard.

It occurred to her that the person who most deserved those two dogs was Sylvia Brown. She had been the one, after all, who had worked with them over and over again, helping to bring them to the top. Amy, of course, would probably not stand for it. But if Sylvia Brown wasn't a murderer, she really did seem to be the logical person to take the dogs. After fifteen minutes Jackie still hadn't thought of a solution, short of using herself as a front should Sylvia want to buy the dogs. And that seemed like drastic cloak-and-dagger stuff. Better, perhaps, not to stir the pot. Better to let sleeping dogs lie.

On the other hand, she had every intention of filling Michael McGowan in on the bit of gossip that Amy had passed along. Were the police aware that Mel Sweeten and Thalia Gilmore were enemies?

When she got home that evening, Jackie's course was made smoother by an unexpected telephone call from Sylvia Brown. She had changed her mind, she told Jackie, and would like to take Jake to the obedience trials on Saturday morning. If Jackie and Peter were still interested?

Jackie, intrigued, accepted. She wondered what on earth had prompted Sylvia's change of heart. She would just have to wait until Saturday—but she was determined to find out.

CHAPTER 16

On Friday afternoon, after a long week, Jackie decided to give Michael McGowan a call. She had to admit to herself that she was just the tiniest bit annoyed with him—he seemed to have been neglecting her of late. He was always happy to invite himself for dinner when he wanted something—when he wanted to borrow Jake for his investigation, for instance—but in between those exigencies he rarely called or came by. Jackie had begun to wonder if he were a fair-weather friend. Or if maybe there were some other, more personal reason why he was keeping her at arm's length from the investigation.

Jackie was looking forward to Saturday. Mel Sweeten's murder still intrigued her, and the obedience competition would give her a much-needed change of pace. In her film history class, they had spent the entire week on the work of Jean-Luc Godard, whom Jackie privately considered a bore and an impostor. But the French filmmaker's work was influential and famous, of that there could be little doubt. So Jackie had forced herself to sit through a screening of *Weekend*, and generously forbore to tell her class that she found Godard's situations contrived and sententious. A few in the class had reached the same conclusion on their own, which had gladdened Jackie's heart, but after giving two hour-long lectures on the Frenchman, she desperately needed to think about something practical, like murder.

Shortly before suppertime, she dialed McGowan's number. He professed himself glad to hear from her, but she wasn't certain. There was an edge to his voice.

"I heard something interesting from Amy Sweeten," she told him.

"Oh, yeah?" McGowan sounded busy, harassed. "What's that?"

"That her husband had an enemy."

"We know that, Jackie. He got himself murdered."

"Michael, please don't be condescending. I mean there was a person that he was feuding with."

"Tell me."

"A woman who breeds beagles. I told you about her—I saw her at the dog show. She's the one that was complaining about the article in that dog newsletter."

"Oh, Thalia Gilmore. Right. Well, we're not really looking into that angle anymore. But thanks for the information. I'll file it, just in case."

Jackie was stung. "But, Michael," she protested, "you're the one that wanted to borrow Jake and go around to dog shows. Now I'm doing all this work for you, and you just brush me off."

McGowan's reticence seemed like treason. She had been such a willing helper when he asked. She had volunteered not only the services of her dog, but also her own time. And now he was acting as though she were some kind of loony. Worse, he was acting as though he were trying to keep her at a distance. Personally. As if she had ever encouraged him!

Quite suddenly, Jackie made up her mind. She was going to beat him to the punch. She would find out who had killed Mel Sweeten.

But she decided to play it fair, and play it safe. She didn't want another moment of panic like the one she'd experienced the other night, all alone in the darkened road with Sylvia Brown. There was no evidence, so far, that the woman was not a killer.

"Well, anyway, Michael, I don't mind if you're not interested, but I'll tell you anyway. First about Thalia Gilmore, and then about Sylvia Brown. I don't want you telling me that I didn't fill you in, in case I come up with the answer before you do."

McGowan laughed. "Okay, Jackie. Listen. Don't be mad at me, okay? If I could tell you everything that's going on at this end, I would. You just have to trust me on this. Detective work has a certain amount of confidentiality to it—and that's for your safety as much as anything else. But I will tell you that I'm working on a very strong lead, one that has nothing to do with dogs or dog shows or someone being jealous of someone else's dog, or anything remotely like that. Okay?"

"But what about Thalia Gilmore?"

"I've talked to her. She admitted that she had reason to hate Mel Sweeten, but she had hated him for years. Besides, her son vouches for her. He lives with her."

"Oh, great."

"I know what you mean. But unless we can impeach her alibi, we'll have to swallow it. Dick Buzone, the man that you love to hate, says that the executive committee ended the meeting at about eight-fifteen. He remembers because he was going to meet a friend, and he was a few minutes late."

"I suppose his friend alibis him too."

"Sure. They went to a party. A big, noisy party at the new club that was opening downtown. A charity benefit, or something, with all the local advertising bigwigs. It was the kind of thing where you don't see your date for hours."

"So he *could* have done it."

"So could you or I, if you think like that. Jackie, trust me on this. There is more to this murder than just dogs and dog shows. Okay?"

"If you say so." Jackie was unconvinced. She wanted to talk to Thalia Gilmore, face-to-face. She was already convinced that Dick Buzone could murder thirty people without giving it a thought, but it would have to profit him greatly. He struck her as the kind of person who never did anything without the assurance of great personal gain.

"Oh, by the way, Michael. There's one other thing I wondered about. About Buzone."

"What's that?"

"Well, he just doesn't seem to be the type of guy who would get involved in a nonprofit thing like dog shows. Plus, I don't think he really likes dogs very much. If I were a dog, I wouldn't go near him. He just doesn't have that doggy personality, if you know what I mean."

"I do," replied McGowan. "He's more like a flounder."

"Not a flounder," said Jackie with spirit. "He's an eel. An eel with hair."

"So he is."

"Right. And maybe there's some dirt on him somewhere."

"You can find dirt on anyone, if you look hard enough. As our political process seems to prove every election year."

"Yes, but—"

"Tell you what," said McGowan, his voice pacifying. He wanted to make Jackie feel better about being left out of the investigation. "Try to dig up some dirt on Buzone from the dog people you see tomorrow. And if there's anything useful for the investigation, I'll fill you in completely. Okay?"

"It's a deal," Jackie answered, somewhat mollified.

CHAPTER 17

Thus on the following Saturday morning, Jackie, Peter, Isaac Cook, Jake, and Sylvia Brown were all piled into Jackie's Jeep, headed for Wardville High School, whose gymnasium and playing fields today would be the setting for the Greater Palmer Canine Obedience Competition.

Peter was thoroughly pleased. At last he'd have a chance to show the world how truly great and impressive a dog Jake was. He and Isaac knew, for a fact, that Jake would win every prize in the book. He was the best-trained dog in the world.

Last night, as the two boys talked on the phone to make arrangements, Isaac had expressed skepticism. He was concerned that "some lady" was going to be putting Jake through his paces. But Peter, having learned of Sylvia's credentials, was quick to put his friend's mind to rest. "It'll be cake for Jake, and we know it," he said. "Jake knows what he knows. The lady doesn't matter."

"Yeah, but what if she says something like 'Get him, Jake'? Remember what happened to my sweater?" Isaac was referring to a training session that he and Peter had had with Jake last fall. That was the day when the boys discovered the range and depth of Jake's training. It had

been an aweseome experience. Jake's power wasn't something to be trifled with.

"Look," Peter had explained patiently. "She's a dog trainer. She won't do anything stupid like that."

Thus encouraged, Isaac had agreed to come along and be
part of Jake's cheering section.

Now as the group headed out toward the school, Sylvia
Brown was offering Jackie an explanation for her change
of heart. "I got to thinking about it, you know—how I
told you that since my friend had died I wasn't sure about
keeping up with the dog-handling routine. But I figured that
that attitude wasn't really in the right spirit. I mean, Mel
wouldn't want me to give up. I know he wouldn't."

"Probably not," concurred Jackie.

"Besides, I've been working with his dogs for a really
long time, and I figure that branching out is going to be
tough for me. Emotionally, and also in the show ring. You
get to know one breed pretty well, but then you're kind of
stuck if someone asks you to take charge of another breed.
Different temperaments, and different things that the judges
look for. There's a lot of work in bringing a dog all the way
to best of breed in a show; and to finish him you really have
to know him."

"I can imagine," said Jackie, who hadn't previously considered the problem. She conjured up an image of the little
white poodle, Serena, that she had seen at the dog show last
Sunday. Certainly that dog had a different temperament—
that dog had been all nerves. Undoubtedly you would have
to know what you were getting into, to successfully handle
a dog like that one. Jackie guessed that being a dog handler
had its subtleties, much like any other profession. "What
made you choose basset hounds in the first place?"

"Oh, I've always loved them. At first for their looks—
they're so low, and long, and have such silky ears, and

their paws are so adorable. But once you start to work with a breed, you find more to like in it than just its cuteness. Bassets are sturdy companions, true blue. I think that's why I like them so much."

There was a traffic jam outside the entrance to Wardville High; the Obedience Competition had apparently drawn a huge crowd. Peter and Isaac took off to look around, while Sylvia put Jake on his lead and went over to the area where the competitors were waiting. To Jackie fell the thankless task of waiting in line at the registration table. She watched her son and his friend as they nudged each other, laughing excitedly, and moved in for a closer look at some of the dogs. Jackie felt real happiness. For Peter, the transition from suburban life to city life had been easy—but a lot of that had to do with Isaac. The boys were such good friends. And of course, Jake had been a big part of it too. Jackie felt quite sure that Jake would win all the prizes, just as Peter had predicted.

As Jackie waited to fill in a card for Jake, she considered what Sylvia Brown had said in the car. Jackie didn't really believe that Sylvia had changed her mind out of fidelity to Mel Sweeten's memory; on the other hand, the woman's reasons for liking basset hounds had sounded, to her, like the truth. It seemed likely to Jackie that something had happened on Wednesday or Thursday to prompt Sylvia's call. She wanted to find out what it was.

The day was quite chilly, but Jackie had brought two large red-and-black checked blankets and several thermoses full of hot chocolate. As she and the boys found a good spot on one of the old benches along the side of the soccer field, there was great promise in the air.

The obedience competition was, to Jackie's mind, more of what a dog show should be all about—it looked like fun. There were fewer competitors, and some of them, like Jake himself, looked a little bit the worse for wear, in spite of the efforts that their owners and handlers were making to groom them for the occasion. But all the dogs, and the people as well, looked positively thrilled to be there. The school's grounds afforded plenty of room for wandering around and exploring, and the competitors' area, from what Jackie could tell, seemed to lack the ominous tension that she had sensed last Sunday at the armory.

Sylvia Brown had explained to them that today's event wasn't an important competition—just a preliminary heat, more of an informal get-together of dog lovers. The place was crowded with contestants and owners; only about twenty-five of the best dogs would be invited to compete in the formal competition two weeks from now.

The result was a carnival atmosphere. Off in a far corner of the large field, some teenagers had established their own competition for Frisbee-catching. At the opposite end, near the back of the gymnasium, a group of small children and their dogs seemed to be playing a canine version of "Duck, Duck, Goose." Jackie felt delighted—she loved to see dogs at play.

Sylvia had taken Jake off to do a few warm-ups with him before entering the competitors' area. The boys had gone off to watch the Frisbee-fetching competition, and Jackie decided to take a look around.

She wandered around among the crowd, slowly making her way toward a small table where coffee and hot chocolate were sold. A few of the faces were familiar to her from Sunday's outing at the armory. One of them was Thalia Gilmore, the beagle lady, hugely attired in a thick woolen suit of a color somewhere between mustard and puce. As she pushed through a knot of people, she reminded Jackie of a magnificent snowplow, or perhaps an icebreaker ship. She moved steadily forward with huge but stately calm, nodding this way and that, and the people parted before her.

Thalia Gilmore was accompanied today not by the sprightly Clematis, who had competed on Sunday at the armory, but by a slightly misshapen liver-and-white basset hound. The dog was indisputably seedy and inclined to bay loudly and long, ignoring all orders to be quiet. The dog seemed to be the only living creature who didn't bow to Thalia Gilmore's will.

Jackie thought about the woman's offer to buy Fred and Karen from Amy Sweeten. This dog must be the "dud" that Amy had mentioned. He certainly didn't look like a show-stopper, that was for certain. But perhaps he had hidden virtues in the area of obedience skills.

Before long Jackie spotted Dick Buzone. Undoubtedly, as president of the local dog club, he had to put in an appearance at every meet. She watched as he approached Sylvia, who seemed bent on ignoring him. He said a few words to her, but she kept her back turned to him. Jackie was struck by something in the attitude of the two of them; there was an unmistakable familiarity in the way that Sylvia snubbed Buzone. It was easy to see.

Before long, the crowd seemed to come to attention. The competition was about to get under way, and Jackie and the boys took their seats. A large, red-faced man in a tweed suit and large tweed hat picked up a megaphone and began to speak to the crowd.

"Ladies and gentlemen, and contestants. Your attention please." The talk of the crowd lowered to a murmur, permitting the voices of the contestants to be heard, variously barking, yelping, and baying. Jackie thought she could pick out the voice of Thalia Gilmore's basset above all the rest of the noise.

"Please, ladies and gentlemen, ask your four-legged friends to be quiet."

Giggling and joking, Jackie and the boys settled into their seats. The competition was called to order, and one by one, dog after dog was put through his paces. The dogs heeled, they sat, they lay down, and they stayed; they bounded from one corner of the show area to another, and they walked sedately back. The retrievers were called upon to fetch things; others were required to stay quite still and ignore tantalizing objects, such as frankfurters, that were placed nearby.

Some of the dogs were real show-offs, but others seemed to take it all in stride. There were one or two excellent performances by golden retrievers, and a dog with no recognizable bloodlines came close to turning in a perfect performance. Thalia Gilmore's basset was as intractable as a goat, prompting great gusts of laughter from the crowd. Poor Thalia herself looked mortified, but the dog seemed to be utterly impervious to the amused scorn of the onlookers.

Jake's turn finally came. Sylvia, who had taken off a baggy sweatsuit to reveal a colorful spandex aerobics costume, led him into the center of the ring. It was hard to say who had more stage presence at that precise instant: Sylvia Brown certainly knew how to get the attention of the crowd, but Jake seemed, for the moment, a born performer. Jackie thought of Rin-Tin-Tin, and smiled. Peter and Isaac were mesmerized; there was no dog on earth like him. The others, good as they had been, seemed like beginners in comparison. They were out of his league.

"Isn't he great, Mom? Isn't he great?"

"Absolutely the best, Petey," said Jackie with real pride in her voice.

"I think Stella could do that," said Isaac, halfheartedly. Stella was one of his dogs. A huge, friendly thing with a coat that looked like a cinnamon bagel, she was part plott hound (Isaac thought) and part mystery dog.

Jake had golden assurance, and he walked with a surefooted and dignified tread. With silent grace he anticipated the orders that the judges called for, and he responded to Sylvia's hands and voice as though he had known her all his life. The audience grew a little quieter in appreciation as Jake unfailingly carried out every command given him. There was never a moment's hesitation; he had done it all so many times before.

He would win, hands down. There was no question of that.

After Jake had had his turn, Jackie and the boys got up to wander around again. Jackie headed over to where Thalia Gilmore, her face red, was trying to coax her basset hound into the back of her station wagon. The dog did not want to make the jump. He looked firmly at his mistress and sat down heavily.

Jackie, with a smile for Thalia Gilmore, stooped down to get a better look at the dog. Imperfect as he was, the basset was nonetheless adorable. She offered this opinion to his owner.

"Adorable. Yes, I suppose he might appear so to the uninitiated," was the stony reply. "Perhaps you'd care to take him home. If so, be my guest. He's all yours."

Jackie laughed. "We have one dog already," she answered easily. "And I think one's enough for now. But surely you don't want to give him away?"

"Don't I?" retorted Thalia Gilmore huffily. "Just look at him. He was supposed to come from champion stock."

"You think he didn't?"

"I know for a fact that he didn't. This dog probably came from the pound. At best. Although I wonder that any self-respecting dog pound would have accepted him in the first place, he's such an utter disgrace—not only to his breed, but to the entire species."

The dog looked mournfully up at Jackie, seeming to beg her indulgence for his appearance. The worry lines on his forehead deepened, and his jowls sagged.

Thalia Gilmore was going on with her tale. "I have been working with beagles for quite some time, but I thought the change would be interesting. My late husband always told me to be sure to trade up. I failed to follow his advice, and look what I'm stuck with."

"What's his name?" asked Jackie, stooping momentarily to stroke the dog's silky ears.

"Raphael. Idiotic name, but that's the name that came on his papers. His obviously forged papers."

"Well, sometimes even the best families have their black sheep," suggested Jackie. "I'm sure nobody could have predicted that he wouldn't be a champion."

"The person who sold him to me for five hundred dollars knew," was the stiff reply. "So much for you, Raphael," she said sternly to the dog. She looked at Jackie fiercely. "I saw you last weekend at the dog show."

Thalia Gilmore pronounced "weekend" with the emphasis on the second syllable—a distinctly British linguistic trick that Jackie had sometimes noticed in American women of a certain age and bearing. She wondered idly where it came from. Too many *Thin Man* movies, perhaps. Thalia Gilmore was certainly no Myrna Loy.

Jackie smiled. "My son and I have recently acquired a dog, and we're checking out all the angles."

"You're thinking of competing?"

"In a way. But last Sunday's performance convinced me that our Jake probably wouldn't make champion. So we thought we'd try obedience competition. He's a really good dog."

"What kind is he?"

"He's a German shepherd."

"Ah." Thalia Gilmore gave Jackie a knowing look. "The ringer."

"Ringer?"

"Yes, a ringer. If it's your shepherd that won the competition today. The one that tart was handling."

"Well—" began Jackie, stunned at the characterization of Sylvia Brown. Clearly, Thalia Gilmore spoke her mind on every subject.

"He's obviously a champion many times over, that dog of yours. Don't try to fool me, young lady. If this were an important competition, I'd have you hauled up before the judges' committee. What I'd like to know is where you got him."

"Actually, believe it or not, he just turned up on our doorstep one morning." Jackie was glad to be able to tell the truth. She didn't much like the suspicious way that Thalia Gilmore was looking at her. "He was hurt, so we took him in."

"I don't believe it," was the matter-of-fact reply. "Not that dog."

"It's true. His owner died, and he had wandered off. We found that much out later."

"Who was his owner? Not Lewis Perkins? He's the only one around here who breeds Alsatians that good."

"No, the man's name was Dugan."

"Dugan, Dugan," pondered Thalia Gilmore aloud. "Not the Dugans from Thornton Hill? I was at school with one of them. A very good family."

"No, I don't think so," said Jackie.

"Well, there really aren't any others." Clearly, Thalia Gilmore felt that if she didn't know a person, the person didn't exist. She harrumphed. "At any rate, I congratulate you. I was always taught to be a graceful loser." She glowered at poor Raphael, who by this time was sleeping soundly on the ground at her feet.

"Maybe he needs a friend," suggested Jackie. "You know, another basset hound. Give him something to look up to, someone to model himself after."

"Too late for that, I'm afraid. But I do plan to get another basset. Two, in fact. I've had my eye on them for three years, and they're the best around. I'm going to buy them, and I shall thus have my revenge on the swindler who sold me this bag of bones." She lifted an eyebrow at the snoozing Raphael. "Come on, you idiotic animal."

She yanked the dog's chain sharply, and Raphael stumbled to his feet. "Nice chatting with you." Thalia Gilmore hoisted Raphael into the back of her station wagon, climbed in the driver's seat, and slammed the door.

Jackie headed back over toward the benches, where the boys were waiting for her excitedly. Peter held up Jake's blue ribbon proudly.

"Whaddaya think about *that,* Mom?"

She tousled his reddish hair. "Just about what we expect of Jake, isn't it?"

"He's a pretty great dog," put in Isaac. "I just wish that everybody could really see him do his stuff."

"Yeah," agreed Peter warmly. "Like going after crooks."

"I think that might scare off some of the other contestants," suggested Jackie. "It's much better if people don't know everything that Jake can do. We'll keep that to ourselves, all right?"

"Yeah," said Isaac. "Not just anybody should know the power of Jake."

"The power of Jake is awesome," averred Peter.

Jackie, looking around for Sylvia Brown, was inclined to agree. She spotted Sylvia, at last. She had once more donned her baggy sweatsuit, and at the far end of the field she was engaged in conversation with a middle-aged man

who had his back toward them. As Jackie watched, Sylvia
pointed in their direction. The man turned, raised a hand
to ward off the glare of the sunlight, and looked toward
where Jackie and the boys were standing. Jackie felt an
unaccountable shiver.

Undoubtedly the man was a stranger—yet as he turned
his back on them once more, Jackie had a peculiar feeling
that there was something familiar about him. The sensation
made her nervous. She watched as the man continued his
conversation with Sylvia, who nodded her head occasion-
ally in Jackie's direction.

"Isaac," said Jackie at last, "will you do something for
me?"

"Sure," said Isaac, who privately adored Peter's mother.

"Go and tell Sylvia Brown that we're ready to go. Peter
and I will meet you at the car."

"Sure," said Isaac again. He sped away across the field,
and Peter and Jackie gathered up the blankets and thermoses,
then they and Jake headed for the Jeep. They had tarried
a long time, accepting congratulations from the other contestants and making small talk; the Jeep was one of the last
cars left in the parking lot.

On the way back to town, there was much exultation
among the little party. Sylvia Brown looked particularly
pleased with herself; Jackie, knowing how very well trained
Jake was, was a bit surprised by the woman's attitude.
Sylvia was smiling to herself, as though she had pulled
off a difficult job.

CHAPTER 18

While Jake and company were enjoying their shining hour at the obedience competition, Michael McGowan was once more interviewing Ned Whiting. It was eleven on Saturday morning, and the precinct-house coffee, having spent three hours on the burner, had already acquired a stale, rotten flavor. McGowan sipped at it anyway, hardly noticing the acrid taste. There was something in the air this morning, a sense that progress would soon be made. But McGowan's face betrayed no hint of the anticipation he felt.

His men and women had talked to every member of the staff at the Senator Theater, where Whiting claimed to have been the night that his uncle was murdered. The Senator was one of the few movie houses in Palmer that hadn't converted itself into a "plex" of some sort. The Senator still had a balcony, and still employed ushers with flashlights to help people find seats in the dark. It was a poor movie house to select for an alibi. Much better to choose the Twelve-plex out at Running Brook Mall, on the road to Wardville. No one at the Senator could place him. What was more, the police had gotten a very lucky break. It was McGowan's hole card, to break down Whiting's alibi.

Today, McGowan was determined to get to the bottom of it. He had Whiting shown into an interrogation room, instead of the office, when he arrived at eleven-fifteen. It was a mean little room, windowless, and it had an unhappy, confessional atmosphere. There was nothing reassuring about the pale blue-gray walls, or the scratched wooden table scarred by endless coffee-cup rings and cigarette burns. The overhead lights were harsh and white. There was nothing to look at, nothing to fix your eye on, except the vacant blue-gray of the walls, and the eyes of the interrogators. It was a room in which many detectives had found a measure of success.

Sergeant Felix Cruz was stationed in an armchair in a corner of the room, his bulk impressive in its immobility. He had come to take notes, but there was also a tape recorder on the table. The video recorder in the corner was ready, if by chance they should hit pay dirt this morning.

After a few preliminaries, McGowan came to the point. "I've had a full report from one of the managing partners at Nash Brothers. You're in trouble, as I'm sure you know by now. I don't think I have to remind you that this is a murder investigation, and anything you say will go into the official record of this interview. Sergeant Cruz has already read you your rights. Is that accurate?"

"Yes." It came out a squeak, and Whiting tried again, clearing his throat. "Yes, that's clear."

Whiting didn't look nearly as sure of himself this morning as he had on Thursday. McGowan knew that Nash Brothers was on the point of dismissing him for failing to keep accurate records. Johnny Shaw had been riding him hard since Thursday. Evidently, he'd taken the wind out of the young man's sails.

"All right then. I want to know exactly what kind of funny business was going on with your uncle's investments."

"Look," said Whiting. "Maybe I should come to the point." He looked pale and haggard, as though he hadn't slept. He gestured to the tape recorder. "Is that thing going?"

"What do you think? It's there for decoration?"

"I could lose my license as a broker."

"You should have thought about that sooner."

Whiting ran a hand through his dark hair, then drummed his fingers nervously on the table before him. His arms were long and skinny. He had dressed as though for the country club—in khaki pants and a bright blue polo shirt—but he had not managed to relax. "Maybe I should get a lawyer."

"You have the right, of course," said McGowan soothingly. "If you think you're ready to confess to your uncle's murder, I would strongly advise that you get yourself the best lawyer you can find. Generally speaking, lawyers are useful things when you're in a situation like this one."

Whiting gave him a contemptuous look, then appeared to make up his mind. "All right. Look—I swear I didn't kill him. I don't need a lawyer. You'll believe me, I promise."

"We'll see."

"I didn't kill him. But you're right that I haven't been exactly square with you. There was something—um— something about the portfolio that wasn't strictly within the rules."

"Such as the fact that you were stealing from him?"

"Oh, no," protested Whiting. "I never took a nickel from Uncle Mel. That is—"

"Not with his knowledge, you mean?"

"No, no. Not at all. It wasn't what I got out of it that was a little off. It was what he was investing."

"What do you mean?" This was unexpected.

"Look—can you imagine that a guy running a boarding school for dogs could salt away a million bucks? For starters, do you know how much he has to pay every year in taxes, insurance, and that kind of crap? He would barely have squeaked by. I know. I went over his books."

McGowan sat back. He was slightly relieved to think that it wasn't possible to make a million dollars in the dog business. Not legally, at least. "So?"

"So—well, when he came to me with a pile of money to invest, I got kind of curious."

"Yes?"

"I didn't ask him outright. He wasn't a very nice guy, and I didn't want to lose the chance of the commission on investing half a million."

"Very noble of you."

"But I couldn't figure out where he got it, because the Dog Academy seemed to have pretty accurate books, records of revenues and so forth. So I did a little snooping around one day at his house. At tax time, last year. I went over there to talk to him about capital gains, tax-free investments, and all that kind of stuff. He was doing his own taxes, and he didn't have the head for it. Doesn't know anything. So I was giving him advice."

"And?"

"Well, the first thing I noticed was that the revenues from the business were pretty good, like I said. But there shouldn't have been enough left over for him to have anything to invest. Let alone the forty grand he'd invested through Nash over the last year."

"What did you do?"

"Okay, I'm telling you." Whiting held up a hand, as though to quiet an insistent child. "He had some emergency out back, where the dog business was. Some old lady wanted to leave her poodle, and she hadn't paid her bill the last time, or something like that. I forget. Uncle Mel's manager came in to get him, because the old lady was being really pushy. He went out to handle it, and I used that opportunity to do a little digging around. I figured that if there was something off about the source of the money, I wanted to know all about it. It made me uncomfortable. I wanted to be ready to protect myself, if anyone came asking questions."

"A wise course, I suppose, under the circumstances," said McGowan sarcastically.

"Yeah, that's what I figured. So I went through all the books, which were right there, all together. Like I said, it was tax time, and I was helping him out. And there was this one ledger that had a bunch of names, dates, and amounts of money. Like that."

"What was suspicious about it?"

"The money never appeared anywhere else, in any of Uncle Mel's financial statements. So I figured it was cash that had been coming in somehow. And he was living off of that, paying the bills with it, and using his income from the business to invest. He would have been caught sooner or later—in fact I don't know quite how he got away with it for so long, unless he'd been doing everything in cash. He had used another broker up until about a year ago, when I went to work at Nash, and all I did was transfer some investments from one of the big New York investment houses. So I don't know, exactly. But it seemed off. Like one of those drawings, where it says 'What's wrong with this picture?' "

"Was it a lot of money?"

"It would have added up, that's for sure, because the book seemed to go back about ten or twelve years. A hundred bucks here, three hundred there—and all on the quiet."

Cruz was hastily making notes; he looked up at McGowan. The police search of the house had revealed no such ledger.

"Any idea where the money was coming from?"

"No. None at all."

"And you never asked your uncle about it?"

"Not for a long time. Then, right around Christmas last year, I found myself a little short of cash."

"Nice."

"Yeah, I always seem to run out right about that time. It's definitely a bummer."

"That wasn't what I meant, exactly. But never mind—go on."

"Huh? Well—anyway. I stopped by to ask Uncle Mel, kind of casually, if he could front me a grand or so. Just so I could get my family a couple of decent Christmas presents. Not for myself."

"No—definitely not for yourself."

"No. I mean, I was planning to go to Acapulco with this chick over New Year's, and I had bought the tickets on credit, so I was up to my limit on my Visa card, and for some reason I was real short of cash. But the loan wasn't for me."

"Believe me, I get the picture," said McGowan.

"So I figured that Uncle Mel could spare it. In cash. So I asked him for a loan, and he said he was all tapped out. So I said, almost without thinking about it, I said, 'What about the money in that ledger?' "

"What was his response?"

"At first he acted like he didn't hear me, or maybe didn't know what I was getting at or something. But I asked him again, and then he wanted to know how I knew about it, and I told him."

"And then?"

"Then he seemed to want to cut me in. I didn't pressure him or anything, I swear it. It was his idea."

"Uh-huh," said McGowan.

"And so he cut me in, but only through what I could earn by investing the money for him. We decided that if I could run a bigger pool of money for him than Nash knew about, put it in some offshore interests, then I could keep a bigger chunk of the investment commission. So the records in the file had to be a little off—because sooner or later somebody would have wanted to know about where the dough came from. So. That's why the portfolio was kind of a mess. It's not like I'm incompetent or anything. I did it on purpose."

Whiting seemed to think that the story demonstrated his skill. He had a satisfied look on his face.

"So you shared the pie with him for a while. And then you decided that Uncle Mel was just in the way of keeping the whole pie for yourself."

"No! No, I swear it. Look, it wasn't just Uncle Mel. He had a friend, a guy that was also getting this money, and I was helping him with his investments too."

"What was his name?"

"I don't know."

"Listen, little man," said McGowan contemptuously. "You're up the creek. The best thing you can do for yourself right now is to come clean, absolutely clean about the whole damn mess. You can be sure Uncle Mel's buddy, if there is such a creature, isn't going to go out on a limb to protect you. So spill it."

Whiting swallowed hard, glancing nervously from McGowan to Cruz and back again.

"I swear. I don't know."

McGowan and Cruz exchanged a look of tired disbelief.

"All right." McGowan returned his gaze to Whiting. "So you were running a pool of untraceable offshore investments for Uncle Melvin. Where did the money come from?"

"I swear I don't know. All I knew about it was what I found out that day last April."

"Okay. So. What do you think about the fact that not one of the employees at the Senator Theater can place you there for the ten o'clock show?"

Whiting shrugged. "It's a big theater."

McGowan nodded. "It's also rather unusual. That is to say, it's kind of an old-fashioned place. With a balcony, and ushers, and the whole works. Did you know that you can rent the whole movie theater for private parties?"

Whiting went pale, but recovered himself quickly. "No. No, I had no idea. Sounds like fun. Is it expensive?"

"Yeah. It's gonna cost you, buddy. Big time." McGowan permitted himself a small smile. "There was a private party at the Senator that night. *Thelma and Louise* was not showing—it was a party for a local group of vintage sci-fi buffs, a double bill of *The Thing* and *Attack of the Killer Tomatoes*."

Whiting gulped.

"So you see," McGowan went on, "I think the time has come for you to tell me what you were doing that night."

"I think I want my lawyer."

"Call him."

Whiting sat perfectly still in his chair. He didn't speak for a full minute. Then he took a deep breath and seemed to reach a conclusion.

"All right. I did go to see Uncle Mel that night. But he was already dead. I got really scared, and just drove away."

"I don't buy it."

"No, honestly. Look, you've just got to believe me."

"Why?"

"Because!" It was the voice of a spoiled child. "Because I didn't do it, I swear." Whiting paused a moment, trying to recover his composure. "Listen. Uncle Mel had called me that day, said he wanted to talk to me."

"He had found out you were stealing from him."

"I *wasn't* stealing, I swear! There was plenty of dough to go around, the way it was coming in from him. No, he just wanted to ask me some questions about a mutual fund, and I told him I'd come over for a drink. His wife was away. She's really a drip."

"Cut the editorializing," said McGowan. "What happened?"

"Well, after work I went out with my buddies, just like I told you. We went to Charlie's Place, drank some brews, and I got a little lit. There was college basketball on the tube, and I forgot all about my appointment with Uncle Mel until the game was nearly over, about quarter of ten, maybe. I had told him I'd be there at nine. So I left."

"We've talked to one or two of your office mates. They say you sat in a booth by yourself most of the evening, staring at your beer. Then you left suddenly."

"Well, I was kind of worried. I'd made a few bad calls for another client, and I was trying to figure a way out of it. I was worrying that he might decide to cut his losses and go."

"So you were consumed with professional self-doubt. Then you took off like a bat out of hell to see your uncle. That was one way to solve the problem about the other client, am I right?"

"Hell, no." Whiting shook his head, like a teacher who cannot make a student understand a simple concept. "No, you have it all wrong. I just forgot I was supposed to go over there, and I didn't want him ticked off at me. So I hurried up."

"What time did you get there?"

"About ten."

"And?"

"I went in the front entrance—the driveway that goes up to the house, you know. Not the driveway that goes in through the Dog Academy entrance."

"And?"

"All the lights were on, so I knew he would still be up. That had been my big worry, because I knew he liked to go to bed real early, and I didn't want to wake him up."

"Right. Very considerate of you."

"You don't have to be so sarcastic," complained Whiting. "Anyway, I rang the doorbell, but there was no answer. The front door wasn't locked, so I went on in. He wasn't inside, so I figured he was out back with his basset hounds."

"So you went out back to look for him."

"Right. The lights were off in the kennels, but those two dogs of his were making a racket. So I called to him, but there was no answer."

"Were you worried?"

"To tell you the truth, I was feeling kind of spooked. I don't like to be outside in the dark at night. I went back into the kitchen, turned on the floodlight, and went back out toward the kennel. That was when I saw him."

"Where?"

"In the third dog run from the house. He was lying on his face. I went up for a closer look. I could tell that he was dead, because his legs and arms were all funny. You couldn't have them that way if they could feel anything. If you know what I mean. Plus, I could see this big chain around his neck, like a dog leash or something."

McGowan's description of the body tallied in every particular with the way the corpse had appeared to the police the following morning. There was no question that the young man had seen it.

"So you went inside to call a doctor, or the police. Am I right?"

"Yes. Well, I did think about that. I went back inside. And then I got to thinking that the police would suspect me.

I got really scared. So I just hopped in my car and drove and drove. I drove about forty miles out into the country, going really fast. Then I kind of came to my senses, and went back home. I figured I'd call the police in the morning, and say what had happened. But by the time the morning came I was scared again."

McGowan stood up, stretched, and glared at Whiting. "You're getting better at storytelling. Maybe you missed your calling. Maybe you should write fairy tales."

"It's the *truth!*" exclaimed Whiting. "I swear it! Look— all you have to do is check out his books. Then you'll have to believe me."

"I don't have to believe you, ever." McGowan gave Cruz a nod. They were through for the moment. "I'm not finished with you yet. But I have other things to attend to. Sergeant Cruz will type a statement for you to sign. You can wait in here until it's ready. We'll decide whether or not to charge you formally with obstruction of justice. For now. The rest will come later. Believe me, it will come."

Whiting slouched down in his chair. "Any chance of a cup of coffee while I wait?"

"Be careful what you wish for," McGowan replied. He nodded to Cruz. "Get him some coffee. That'll teach him."

CHAPTER 19

McGowan owed Jackie a telephone call. He had been giving her the brush-off for days now, and there was no reason for it, really, except the pressures of the job. Now that he had something more solid to go on, he was feeling a little bit like conversation.

The case was beginning to break wide open. McGowan had told Cruz, when they were finished taking Whiting's statement, that they were almost there. It would be a mere matter of days before the nephew decided to come clean with the whole truth. They needed to play their cards right, he told Cruz. But the two men were experienced at the game. They knew how to bluff their way past a full house with nothing but a pair of tens.

McGowan didn't bother to contain his satisfaction as he spoke to Jackie.

"I just wanted to say thank you for being patient with me. I think we've got our man, or we're close to it. Want to hear all about it?"

"Of course I do. That's really exciting, Michael."

McGowan filled Jackie in, from the beginning. He told her all about Whiting's claim that there was a secret fund of cash that necessitated the keeping of misleading records.

"I've never heard such a cock-and-bull story in my life," said McGowan contemptuously.

"You don't believe him, then."

"Of course not. He's been lying since the day he was born, that one, but he still hasn't got the hang of doing it very well. No. He was stealing his uncle blind, he was making unauthorized investments, or maybe he was failing to invest the money that his uncle asked him to invest. One way or another, he was playing fast and loose with half a million dollars."

"That's a *lot* of money, Michael."

"I know. I wish I were in the dog business."

"But does the story seem off-base to you?"

"Of course it does. He even admits he was there the night his uncle was killed."

"Oh! Tell me about it."

McGowan told her about the broken alibi and the way that Whiting had sulked over his beer at Charlie's Place before rushing off to his uncle's house. "Every time we get him down at the precinct house, he gets one step closer to telling us the truth. It's just a matter of time, now. But we've got him. We're sure of that."

"Congratulations," replied Jackie gently.

"Thanks. You know, now that I've had a few conversations with him, I'm surprised he had the brains to carry it out. At a guess, I'd say he has trouble tying his shoes."

"I didn't know murderers were supposed to be smart."

"He's what I'd call subnormally intelligent. He can read and write, I suppose, but about living in the world he has not got a clue. Don't know how he got a job at Nash Brothers."

"Connections," said Jackie. "His mother's uncle was one of the firm's founders. A long time ago."

"Now, how do you know that?"

"I don't know. That's just a part of Palmer history. Just one of the things you pick up on."

"Well, thank you for the history lesson," said McGowan gravely.

"You're welcome. What's your next step going to be?"

"We'll let him twist for a day or two, then get him back in here. He'll break."

"Well, let me know, won't you, how it turns out?"

"I will. And when we've got it all neatly packaged up, how about going to dinner with me?"

"Anytime," said Jackie, surprised at herself. She wasn't sure that going *out* to dinner with McGowan had the same innocence as letting him come around to their house for spaghetti every now and then. But it was too late to change her answer. She would just have to live with it. "Anytime," she repeated.

"I'm going to hold you to that."

As Jackie hung up the phone in her kitchen, she thought about what McGowan had told her. She wasn't surprised to hear that Whiting had been up to no good with his uncle's investments. There was an awful lot of that kind of thing going around these days. But she wasn't at all sure she bought the angle that he'd killed his uncle. Surely that was like killing the goose that laid the golden eggs? Besides, Jackie was convinced that there was something more to the whole affair. She was not satisfied that it boiled down to a question of money—that seemed too neat.

As she started to organize dinner for herself and Peter, she thought over everything she had seen and heard of the world that Mel Sweeten had moved in. Amy had been right, Jackie reflected, to characterize some of the participants as "disgustingly competitive." Not all were that way, of course—the man with the poodle, whom she had met on

Sunday, had been quite nice, despite being totally preoccupied with his little Serena. And this afternoon's excursion had certainly been fun. Sylvia Brown had been positively lighthearted. But a few of the people she had met were in deadly earnest about their dogs. They seemed to be so worried about winning that they didn't have the energy left to enjoy themselves, much less enjoy their dogs.

Jackie was struck by a sudden idea.

"Peter!" she called upstairs.

"Yes, Mom?" Peter appeared at the top of the stairs.

"I have to go out on an errand. Why don't you give Isaac a call and see if you can go over there for a while. For supper, if they'll have you." Jackie knew that Peter was welcome at Isaac's house at any time of day or night. Isaac's mother was an easygoing woman, and she liked Peter quite a lot. It was soon arranged.

Peter and Jackie and Jake headed for Isaac's house. Jackie stopped in at the Cooks' house to say a quick hello before she and Jake continued their course toward Linden Lane, where Sylvia Brown lived in a small ground-floor apartment of a townhouse. Jackie had dropped her off here this afternoon, after Jake's triumph at the obedience competition.

With a start, Jackie realized that she had forgotten to tell Michael McGowan about the obedience competition. Not that Jake's blue ribbon would come as a surprise to anyone—but still, McGowan deserved to be clued in. She would tell him tomorrow—by which time she also hoped to have some additional information for him about the case.

As she reached the door, she wondered briefly if she was making a big mistake. She was convinced that Michael McGowan was wrong about the nephew. No matter what kind of a crook he was, she was utterly sure that there was more to Mel Sweeten's death than mere money. There was something about the way he had been killed that spoke volumes. He had been choked to death by a dog collar, in one of his own dog runs.

Surely the nephew wouldn't have been so picturesque? Surely the manner of Sweeten's death pointed in one direction only?

But it was going to be difficult to prove, and in the meantime, people might be at risk.

She buzzed Sylvia's doorbell, and the intercom clicked.

At six-fifteen that evening, a satisfied Michael McGowan leaned back in his desk chair. His long, restless fingers toyed with a rubber band, a habit he found both stimulating to his mental processes and intimidating to suspects. He kept his eyes firmly fixed on Cosmo Gordon, who had dropped by to hear the news about the Sweeten case.

"I'm glad you came by," he said. "I'll tell you about the Whiting kid in a minute. But in the meantime, I have good news for you. We've found the gun that killed Matt Dugan."

Gordon looked gratified. "Where?"

"Not far from where he was killed. Looks like a mob weapon. Serial number filed off, the whole bit. But the boys and girls down in the ballistics lab say it's a make."

"Where did it come from?"

"That's the usual problem. But believe it or not, we may have a break. You ever hear of a guy called Shorty, who lives down on Front Street?"

"Sure. Gunrunner for the big boys."

"That's the one. Well, his kid got beat up kind of badly last week. In the hospital and everything. So Shorty's been on the horn to Cruz. Wants to talk about a few things."

"That's good."

"Yeah. Too bad about the kid. He lost an eye. But it may be good for the city in the long run. There are times when you just have to take the utilitarian viewpoint in this job."

"I'm with you," said Gordon. "There are times when the utilitarian viewpoint is the only one left."

"That too."

"Keep me posted, will you?"

"Of course. What did you get from the lab on that letter?"

"Nothing," said Gordon, shaking his head. "I didn't expect anything. But I'm worried about Nancy. She was at home with me the night that Dugan came over. The boys who sent me that letter know that Dugan came to the house. Probably they were having him watched. So they know Nancy was at home. But they have no way of knowing that she wasn't in the room when he began to talk about conspiracies."

"No." McGowan considered it for a bit. He saw an opening. "On the other hand, don't overestimate these guys. Remember that you're dealing with a fairly primitive bunch. They're right about at the level of the Cro-Magnon man in terms of social development."

McGowan was famous on the Palmer police force for his exceptionally enlightened view of modern society. Gordon, like others, was used to the young lieutenant's lectures on the equality of women. Unlike many others, Gordon was wholeheartedly in McGowan's camp. Their high regard for women, and their outspoken belief in equal pay for equal work, was one of the bonds that united them.

McGowan was warming to his theme. He smiled and shot his rubber band up at the overhead light, hitting the little metal hood that covered the bulb. His effort was rewarded with a resounding *ping!* He picked up another rubber band and continued his lecture.

"One aspect of the caveman personality is total insecurity around women, the need to subjugate them or keep them 'in their place,' wherever they think that is. By force, when necessary, or just by brutish emotional intimidation—by being nasty to them. Another aspect of that personality is, of course, the need to go around shooting people you don't like. But remember—it would never occur to these goons that you might want Nancy around when something important was being discussed. They whisper about things, or send their wives out of the room, unless the topic is food."

"Good point," replied Gordon, who had been following McGowan's reasoning. He grinned. "It hadn't occurred to me, but you're right, of course. They'd assume that Dugan and I would talk privately." There was genuine relief in his tone.

"There's one other thing you should know about the Dugan case," said McGowan. His tone was suddenly quite serious. "I got a call this afternoon from Cornelius Mitchell, the K-9 man."

"And?"

"And he had a call last week, from some man who wanted to know what had happened to Dugan's dog."

Gordon looked alarmed. This was just the kind of development he and McGowan had been worried about. Jackie's safety, they felt, depended on keeping Jake's identity a secret. They were sure that whoever had killed Dugan wanted to get to Jake—the dog had, after all, been a witness to his master's murder. And although he couldn't testify in a court of law, Jake was certainly capable of carrying out his own form of justice, if and when he got his chance. "Mitchell didn't tell the man anything, did he?"

"No. No, he has brains, that Mitchell. Even tried to get a trace on the call, while he pretended to look through the files. But whoever it was must have figured out what was going on, because he hung up."

"Have you told Jackie about it?"

McGowan shook his head. "I only just heard about it myself. I tried reaching her, but I guess she and Peter have gone out for the evening. There's no answer at her house."

"Well, you can tell her tomorrow. I'm sure that between now and then, she won't put herself at risk." He shot another rubber band at the light overhead. *Ping!*

CHAPTER 20

Sylvia Brown's voice came crackling through the intercom at her apartment door.

"Yes?"

"Sylvia, hi. It's Jackie. Got a minute?"

"Um—"

"Just a minute, really."

Jackie could hear a hurried movement. Then the front door buzzed, and Jackie and Jake went on into the vestibule.

"Hi," said Sylvia, opening her apartment door just a crack. "Oh. I see you've brought Jake."

"I wanted to talk to you," said Jackie.

"Well, I'm kind of busy right now." She looked pointedly at her watch. "I have to take a shower and get dressed. I'm going out a little later."

"It's important."

Sylvia looked thoughtful for a moment. "Okay." She swung the door wide to let Jackie and Jake pass.

Sylvia Brown's living room was small and sparsely furnished, but everything she had, thought Jackie, was in excellent taste. Sylvia clearly had an artistic streak, which manifested itself everywhere. Old crates, covered with bits of exotic-looking, hand-dyed cloth, served as end tables. There was a tiny fireplace, which had been fitted out a century ago for gas jets; the gingerbread wrought-iron grill in front of it had been painted brilliant colors. The curtains were colorful too, and the walls were hung with a series of watercolors—beach scenes, a stream, a farmhouse. There wasn't a hint of a basset hound among them.

Instinctively, and on purely aesthetic grounds, Jackie rejected the notion that Sylvia Brown had had an affair with Mel Sweeten. Sylvia Brown, Jackie thought, was probably capable of compromising herself, but not with a man who, in utter seriousness, had decorated his house with basset-hound lamps and basset-hound nut dishes. Jackie didn't see how it was possible; the two sensibilities would just not work together.

But she reminded herself that Amy Sweeten, as an art historian, presumably had a certain amount of taste as well. Maybe Mel Sweeten had been somehow devastatingly attractive to artistic women.

Sylvia, after greeting Jake with the enthusiasm due him, gestured Jackie to a chair and took a seat on the sofa. Jake found himself a comfortable spot halfway between the two women and put his nose down on his front paws.

"Okay," said Sylvia. "I guess it must be important, since you could have telephoned. I'm in the book."

Now that Jackie was here, she didn't quite know how to start. She had planned to start by talking about the rumors of the affair, but now that whole idea seemed an absurdity.

"Look—you'll probably think I'm crazy," Jackie began at last, "but I think maybe I can help you. If you're in a jam. Which I think you are."

"What makes you think so?"

"A lot of things. Mainly that you changed your mind and came with us today to the obedience competition. You said you needed practice with other breeds, but I think that was just an excuse."

"You're right," said Sylvia. Jackie waited, but the woman didn't elaborate. At last Jackie started up again.

"So. Okay, you wanted either to get something from me, or to talk to me. I figure that if you wanted to get something from me you would have worked on me, but you didn't. So that means you wanted to tell me something. The fact that you didn't manage to get it out means that it's hard to talk about. So I figure you're in a bind of some kind. And I thought maybe if I came over here and asked you, you'd talk."

Sylvia Brown laughed. "You should have been a psychologist. Or a detective."

"Am I right?"

"Yes, you are." Again, Sylvia grew silent. It began to look like Jackie would have to play Twenty Questions all evening. She decided to cut to the chase.

"Okay. You'd like to help the police get to the bottom of Mel Sweeten's murder. But you just don't know how to go about it. Am I right?"

Sylvia shook her long blond hair back out of her face and gave Jackie an appraising look. "How do you mean?"

"I mean this—that there was something going on."

"Hey, not you too! I am getting awfully tired of having people accuse me of carrying on." Sylvia looked disappointed. She had expected more from Jackie.

"I don't mean with Mel." Jackie looked her straight in the eye. "I don't believe you were having any kind of affair with him. But I do believe there was something up. Am I right?"

"Such as?"

"I couldn't really say. I'm here to get it from you. All I know is that Mel Sweeten was getting a lot of money from somewhere, and it wasn't from the Dog Academy. But the only thing he was interested in was dogs. So. Where was it coming from?"

Sylvia Brown looked uncomfortable. She hadn't expected the direct approach, clearly. She said nothing.

"You see," Jackie went on, "I don't really care about whatever little swindle is going on in the dog-show world. I doubt the police care, either. But Mel Sweeten was murdered, and I have a feeling that his killer might not want to stop there. So, since I like you, and think you have a lot of talent, I thought I'd try to talk some sense into you. Before it's too late. You may not even have to face a criminal charge, if you go to the police yourself. That's really all I came to say. I don't know if you've changed your mind about wanting to talk. But if you have, I suggest you call Michael McGowan and tell him what you know."

"I can't," said Sylvia in a quiet voice.

"Why not?"

"I'm terrified." She had gone suddenly ashen. "Don't you see? If anyone finds out I've gone to the police, I'll be next."

"If you help the police find the murderer, you won't have anything to worry about. Nothing at all."

"I doubt that." Sylvia Brown laughed.

"Why don't you try talking to me, then? I can't promise you anything—but I do sort of have an in with the police."

"So I've heard." Sylvia chuckled.

"What do you mean?"

"I mean that Dick Buzone sent you to talk to me so that he could figure out just how much the police knew. He says the detective is your boyfriend."

"He's wrong." Jackie felt a slow flush spread up her cheeks.

"What would you call him, then?" Sylvia was genuinely curious.

"He's a friend of the family."

"Oh."

For half a second, Jackie thought she detected a look of gratification on Sylvia's face. She felt a knot of anxiety beginning to form in her stomach, but she told herself sternly to keep her mind on the job. Being jealous of Sylvia could wait. What was important right now was Sylvia's safety.

"A good friend," Jackie added, not able to stop herself. "All right." Her tone was once again businesslike. "Why did Dick Buzone want to know about the police case?"

Sylvia sighed. "He had something going. He works as a judge, you know, at most of the big shows in the area."

"So I gathered. And I hear he isn't very popular with the owners and handlers."

"No," agreed Sylvia. "And with good reason. He takes bribes."

"So that's it," said Jackie. "I knew he was up to something."

"You did?"

"Well, he doesn't strike me as much of a dog person. I've seen him at two dog shows now, if you count today's competition, and he never really so much as glances at the dogs that are competing. It's as though he has his mind all made up at the beginning."

"I tried to tell him not to be so obvious about it," said Sylvia.

"All right. So he takes bribes. Big ones? Little ones? How does it work?"

"He puts out a little magazine. Maybe you've seen it— *The Canine Chronicle*."

Jackie nodded. "Yes, I've seen it. Articles on puppy cuts for poodles, and so forth."

"Right. Well, Dick has a system. He puts you on the mailing list for the magazine, and you pay a subscription rate of anywhere from ten bucks to a hundred bucks a copy. Depending. He can pretty much size up who can afford what."

"Whew!"

"I know. Ridiculous, isn't it? And subscribing for a year only puts you on the short list, for winning best of breed, or winning in a puppy class. To get on the best of show list, you have to have subscribed for two years. And after the two years, you have to pay five hundred dollars a year to stay on the list."

"Complicated. But what's the point of it all?"

"Oh, that's easy. The point is finishing your dog."

"Finishing."

"Getting your championship points. Because then you can breed your dog and sell the puppies for a lot of money. So you get your money back, in the long run."

"How many people are on the list?"

"Oh, I guess about fifty or sixty every year. Dick judges about twenty big shows, and he can give two awards in each show. There are always some subscribers left over, who have to resubscribe. It's quite a nice little racket."

Jackie grew thoughtful a moment. "I thought there was something odd about that newsletter," she said.

"Yeah. Well, it isn't just a one-way transaction all the time. Subscribers get to run advertisements if they want to, so sometimes it works out well for both sides."

"And what's your role, if you don't mind my asking?"

"Oh, nothing too big, really. Just to talk to people at shows, find out who might be willing to cough up the dough, and get back to Dick with their names."

"Set them up, kind of."

"Yeah, more or less." Sylvia was quiet a moment. "When I started out helping Dick, about three years ago, I thought he was just being friendly. He said he wanted to help me get to know all the right people, since I was thinking about becoming a professional handler. He gave me this long song and dance about how the dog-show circuit is really a people thing, more than a dog thing, and so it would be a good boost to my career if he helped me."

"And did he help you?"

"No. Well, yes, I suppose in a way he did, at first. But then he began to pump me for information about the people I was working for."

"Didn't you think that was suspicious?"

"Of course I did. But by that time I had figured out that he's a pretty nasty character. So I kept up the pretense, until I could find out what he was using the information for."

"And then?"

"Then I accused him of extorting money from people under the promise of gain, and that I'd go to the Am-DOG authorities. But he just laughed at me, and said I'd be totally out of work, because everyone would say that *I'd* been in it with him; that I'd been digging up all kinds of information on people. Which was true." She made a face. "He had me in a corner."

"Quite the prince, isn't he?" commented Jackie.

"Yeah. Prince of creeps. Well, I didn't have any hard evidence against him, and I figured that he had a point about my complicity. So I kept quiet, which wasn't right. But at least I had the integrity to cut him off."

"You stopped."

"Yeah, I refused to do any more work for him. Plus, I decided that I would ease out of the dog world into something a little less cutthroat. That's why I got my certification to teach aerobics."

Jackie could understand that it must have been a tough position for Sylvia. She could sympathize with the difficulty of the predicament, but she liked to think that in the same circumstances she would have blown the whistle—job or no job. It was hard to say.

"So," said Jackie thoughtfully, "pretty much all the championship points that he's awarded in the last three years have been as a direct result of bribes."

"Well, yes and no. Sometimes there's really not *that* much difference in conformation to the standard. Most judges have preferences; Dick just preferred those who paid for the honor."

"I don't think I know what you mean," replied Jackie.

"Okay, look. Say you have a dog show, and there are five winners competing for best in show. They've all won best of breed, already, because that's the way a dog show works."

"Right," said Jackie, who had gathered as much in her brief visit to the show at the armory last Sunday.

"So if the prize goes to, say, Jake here, instead of to a toy poodle, it's really got a lot to do with how much the judges like shepherds in general, as compared to toy poodles."

"I see."

"People who enter dog shows choose their judges carefully. Because it's really hard, if your dog wins best of breed, and then he gets shot down for best in show just because the judge doesn't like his kind. But that has been known to happen, believe me."

"It's subjective."

"Exactly. So—Dick's choices are subjective too. How much everyone has paid him, and whether he wants to make them go on paying and paying. There are a few people whose money he's been taking for thirteen years, and still he's never given them best in show."

"Why do they keep trying?"

"God only knows," replied Sylvia. "You would think that they would figure out that he'd never come through."

Jackie grew thoughtful. "Where did Mel Sweeten figure into all of this?"

"Oh—he was taking about half the cut. Supposedly the whole scheme was his idea. At least that's what Dick told me, although I never am quite sure how much of what Dick says to believe."

Jackie nodded. It fit with what Michael had told her this afternoon about the nephew and the mysterious income.

"Who else knew about their little game?"

"Besides me?" Sylvia shook her head. "Nobody."

"Are you sure?"

"Positive. They thought it was a scream. Mel especially, because Dick was always making his bassets champions. Then Mel would give him a little kickback on the stud fee, or something."

"What a pair."

"I know. They were pretty awful."

"Tell me, Sylvia," Jackie began, but the other woman cut her off.

"Let me guess. You heard the rumors about me and Mel. You also know I was handling his bassets. Now you know that I knew he was a crook. You want to know what was going on. Right?"

"Right," said Jackie.

"Not much. Just this: I adore Fred and Karen. I've been working with them, and placing Karen's puppies, and finding mates for Fred, for three years—and I'm just crazy about them. That's all."

For some reason, Jackie found this explanation utterly

compelling. It answered every question, it left no loose ends, no "what-ifs" lying about.

Now that she had her answers about Sylvia Brown, Jackie decided it was high time to confront the murderer of Mel Sweeten. She thanked Sylvia for her time and took her leave, considering, on her way home, what would be the best way to approach the next person on her list.

The very first thing to do was to call Michael McGowan and tell him what her plan was. Jake or no Jake, she didn't relish the idea of a confrontation without knowing that help would soon be on the way.

CHAPTER 21

"Wait a second, Jackie. Hold on, would you? Just let me turn down the volume so I can hear you." Michael McGowan had just settled himself in front of the television. The Lakers were playing the Celtics. The beer was cold, the pretzels were crisp, and he was exhausted. What he clearly did not want was to talk about the murder of Mel Sweeten.

"But, Michael, there's no time to lose. I tell you that Dick Buzone's life is in danger."

He caught the end of this frantic statement as he returned to the telephone. One of these days, McGowan often vowed, he would buy a new television with remote control. But on a lieutenant's salary, after alimony payments every month, there was never enough left over for that dream machine.

"Okay," he said. "Start again."

Jackie repeated her assertion.

"You're not serious."

"Of course I am. Listen." She told him about her visit to Sylvia Brown's apartment. "Michael, that kid Whiting was telling you the truth. There was a slush fund. It was the subscription list for that stupid newsletter."

McGowan could have kicked himself. Jackie had pestered him and pestered him about that subscription list, and he had dismissed everything she said. Now it looked like he had been a little too high-and-mighty.

Worse yet, it looked like his case against Ned Whiting would collapse. If there had been a slush fund, then maybe there was truth in his account of having found his uncle dead. "Just what I needed," said McGowan ungratefully. "I'm back at square one."

"No, you're not. Michael, I think I know who killed Mel Sweeten."

"Do tell."

So Jackie told, and told him her reasons for thinking so. Then she told him what she thought they ought to do about it. She had a plan, but she needed his help. Would he make one little telephone call for her?

McGowan listened to her plan in amazed silence. While he had been concentrating on Ned Whiting, Jackie Walsh had seen clear through to the bottom of the problem. Feeling slightly sheepish, he agreed to her plan, with one proviso— that she would take Jake with her.

"Of course I will. What, you think I'm crazy or some-thing? I'm not going all the way out there to face a murderer without my bodyguard."

"I'll meet you there in twenty-five minutes," said McGowan.

In less than that time, in twenty minutes, Jackie and Jake had arrived at Mel Sweeten's Dog Academy. The lights were blazing in the house; Jackie had expected Amy to be at home. She had the feeling that Amy was almost always at home, at least when the library was shut.

She and Jake made their way up the darkened path, past Fred and Karen, who set about howling magnificently at the intruders. That was what Jackie wanted—she wanted to get them stirred up, the way they had been the night that Mel Sweeten was killed.

She wanted to hear how they responded to the presence of something that they were afraid of. Tonight, it was Jake, who gave off immense vibes of power and authority, even in the dark, even on territory that was clearly not his own.

That night, it had been Mel Sweeten's murderer—a person that the bassets loathed and feared.

As Jackie and Jake arrived at the front door, another car pulled up in the driveway. Jackie recognized the station wagon that Thalia Gilmore had been driving that morning at the obedience competition. Jackie didn't wait for Thalia, but knocked straightaway at the front door.

Amy answered in less than five seconds. She must have been pacing in the hallway.

"Jackie!" she said in stunned surprise. "What are you doing here?"

"May I come in?"

"Um, sure. Do you mind leaving your dog outside?"

Thalia Gilmore arrived huffing and puffing. "What is all this about?" she demanded.

"It's about the night that Mel Sweeten was murdered," said Jackie quietly. "And no, Amy, I'd prefer to bring Jake inside with me. If it's all the same to you."

Amy Sweeten, looking mystified, shrugged her shoulders and led the way into the living room, with the two other women and Jake on her heels.

"What do you mean it's about that night?" Thalia Gilmore bellowed. "I have never heard anything so absurd in my life." She turned to give Amy an indignant stare. "Who *is* this woman that you let her push you around, Mrs. Sweeten?"

"She's a colleague," replied Amy in a level voice. She was regarding Jackie warily. "She's a member of the faculty at Rodgers University."

"Well, what on earth is she doing here, at this time of night, with her dog?"

"I'm not sure," replied Amy in a faint voice.

"I'm here conducting a little experiment," said Jackie. "And I needed your help, Mrs. Gilmore."

"My help? This is absurd. It's outrageous. I came here to ask Mrs. Sweeten a question or two, not to play some silly game with you. I'm going *straight* home."

"I really wish you'd stay," Jackie replied. "You're the only person who can help us."

"How can I *possibly* help you, child?"

"Mrs. Gilmore, you were here that night."

"Of course I was. Everyone knows that. I'm a member of the executive committee of the Greater Palmer Dog Fanciers Association."

"You remember, don't you, the noise that the dogs made in the middle of your meeting?"

"I most certainly do. A horrid racket, perfectly dreadful. Mel had to go outside and quiet them down."

"When he returned to the room, how did he look?"

"Shaken. But I thought—that is to say, I had rather been hoping that he had decided to confess his treachery to me. He had poisoned my Clematis, down in Philadelphia, made her terribly ill so that she couldn't compete. That was the day she was supposed to have won best in show too."

Thalia Gilmore looked suddenly alarmed. "I mean to say—"

"I know exactly what you mean to say, Mrs. Gilmore. You mean to say that you had been one of Dick Buzone's 'subscribers' for many years, and he had put you off, continually. But with Clematis you really thought you had a chance of winning, and then she was ill."

"That's right. And one of Karen's pups, well not a pup any longer, she's two or three by now—anyway, one of

Mel's dogs, in effect, won not only best in the Hound class but also won best of show. It was *terribly* unfair. And Mel Sweeten ought to have been shot for doing such a thing." The blood drained from Thalia Gilmore's face as she realized her gaffe. "Oh, I'm so *dreadfully* sorry, Mrs. Sweeten, I didn't mean—"

"Don't give it a thought, Mrs. Gilmore," Amy replied. "Would anyone like a cup of tea or anything? Or maybe just tell me why you're here."

"Mrs. Gilmore wants to buy Fred and Karen, Amy." She gave Thalia Gilmore a look; and that large lady, for once, kept her mouth shut. Jackie went on. "I told her that you were interested in her offer, but I thought it was a little low. She has agreed to pay five thousand for the pair of them."

"Great," said Amy. "The sooner the better. I can use the money, and all of our cash is tied up in probate. Everything was in Mel's name." She smiled her pale little smile.

"Well, my dear," said Thalia Gilmore, rising magnificently to the occasion, "I have brought my checkbook with me. I'm all ready to go."

"The only thing is," Jackie interrupted, with a hard, even stare at the astonished Thalia Gilmore, "that Mrs. Gilmore would like to take a look at the dogs before she writes the check."

"I certainly would. My late husband always told me that I ought to look before I leapt. He was a very wise man." She addressed Amy. "Would you do me the kindness, my dear, of bringing the dogs inside so that I can take one last look at them before I sign on the dotted line?"

"Sure," said Amy. "Jackie, you know more about dogs than I do. Would you let them in? And I'll make a pot of tea."

"I think I'd better stay here with Jake, Amy. I'm the only one in this room who can control him, and I would hate for anything to happen to Fred and Karen. Just go get them and bring them in the kitchen. Then I'll take Jake out."

Amy Sweeten, looking visibly reluctant, complied.

A minute passed. And then, with a noise like something out of the nether world, Fred and Karen set up their alarm call. Thalia Gilmore gave Jackie a questioning look, but didn't say a word.

In another minute or two, Amy had come back inside.

"They're really stubborn," she said lamely. "You'd better go on out and have a look for yourself, Mrs. Gilmore."

"They hate you, don't they, Amy?" asked Jackie.

"They're just stupid dogs. Go on outside, Mrs. Gilmore. They're right in their pen."

"They hate you and they fear you," said Jackie in a flat, calm, implacable voice. She turned to Thalia Gilmore. "Is that the noise they made the night that you were here?"

"Yes," said Thalia Gilmore. "I'd never heard anything like it. Certainly not out of Fred and Karen. But that was it."

Jackie returned her gaze to Amy, who was looking stricken. "They hate you and they fear you, Amy, because you have always hated them," said Jackie, her voice quiet and calm. "And because you murdered their friend. They despise you and revile you, and call out in a wild voice whenever you come near. Isn't that so, Amy?"

Amy Sweeten had gone a pale, dead gray. She was breathing rapidly, in shallow little breaths, and staring hard at Jackie. Finally she found the breath to speak.

"No. You're wrong."

"I'm not wrong. If I'm wrong, go and get those dogs for me, and bring them inside. They'll tell you who's right and who's wrong."

"No, I can't," said Amy, her eyes wild. "They're just stupid dogs."

"Go and get them," repeated Jackie.

"I can't. I can't." Amy's voice broke, and her thin little body was racked with sobs. "I can't, I can't, I can't. They'll kill me."

"Who will?" persisted Jackie in the same low, level voice. "Who will kill you?"

"They will, they'll kill me, they'll tear me apart. They were there!" She sank onto the sofa, her voice hysterical. "They know!"

"What do the bassets know, Amy?"

"They know that I killed Mel!" Now Amy's whole body shook as if she were sobbing, but her eyes were dry. Jackie went quickly and quietly to the front door and opened it. Michael McGowan was there. Jackie nodded and led him in.

Amy was hugging her knees to her chest, rocking back and forth on the sofa, sobbing great huge dry sobs. "I killed him! I killed him!" she cried out, again and again. "I did it, and the bassets know! The bassets know!"

CHAPTER 22

The following day, Jackie invited Sylvia Brown and Thalia Gilmore to lunch, and refused to take no for an answer. Sylvia promised to give all the statements necessary to the police about the extortion racket. McGowan had phoned her that morning, and he seemed to feel that no charges would be pressed against her.

Thalia, of course, knew the reason for being summoned to Jackie's. She had totally recovered her magnificent aplomb, and was reveling in her important role of the evening before. Sylvia was amazed at the tale. Michael McGowan arrived just in time for dessert, to hear Thalia Gilmore doing quite a passable imitation of Fred's and Karen's wailing. The noise roused Jake, who had been drowsing under the kitchen table. Peter and Isaac, playing Game Boy in the den, emerged to find out what all the noise was about.

McGowan settled down familiarly at the kitchen table.

"We've got the full confession. You were absolutely right, Jackie. The woman is crazy."

"Who's crazy, Mom?"

"A lady who murdered her husband, sweetie."

"And you caught the murderer?" Peter beamed and poked Isaac in the ribs. That made it two to zero. Isaac's mother hadn't caught any murderers.

"Jake and I did, honey. I'll tell you all about it. Do us a favor, though, and run along. Okay?"

Peter knew that his mother only sent him out of the room when he was likely to get a better version of the story later—when she didn't have to be polite in front of strangers. So he dragged the protesting Isaac back to the den. "It's better this way, I promise," said Peter. "You can stay for supper."

"Okay."

The group in the kitchen listened fascinated as McGowan told them the whole story. "She turned up at the Dog Academy at about eight o'clock. She was going to poison the bassets. But as you know, they made a terrible racket. Mel Sweeten came out of the house; he knew that the dogs only made that kind of noise when they were really upset about something."

"That's true," put in Sylvia, who knew Fred and Karen better than anyone else, except Mel Sweeten. "They always made that noise when Amy was anywhere around. They just *hated* her."

"So she hid in the bushes behind the dog runs, while Mel quieted the dogs down. Apparently he knew that she must be there. He called her name a couple of times, but got no answer. So he went back inside."

"No *wonder* he looked so upset," said Thalia Gilmore.

"He had suspected Amy of trying to poison the dogs once before," put in Sylvia. "But he couldn't prove it. All he knew was that she was insanely jealous of them."

"What did she do—jump him when he came back outside?" asked Jackie.

"Not exactly. She says Mel came out and looked around a little bit. Then he sat down, and after a while he fell asleep. I suppose he was trying to stand guard over the dogs or something, in case she was still around." McGowan shook his head. "He knew how much she resented them. Once he was asleep, she had her opportunity. I don't know if he was even aware of what was happening."

"You can't really blame the poor thing for being jealous," said Thalia. "He was a total nut about those dogs. And as far as I could tell, he never gave her a thought."

"You're wrong about that," said Sylvia. "He was terribly worried about her mental condition. She apparently had decided to do her doctoral thesis on dogs in art, which the university thought was a bad idea. But she was persisting, finding every portrait that had ever been done of a dog, finding every casual dog that ever appeared in a painting. She was hunting for bassets, but they were scarce. It was really spooky. Mel was wondering how to get help for her."

"You didn't help things, my dear," reproved Thalia Gilmore. "Just look at you."

"I can't help the way I look, Mrs. Gilmore. Mel and I were never anything but friends. And even not such good friends toward the end. My real friends in the dog-show circuit were Fred and Karen."

"Hmph," said Thalia Gilmore.

"What about the nightgown, Michael?" asked Jackie.

"There never was any nightgown. If we'd gotten around to it, we'd have found out that her story didn't check out. She admitted to me in her confession this morning that she had made that whole thing up. Oh, she *was* convinced he was fooling around, but she had no evidence. She just decided to focus her accusations on Sylvia. To cast suspicion around."

Jackie shivered. "In a way, I feel sorry for her. But I feel sorry for Mel too. I'll bet she was constantly on his back, spying on him. . . . There's something so ugly about a marriage without any love or trust."

"Speaking of spies, Jackie," said Sylvia, "there was a guy at the obedience competition the other day asking me all kinds of questions about Jake. And about you."

McGowan and Jackie exchanged a look. "Why?" asked the detective.

Sylvia shrugged. "Got me. I told him that Jake belonged to Jackie, because he could have found that out from anyone. Then he kind of took off. Hey, what's it all about?" She had noticed the anxious look in McGowan's eyes.

He explained briefly the circumstances of Jake's arrival.

"He's a *police* dog?" Sylvia was disbelieving. Then she nodded. "I wondered where he'd learned his stuff."

"Please don't mention it to anyone, under any circumstances," cautioned McGowan. "Jackie and Peter aren't really safe until we can get the guy who murdered Matt Dugan. And the people he works for."

"Well," said Sylvia, "if that's your next case, maybe I can help. Here." She fished in her wallet and dug out a scrap of paper. "This is the license of the car that guy was driving yesterday."

She smiled at the astonished group. "My father always taught me to be on the lookout for creeps. I think I'm finally learning to follow his advice." She handed the slip of paper to Jackie. "I think this will be your next case. Yours and Jake's."

Jake, from under the kitchen table, let out a low *woof.* He was evidently ready to solve his own mystery.

Gabelle had to do with the collection of rent and taxes—
though it was but a small instalment of taxes, and no rent at
all, that Gabelle had got in those latter days—became impatient for an interview with him, and, surrounding his house,
summoned him to come forth for personal conference.
Whereupon, Monsieur Gabelle did heavily bar his door, and
retire to hold counsel with himself. The result of that conference was, that Gabelle again withdrew himself to his
house-top behind his stack of chimneys; this time resolved,
if his door were broken in (he was a small Southern man of
retaliative temperament), to pitch himself head foremost
over the parapet, and crush a man or two below.

Probably, Monsieur Gabelle passed a long night up there
with the distant château for fire and candle, and the beating
at his door, combined with the joy-ringing for music; not to
mention his having an ill-omened lamp slung across the
road before his posting-house gate, which the village
showed a lively inclination to displace in his favour. A trying
suspense, to be passing a whole summer night on the brink
of the black ocean, ready to take that plunge into it upon
which Monsieur Gabelle had resolved! But, the friendly
dawn appearing at last, and the rush-candles of the village
guttering out, the people happily dispersed, and Monsieur
Gabelle came down bringing his life with him for that while.

Within a hundred miles, and in the light of other fires,
there were other functionaries less fortunate, that night and
other nights, whom the rising sun found hanging across
once-peaceful streets, where they had been born and bred;
also, there were other villagers and townspeople less fortunate than the mender of roads and his fellows, upon whom
the functionaries and soldiery turned with success, and
whom they strung up in their turn. But, the fierce figures
were steadily wending East, West, North, and South, be
that as it would; and whosoever hung, fire burned. The alti-
tude of the gallows that would turn to water and quench it,
no functionary, by any stretch of mathematics, was able to
calculate successfully.

24

DRAWN TO THE LOADSTONE ROCK

◆

IN SUCH risings of fire and risings of sea—the firm earth shaken by the rushes of an angry ocean which had now no ebb, but was always on the flow, higher and higher, to the terror and wonder of the beholders on the shore—three years of tempest were consumed. Three more birthdays of little Lucie had been woven by the golden thread into the peaceful tissue of the life of her home.

Many a night and many a day had its inmates listened to the echoes in the corner, with hearts that failed them when they heard the thronging feet. For, the footsteps had become to their minds as the footsteps of a people, tumultuous under a red flag and with their country declared in danger, changed into wild beasts, by terrible enchantment long persisted in.

Monseigneur, as a class, had dissociated himself from the phenomenon of his not being appreciated: of his being so little wanted in France, as to incur considerable danger of receiving his dismissal from it, and this life together. Like the fabled rustic who raised the Devil with infinite pains, and was so terrified at the sight of him that he could ask the Enemy no question, but immediately fled; so, Monseigneur, after boldly reading the Lord's Prayer backwards[27] for a

great number of years and performing many other potent
spells for compelling the Evil One, no sooner beheld him in
his terrors than he took to his noble heels.

The shining Bull's Eye of the Court was gone, or it would
have been the mark for a hurricane of national bullets. It
had never been a good eye to see with—had long had the
mote in it of Lucifer's pride, Sardanapalus's luxury,[28] and a
mole's blindness—but it had dropped out and was gone.
The Court, from that exclusive inner circle to its outermost
rotten ring of intrigue, corruption, and dissimulation, was
all gone together. Royalty was gone; had been besieged in
its Palace and "suspended," when the last tidings came over.

The August of the year one thousand seven hundred and
ninety-two was come, and Monseigneur was by this time
scattered far and wide.

As was natural, the head-quarters and great gathering-
place of Monseigneur, in London, was Tellson's Bank.
Spirits are supposed to haunt the places where their bodies
most resorted, and Monseigneur without a guinea haunted
the spot where his guineas used to be. Moreover, it was the
spot to which such French intelligence as was most to be
relied upon, came quickest. Again: Tellson's was a munifi-
cent house, and extended great liberality to old customers
who had fallen from their high estate. Again: those nobles
who had seen the coming storm in time, and anticipating
plunder of confiscation, had made provident remittances to
Tellson's, were always to be heard of there by their needy
brethren. To which it must be added that every new comer
from France reported himself and his tidings at Tellson's,
almost as a matter of course. For such variety of reasons,
Tellson's was at that time, as to French intelligence, a kind
of High Exchange; and this was so well known to the public,
and the inquiries made there were in consequence so
numerous, that Tellson's sometimes wrote the latest news
out in a line or so and posted it in the Bank windows, for all
who ran through Temple Bar to read.

On a steamy, misty afternoon, Mr. Lorry sat at his desk,

and Charles Darnay stood leaning on it, talking with him in a low voice. The penitential den once set apart for interviews with the House, was now the news-Exchange, and was filled to overflowing. It was within half an hour or so of the time of closing.

"But, although you are the youngest man that ever lived," said Charles Darnay, rather hesitating, "I must still suggest to you——"

"I understand. That I am too old?" said Mr. Lorry.

"Unsettled weather, a long journey, uncertain means of travelling, a disorganised country, a city that may not be even safe for you."

"My dear Charles," said Mr. Lorry, with cheerful confidence, "you touch some of the reasons for my going: not for my staying away. It is safe enough for me; nobody will care to interfere with an old fellow of hard upon fourscore when there are so many people there much better worth interfering with. As to its being a disorganised city, if it were not a disorganised city there would be no occasion to send somebody from our House here to our House there, who knows the city and the business, of old, and is in Tellson's confidence. As to the uncertain travelling, the long journey, and the winter weather, if I were not prepared to submit myself to a few inconveniences for the sake of Tellson's, after all these years, who ought to be?"

"I wish I were going myself," said Charles Darnay, somewhat restlessly, and like one thinking aloud.

"Indeed! You are a pretty fellow to object and advise!" exclaimed Mr. Lorry. "You wish you were going yourself? And you a Frenchman born? You are a wise counsellor."

"My dear Mr. Lorry, it is because I am a Frenchman born, that the thought (which I did not mean to utter here, however) has passed through my mind often. One cannot help thinking, having had some sympathy for the miserable people, and having abandoned something to them," he spoke here in his former thoughtful manner, "that one might be listened to, and might have the power to persuade to some restraint. Only last night, after you had left us, when I was talking to Lucie——"

"When you were talking to Lucie," Mr. Lorry repeated. "Yes. I wonder you are not ashamed to mention the name of Lucie! Wishing you were going to France at this time of day!"

"However, I am not going," said Charles Darnay, with a smile. "It is more to the purpose that you say you are."

"And I am in plain reality. The truth is, my dear Charles," Mr. Lorry glanced at the distant House, and lowered his voice, "you can have no conception of the difficulty with which our business is transacted, and of the peril in which our books and papers over yonder are involved. The Lord above knows what the compromising consequences would be to numbers of people, if some of our documents were seized or destroyed; and they might be, at any time, you know, for who can say that Paris is not set a-fire to-day or sacked to-morrow! Now, a judicious selection from these, with the least possible delay, and the burying of them, or otherwise getting of them out of harm's way is within the power (without loss of precious time) of scarcely any one but myself, if any one. And shall I hang back, when Tellson's knows this and says this— Tellson's, whose bread I have eaten these sixty years— because I am a little stiff about the joints? Why, I am a boy, sir, to half a dozen old codgers here!"

"How I admire the gallantry of your youthful spirit, Mr. Lorry."

"Tut! Nonsense, sir!—And, my dear Charles," said Mr. Lorry, glancing at the House again, "you are to remember, that getting things out of Paris at this present time, no matter what things, is next to an impossibility. Papers and precious matters were this very day brought to us here (I speak in strict confidence; it is not business-like to whisper it, even to you), by the strangest bearers you can imagine, every one of whom had his head hanging on by a single hair as he passed the Barriers. At another time, our parcels would come and go, as easily as in business-like Old England; but now, everything is stopped."

"And do you really go to-night?"

"I really go to-night, for the case has become too pressing to admit of delay."

"And do you take no one with you?"

"All sorts of people have been proposed to me, but I will have nothing to say to any of them. I intend to take Jerry. Jerry has been my body-guard on Sunday nights for a long time past, and I am used to him. Nobody will suspect Jerry of being anything but an English bull-dog, or of having any design in his head but to fly at anybody who touches his master."

"I must say again that I heartily admire your gallantry and youthfulness."

"I must say again, nonsense, nonsense! When I have executed this little commission, I shall, perhaps, accept Tellson's proposal to retire and live at my ease. Time enough, then, to think about growing old."

This dialogue had taken place at Mr. Lorry's usual desk, with Monseigneur swarming within a yard or two of it, boastful of what he would do to avenge himself on the rascal-people before long. It was too much the way of Monseigneur under his reverses as a refugee, and it was much too much the way of native British orthodoxy, to talk of this terrible Revolution as if it were the one only harvest ever known under the skies that had not been sown—as if nothing had ever been done, or omitted to be done, that had led to it—as if observers of the wretched millions in France, and of the misused and perverted resources that should have made them prosperous, had not seen it inevitably coming, years before, and had not in plain words recorded what they saw. Such vapouring, combined with the extravagant plots of Monseigneur for the restoration of a state of things that had utterly exhausted itself, and worn out heaven and earth as well as itself, was hard to be endured without some remonstrance by any sane man who knew the truth. And it was such vapouring all about his ears, like a troublesome confusion of blood in his own head, added to a latent uneasiness in his mind, which had already made Charles Darnay restless, and which still kept him so.

Among the talkers, was Stryver, of the King's Bench Bar, far on his way to state promotion, and, therefore, loud on the theme: broaching to Monseigneur, his devices for blowing the people up and exterminating them from the face of the earth, and doing without them: and for accomplishing many similar objects akin in their nature to the abolition of eagles by sprinkling salt on the tails of the race. Him, Darnay heard, with a particular feeling of objection; and Darnay stood divided between going away that he might hear no more, and remaining to interpose his word, when the thing that was to be, went on to shape itself out.

The House approached Mr. Lorry, and laying a soiled and unopened letter before him, asked if he had yet discovered any traces of the person to whom it was addressed? The House laid the letter down so close to Darnay that he saw the direction—the more quickly because it was his own right name. The address, turned into English, ran:

"Very pressing. To Monsieur heretofore the Marquis St. Evrémonde, of France. Confided to the cares of Messrs. Tellson and Co., Bankers, London, England."

On the marriage morning, Dr. Manette had made it his one urgent and express request to Charles Darnay, that the secret of his name should be—unless he, the Doctor, dissolved the obligation—kept inviolate between them. Nobody else knew it to be his name; his own wife had no suspicion of the fact; Mr. Lorry could have none.

"No," said Mr. Lorry, in reply to the House; "I have referred it, I think, to everybody now here, and no one can tell me where this gentleman is to be found."

The hands of the clock verging upon the hour of closing the Bank, there was a general set of the current of talkers past Mr. Lorry's desk. He held the letter out inquiringly; and Monseigneur looked at it, in the person of this plotting and indignant refugee; and This, That, and The Other, all had something disparaging to say, in French or in English, concerning the Marquis who was not to be found.

"Nephew, I believe—but in any case degenerate successor—of the polished Marquis who was murdered," said one. "Happy to say I never knew him."

"A craven who abandoned his post," said another—this Monseigneur had been got out of Paris, legs uppermost and half suffocated, in a load of hay—"some years ago."

"Infected with the new doctrines," said a third, eyeing the direction through his glass in passing; "set himself in opposition to the last Marquis, abandoned the estates when he inherited them, and left them to the ruffian herd. They will recompense him now, I hope, as he deserves."

"Hey?" cried the blatant Stryver. "Did he though? Is that the sort of fellow? Let us look at his infamous name. D—n the fellow!"

Darnay, unable to restrain himself any longer, touched Mr. Stryver on the shoulder, and said:

"I know the fellow."

"Do you, by Jupiter?" said Stryver. "I am sorry for it."

"Why?"

"Why, Mr. Darnay? D'ye hear what he did? Don't ask, why in these times."

"But I do ask why?"

"Then I tell you again, Mr. Darnay, I am sorry for it. I am sorry to hear you putting any such extraordinary questions. Here is a fellow who, infected by the most pestilent and blasphemous code of devilry that ever was known, abandoned his property to the vilest scum of the earth that ever did murder by wholesale, and you ask me why I am sorry that a man who instructs youth knows him? Well, but I'll answer you. I am sorry because I believe there is contamination in such a scoundrel. That's why."

Mindful of the secret, Darnay with great difficulty checked himself, and said: "You may not understand the gentleman."

"I understand how to put *you* in a corner, Mr. Darnay,"

said Bully Stryver, "and I'll do it. If this fellow is a gentle-man, I *don't* understand him. You may tell him so, with my compliments. You may also tell him, from me, that after abandoning his worldly goods and position to this butcherly mob, I wonder he is not at the head of them. But, no, gen-tlemen," said Stryver, looking all round, and snapping his fingers, "I know something of human nature, and I tell you that you'll never find a fellow like this fellow, trusting him-self to the mercies of such precious *protégés*. No, gentle-men; he'll always show 'em a clean pair of heels very early in the scuffle, and sneak away."

With these words and a final snap of his fingers, Mr. Stryver shouldered himself into Fleet-street, amidst the general approbation of his hearers. Mr. Lorry and Charles Darnay were left alone at the desk in the general departure from the Bank.

"Will you take charge of the letter?" said Mr. Lorry. "You know where to deliver it?"

"I do."

"Will you undertake to explain, that we suppose it to have been addressed here, on the chance of our knowing where to forward it, and that it has been here some time?"

"I will do so. Do you start for Paris from here?"

"From here, at eight."

"I will come back to see you off."

Very ill at ease with himself, and with Stryver and most other men, Darnay made the best of his way into the quiet of the Temple, opened the letter and read it. These were its contents:

Prison of the Abbaye, PARIS
June 21, 1792

MONSIEUR HERETOFORE THE MARQUIS

After having long been in danger of my life at the hands of the village, I have been seized, with great violence and indignity, and brought a long journey on foot to Paris. On the road I have suffered a great deal. Nor is that all; my house has been destroyed—razed to the ground.

The crime for which I am imprisoned, Monsieur heretofore the Marquis, and for which I shall be summoned before the tribunal, and shall lose my life (without your so generous help), is, they tell me, treason against the majesty of the people, in that I have acted against them for an emigrant. It is in vain I represent that I have acted for them, and not against, according to your commands. It is in vain I represent that, before the sequestration of emigrant property, I have remitted the imposts they have ceased to pay; that I had collected no rent; that I had had recourse to no process. The only response is, that I have acted for an emigrant, and where is that emigrant?

Ah! most gracious Monsieur heretofore the Marquis, where is that emigrant? I cry in my sleep where is he? I demand of Heaven, will he not come to deliver me? No answer. Ah Monsieur heretofore the Marquis, I send my desolate cry across the sea, hoping it may perhaps reach your ears through the great bank of Tilson known at Paris!

For the love of Heaven, of justice, of generosity, of the honour of your noble name, I supplicate you, Monsieur heretofore the Marquis, to succour and release me. My fault is, that I have been true to you. Oh Monsieur heretofore the Marquis, I pray you be you true to me!

From this prison here of horror, whence I every hour tend nearer and nearer to destruction, I send you, Monsieur heretofore the Marquis, the assurance of my dolorous and unhappy service.

> Your afflicted,
> GABELLE

The latent uneasiness in Darnay's mind was roused to vigorous life by this letter. The peril of an old servant and a good one, whose only crime was fidelity to himself and his family, stared him so reproachfully in the face, that, as he walked to and fro in the Temple considering what to do, he almost hid his face from the passers-by.

He knew very well, that in his horror of the deed which had culminated the bad deeds and bad reputation of the old family house, in his resentful suspicions of his uncle, and in the aversion with which his conscience regarded the crumbling fabric that he was supposed to uphold, he had acted imperfectly. He knew very well, that in his love for Lucie, his renunciation of his social place, though by no means new to his own mind, had been hurried and incomplete. He knew that he ought to have systematically worked it out and supervised it, and that he had meant to do it, and that it had never been done.

The happiness of his own chosen English home, the necessity of being always actively employed, the swift changes and troubles of the time which had followed on one another so fast, that the events of this week annihilated the immature plans of last week, and the events of the week following made all new again; he knew very well, that to the force of these circumstances he had yielded:—not without disquiet, but still without continuous and accumulating resistance. That he had watched the times for a time of action, and that they had shifted and struggled until the time had gone by, and the nobility were trooping from France by every highway and byway, and their property was in course of confiscation and destruction, and their very names were blotting out, was as well known to himself as it could be to any new authority in France that might impeach him for it.

But, he had oppressed no man, he had imprisoned no man; he was so far from having harshly exacted payment of his dues, that he had relinquished them of his own will, thrown himself on a world with no favour in it, won his own private place there, and earned his own bread.

Monsieur Gabelle had held the impoverished and involved estate on written instructions, to spare the people, to give them what little there was to give—such fuel as the heavy creditors would let them have in the winter, and such produce as could be saved from the same grip in the summer—and no doubt he had put the fact in plea and proof, for his own safety, so that it could not but appear now.

This favoured the desperate resolution Charles Darnay had begun to make, that he would go to Paris.

Yes. Like the mariner in the old story, the winds and streams had driven him within the influence of the Loadstone Rock, and it was drawing him to itself, and he must go. Everything that arose before his mind drifted him on, faster and faster, more and more steadily, to the terrible attraction. His latent uneasiness had been, that bad aims were being worked out in his own unhappy land by bad instruments, and that he who could not fail to know that he was better than they, was not there, trying to do something to stay bloodshed, and assert the claims of mercy and humanity. With this uneasiness half stifled, and half reproaching him, he had been brought to the pointed comparison of himself with the brave old gentleman in whom duty was so strong; upon that comparison (injurious to himself) had instantly followed the sneers of Monseigneur, which had stung him bitterly, and those of Stryver, which above all were coarse and galling, for old reasons. Upon those, had followed Gabelle's letter: the appeal of an innocent prisoner, in danger of death, to his justice, honour, and good name.

His resolution was made. He must go to Paris.

Yes. The Loadstone Rock was drawing him, and he must sail on, until he struck. He knew of no rock; he saw hardly any danger. The intention with which he had done what he had done, even although he had left it incomplete, presented it before him in an aspect that would be gratefully acknowledged in France on his presenting himself to assert it. Then, that glorious vision of doing good, which is so often the sanguine mirage of so many good minds, arose before him, and he even saw himself in the illusion with some influence to guide this raging Revolution that was running so fearfully wild.

As he walked to and fro with his resolution made, he considered that neither Lucie nor her father must know of it until he was gone. Lucie should be spared the pain of separation; and her father, always reluctant to turn his thoughts toward the dangerous ground of old, should come to the knowledge of the step, as a step taken, and not in the balance of suspense and doubt. How much of the incompleteness of his situation was referable to her father, through the painful anxiety to avoid reviving old associations of France in his mind, he did not discuss with himself. But, that circumstance, too, had had its influence in his course.

He walked to and fro, with thoughts very busy, until it was time to return to Tellson's and take leave of Mr. Lorry. As soon as he arrived in Paris he would present himself to this old friend, but he must say nothing of his intention now.

A carriage with post-horses was ready at the Bank door, and Jerry was booted and equipped.

"I have delivered that letter," said Charles Darnay to Mr. Lorry. "I would not consent to your being charged with any written answer, but perhaps you will take a verbal one?"

"That I will, and readily," said Mr. Lorry, "if it is not dangerous."

"Not at all. Though it is to a prisoner in the Abbaye."

"What is his name?" said Mr. Lorry, with his open pocketbook in his hand.

"Gabelle."

"Gabelle. And what is the message to the unfortunate Gabelle in prison?"

"Simply, 'that he has received the letter, and will come.' "

"Any time mentioned?"

"He will start upon his journey to-morrow night."

"Any person mentioned?"

"No."

He helped Mr. Lorry to wrap himself in a number of coats and cloaks, and went out with him from the warm atmosphere of the old Bank, into the misty air of Fleet-street. "My love to Lucie, and to little Lucie," said Mr. Lorry at parting, "and take precious care of them till I come back." Charles Darnay shook his head and doubtfully smiled, as the carriage rolled away.

That night—it was the fourteenth of August—he sat up late, and wrote two fervent letters; one was to Lucie, explaining the strong obligation he was under to go to Paris, and showing her, at length, the reasons that he had, for feeling confident that he could become involved in no personal danger there; the other was to the Doctor, confiding Lucie and their dear child to his care, and dwelling on the same topics with the strongest assurances. To both, he wrote that he would despatch letters in proof of his safety, immediately after his arrival.

It was a hard day, that day of being among them, with the first reservation of their joint lives on his mind. It was a hard matter to preserve the innocent deceit of which they were profoundly unsuspicious. But, an affectionate glance at his wife, so happy and busy, made him resolute not to tell her what impended (he had been half moved to do it, so strange it was to him to act in anything without her quiet aid), and the day passed quickly. Early in the evening he embraced her, and her scarcely less dear namesake, pretending that he would return by-and-by (an imaginary engagement took him out, and he had secreted a valise of clothes ready), and so he emerged into the heavy mist of the heavy streets, with a heavier heart.

The unseen force was drawing him fast to itself, now, and all the tides and winds were setting straight and strong towards it. He left his two letters with a trusty porter, to be delivered half an hour before midnight, and no sooner;

took horse for Dover; and began his journey. "For the love of Heaven, of justice, of generosity, of the honour of your noble name!" was the poor prisoner's cry with which he strengthened his sinking heart, as he left all that was dear on earth behind him, and floated away for the Loadstone Rock.

Book the Third
THE TRACK OF A STORM

1

In Secret

THE traveller fared slowly on his way, who fared towards Paris from England in the autumn of the year one thousand seven hundred and ninety-two. More than enough of bad roads, bad equipages, and bad horses, he would have encountered to delay him, though the fallen and unfortunate King of France had been upon his throne in all his glory; but, the changed times were fraught with other obstacles than these. Every town-gate and village taxing-house had its band of citizen-patriots, with their national muskets in a most explosive state of readiness, who stopped all comers and goers, cross-questioned them, inspected their papers, looked for their names in lists of their own, turned them back, or sent them on, or stopped them and laid them in hold, as their capricious judgment or fancy deemed best for the dawning Republic One and Indivisible, of Liberty, Equality, Fraternity, or Death.

A very few French leagues of his journey were accomplished, when Charles Darnay began to perceive that for him along these country roads there was no hope of return until he should have been declared a good citizen at Paris. Whatever might befall now, he must on to his journey's end.

Not a mean village closed upon him, not a common barrier dropped across the road behind him, but he knew it to be another iron door in the series that was barred between him and England. The universal watchfulness so encompassed him, that if he had been taken in a net, or were being forwarded to his destination in a cage, he could not have felt his freedom more completely gone.

This universal watchfulness not only stopped him on the highway twenty times in a stage, but retarded his progress twenty times in a day, by riding after him and taking him back, riding before him and stopping him by anticipation, riding with him and keeping him in charge. He had been days upon his journey in France alone, when he went to bed tired out, in a little town on the high road, still a long way from Paris.

Nothing but the production of the afflicted Gabelle's letter from his prison of the Abbaye would have got him on so far. His difficulty at the guard-house in this small place had been such, that he felt his journey to have come to a crisis. And he was, therefore, as little surprised as a man could be, to find himself awakened at the small inn to which he had been remitted until morning, in the middle of the night.

Awakened by a timid local functionary and three armed patriots in rough red caps and with pipes in their mouths, who sat down on the bed.

"Emigrant," said the functionary, "I am going to send you on to Paris, under an escort."

"Citizen, I desire nothing more than to get to Paris, though I could dispense with the escort."

"Silence!" growled a red-cap, striking at the coverlet with the butt-end of his musket. "Peace, aristocrat!"

"It is as the good patriot says," observed the timid functionary. "You are an aristocrat, and must have an escort— and must pay for it."

"I have no choice," said Charles Darnay.

"Choice! Listen to him!" cried the same scowling red-cap. "As if it was not a favour to be protected from the lamp-iron!"

"It is always as the good patriot says," observed the functionary. "Rise and dress yourself, emigrant."

Darnay complied, and was taken back to the guardhouse, where other patriots in rough red caps were smoking, drinking, and sleeping, by a watch-fire. Here he paid a heavy price for his escort, and hence he started with it on the wet, wet roads at three o'clock in the morning.

The escort were two mounted patriots in red caps and tricoloured cockades,[1] armed with national muskets and sabres, who rode one on either side of him. The escorted governed his own horse, but a loose line was attached to his bridle, the end of which one of the patriots kept girded round his wrist. In this state they set forth with the sharp rain driving in their faces: clattering at a heavy dragoon trot over the uneven town pavement, and out upon the mire-deep roads. In this state they traversed without change, except of horses and pace, all the mire-deep leagues that lay between them and the capital.

They travelled in the night, halting an hour or two after daybreak, and lying by until the twilight fell. The escort were so wretchedly clothed, that they twisted straw round their bare legs, and thatched their ragged shoulders to keep the wet off. Apart from the personal discomfort of being so attended, and apart from such considerations of present danger as arose from one of the patriots being chronically drunk, and carrying his musket very recklessly, Charles Darnay did not allow the restraint that was laid upon him to awaken any serious fears in his breast; for, he reasoned with himself that it could have no reference to the merits of an individual case that was not yet stated, and of representations, confirmable by the prisoner in the Abbaye, that were not yet made.

But when they came to the town of Beauvais—which they did at eventide, when the streets were filled with people—he could not conceal from himself that the aspect of affairs was very alarming. An ominous crowd gathered to see him dismount at the posting-yard, and many voices called out loudly, "Down with the emigrant!"

He stopped in the act of swinging himself out of his saddle, and resuming it as his safest place, said:

"Emigrant, my friends! Do you not see me here, in France, of my own will?"

"You are a cursed emigrant," cried a farrier, making at him in a furious manner through the press, hammer in hand; "and you are a cursed aristocrat!"

The postmaster interposed himself between this man and the rider's bridle (at which he was evidently making), and soothingly said, "Let him be; let him be! He will be judged at Paris."

"Judged!" repeated the farrier, swinging his hammer. "Ay! and condemned as a traitor." At this the crowd roared approval.

Checking the postmaster, who was for turning his horse's head to the yard (the drunken patriot sat composedly in his saddle looking on, with the line round his wrist), Darnay said, as soon as he could make his voice heard:

"Friends, you deceive yourselves, or you are deceived. I am not a traitor."

"He lies!" cried the smith. "He is a traitor since the decree. His life is forfeit to the people. His cursed life is not his own!"

At that instant when Darnay saw a rush in the eyes of the crowd, which another instant would have brought upon him, the postmaster turned his horse into the yard, the escort rode in close upon his horse's flanks, and the postmaster shut and barred the crazy double gates. The farrier struck a blow upon them with his hammer, and the crowd groaned; but no more was done.

"What is this decree that the smith spoke of?" Darnay asked the postmaster, when he had thanked him, and stood beside him in the yard.

"Truly, a decree for selling the property of emigrants."

"When passed?"

"On the fourteenth."

"The day I left England!"

"Everybody says it is but one of several, and that there will be others—if there are not already—banishing all emigrants, and condemning all to death who return. That is what he meant when he said your life was not your own."

"But there are no such decrees yet?"

"What do I know!" said the postmaster, shrugging his shoulders; "there may be, or there will be. It is all the same. What would you have?"

They rested on some straw in a loft until the middle of the night, and then rode forward again when all the town was asleep. Among the many wild changes observable on familiar things which made this wild ride unreal, not the least was the seeming rarity of sleep. After long and lonely spurring over dreary roads, they would come to a cluster of poor cottages, not steeped in darkness, but all glittering with lights, and would find the people, in a ghostly manner in the dead of the night, circling hand in hand round a shrivelled tree of Liberty, or all drawn up together singing a Liberty song. Happily, however, there was sleep in Beauvais that night to help them out of it, and they passed on once more into solitude and loneliness: jingling through the untimely cold and wet, among impoverished fields that had yielded no fruits of the earth that year, diversified by the blackened remains of burnt houses, and by the sudden emergence from ambuscade, and sharp reining up across their way, of patriot patrols on the watch on all the roads.

Daylight at last found them before the wall of Paris. The barrier was closed and strongly guarded when they rode up to it.

"Where are the papers of this prisoner?" demanded a resolute-looking man in authority, who was summoned out by the guard.

Naturally struck by the disagreeable word, Charles Darnay requested the speaker to take notice that he was a free traveller and French citizen, in charge of an escort which the disturbed state of the country had imposed upon him, and which he had paid for.

"Where," repeated the same personage, without taking any heed of him whatever, "are the papers of this prisoner?"

The drunken patriot had them in his cap, and produced them. Casting his eyes over Gabelle's letter, the same personage in authority showed some disorder and surprise and looked at Darnay with a close attention.

He left escort and escorted without saying a word, however, and went into the guard-room; meanwhile they sat upon their horses outside the gate. Looking about him while in this state of suspense, Charles Darnay observed that the gate was held by a mixed guard of soldiers and patriots, the latter far outnumbering the former; and that while ingress into the city for peasants' carts bringing in supplies, and for similar traffic and traffickers, was easy enough, egress, even for the homeliest people, was very difficult. A numerous medley of men and women, not to mention beasts and vehicles of various sorts, was waiting to issue forth; but the previous identification was so strict, that they filtered through the barrier very slowly. Some of these people knew their turn for examination to be so far off, that they lay down on the ground to sleep or smoke, while others talked together, or loitered about. The red cap and tricolour cockade were universal, both among men and women.

When he had sat in his saddle some half-hour, taking note of these things, Darnay found himself confronted by the same man in authority, who directed the guard to open the barrier. Then he delivered to the escort, drunk and sober, a receipt for the escorted and requested him to dismount. He did so, and the two patriots, leading his tired horse, turned and rode away without entering the city.

He accompanied his conductor into a guard-room, smelling of common wine and tobacco, where certain soldiers and patriots, asleep and awake, drunk and sober, and in various neutral states between sleeping and waking, drunkenness and sobriety, were standing and lying about. The light in the guard-house, half derived from the waning oil lamps of the night, and half from the overcast day, was in a correspondingly uncertain condition. Some registers were lying open on a desk, and an officer of a coarse, dark aspect, presided over these.

"Citizen Defarge," said he to Darnay's conductor, as he took a slip of paper to write on. "Is this the emigrant Evrémonde?"

"This is the man."

"Your age, Evrémonde?"

"Thirty-seven."

"Married, Evrémonde?"

"Yes."

"Where married?"

"In England."

"Without doubt. Where is your wife, Evrémonde?"

"In England."

"Without doubt. You are consigned, Evrémonde, to the prison of La Force."

"Just Heaven!" exclaimed Darnay. "Under what law, and for what offence?"

The officer looked up from his slip of paper for a moment.

"We have new laws, Evrémonde, and new offences, since you were here." He said it with a hard smile, and went on writing.

"I entreat you to observe that I have come here voluntarily, in response to that written appeal of a fellow-countryman which lies before you. I demand no more than the opportunity to do so without delay. Is not that my right?"

"Emigrants have no rights, Evrémonde," was the stolid reply. The officer wrote until he had finished, read over to himself what he had written, sanded it, and handed it to Defarge, with the words, "In secret."

Defarge motioned with the paper to the prisoner that he must accompany him. The prisoner obeyed, and a guard of two armed patriots attended them.

"Is it you," said Defarge, in a low voice, as they went down the guard-house steps and turned into Paris, "who married the daughter of Doctor Manette, once a prisoner in the Bastille that is no more²?"

"Yes," replied Darnay, looking at him with surprise.

"My name is Defarge, and I keep a wine-shop in the Quarter Saint Antoine. Possibly you have heard of me."

"My wife came to your house to reclaim her father? Yes!"

The word "wife" seemed to serve as a gloomy reminder to Defarge, to say with sudden impatience, "In the name of that sharp female newly-born, and called La Guillotine, why did you come to France?"

"You heard me say why, a minute ago. Do you not believe it is the truth?"

"A bad truth for you," said Defarge, speaking with knitted brows, and looking straight before him.

"Indeed I am lost here. All here is so unprecedented, so changed, so sudden and unfair, that I am absolutely lost. Will you render me a little help?"

"None." Defarge spoke, always looking straight before him.

"Will you answer me a single question?"

"Perhaps. According to its nature. You can say what it is."

"In this prison that I am going to so unjustly, shall I have some free communication with the world outside?"

"You will see."

"I am not to be buried there, prejudiced, and without any means of presenting my case?"

"You will see. But, what then? Other people have been similarly buried in worse prisons, before now."

"But never by me, Citizen Defarge."

Defarge glanced darkly at him for answer, and walked on in a steady and set silence. The deeper he sank into this silence, the fainter hope there was—or so Darnay thought—of his softening in any slight degree. He, therefore, made haste to say:

"It is of the utmost importance to me (you know, Citizen, even better than I do, of how much importance), that I should be able to communicate to Mr. Lorry of Tellson's Bank, an English gentleman who is now in Paris, the simple fact without comment, that I have been thrown into the prison of La Force. Will you cause that to be done for me?"

"I will do," Defarge doggedly rejoined, "nothing for you. My duty is to my country and the People. I am the sworn servant of both, against you. I will do nothing for you."

Charles Darnay felt it hopeless to entreat him further, and his pride was touched besides. As they walked on in silence, he could not but see how used the people were to the spectacle of prisoners passing along the streets. The very children scarcely noticed him. A few passers turned their heads, and a few shook their fingers at him as an aristocrat; otherwise that a man in good clothes should be going to prison, was no more remarkable than that a labourer in working clothes should be going to work. In one narrow, dark, and dirty street through which they passed, an excited orator, mounted on a stool, was addressing an excited audience on the crimes against the people, of the king and the royal family. The few words that he caught from this man's lips, first made it known to Charles Darnay that the king was in prison, and that the foreign ambassadors had one and all left Paris. On the road (except at Beauvais) he had heard absolutely nothing. The escort and the universal watchfulness had completely isolated him.

That he had fallen among far greater dangers than those which had developed themselves when he left England, he of course knew now. That perils had thickened about him fast, and might thicken faster and faster yet, he of course knew now. He could not but admit to himself that he might not have made this journey, if he could have foreseen the events of a few days. And yet his misgivings were not so dark as, imagined by the light of this later time, they would appear. Troubled as the future was, it was the unknown future, and in its obscurity there was ignorant hope. The horrible massacre, days and nights long, which, within a few rounds of the clock, was to set a great mark of blood upon the blessed garnering time of harvest, was as far out of his knowledge as if it had been a hundred thousand years away. The "sharp female newly-born, and called La Guillotine," was hardly known to him, or to the generality of people, by name. The frightful deeds that were to be soon done, were probably unimagined at that time in the brains of the doers. How could they have a place in the shadowy conceptions of a gentle mind?

Of unjust treatment in detention and hardship, and in cruel separation from his wife and child, he foreshadowed the likelihood, or the certainty; but, beyond this, he dreaded nothing distinctly. With this on his mind, which was enough to carry him into a dreary prison court-yard, he arrived at the prison of La Force.

A man with a bloated face opened the strong wicket, to whom Defarge presented "The Emigrant Evrémonde."

"What the Devil! How many more of them!" exclaimed the man with the bloated face.

Defarge took his receipt without noticing the exclamation, and withdrew, with his two fellow-patriots.

"What the Devil, I say again!" exclaimed the gaoler, left with his wife. "How many more!"

The gaoler's wife, being provided with no answer to the question, merely replied, "One must have patience, my dear!" Three turnkeys who entered responsive to a bell she rang, echoed the sentiment, and one added. "For the love of Liberty"; which sounded in that place like an inappropriate conclusion.

The prison of La Force was a gloomy prison, dark and filthy, and with a horrible smell of foul sleep in it. Extraordinary how soon the noisome flavour of imprisoned sleep, becomes manifest in all such places that are ill cared for!

"In secret, too," grumbled the gaoler, looking at the written paper. "As if I was not already full to bursting!"

He stuck the paper on a file, in an ill-humour, and Charles Darnay awaited his further pleasure for half an hour: sometimes, pacing to and fro in the strong arched room: sometimes, resting on a stone seat: in either case detained to be imprinted on the memory of the chief and his subordinates.

"Come!" said the chief, at length taking up his keys, "come with me, Emigrant."

Through the dismal prison twilight, his new charge accompanied him by corridor and staircase, many doors clanging and locking behind them, until they came into a large, low, vaulted chamber, crowded with prisoners of both sexes. The women were seated at a long table, reading and writing, knitting, sewing, and embroidering; the men were for the most part standing behind their chairs, or lingering up and down the room.

In the instinctive association of prisoners with shameful crime and disgrace, the newcomer recoiled from this company. But the crowning unreality of his long unreal ride, was, their all at once rising to receive him, with every refinement of manner known to the time, and with all the engaging graces and courtesies of life.

So strangely clouded were these refinements by the prison manners and gloom, so spectral did they become in the inappropriate squalor and misery through which they were seen, that Charles Darnay seemed to stand in company of the dead. Ghosts all! The ghost of beauty, the ghost of stateliness, the ghost of elegance, the ghost of pride, the ghost of frivolity, the ghost of wit, the ghost of youth, the ghost of age, all waiting their dismissal from the desolate shore, all turning on him eyes that were changed by the death they had died in coming there.

It struck him motionless. The gaoler standing at his side, and the other gaolers moving about, who would have been well enough as to appearance in the ordinary exercise of their functions, looked so extravagantly coarse contrasted with sorrowing mothers and blooming daughters who were there—with the apparitions of the coquette, the young beauty, and the mature woman delicately bred—that the inversion of all experience and likelihood which the scene of shadows presented, was heightened to its utmost. Surely, ghosts all. Surely, the long unreal ride some progress of disease that had brought him to these gloomy shades!

"In the name of the assembled companions in misfortune," said a gentleman of courtly appearance and address, coming forward, "I have the honour of giving you welcome to La Force, and of condoling with you on the calamity that has brought you among us. May it soon terminate happily! It would be an impertinence elsewhere, but it is not so here, to ask your name and condition?"

Charles Darnay roused himself, and gave the required information, in words as suitable as he could find.

"But I hope," said the gentleman, following the chief gaoler with his eyes, who moved across the room, "that you are not in secret?"

"I do not understand the meaning of the term, but I have heard them say so."

"Ah, what a pity! We so much regret it! But take courage; several members of our society have been in secret, at first, and it has lasted but a short time." Then he added, raising his voice, "I grieve to inform the society—in secret."

There was a murmur of commiseration as Charles Darnay crossed the room to a grated door where the gaoler awaited him, and many voices—among which, the soft and compassionate voices of women were conspicuous—gave him good wishes and encouragement. He turned at the grated door, to render the thanks of his heart; it closed under the gaoler's hand; and the apparitions vanished from his sight for ever.

The wicket opened on a stone staircase, leading upward. When they had ascended forty steps (the prisoner of half an hour already counted them), the gaoler opened a low black door, and they passed into a solitary cell. It struck cold and damp, but was not dark.

"Yours," said the gaoler.

"Why am I confined alone?"

"How do I know!"

"I can buy pen, ink, and paper?"

"Such are not my orders. You will be visited, and can ask then. At present, you may buy your food, and nothing more."

There were in the cell, a chair, a table, and a straw mattress. As the gaoler made a general inspection of these objects, and of the four walls, before going out, a wandering fancy wandered through the mind of the prisoner leaning against the wall opposite to him, that this gaoler was so unwholesomely bloated, both in face and person, as to look like a man who had been drowned and filled with water. When the gaoler was gone, he thought in the same wandering way. "Now am I left, as if I were dead." Stopping then, to look down at the mattress, he turned from it with a sick feeling, and thought, "And here in these crawling creatures is the first condition of the body after death."

"Five paces by four and a half, five paces by four and a half, five paces by four and a half." The prisoner walked to and fro in his cell, counting its measurements, and the roar of the city arose like muffled drums with a wild swell of voices added to them. "He made shoes, he made shoes, he made shoes." The prisoner counted the measurement again, and paced faster, to draw his mind with him from that latter repetition. "The ghosts that vanished when the wicket closed. There was one among them, the appearance of a lady dressed in black, who was leaning in the embrasure of a window, and she had a light shining upon her golden hair, and she looked like . . . Let us ride on again, for God's sake, through the illuminated villages with the people all awake! . . . He made shoes, he made shoes, he made shoes. . . . Five paces by four and a half." With such scraps tossing and rolling upward from the depths of his mind, the prisoner walked faster and faster, obstinately counting and counting; and the roar of the city changed to this extent—that it still rolled in like muffled drums, but with the wail of voices that he knew, in the swell that rose above them.

2

THE GRINDSTONE

TELLSON'S BANK, established in the Saint Germain Quarter of Paris, was in a wing of a large house, approached by a court-yard and shut off from the street by a high wall and a strong gate. The house belonged to a great nobleman who had lived in it until he made a flight from the troubles, in his own cook's dress, and got across the borders. A mere beast of the chase flying from hunters, he was still in his metempsychosis no other than the same Monseigneur, the preparation of whose chocolate for whose lips had once occupied three strong men besides the cook in question.

Monseigneur gone, and the three strong men absolving themselves from the sin of having drawn his high wages, by being more than ready and willing to cut his throat on the altar of the drawing Republic One and Indivisible, of Liberty, Equality, Fraternity, or Death, Monseigneur's house had been first sequestrated, and then confiscated. For, all things move so fast, and decree following decree with that fierce precipitation, that now upon the third night of the autumn month of September, patriot emissaries of the law were in possession of Monseigneur's house, and had marked it with the tricolour, and were drinking brandy in its state apartments.

A place of business in London like Tellson's place of business in Paris, would soon have driven the House out of its mind and into the *Gazette*. For, what would staid British responsibility and respectability have said to orange-trees in boxes in a Bank court-yard, and even to a Cupid over the counter? Yet such things were. Tellson's had whitewashed the Cupid, but he was still to be seen on the ceiling, in the coolest linen, aiming (as he very often does) at money from morning to night. Bankruptcy must inevitably have come of this young Pagan, in Lombard-street, London, and also of a curtained alcove in the rear of the immortal boy, and also of a looking-glass let into the wall, and also of clerks not at all old, who danced in public on the slightest provocation. Yet, a French Tellson's could get on with these things exceedingly well, and, as long as the times held together, no man had taken fright at them, and drawn out his money.

What money would be drawn out of Tellson's henceforth, and what would lie there, lost and forgotten; what plate and jewels would tarnish in Tellson's hiding-places, while the depositors rusted in prisons, and when they should have violently perished; how many accounts with Tellson's never to be balanced in this world, must be carried over into the next; no man could have said, that night, any more than Mr. Jarvis Lorry could, though he thought heavily of these questions. He sat by a newly-lighted wood fire (the blighted and unfruitful year was prematurely cold), and on his honest and courageous face there was a deeper shade than the pendent lamp could throw, or any object in the room distortedly reflect—a shade of horror.

He occupied rooms in the Bank, in his fidelity to the House of which he had grown to be a part, like strong root-ivy. It chanced that they derived a kind of security from the patriotic occupation of the main building, but the true-hearted old gentleman never calculated about that. All such circumstances were indifferent to him, so that he did his duty. On the opposite side of the courtyard, under a colon-nade, was extensive standing for carriages—where, indeed, some carriages of Monseigneur yet stood. Against two of the pillars were fastened two great flaring flambeaux, and in the light of these, standing out in the open air, was a large grindstone: a roughly mounted thing which appeared to have hurriedly been brought there from some neighbouring smithy, or other workshop. Rising and looking out of the window at these harmless objects, Mr. Lorry shivered, and retired to his seat by the fire. He had opened, not only the glass window, but the lattice blind outside it, and he had closed both again, and he shivered through his frame.

From the streets beyond the high wall and the strong gate, there came the usual night hum of the city, with now and then an indescribable ring in it, weird and unearthly, as if some unwonted sounds of a terrible nature were going up to Heaven.

"Thank God," said Mr. Lorry, clasping his hands, "that no one near and dear to me is in this dreadful town tonight. May He have mercy on all who are in danger!"

Soon afterwards the bell at the great gate sounded, and he thought, "They have come back!" and sat listening. But, there was no loud irruption into the court-yard, as he had expected, and he heard the gate clash again, and all was quiet.

The nervousness and dread that were upon him inspired that vague uneasiness respecting the Bank, which a great change would naturally awaken, with such feelings roused. It was well guarded, and he got up to go among the trusty people watching it, when his door suddenly opened, and two figures rushed in, at sight of which he fell back in amazement.

Lucie and her father! Lucie with her arms stretched out to him, and with that old look of earnestness so concen-trated and intensified, that it seemed as though it had been stamped upon her face expressly to give force and power to it in this one passage of her life.

"What is this?" cried Mr. Lorry, breathless and confused. "What is the matter? Lucie! Manette! What has happened? What has brought you here? What is it?"

With the look fixed upon him, in her paleness and wildness, she panted out in his arms, imploringly, "O my dear friend! My husband!"

"Your husband, Lucie?"

"Charles."

"What of Charles?"

"Here."

"Here, in Paris?"

"Has been here some days—three or four—I don't know how many—I can't collect my thoughts. An errand of generosity brought him here unknown to us; he was stopped at the barrier, and sent to prison."

The old man uttered an irrepressible cry. Almost at the same moment, the bell of the great gate rang again, and a loud noise of feet and voices came pouring into the court-yard.

"What is that noise?" said the Doctor, turning towards the window.

"Don't look!" cried Mr. Lorry. "Don't look out! Manette, for your life, don't touch the blind!"

The Doctor turned, with his hand upon the fastening of the window, and said, with a cool, bold smile:

"My dear friend, I have a charmed life in this city. I have been a Bastille prisoner. There is no patriot in Paris—in Paris? In France—who, knowing me to have been a prisoner in the Bastille, would touch me, except to overwhelm me with embraces, or carry me in triumph. My old pain has given me a power that has brought us through the barrier, and gained us news of Charles there, and brought us here. I knew it would be so; I knew I could help Charles out of all danger; I told Lucie so.—What is that noise?" His hand was again upon the window.

"Don't look!" cried Mr. Lorry, absolutely desperate. "No, Lucie, my dear, nor you!" He got his arm around her, and held her. "Don't be so terrified, my love. I solemnly swear to you that I know of no harm having happened to Charles; that I had no suspicion even of his being in this fatal place. What prison is he in?"

"La Force!"

"La Force! Lucie, my child, if ever you were brave and serviceable in your life—and you were always both—you will compose yourself now, to do exactly as I bid you; for more depends upon it than you can think, or I can say. There is no help for you in any action on your part to-night; you cannot possibly stir out. I say this, because what I must bid you to do for Charles's sake, is the hardest thing to do of all. You must instantly be obedient, still and quiet. You must let me put you in a room at the back here. You must leave your father and me alone for two minutes, and as there are Life and Death in the world you must not delay."

"I will be submissive to you. I see in your face that you know I can do nothing else than this. I know you are true."

The old man kissed her, and hurried her into his room, and turned the key; then came hurrying back to the Doctor, and opened the window and partly opened the blind, and put his hand upon the Doctor's arm, and looked out with him into the court-yard.

Looked out upon a throng of men and women: not enough in number, or near enough, to fill the court-yard: not more than forty or fifty in all. The people in possession of the house had let them in at the gate, and they rushed in to work at the grindstone; it had evidently been set up there for their purpose, as in a convenient and retired spot.

But such awful workers, and such awful work!

The grindstone had a double handle, and turning at it madly were two men, whose faces, as their long hair flapped back when the whirlings of the grindstone brought their faces up, were more horrible and cruel than the visages of the wildest savages in their most barbarous disguise. False eyebrows and false moustaches were stuck upon them, and their hideous countenances were all bloody and sweaty, and all awry with howling, and all staring and glaring with beastly excitement and want of sleep. As these ruffians turned and turned, their matted locks now flung forward over their eyes, now flung backward over their necks, some women held wine to their mouths that they might drink; and what with dropping blood, and what with dropping wine, and what with the stream of sparks struck out of the stone, all their wicked atmosphere seemed gore and fire. The eye could not detect one creature in the group free from the smear of blood. Shouldering one another to get next at the sharpening-stone, were men stripped to the waist, with the stain all over their limbs and bodies; men in all sorts of rags, with the stain upon those rags; men devilishly set off with spoils of women's lace and silk and ribbon, with the stain dyeing those trifles through and through. Hatchets, knives, bayonets, swords, all brought to be sharpened, were all red with it. Some of the hacked swords were tied to the wrist of those who carried them, with strips of linen and fragments of dress: ligatures various in kind, but all deep of the one colour. And as the frantic wielders of these weapons snatched them from the stream of sparks and tore away into the streets, the same red hue was red in their frenzied eyes;—eyes which any unbrutalised beholder would have given twenty years of life, to petrify with a well directed gun.

All this was seen in a moment, as the vision of a drowning man, or of any human creature at any very great pass, could see a world if it were there. They drew back from the window, and the Doctor looked for explanation in his friend's ashy face.

"They are," Mr. Lorry whispered the words, glancing fearfully around at the locked room, "murdering the prisoners. If you are sure of what you say; if you really have the power you think you have—as I believe you have—make yourself known to these devils, and get taken to La Force. It may be too late, I don't know, but let it not be a minute later!"

Doctor Manette pressed his hand, hastened bareheaded out of the room, and was in the court-yard when Mr. Lorry regained the blind.

His streaming white hair, his remarkable face, and the impetuous confidence of his manner, as he put the weapons aside like water, carried him in an instant to the heart of the concourse at the stone. For a few minutes there was a pause, and a hurry, and a murmur, and the unintelligible sound of his voice; and then Mr. Lorry saw him, surrounded by all, and in the midst of a line of twenty men long, all linked shoulder to shoulder, and hand to shoulder, hurried out with cries—"Live the Bastille prisoner! Help for the Bastille prisoner's kindred in La Force! Room for the Bastille prisoner in front there! Save the prisoner Evrémonde at La Force!" and a thousand answering shouts.

He closed the lattice again with a fluttering heart, closed the window and the curtain, hastened to Lucie, and told her that her father was assisted by the people, and gone in search of her husband. He found her child and Miss Pross with her; but, it never occurred to him to be surprised by their appearance until a long time afterwards, when he sat watching them in such quiet as the night knew.

Lucie had, by that time, fallen into a stupor on the floor at his feet, clinging to his hand. Miss Pross had laid the child down on his own bed, and her head had gradually fallen on the pillow beside her pretty charge. O the long, long night, with the moans of the poor wife! And O the long, long night, with no return of her father and no tidings!

Twice more in the darkness the bell at the great gate sounded, and the irruption was repeated, and the grindstone whirled and spluttered. "What is it?" cried Lucie, affrighted, "Hush! The soldiers' swords are sharpened there," said Mr. Lorry. "The place is national property now, and used as a kind of armoury, my love."

Twice more in all; but, the last spell of work was feeble and fitful. Soon afterwards the day began to dawn, and he softly detached himself from the clasping hand, and cautiously looked out again. A man, so besmeared that he might have been a sorely wounded soldier creeping back to consciousness on a field of slain, was rising from the pavement by the side of the grindstone, and looking about him with a vacant air. Shortly, this worn-out murderer descried in the imperfect light one of the carriages of Monseigneur, and, staggering to that gorgeous vehicle, climbed in at the door, and shut himself up to take his rest on its dainty cushions.

The great grindstone, Earth, had turned when Mr. Lorry looked out again, and the sun was red on the courtyard. But, the lesser grindstone stood alone there in the calm morning air, with a red upon it that the sun had never given, and would never take away.

3

The Shadow

⚜

ONE of the first considerations which arose in the business mind of Mr. Lorry when business hours came round, was this:—that he had no right to imperil Tellson's by sheltering the wife of an emigrant prisoner under the Bank roof. His own possessions, safety, life, he would have hazarded for Lucie and her child, without a moment's demur; but the great trust he held was not his own, and as to that business charge he was a strict man of business.

At first, his mind reverted to Defarge, and he thought of finding out the wine-shop again and taking counsel with its master in reference to the safest dwelling-place in the distracted state of the city. But, the same consideration that suggested him, repudiated him; he lived in the most violent Quarter, and doubtless was influential there, and deep in its dangerous workings.

Noon coming, and the Doctor not returning, and every minute's delay tending to compromise Tellson's, Mr. Lorry advised with Lucie. She said that her father had spoken of hiring a lodging for a short term, in that Quarter, near the Banking-house. As there was no business objection to this, and as he foresaw that even if it were all well with Charles, and he were to be released, he could not hope to leave the city, Mr. Lorry went out in quest of such a lodging, and found a suitable one, high up in a removed by-street where the closed blinds in all the other windows of a high melancholy square of buildings marked deserted homes.

To this lodging he at once removed Lucie and her child, and Miss Pross; giving them what comfort he could, and much more than he had himself. He left Jerry with them, as a figure to fill a doorway that would bear considerable knocking on the head, and returned to his own occupations. A disturbed and doleful mind he brought to bear upon them; and slowly and heavily, the day lagged on with him.

It wore itself out, and wore him out with it, until the Bank closed. He was again alone in his room of the previous night, considering what to do next, when he heard a foot upon the stair. In a few moments a man stood in his presence, who, with a keenly observant look at him, addressed him by his name.

"Your servant," said Mr. Lorry. "Do you know me?"

He was a strongly made man with dark curling hair, from forty-five to fifty years of age. For answer he repeated without any change of emphasis, the words:

"Do you know me?"

"I have seen you somewhere."

"Perhaps at my wine-shop?"

Much interested and agitated, Mr. Lorry said: "You come from Doctor Manette?"

"Yes, I come from Doctor Manette."

"And what says he? What does he send me?"

Defarge gave into his anxious hand, an open scrap of paper. It bore the words in the Doctor's writing:

> Charles is safe, but I cannot safely leave this place yet. I have obtained the favour that the bearer has a short note from Charles to his wife. Let the bearer see his wife.

It was dated from La Force, within an hour.

"Will you accompany me," said Mr. Lorry, joyfully relieved after reading this note aloud, "to where his wife resides?"

"Yes," returned Defarge.

Scarcely noticing as yet, in what a curiously reserved and mechanical way Defarge spoke, Mr. Lorry put on his hat and they went down into the court-yard. There they found two women; one knitting.

"Madame Defarge, surely!" said Mr. Lorry, who had left her in exactly the same attitude some seventeen years ago.

"It is she," observed her husband.

"Does Madame go with us?" inquired Mr. Lorry, seeing that she moved as they moved.

"Yes. That she may be able to recognise the faces and know the persons. It is for their safety."

Beginning to be struck by Defarge's manner, Mr. Lorry looked dubiously at him, and led the way. Both the women followed; the second woman being The Vengeance.

They passed through the intervening streets as quickly as they might, ascended the staircase of the new domicile, were admitted by Jerry, and found Lucie weeping, alone. She was thrown into a transport by the tidings Mr. Lorry gave her of her husband, and clasped the hand that delivered his note— little thinking what it had been doing near him in the night, and might, but for a chance, have done for him.

DEAREST—

Take courage. I am well, and your father has influence around me. You cannot answer this. Kiss our child for me.

That was all the writing. It was so much, however, to her who received it, that she turned from Defarge to his wife, and kissed one of the hands that knitted. It was a passionate, loving, thankful, womanly action, but the hand made no response—dropped cold and heavy, and took to its knitting again.

There was something in its touch that gave Lucie a check. She stopped in the act of putting the note in her bosom, and, with her hands yet at her neck, looked terrified at Madame Defarge. Madame Defarge met the lifted eyebrows and forehead with a cold, impassive stare.

"My dear," said Mr. Lorry, striking in to explain; "there are frequent risings in the streets; and, although it is not likely they will ever trouble you, Madame Defarge wishes to see those whom she has the power to protect at such times, to the end that she may know them—that she may identify them. I believe," said Mr. Lorry, rather halting in his reassuring words, as the stony manner of all the three impressed itself upon him more and more, "I state the case, Citizen Defarge?"

Defarge looked gloomily at his wife, and gave no other answer than a gruff sound of acquiescence.

"You had better, Lucie," said Mr. Lorry, doing all he could to propitiate, by tone and manner, "have the dear child here, and our good Pross. Our good Pross, Defarge, is an English lady, and knows no French."

The lady in question, whose rooted conviction that she was more than a match for any foreigner, was not to be shaken by distress and danger, appeared with folded arms, and observed in English to The Vengeance, whom her eyes first encountered, "Well, I am sure, Boldface! I hope *you* are pretty well!" She also bestowed a British cough on Madame Defarge; but, neither of the two took much heed of her.

"Is that his child?" said Madame Defarge, stopping in her work for the first time and pointing her knitting-needle at little Lucie as if it were the finger of Fate.

"Yes, Madame," answered Mr. Lorry; "this is our poor prisoner's darling daughter, and only child."

The shadow attendant on Madame Defarge and her party seemed to fall so threatening and dark on the child, that her mother instinctively kneeled on the ground beside her, and held her to her breast. The shadow attendant on

Madame Defarge and her party seemed then to fall, threatening and dark, on both the mother and the child.

"It is enough, my husband," said Madame Defarge. "I have seen them. We may go."

But the suppressed manner had enough of menace in it—not visible and presented, but indistinct and withheld—to alarm Lucie into saying, as she laid her appealing hand on Madame Defarge's dress:

"You will be good to my poor husband. You will do him no harm. You will help me to see him if you can?"

"Your husband is not my business here," returned Madame Defarge, looking down at her with perfect composure. "It is the daughter of your father who is my business here."

"For my sake, then, be merciful to my husband. For my child's sake! She will put her hands together and pray you to be merciful. We are more afraid of you than of these others."

Madame Defarge received it as a compliment, and looked at her husband. Defarge, who had been uneasily biting his thumb-nail and looking at her, collected his face into a sterner expression.

"What is that your husband says in that little letter?" asked Madame Defarge, with a lowering smile. "Influence; he says something touching influence?"

"That my father," said Lucie, hurriedly taking the paper from her breast, but with her alarmed eyes on her questioner and not on it, "has much influence around him."

"Surely it will release him!" said Madame Defarge. "Let it do so."

"As a wife and mother," cried Lucie most earnestly, "I implore you to have pity on me and not exercise any power that you possess, against my innocent husband, but to use it in his behalf. O sister-woman, think of me. As a wife and mother!"

Madame Defarge looked, coldly as ever, at the suppliant, and said, turning to her friend The Vengeance:

"The wives and mothers we have been used to see, since we were as little as this child, and much less, have not been greatly considered? We have known *their* husbands and fathers laid in prison and kept from them, often enough? All our lives, we have seen our sister-women suffer, in themselves and in their children, poverty, nakedness, hunger, thirst, sickness, misery, oppression, and neglect of all kinds?"

"We have seen nothing else," returned The Vengeance.

"We have borne this a long time," said Madame Defarge, turning her eyes again upon Lucie. "Judge you! Is it likely that the trouble of one wife and mother would be much to us now?"

She resumed her knitting and went out. The Vengeance followed. Defarge went last, and closed the door.

"Courage, my dear Lucie," said Mr. Lorry, as he raised her. "Courage, courage! So far all goes well with us—much, much better than it has of late gone with many poor souls. Cheer up, and have a thankful heart."

"I am not thankless, I hope, but that dreadful woman seems to throw a shadow on me and on all my hopes."

"Tut, tut!" said Mr. Lorry; "what is this despondency in the brave little breast? A shadow indeed! No substance in it, Lucie."

But the shadow of the manner of these Defarges was dark upon himself, for all that, and in his secret mind it troubled him greatly.

4

CALM IN STORM

◆

DOCTOR MANETTE did not return until the morning of the fourth day of his absence. So much of what had happened in that dreadful time as could be kept from the knowledge of Lucie was so well concealed from her, that not until long afterwards, when France and she were far apart, did she know that eleven hundred defenceless prisoners of both sexes and all ages had been killed by the populace; that four days and nights had been darkened by this deed of horror; and that the air around her had been tainted by the slain. She only knew that there had been an attack upon the prisons, that all political prisoners had been in danger, and that some had been dragged out by the crowd and murdered.

To Mr. Lorry, the Doctor communicated under an injunction of secrecy on which he had no need to dwell, that the crowd had taken him through a scene of carnage to the prison La Force. That, in the prison he had found a self-appointed Tribunal sitting, before which the prisoners were brought singly, and by which they were rapidly ordered to be put forth to be massacred, or to be released, or (in a few cases) to be sent back to their cells. That, presented by his

conductors to this Tribunal, he had announced himself by
name and profession as having been for eighteen years a
secret and unaccused prisoner in the Bastille; that, one of
the body so sitting in judgment had risen and identified
him, and that this man was Defarge.

That, hereupon he had ascertained, through the registers on the table, that his son-in-law was among the living
prisoners, and had pleaded hard to the tribunal—of whom
some members were asleep and some awake, some dirty
with murder and some clean, some sober and some not—
for his life and liberty. That, in the first frantic greetings lav-
ished on himself as a notable sufferer under the overthrown system, it had been accorded to him to have Charles
Darnay brought before the lawless Court, and examined.
That, he seemed on the point of being at once released,
when the tide in his favour met with some unexplained
check (not intelligible to the Doctor), which led to a few
words of secret conference. That, the man sitting as
President had then informed Doctor Manette that the prisoner must remain in custody, but should, for his sake, be
held inviolate in safe custody. That, immediately, on a sig-
nal, the prisoner was removed to the interior of the prison
again; but, that he, the Doctor, had then so strongly pleaded
for permission to remain and assure himself that his son-in-
law was, through no malice or mischance, delivered to the
concourse whose murderous yells outside the gate had
often drowned the proceedings, that he had obtained the
permission, and had remained in that Hall of Blood until
the danger was over.

The sights he had seen there, with brief snatches of food
and sleep by intervals, shall remain untold. The mad joy
over the prisoners who were saved, had astounded him
scarcely less than the mad ferocity against those who were
cut to pieces. One prisoner there was, he said, who had
been discharged into the street free, but at whom a mistaken savage had thrust a pike as he passed out. Being
besought to go to him and dress the wound, the Doctor had

passed out at the same gate, and found him in the arms of a company of Samaritans, who were seated on the bodies of their victims. With an inconsistency as monstrous as anything in this awful nightmare, they had helped the healer, and tended the wounded man with the gentlest solicitude—had made a litter for him and escorted him carefully from the spot—had then caught up their weapons and plunged anew into a butchery so dreadful, that the Doctor had covered his eyes with his hands, and swooned away in the midst of it.

As Mr. Lorry received these confidences, and as he watched the face of his friend now sixty-two years of age, a misgiving arose within him that such dreadful experiences would revive the old danger. But, he had never seen his friend in his present aspect: he had never at all known him in his present character. For the first time the Doctor felt, now, that his suffering was strength and power. For the first time he felt that in that sharp fire, he had slowly forged the iron which could break the prison door of his daughter's husband, and deliver him. "It all tended to a good end, my friend; it was not mere waste and ruin. As my beloved child was helpful in restoring me to myself, I will be helpful now in restoring the dearest part of herself to her; by the aid of Heaven I will do it!" Thus, Doctor Manette. And when Jarvis Lorry saw the kindled eyes, the resolute face, the calm strong look and bearing of the man whose life always seemed to him to have been stopped, like a clock, for so many years, and then set going again with an energy which had lain dormant during the cessation of its usefulness, he believed.

Greater things than the Doctor had at that time to contend with, would have yielded before his persevering purpose. While he kept himself in his place, as a physician, whose business was with all degrees of mankind, bond and free, rich and poor, bad and good, he used his personal influence so wisely, that he was soon the inspecting physician of three prisons, and among them of La Force. He could now assure Lucie that her husband was no longer confined alone, but was mixed with the general body of prisoners; he saw her husband weekly, and brought sweet messages to her, straight from his lips; sometimes her husband himself sent a letter to her (though never by the Doctor's hand), but she was not permitted to write to him: for, among the many wild suspicions of plots in the prisons, the wildest of all pointed at emigrants who were known to have made friends or permanent connections abroad.

This new life of the Doctor's was an anxious life, no doubt; still, the sagacious Mr. Lorry saw that there was a new sustaining pride in it. Nothing unbecoming tinged the pride; it was a natural and worthy one; but he observed it as a curiosity. The Doctor knew, that up to that time, his imprisonment had been associated in the minds of his daughter and his friend, with his personal affliction, deprivation, and weakness. Now that this was changed, and he knew himself to be invested through that old trial with forces to which they both looked for Charles's ultimate safety and deliverance, he became so far exalted by the change, that he took the lead and direction, and required them as the weak, to trust to him as the strong. The preceding relative positions of himself and Lucie were reversed, yet only as the liveliest gratitude and affection could reverse them, for he could have had no pride but in rendering some service to her who had rendered so much to him. "All curious to see," thought Mr. Lorry, in his amiably shrewd way, "but all natural and right; so, take the lead, my dear friend, and keep it; it couldn't be in better hands."

But, though the Doctor tried hard, and never ceased trying, to get Charles Darnay set at liberty, or at least to get him brought to trial, the public current of the time set too strong and fast for him. The new era began; the king was tried, doomed and beheaded; the Republic of Liberty, Equality, Fraternity, or Death, declared for victory or death against the world in arms; the black flag waved night and day from the great towers of Notre Dame; three hundred thousand men, summoned to rise against the tyrants of the earth, rose from all the varying soils of France, as if the dragon's teeth had been sown broadcast, and had yielded fruit equally on hill and plain, on rock, in gravel, and alluvial mud, under the bright sky of the South and under the clouds of the North, in fell and forest, in the vineyards and the olive-grounds and among the cropped grass and the stubble of the corn, along the fruitful banks of the broad rivers, and in the sand of the seashore. What private solicitude could rear itself against the deluge of the Year One of Liberty—the deluge rising from below, not falling from above, and with the windows of Heaven shut, not opened!

There was no pause, no pity, no peace, no interval of relenting rest, no measurement of time. Though days and nights circled as regularly as when time was young, and the evening and morning were the first day, other count of time there was none. Hold of it was lost in the raging fever of a nation, as it is in the fever of one patient. Now, breaking the unnatural silence of a whole city, the executioner showed the people the head of the king—and now, it seemed almost in the same breath, the head of his fair wife which had had eight weary months of imprisoned widowhood and misery, to turn it grey.

And yet, observing the strange law of contradiction which obtains in all such cases, the time was long, while it flamed by so fast. A revolutionary tribunal in the capital, and forty or fifty thousand revolutionary committees all over the land; a law of the Suspected, which struck away all security for liberty or life, and delivered over any good and innocent person to any bad and guilty one; prisons gorged with people who had committed no offence, and could obtain no hearing; these things became the established order and nature of appointed things, and seemed to be ancient usage before they were many weeks old. Above all, one hideous figure grew as familiar as if it had been before the general gaze from the foundations of the world—the figure of the sharp female called La Guillotine.

It was the popular theme for jests; it was the best cure for headache, it infallibly prevented the hair from turning grey, it imparted a peculiar delicacy to the complexion, it was the National Razor which shaved close: who kissed La Guillotine, looked through the window and sneezed into the sack. It was the sign of the regeneration of the human race. It superseded the Cross. Models of it were worn on breasts from which the Cross was discarded, and it was bowed down to and believed in where the Cross was denied.

It sheared off heads so many, that it, and the ground it most polluted, were a rotten red. It was taken to pieces, like a toy-puzzle for a young Devil, and was put together again when the occasion wanted it. It hushed the eloquent, struck down the powerful, abolished the beautiful and good. Twenty-two friends of high public mark, twenty-one living and one dead, it had lopped the heads off, in one morning, in as many minutes. The name of the strong man of Old Scripture[3] had descended to chief functionary who worked it; but, so armed, he was stronger than his name-sake, and blinder, and tore away the gates of God's own Temple every day.

Among these terrors, and the brood belonging to them, the Doctor walked with a steady head; confident in his power, cautiously persistent in his end, never doubting that he would have Lucie's husband at last. Yet the current of the time swept by, so strong and deep, and carried the time away so fiercely, that Charles had lain in prison one year and three months when the Doctor was thus steady and confident. So much more wicked and distracted had the Revolution grown in that December month, that the rivers of the South were encumbered with the bodies of the violently drowned by night, and prisoners were shot in lines and squares under the southern wintry sun. Still, the Doctor walked among the terrors with a steady head. No man better known than he, in Paris at that day; no man in a stranger situation. Silent, humane, indispensable in hospital and prison, using his art equally among assassins and victims, he was a man apart. In the exercise of his skill, the appearance and the story of the Bastille Captive removed him from all other men. He was not suspected or brought in question, any more than if he had indeed been recalled to life some eighteen years before, or were a spirit moving among mortals.

5

THE WOOD-SAWYER

ONE year and three months. During all that time Lucie was never sure, from hour to hour, but that the Guillotine would strike off her husband's head next day. Every day, through the stony streets, the tumbrils now jolted heavily, filled with Condemned. Lovely girls; bright women, brown-haired, black-haired, and grey; youths; stalwart men and old; gentle born and peasant born; all red wine for La Guillotine, all daily brought into light from the dark cellars of the loathsome prisons, and carried to her through the streets to slake her devouring thirst. Liberty, Equality, Fraternity, or Death;—the last, much the easiest to bestow, O Guillotine!

If the suddenness of her calamity, and the whirling wheels of the time, had stunned the Doctor's daughter into awaiting the result in idle despair, it would but have been with her as it was with many. But, from the hour when she had taken the white head to her fresh young bosom in the garret of Saint Antoine, she had been true to her duties. She was truest to them in the season of trial, as all the quietly loyal and good will always be.

As soon as they were established in their new residence,

and her father had entered on the routine of his avocations, she arranged the little household as exactly as if her husband had been there. Everything had its appointed place and its appointed time. Little Lucie she taught, as regularly, as if they had all been united in their English home. The slight devices with which she cheated herself into the show of a belief that they would soon be reunited—the little preparations for his speedy return, the setting aside of his chair and his books—these, and the solemn prayer at night for one dear prisoner especially, among the many unhappy souls in prison and the shadow of death—were almost the only outspoken reliefs of her heavy mind.

She did not greatly alter in appearance. The plain dark dresses, akin to mourning dresses, which she and her child wore, were as neat and as well attended to as the brighter clothes of happy days. She lost her colour, and the old and intent expression was a constant, not an occasional, thing; otherwise, she remained very pretty and comely. Sometimes, at night on kissing her father, she would burst into the grief she had repressed all day, and would say that her sole reliance, under Heaven, was on him. He always resolutely answered: "Nothing can happen to him without my knowledge, and I know that I can save him, Lucie."

They had not made the round of their changed life many weeks, when her father said to her, on coming home one evening:

"My dear, there is an upper window in the prison, to which Charles can sometimes gain access at three in the afternoon. When he can get to it—which depends on many uncertainties and incidents—he might see you in the street, he thinks, if you stood in a certain place that I can show you. But you will not be able to see him, my poor child, and even if you could, it would be unsafe for you to make a sign of recognition."

"Oh show me the place, my father, and I will go there every day."

From that time, in all weathers, she waited there two hours. As the clock struck two, she was there, and at four she turned resignedly away. When it was not too wet or inclement for her child to be with her, they went together; at other times she was alone; but, she never missed a single day.

It was the dark and dirty corner of a small winding street. The hovel of a cutter of wood into lengths for burning was the only house at that end; all else was wall. On the third day of her being there, he noticed her.

"Good day, citizeness."

"Good day, citizen."

This mode of address was now prescribed by decree. It had been established voluntarily some time ago, among the more thorough patriots; but, was now law for everybody.

"Walking here again, citizeness?"

"You see me, citizen!"

The wood-sawyer, who was a little man with a redundancy of gesture (he had once been a mender of roads), cast a glance at the prison, pointed at the prison, and putting his ten fingers before his face to represent bars, peeped through them jocosely.

"But it's not my business," said he. And went on sawing his wood.

Next day he was looking out for her, and accosted her the moment she appeared.

"What! Walking here again, citizeness?"

"Yes, citizen."

"Ah! A child too! Your mother, is it not, my little citizeness?"

"Do I say yes, mamma?" whispered little Lucie, drawing close to her.

"Yes, dearest."

"Yes, citizen."

"Ah! But it's not my business. My work is my business. See my saw! I call it my Little Guillotine. La, la, la; La, la, la! And off his head comes!"

The billet fell as he spoke, and he threw it into a basket.

"I call myself the Samson of the firewood guillotine. See here again! Loo, loo, loo; Loo, loo, loo! And off *her* head comes! Now, a child. Tickle, tickle; Pickle, pickle! And off its head comes. All the family!"

Lucie shuddered as he threw two more billets into his basket, but it was impossible to be there while the wood-sawyer was at work, and not be in his sight. Thenceforth, to secure his good will, she always spoke to him first, and often gave him drink-money, which he readily received.

He was an inquisitive fellow, and sometimes when she had quite forgotten him in gazing at the prison roof and grates, and in lifting her heart up to her husband, she would come to herself to find him looking at her, with his knee on his bench and his saw stopped in its work. "But it's not my business!" he would generally say at those times, and would briskly fall to his sawing again.

In all weathers, in the snow and frost of winter, in the bitter winds of spring, in the hot sunshine of summer, in the rains of autumn, and again in the snow and frost of winter, Lucie passed two hours of every day at this place; and every day on leaving it, she kissed the prison wall. Her husband saw her (so she learned from her father) it might be once in five or six times: it might be twice or thrice running: it might be, not for a week or a fortnight together. It was enough that he could and did see her when the chances served, and on that possibility she would have waited out the day, seven days a week.

These occupations brought her round to the December month, wherein her father walked among the terrors with a steady head. On a lightly-snowing afternoon she arrived at the usual corner. It was a day of some wild rejoicing, and a festival. She had seen the houses, as she came along, decorated with little pikes, and with little red caps stuck upon them; also, with tricoloured ribbons; also, with the standard inscription (tricoloured letters were the favourite), Republic One and Indivisible. Liberty, Equality, Fraternity, or Death!

The miserable shop of the wood-sawyer was so small, that its whole surface furnished very indifferent space for this legend. He had got somebody to scrawl it up for him, however, who had squeezed Death in with most inappropriate difficulty. On his house-top, he displayed pike and cap, as a good citizen must, and in a window he had stationed his saw inscribed as his "Little Sainte Guillotine"—for the great sharp female was by that time popularly canonised. His shop was shut and he was not there, which was a relief to Lucie, and left her quite alone.

But, he was not far off, for presently she heard a troubled movement and a shouting coming along, which filled her with fear. A moment afterwards, and a throng of people came pouring round the corner by the prison wall, in the midst of which was the wood-sawyer hand in hand with The Vengeance. There could not be fewer than five hundred people, and they were dancing like five thousand demons. There was no other music than their own singing. They danced to the popular Revolution song,[4] keeping a ferocious time that was like a gnashing of teeth in unison. Men and women danced together, women danced together, men danced together, as hazard had brought them together. At first, they were a mere storm of coarse red caps and coarse woollen rags; but, as they filled the place, and stopped to dance about Lucie, some ghastly apparition of a dance-figure gone raving mad arose among them. They advanced, retreated, struck at one another's hands, clutched at one another's heads, spun round alone, caught one another and spun round in pairs, until many of them dropped. While those were down, the rest linked hand in hand, and all spun round together: then the ring broke, and in separate rings of two and four they turned and turned until they all stopped at once, began again, struck, clutched, and tore, and then reversed the spin, and all spun round another way. Suddenly they stopped again, paused, struck out the time afresh, formed into lines the width of the public way, and, with their heads low down and their hands high up, swooped screaming off. No fight could have been half so terrible as this dance. It was so emphatically a fallen sport—a something, once innocent, delivered over to all devilry—a healthy pastime changed into a means of angering the blood, bewildering the senses, and stealing the heart. Such grace as was visible in it, made it the uglier, showing how warped and perverted all things good by nature were become. The maidenly bosom bared to this, the pretty almost-child's head thus distracted, the delicate foot mincing in this slough of blood and dirt, were types of the disjointed time.

This was the Carmagnole. As it passed, leaving Lucie frightened and bewildered in the doorway of the wood-sawyer's house, the feathery snow fell as quietly and lay as white and soft, as if it had never been.

"O my father!" for he stood before her when she lifted up the eyes she had momentarily darkened with her hand; "such a cruel, bad sight."

"I know, my dear, I know. I have seen it many times. Don't be frightened. Not one of them would harm you."

"I am not frightened for myself, my father. But when I think of my husband, and the mercies of these people——"

"We will set him above their mercies very soon. I left him climbing to the window, and I came to tell you. There is no one here to see you. You may kiss your hand towards the highest shelving roof."

"I do so, father, and I send him my Soul with it!"

"You cannot see him, my poor dear?"

"No, father," said Lucie, yearning and weeping as she kissed her hand, "no."

A footstep in the snow. Madame Defarge. "I salute you, citizeness," from the Doctor. "I salute you, citizen." This in passing. Nothing more. Madame Defarge gone, like a shadow over the white road.

"Give me your arm, my love. Pass from here with an air

of cheerfulness and courage, for his sake. That was well done"; they had left the spot; "it shall not be in vain. Charles is summoned for to-morrow."

"For to-morrow!"

"There is no time to lose. I am well prepared, but there are precautions to be taken, that could not be taken until he was actually summoned before the Tribunal. He has not received the notice yet, but I know that he will presently be summoned for to-morrow, and removed to the Conciergerie[5]; I have timely information. You are not afraid?"

She could scarcely answer, "I trust in you."

"Do so implicitly. Your suspense is nearly ended, my darling; he shall be restored to you within a few hours; I have encompassed him with every protection. I must see Lorry."

He stopped. There was a heavy lumbering of wheels within hearing. They both knew too well what it meant. One. Two. Three. Three tumbrils faring away with their dread loads over the hushing snow.

"I must see Lorry," the Doctor repeated, turning her another way.

The staunch old gentleman was still in his trust; had never left it. He and his books were in frequent requisition as to property confiscated and made national. What he could save for the owners, he saved. No better man living to hold fast by what Tellson's had in keeping, and to hold his peace.

A murky red and yellow sky, and a rising mist from the Seine, denoted the approach of darkness. It was almost dark when they arrived at the Bank. The stately residence of Monseigneur was altogether blighted and deserted. Above a heap of dust and ashes in the court, ran the letters: National Property. Republic One and Indivisible. Liberty, Equality, Fraternity, or Death!

Who could that be with Mr. Lorry—the owner of the riding-coat upon the chair—who must not be seen? From

whom newly arrived, did he come out, agitated and surprised, to take his favourite in his arms? To whom did he
appear to repeat her faltering words, when, raising his voice
and turning his head towards the door of the room from
which he had issued, he said: "Removed to the
Conciergerie, and summoned for to-morrow?"

6

TRIUMPH

THE dread Tribunal of five Judges, Public Prosecutor, and determined Jury, sat every day. Their lists went forth every evening, and were read out by the gaolers of the various prisons to their prisoners. The standard gaoler-joke was, "Come out and listen to the Evening Paper, you inside there!"

"Charles Evrémonde, called Darnay!"

So at last began the Evening Paper at La Force.

When a name was called, its owner stepped apart into a spot reserved for those who were announced as being thus fatally recorded. Charles Evrémonde, called Darnay, had reason to know the usage; he had seen hundreds pass away so.

His bloated gaoler, who wore spectacles to read with, glanced over them to assure himself that he had taken his place, and went through the list, making a similar short pause at each name. There were twenty-three names, but only twenty were responded to; for one of the prisoners so summoned had died in gaol and been forgotten, and two had already been guillotined and forgotten. The list was read, in the vaulted chamber where Darnay had seen the associated prisoners on the night of his arrival. Every one of those had perished in the massacre; every human creature he had since cared for and parted with, had died on the scaffold.

There were hurried words of farewell and kindness, but the parting was soon over. It was the incident of every day, and the society of La Force were engaged in the preparation of some games of forfeits and a little concert, for that evening. They crowded to the grates and shed tears there; but, twenty places in the projected entertainments had to be refilled, and the time was, at best, short to the lockup hour, when the common rooms and corridors would be delivered over to the great dogs who kept watch there through the night. The prisoners were far from insensible or unfeeling; their ways arose out of the condition of the time. Similarly, though with a subtle difference, a species of fervour or intoxication, known, without doubt, to have led some persons to brave the guillotine unnecessarily, and to die by it, was not mere boastfulness, but a wild infection of the wildly shaken public mind. In seasons of pestilence, some of us will have a secret attraction to the disease—a terrible passing inclination to die of it. And all of us have like wonders hidden in our breasts, only needing circumstances to evoke them.

The passage to the Conciergerie was short and dark; the night in its vermin-haunted cells was long and cold. Next day, fifteen prisoners were put to the bar before Charles Darnay's name was called. All the fifteen were condemned, and the trials of the whole occupied an hour and a half.

"Charles Evrémonde, called Darnay," was at length arraigned.

His judges sat upon the Bench in feathered hats; but the rough red cap and tricoloured cockade was the headdress otherwise prevailing. Looking at the Jury and the turbulent audience, he might have thought that the usual order of things was reversed, and that the felons were trying the honest men. The lowest, crudest, and worst populace of a city, never without its quantity of low, cruel, and bad, were the directing spirits of the scene: noisily commenting, applauding, disapproving, anticipating, and precipitating the result, without a check. Of the men, the greater part were armed in various ways; of the women, some wore knives, some daggers, some ate and drank as they looked on, many knitted. Among these last, was one, with a spare piece of knitting under her arm as she worked. She was in a front row, by the side of a man whom he had never seen since his arrival at the Barrier, but whom he directly remembered as Defarge. He noticed that she once or twice whispered in his ear, and that she seemed to be his wife; but, what he most noticed in the two figures was, that although they were posted as close to himself as they could be, they never looked towards him. They seemed to be waiting for something with a dogged determination, and they looked at the Jury, but at nothing else. Under the President sat Doctor Manette, in his usual quiet dress. As well as the prisoner could see, he and Mr. Lorry were the only two men there, unconnected with the Tribunal, who wore their usual clothes, and had not assumed the coarse garb of the Carmagnole.

Charles Evrémonde, called Darnay, was accused by the public prosecutor as an emigrant, whose life was forfeit to the Republic, under the decree which banished all emigrants on pain of Death. It was nothing that the decree bore date since his return to France. There he was, and there was the decree; he had been taken in France, and his head was demanded.

"Take off his head!" cried the audience. "An enemy to the Republic!"

The President rang his bell to silence those cries, and asked the prisoner whether it was not true that he had lived many years in England?

Undoubtedly it was.

Was he not an emigrant then? What did he call himself?

Not an emigrant, he hoped, within the sense and spirit of the law.

Why not? the President desired to know.

Because he had voluntarily relinquished a title that was distasteful to him, and a station that was distasteful to him, and had left his country—he submitted before the word emigrant in the present acceptation by the Tribunal was in use—to live by his own industry in England, rather than on the industry of the overladen people of France.

What proof had he of this?

He handed in the name of two witness; Théophile Gabelle, and Alexandre Manette.

But he had married in England? the President reminded him.

True, but not an English woman.

A citizeness of France?

Yes. By birth.

Her name and family?

"Lucie Manette, only daughter of Doctor Manette, the good physician who sits there."

This answer had a happy effect upon the audience. Cries in exaltation of the well-known good physician rent the hall. So capriciously were the people moved, that tears immediately rolled down several ferocious countenances which had been glaring at the prisoner a moment before, as if with impatience to pluck him out into the streets and kill him.

On these few steps of his dangerous way, Charles Darnay had set his foot according to Doctor Manette's reiterated instructions. The same cautious counsel directed every step that lay before him, and had prepared every inch of his road.

The President asked, why had he returned to France when he did, and not sooner?

He had not returned sooner, he replied, simply because he had no means of living in France, save those he had resigned; whereas, in England, he lived by giving instruction in the French language and literature. He had returned when he did, on the pressing and written entreaty of a French citizen, who represented that his life was endangered by his absence. He had come back, to save a citizen's life, and to bear his testimony, at whatever personal hazard, to the truth. Was that criminal in the eyes of the Republic?

The populace cried enthusiastically, "No!" and the President rang his bell to quiet them. Which it did not, for they continued to cry "No!" until they left off, of their own will.

The President required the name of that citizen? The accused explained that the citizen was his first witness. He also referred with confidence to the citizen's letter, which had been taken from him at the Barrier, but which he did not doubt would be found among the papers then before the President.

The doctor had taken care that it should be there—had assured him that it would be there—and at this stage of the proceedings it was produced and read. Citizen Gabelle was called to confirm it, and did so. Citizen Gabelle hinted, with infinite delicacy and politeness, that in the pressure of business imposed on the Tribunal by the multitude of enemies of the Republic with which it had to deal, he had been slightly overlooked in his prison of the Abbaye—in fact, had rather passed out of the Tribunal's patriotic remembrance—until three days ago; when he had been summoned before it, and had been set at liberty on the Jury's declaring themselves satisfied that the accusation against him was answered, as to himself, by the surrender of the citizen Evrémonde, called Darnay.

Doctor Manette was next questioned. His high personal popularity, and the clearness of his answers, made a great impression: but, as he proceeded, as he showed that the accused was his first friend on his release from his long imprisonment; that, the accused had remained in England, always faithful and devoted to his daughter and himself in their exile; that, so far from being in favour with the Aristocrat government there, he had actually been tried for his life by it, as the foe of England and friend of the United States—as he brought these circumstances into view, with the greatest discretion and with the straightforward force of truth and earnestness, the Jury and the populace became one. At last, when he appealed by name to Monsieur Lorry, an English gentleman then and there present, who, like himself, had been a witness on that English trial and could corroborate his account of it, the Jury declared that they had heard enough, and that they were ready with their votes if the President were content to receive them.

At every vote (the Jurymen voted aloud and individually), the populace set up a shout of applause. All the voices were in the prisoner's favour, and the President declared him free.

Then, began one of those extraordinary scenes with which the populace sometimes gratified their fickleness, or their better impulses towards generosity and mercy, or which they regarded as some set-off against their swollen account of cruel rage. No man can decide now to which of these motives such extraordinary scenes were referable; it is probable, to a blending of all three, with the second predominating. No sooner was the acquittal pronounced, than tears were shed as freely as blood at another time, and such fraternal embraces were bestowed upon the prisoner by as many of both sexes as could rush at him, that after his long and unwholesome confinement he was in danger of fainting from exhaustion; none the less because he knew very well, that the very same people, carried by another current, would have rushed at him with the very same intensity, to rend him to pieces and strew him over the streets.

His removal, to make way for other accused persons who were to be tried, rescued him from these caresses for the moment. Five were to be tried together, next, as enemies of the Republic, forasmuch as they had not assisted it by word or deed. So quick was the Tribunal to compensate itself and the nation for a chance lost, that these five came down to him before he left the place, condemned to die within twenty-four hours. The first of them told him so, with the customary prison sign of Death—a raised finger—and they all added in words, "Long live the Republic!"

The five had had, it is true, no audience to lengthen their proceedings, for when he and Doctor Manette emerged from the gate, there was a great crowd about it, in which there seemed to be every face he had seen in Court, except two, for which he looked in vain. On his coming out, the concourse made at him anew, weeping, embracing, and shouting, all by turns and all together, until the very tide of the river on the bank of which the mad scene was acted, seemed to run mad, like the people on the shore.

They put him into a great chair they had among them, and which they had taken either out of the Court itself, or one of its rooms or passages. Over the chair they had thrown a red flag, and to the back of it they had bound a pike with a red cap on its top. In this car of triumph, not even the Doctor's entreaties could prevent his being carried to his home on men's shoulders, with a confused sea of red caps heaving about him, and casting up to sight from the stormy deep such wrecks of faces, that he more than once misdoubted his mind being in confusion, and that he was in the tumbril on his way to the Guillotine.

In wild dreamlike procession, embracing whom they met and pointing him out, they carried him on. Reddening the snowy streets with the prevailing Republican colour, in winding and tramping through them, as they had reddened them below the snow with a deeper dye, they carried him thus into the court-yard of the building where he lived. Her father had gone on before, to prepare her, and when her husband stood upon his feet, she dropped insensible in his arms.

As he held her to his heart and turned her beautiful head between his face and the brawling crowd, so that his tears and her lips might come together unseen, a few of the people fell to dancing. Instantly, all the rest fell to dancing, and the court-yard overflowed with the Carmagnole. Then, they elevated into the vacant chair a young woman from the crowd to be carried as the Goddess of Liberty,[6] and then swelling and overflowing out into the adjacent streets, and along the river's bank, and over the bridge, the Carmagnole absorbed them every one and whirled them away.

After grasping the Doctor's hand, as he stood victorious and proud before him; after grasping the hand of Mr. Lorry, who came panting in breathless from his struggle against the waterspout of the Carmagnole; after kissing little Lucie, who was lifted up to clasp her hands round his neck; and after embracing the ever zealous and faithful Pross who lifted her; he took his wife in his arms, and carried her up to their rooms.

"Lucie! My own! I am safe."

"O dearest Charles, let me thank God for this on my knees as I have prayed to Him."

They all reverently bowed their heads and hearts. When she was again in his arms, he said to her——

"And now speak to your father, dearest. No other man in all this France could have done what he has done for me."

She laid her head upon her father's breast, as she had laid his poor head on her own breast, long, long ago. He was happy in the return he had made her, he was recompensed for his suffering, he was proud of his strength. "You must not be weak, my darling," he remonstrated; "don't tremble so. I have saved him."

7

A Knock at the Door

———❦———

"**I** HAVE saved him." It was not another of the dreams in which he had often come back; he was really here. And yet his wife trembled, and a vague but heavy fear was upon her.

All the air round was so thick and dark, the people were so passionately revengeful and fitful, the innocent were so constantly put to death on vague suspicion and black malice, it was so impossible to forget that many as blameless as her husband and as dear to others as he was to her, every day shared the fate from which he had been clutched, that her heart could not be as lightened of its load as she felt it ought to be. The shadows of the wintry afternoon were beginning to fall, and even now the dreadful carts were rolling through the streets. Her mind pursued them, looking for him among the condemned; and then she clung closer to his real presence and trembled more.

Her father, cheering her, showed a compassionate superiority to this woman's weakness, which was wonderful to see. No garret, no shoemaking, no One Hundred and Five, North Tower, now! He had accomplished the task he had set himself, his promise was redeemed, he had saved Charles. Let them all lean upon him.

Their housekeeping was of a very frugal kind: not only because that was the safest way of life, involving the least offence to the people, but because they were not rich, and Charles, throughout his imprisonment, had had to pay heavily for his bad food, and for his guard, and towards the living of the poorer prisoners. Partly on this account, and partly to avoid a domestic spy, they kept no servant; the citizen and citizeness who acted as porters at the court-yard gate, rendered them occasional service; and Jerry (almost wholly transferred to them by Mr. Lorry) had become their daily retainer, and had his bed there every night.

It was an ordinance of the Republic One and Indivisible, of Liberty, Equality, Fraternity, or Death, that on the door or door-post of every house, the name of every inmate must be legibly inscribed in letters of a certain size, at a certain convenient height from the ground. Mr. Jerry Cruncher's name, therefore, duly embellished the door-post down below; and, as the afternoon shadows deepened, the owner of that name himself appeared, from overlooking a painter whom Doctor Manette had employed to add to the list the name of Charles Evrémonde, called Darnay.

In the universal fear and distrust that darkened the time, all the usual harmless ways of life were changed. In the Doctor's little household, as in very many others, the articles of daily consumption that were wanted were purchased every evening, in small quantities and at various small shops. To avoid attracting notice, and to give as little occasion as possible for talk and envy, was the general desire.

For some months past, Miss Pross and Mr. Cruncher had discharged the office of purveyors; the former carrying the money; the latter, the basket. Every afternoon at about the time when the public lamps were lighted, they fared forth on this duty, and made and brought home such purchases as were needful. Although Miss Pross, through her long associations with a French family, might have known as much of their language as of her own, if she had had a mind, she had no mind in that direction; consequently she knew no more of that "nonsense" (as she was pleased to call it) than Mr. Cruncher did. So her manner of marketing was to plump a noun-substantive at the head of a shop-keeper without any introduction in the nature of an article, and, if it happened not to be the name of the thing she wanted, to look round for that thing, lay hold of it, and hold on by it until the bargain was concluded. She always made a bargain for it, by holding up, as a statement of its just price, one finger less than the merchant held up, whatever his number might be.

"Now, Mr. Cruncher," said Miss Pross, whose eyes were red with felicity; "if you are ready, I am."

Jerry hoarsely professed himself at Miss Pross's service. He had worn all his rust off long ago, but nothing would file his spiky head down.

"There's all manner of things wanted," said Miss Pross, "and we shall have a precious time of it. We want wine, among the rest. Nice toasts these Redheads will be drinking, wherever we buy it."

"It will be much the same to your knowledge, miss, I should think," retorted Jerry, "whether they drink your health or the Old Un's."

"Who's he?" said Miss Pross.

Mr. Cruncher, with some diffidence, explained himself as meaning "Old Nick's."

"Ha!" said Miss Pross, "it doesn't need an interpreter to explain the meaning of these creatures. They have but one, and it's Midnight Murder, and Mischief."

"Hush, dear! Pray, pray, be cautious!" cried Lucie.

"Yes, yes, yes, I'll be cautious," said Miss Pross; "but I may say among ourselves, that I do hope there will be no oniony and tobaccoy smotherings in the form of embracings all round, going on in the streets. Now, Ladybird, never you stir from that fire till I come back! Take care of the dear husband you have recovered, and don't move your pretty head from his shoulder as you have it now, till you see me again! May I ask a question, Doctor Manette, before I go?"

"I think you may take that liberty," the doctor answered, smiling.

"For gracious sake, don't talk about Liberty; we have quite enough of that," said Miss Pross.

"Hush, dear! Again?" Lucie remonstrated.

"Well, my sweet," said Miss Pross, nodding her head emphatically, "the short and the long of it is, that I am a subject of His Most Gracious Majesty King George the Third"; Miss Pross curtseyed at the name; "and as such, my maxim is, Confound their politics, Frustrate their knavish tricks, On him our hopes we fix, God save the King!"

Mr. Cruncher in an access of loyalty, growlingly repeated the words after Miss Pross, like somebody at church.

"I am glad you have so much of the Englishman in you, though I wish you had never taken that cold in your voice," said Miss Pross, approvingly. "But the question, Doctor Manette. Is there"—it was the good creature's way to affect to make light of anything that was a great anxiety with them all, and to come at it in this chance manner—"is there any prospect yet, of our getting out of this place?"

"I fear not yet. It would be dangerous for Charles yet."

"Heigh-ho-hum!" said Miss Pross, cheerfully repressing a sigh as she glanced at her darling's golden hair in the light of the fire, "then we must have patience and wait; that's all. We must hold up our heads and fight low, as my brother Solomon used to say. Now, Mr. Cruncher!—Don't you move, Ladybird!"

They went out, leaving Lucie, and her husband, her father and the child, by a bright fire. Mr. Lorry was expected back presently from the Banking House. Miss Pross had lighted the lamp, but had put it aside in a corner, that they might enjoy the fire-light undisturbed. Little Lucie sat by her grandfather with her hands clasped through his arm: and he, in a tone not rising much above a whisper, began to tell her a story of a great and powerful

Fairy who had opened a prison-wall and let out a captive who had once done the Fairy a service. All was subdued and quiet, and Lucie was more at ease than she had been.

"What is that?" she cried, all at once.

"My dear!" said her father, stopping in his story, and laying his hand on hers, "command yourself. What a disordered state you are in! The least thing—nothing—startles you! *You*, your father's daughter!"

"I thought, my father," said Lucie, excusing herself, with a pale face and in a faltering voice, "that I heard strange feet upon the stairs."

"My love, the staircase is as still as Death."

As he said the word, a blow was struck upon the door.

"Oh father, father. What can this be! Hide Charles. Save him!"

"My child," said the Doctor, rising, and laying his hand upon her shoulder, "I *have* saved him. What weakness is this, my dear! Let me go to the door."

He took the lamp in his hand, crossed the two intervening outer rooms, and opened it. A rude clattering of feet over the floor, and four rough men in red caps, armed with sabres and pistols, entered the room.

"The Citizen Evrémonde, called Darnay," said the first.

"Who seeks him?" answered Darnay.

"I seek him. We seek him. I know you, Evrémonde; I saw you before the Tribunal to-day. You are again the prisoner of the Republic."

The four surrounded him where he stood with his wife and child clinging to him.

"Tell me how and why I am again a prisoner?"

"It is enough that you return straight to the Conciergerie, and will know to-morrow. You are summoned for to-morrow."

Dr. Manette, whom this visitation had so turned into stone, that he stood with the lamp in his hand, as if he were a statue made to hold it, moved after these words were spoken, put the lamp down, and confronting the speaker, and taking him, not ungently, by the loose front of his red woollen shirt, said:

"You know him, you have said. Do you know me?"

"Yes, I know you, Citizen Doctor."

"We all know you, Citizen Doctor," said the other three.

He looked abstractedly from one to another, and said, in a lower voice, after a pause:

"Will you answer this question to me then? How does this happen?"

"Citizen Doctor," said the first, reluctantly, "he has been denounced to the Section of Saint Antoine. This citizen," pointing out the second who had entered, "is from Saint Antoine."

The citizen here indicated nodded his head, and added:

"He is accused by Saint Antoine."

"Of what?" asked the Doctor.

"Citizen Doctor," said the first, with his former reluctance, "ask no more. If the Republic demands sacrifices from you, without doubt you as a good patriot will be happy to make them. The Republic goes before all. The People is supreme. Evrémonde, we are pressed."

"One word," the Doctor entreated. "Will you tell me who denounced him?"

"It is against rule," answered the first; "but you can ask Him of Saint Antoine here."

The Doctor turned his eyes upon that man. Who moved uneasily on his feet, rubbed his beard a little, and at length said:

"Well! Truly it is against rule. But he is denounced—and gravely—by the Citizen and Citizeness Defarge. And by one other."

"What other?"

"Do *you* ask, Citizen Doctor?"

"Yes."

"Then," said he of Saint Antoine, with a strange look, "you will be answered to-morrow. Now, I am dumb!"

8

A HAND AT CARDS

HAPPILY unconscious of the new calamity at home, Miss Pross threaded her way along the narrow streets and crossed the river by the bridge of the Pont-Neuf, reckoning in her mind the number of indispensable purchases she had to make. Mr. Cruncher, with the basket, walked at her side. They both looked to the right and to the left into most of the shops they passed, had a wary eye for all gregarious assemblages of people, and turned out of their road to avoid any very excited group of talkers. It was a raw evening, and the misty river, blurred to the eye with blazing lights and to the ear with harsh noises, showed where the barges were stationed in which the smiths worked, making guns for the Army of the Republic. Woe to the man who played tricks with *that* Army, or got undeserved promotion in it! Better for him that his beard had never grown, for the National Razor shaved him close.

Having purchased a few small articles of grocery, and a measure of oil for the lamp, Miss Pross bethought herself of the wine they wanted. After peeping into several wineshops, she stopped at the sign of The Good Republican Brutus of Antiquity, not far from the National Palace, once (and twice) the Tuileries, where the aspect of things rather took her fancy. It had a quieter look than any other place of the same description they had passed, and though red with patriotic caps, was not so red as the rest. Sounding Mr. Cruncher, and finding him of her opinion, Miss Pross resorted to The Good Republican Brutus of Antiquity, attended by her cavalier.

Slightly observant of the smoky lights; of the people pipe in mouth, playing with limp cards and yellow dominoes; of the one bare-breasted, bare-armed, soot-begrimed workman reading a journal aloud, and of the others listening to him; of the weapons worn, or laid aside to be resumed; of the two or three customers fallen forward asleep, who in the popular high-shouldered shaggy black spencer looked, in that attitude, like slumbering bears or dogs; the two outlandish customers approached the counter, and showed what they wanted.

As their wine was measuring out, a man parted from another man in a corner, and rose to depart. In going, he had to face Miss Pross. No sooner did he face her, than Miss Pross uttered a scream, and clapped her hands.

In a moment, the whole company were on their feet. That somebody was assassinated by somebody vindicating a difference of opinion was the likeliest occurrence. Everybody looked to see somebody fall, but only saw a man and a woman standing staring at each other; the man with all the outward aspect of a Frenchman and a thorough Republican; the woman, evidently English.

What was said in this disappointing anti-climax, by the disciples of The Good Republican Brutus of Antiquity, except that it was something very voluble and loud, would have been as so much Hebrew or Chaldean to Miss Pross and her protector, though they had been all ears. But, they had no ears for anything in their surprise. For, it must be recorded, that not only was Miss Pross lost in amazement and agitation, but, Mr. Cruncher—though it seemed on his own separate and individual account—was in a state of the greatest wonder.

"What is the matter?" said the man who had caused Miss Pross to scream; speaking in a vexed, abrupt voice (though in a low tone), and in English.

"Oh, Solomon, dear Solomon!" cried Miss Pross, clapping her hands again. "After not setting eyes upon you or hearing of you for so long a time, do I find you here!"

"Don't call me Solomon. Do you want to be the death of me?" asked the man, in a furtive, frightened way.

"Brother, brother!" cried Miss Pross, bursting into tears. "Have I ever been so hard with you that you ask me such a cruel question?"

"Then hold your meddlesome tongue," said Solomon, "and come out, if you want to speak to me. Pay for your wine, and come out. Who's this man?"

Miss Pross, shaking her loving and dejected head at her by no means affectionate brother, said through her tears, "Mr. Cruncher."

"Let him come out too," said Solomon. "Does he think me a ghost?"

Apparently, Mr. Cruncher did, to judge from his looks. He said not a word, however, and Miss Pross, exploring the depths of her reticule through her tears with great difficulty, paid for her wine. As she did so, Solomon turned to the followers of The Good Republican Brutus of Antiquity, and offered a few words of explanation in the French language, which caused them all to relapse into their former places and pursuits.

"Now," said Solomon, stopping at the dark street corner, "what do you want?"

"How dreadfully unkind in a brother nothing has ever turned my love away from!" cried Miss Pross, "to give me such a greeting, and show me no affection."

"There. Con-found it! There," said Solomon, making a dab at Miss Pross's lips with his own. "Now are you content?"

Miss Pross only shook her head and wept in silence.

"If you expect me to be surprised," said her brother Solomon, "I am not surprised; I knew you were here; I know of most people who are here. If you really don't want to endanger my existence—which I half believe you do—go your ways as soon as possible, and let me go mine. I am busy. I am an official."

"My English brother Solomon," mourned Miss Pross, casting up her tear-fraught eyes, "that had the makings in him of one of the best and greatest of men in his native country, an official among foreigners, and such foreigners! I would almost sooner have seen the dear boy lying in his——"

"I said so!" cried her brother, interrupting. "I knew it. You want to be the death of me. I shall be rendered Suspected, by my own sister. Just as I am getting on!"

"The gracious and merciful Heavens forbid!" cried Miss Pross. "Far rather would I never see you again, dear Solomon, though I have ever loved you truly, and ever shall. Say but one affectionate word to me, and tell me there is nothing angry or estranged between us, and I will detain you no longer."

Good Miss Pross! As if the estrangement between them had come of any culpability of hers. As if Mr. Lorry had not known it for a fact years ago, in the quiet corner in Soho, that this precious brother had spent her money and left her!

He was saying the affectionate word, however, with a far more grudging condescension and patronage than he could have shown if their relative merits and positions had been reversed (which is invariably the case, all the world over), when Mr. Cruncher, touching him on the shoulder, hoarsely and unexpectedly interposed with the following singular question:

"I say! Might I ask the favour? As to whether your name is John Solomon, or Solomon John?"

The official turned towards him with a sudden distrust. He had not previously uttered a word.

"Come!" said Mr. Cruncher. "Speak out, you know." (Which, by the way, was more than he could do himself) "John Solomon, or Solomon John? She calls you Solomon, and she must know, being your sister. And *I* know you're John, you know. Which of the two goes first? And regarding that name of Pross, likewise. That warn't your name over the water."

"What do you mean?"

"Well, I don't know all I mean, for I can't call to mind what your name was, over the water."

"No?"

"No. But I'll swear it was a name of two syllables."

"Indeed?"

"Yes. T'other one's was one syllable. I know you. You was a spy-witness at the Bailey. What, in the name of the Father of Lies, own father to yourself, was you called at that time?"

"Barsad," said another voice, striking in.

"That's the name for a thousand pound!" cried Jerry.

The speaker who struck in, was Sydney Carton. He had his hands behind him under the skirts of his riding-coat, and he stood at Mr. Cruncher's elbow as negligently as he might have stood at the Old Bailey itself.

"Don't be alarmed, my dear Miss Pross. I arrived at Mr. Lorry's, to his surprise, yesterday evening; we agreed that I would not present myself elsewhere until all was well, or unless I could be useful; I present myself here, to beg a little talk with your brother. I wish you had a better employed brother than Mr. Barsad. I wish for your sake Mr. Barsad was not a Sheep of the Prisons."

Sheep was a cant word of the time for a spy, under the gaolers. The spy, who was pale, turned paler, and asked him how he dared——

"I'll tell you," said Sydney. "I lighted on you, Mr. Barsad, coming out of the prison of the Conciergerie while I was contemplating the walls, an hour or more ago. You have a face to be remembered, and I remember faces well. Made curious by seeing you in that connection, and having a reason, to which you are no stranger, for associating you with the misfortunes of a friend now very unfortunate, I walked in your direction. I walked into the wine-shop here, close after you, and sat near you. I had no difficulty in deducing from your unreserved conversation, and the rumour openly going about among your admirers, the nature of your calling. And gradually, what I had done at random, seemed to shape itself into a purpose, Mr. Barsad."

"What purpose?" the spy asked.

"It would be troublesome, and might be dangerous, to explain in the street. Could you favour me, in confidence, with some minutes of your company—at the office of Tellson's Bank, for instance?"

"Under a threat?"

"Oh! Did I say that?"

"Then, why should I go there?"

"Really, Mr. Barsad, I can't say, if you can't."

"Do you mean that you won't say, sir?" the spy irresolutely asked.

"You apprehend me very clearly, Mr. Barsad. I won't."

Carton's negligent recklessness of manner came powerfully in aid of his quickness and skill, in such a business as he had in his secret mind, and with such a man as he had to do with. His practised eye saw it, and made the most of it.

"Now, I told you so," said the spy, casting a reproachful look at his sister; "if any trouble comes of this, it's your doing."

"Come, come, Mr. Barsad!" exclaimed Sydney. "Don't be ungrateful. But for my great respect for your sister, I might not have led up so pleasantly to a little proposal that I wish to make for our mutual satisfaction. Do you go with me to the Bank?"

"I'll hear what you have got to say. Yes, I'll go with you."

"I propose that we first conduct your sister safely to the corner of her own street. Let me take your arm, Miss Pross.

This is not a good city, at this time, for you to be out in, unprotected; and, as your escort knows Mr. Barsad, I will invite him to Mr. Lorry's with us. Are we ready? Come then!"

Miss Pross recalled soon afterwards, and to the end of her life remembered, that as she pressed her hands on Sydney's arm and looked up in his face, imploring him to do no hurt to Solomon, there was a braced purpose in the arm and a kind of inspiration in the eyes, which not only contradicted his light manner, but changed and raised the man. She was too much occupied then with fears for the brother who so little deserved her affection, and with Sydney's friendly reassurances, adequately to heed what she observed.

They left her at the corner of the street, and Carton led the way to Mr. Lorry's, which was within a few minutes' walk. John Barsad, or Solomon Pross, walked at his side.

Mr. Lorry had just finished his dinner, and was sitting before a cheery little log or two of fire—perhaps looking into their blaze for the picture of that younger elderly gentleman from Tellson's, who had looked into the red coals at the Royal George at Dover, now a good many years ago. He turned his head as they entered, and showed the surprise with which he saw a stranger.

"Miss Pross's brother, sir," said Sydney. "Mr. Barsad."

"Barsad?" repeated the old gentleman, "Barsad? I have an association with the name—and with the face."

"I told you you had a remarkable face, Mr. Barsad," observed Carton, coolly. "Pray sit down."

As he took a chair himself, he supplied the link that Mr. Lorry wanted, by saying to him with a frown, "Witness at that trial." Mr. Lorry immediately remembered, and regarded his new visitor with an undisguised look of abhorrence.

"Mr. Barsad has been recognized by Miss Pross as the affectionate brother you have heard of," said Sydney, "and has acknowledged the relationship. I pass to worse news. Darnay has been arrested again."

Struck with consternation, the old gentleman exclaimed, "What do you tell me! I left him safe and free within these two hours, and am about to return to him!"

"Arrested for all that. When was it done, Mr. Barsad?"

"Just now, if at all."

"Mr. Barsad is the best authority possible, sir," said Sydney, "and I have it from Mr. Barsad's communication to a friend and brother Sheep over a bottle of wine, that the arrest has taken place. He left the messengers at the gate, and saw them admitted by the porter. There is no earthly doubt that he is retaken."

Mr. Lorry's business eye read in the speaker's face that it was loss of time to dwell upon the point. Confused, but sensible that something might depend on his presence of mind, he commanded himself, and was silently attentive.

"Now, I trust," said Sydney to him, "that the name and influence of Doctor Manette may stand him in as good stead to-morrow—you said he would be before the Tribunal again to-morrow, Mr. Barsad?——"

"Yes; I believe so."

"—In as good stead to-morrow as to-day. But it may not be so. I own to you, I am shaken, Mr. Lorry, by Doctor Manette's not having had the power to prevent this arrest."

"He may not have known of it beforehand," said Mr. Lorry.

"But that very circumstance would be alarming, when we remember how identified he is with his son-in-law."

"That's true," Mr. Lorry acknowledged, with his troubled hand at his chin, and his troubled eyes on Carton.

"In short," said Sydney, "this is a desperate time, when desperate games are played for desperate stakes. Let the Doctor play the winning game; I will play the losing one. No man's life here is worth purchase. Any one carried home by the people to-day, may be condemned to-morrow. Now, the stake I have resolved to play for, in case of the worst, is a friend in the Conciergerie. And the friend I purpose to myself to win, is Mr. Barsad."

"You need have good cards, sir," said the spy.

"I'll run them over. I'll see what I hold,—Mr. Lorry, you know what a brute I am; I wish you'd give me a little brandy."

It was put before him, and he drank off a glassful—drank off another glassful—pushed the bottle thoughtfully away.

"Mr. Barsad," he went on, in the tone of one who really was looking over a hand at cards: "Sheep of the prisons, emissary of Republican committees, now turnkey, now prisoner, always spy and secret informer, so much the more valuable here for being English that an Englishman is less open to suspicion of subornation in those characters than a Frenchman, represents himself to his employers under a false name. That's a very good card. Mr. Barsad, now in the employ of the republican French government, was formerly in the employ of the aristocratic English government, the enemy of France and freedom. That's an excellent card. Inference clear as day in this region of suspicion, that Mr. Barsad, still in the pay of the aristocratic English government, is the spy of Pitt, the treacherous foe of the Republic crouching in its bosom, the English traitor and agent of all mischief so much spoken of and so difficult to find. That's a card not to be beaten. Have you followed my hand, Mr. Barsad?"

"Not to understand your play," returned the spy, somewhat uneasily.

"I play my Ace, Denunciation of Mr. Barsad to the nearest Section Committee. Look over your hand, Mr. Barsad, and see what you have. Don't hurry."

He drew the bottle near, poured out another glassful of brandy, and drank it off. He saw that the spy was fearful of his drinking himself into a fit state for the immediate denunciation of him. Seeing it, he poured out and drank another glassful.

"Look over your hand carefully, Mr. Barsad. Take time."

It was a poorer hand than he suspected. Mr. Barsad saw losing cards in it that Sydney Carton knew nothing of. Thrown out of his honourable employment in England, through too much unsuccessful hard swearing there—not because he was not wanted there; our English reasons for vaunting our superiority to secrecy and spies are of very modern date—he knew that he had crossed the Channel, and accepted service in France: first, as a tempter and an eavesdropper among his own countrymen there: gradually, as a tempter and an eavesdropper among the natives. He knew that under the overthrown government he had been a spy upon Saint Antoine and Defarge's wine-shop; had received from the watchful police such heads of information concerning Doctor Manette's imprisonment, release, and history, as should serve him for an introduction to familiar conversation with the Defarges; and tried them on Madame Defarge, and had broken down with them signally. He always remembered with fear and trembling, that that terrible woman had knitted when he talked with her, and had looked ominously at him as her fingers moved. He had since seen her, in the Section of Saint Antoine, over and over again produce her knitted registers, and denounce people whose lives the guillotine then surely swallowed up. He knew, as every one employed as he was did, that he was never safe; that flight was impossible; that he was tied fast under the shadow of the axe; and that in spite of his utmost tergiversation and treachery in furtherance of the reigning terror, a word might bring it down upon him. Once denounced, and on such grave grounds as had just now been suggested to his mind, he foresaw that the dreadful woman of whose unrelenting character he had seen many proofs, would produce against him that fatal register, and would quash his last chance of life. Besides that all secret men are men soon terrified, here were surely cards enough of one black suit, to justify the holder in growing rather livid as he turned them over.

"You scarcely seem to like your hand," said Sydney, with the greatest composure. "Do you play?"

"I think, sir," said the spy, in the meanest manner, as he turned to Mr. Lorry, "I may appeal to a gentleman of your years and benevolence, to put it to this other gentleman, so much your junior, whether he can under any circumstances reconcile it to his station to play that Ace of which he has spoken. I admit that *I* am a spy, and that it is considered a discreditable station—though it must be filled by somebody; but this gentleman is no spy, and why should he so demean himself as to make himself one?"

"I play my Ace, Mr. Barsad," said Carton, taking the answer on himself, and looking at his watch, "without any scruple, in a very few minutes."

"I should have hoped, gentlemen both," said the spy, always striving to hook Mr. Lorry into the discussion, "that your respect for my sister——"

"I could not better testify my respect for your sister than by finally relieving her of her brother," said Sydney Carton.

"You think not, sir?"

"I have thoroughly made up my mind about it."

The smooth manner of the spy, curiously in dissonance with his ostentatiously rough dress, and probably with his usual demeanour, received such a check from the inscrutability of Carton,—who was a mystery to wiser and honester men than he,—that it faltered here and failed him. While he was at a loss, Carton said, resuming his former air of contemplating cards:

"And indeed, now I think again, I have a strong impression that I have another good card here, not yet enumerated. That friend and fellow-Sheep, who spoke of himself as pasturing in the country prisons; who was he?"

"French. You don't know him," said the spy, quickly.

"French, eh?" replied Carton, musing, and not appearing to notice him at all, though he echoed his word. "Well, he may be."

"Is, I assure you," said the spy; "though it's not important."

"Though it's not important," repeated Carton, in the same mechanical way—"though it's not important—No, it's not important. No. Yet I know the face."

"I think not. I am sure not. It can't be," said the spy.

"It—can't—be," muttered Sydney Carton, retrospectively, and filling his glass (which fortunately was a small one) again. "Can't—be. Spoke good French. Yet like a foreigner, I thought."

"Provincial," said the spy.

"No. Foreign!" cried Carton, striking his open hand on the table, as a light broke clearly on his mind. "Cly! Disguised, but the same man. We had that man before us at the Old Bailey."

"Now, there you are hasty, sir," said Barsad, with a smile that gave his aquiline nose an extra inclination to one side; "there you really give me an advantage over you. Cly (who I will unreservedly admit, at this distance of time, was a partner of mine) has been dead several years. I attended him in his last illness. He was buried in London, at the church of Saint Pancras-in-the-Fields. His unpopularity with the blackguard multitude at the moment prevented my following his remains, but I helped to lay him in his coffin."

Here, Mr. Lorry became aware, from where he sat, of a most remarkable goblin shadow on the wall. Tracing it to its source, he discovered it to be caused by a sudden extraordinary rising and stiffening of all the risen and stiff hair on Mr. Cruncher's head.

"Let us be reasonable," said the spy, "and let us be fair. To show you how mistaken you are, and what an unfounded assumption yours is, I will lay before you a certificate of Cly's burial, which I happen to have carried in my pocketbook," with a hurried hand he produced and opened it, "ever since. There it is. Oh, look at it, look at it! You may take it in your hand; it's no forgery."

Here, Mr. Lorry perceived the reflection on the wall to elongate, and Mr. Cruncher rose and stepped forward. His hair could not have been more violently on end, if it had been that moment dressed by the Cow with the crumpled horn in the house that Jack built.

Unseen by the spy, Mr. Cruncher stood at his side, and touched him on the shoulder like a ghostly bailiff.

"That there Roger Cly, master," said Mr. Cruncher, with a taciturn and iron-bound visage. "So *you* put him in his coffin?"

"I did."

"Who took him out of it?"

Barsad leaned back in his chair, and stammered. "What do you mean?"

"I mean," said Mr. Cruncher, "that he warn't never in it. No! Not he! I'll have my head took off, if he was ever in it."

The spy looked around at the two gentlemen; they both looked in unspeakable astonishment at Jerry.

"I tell you," said Jerry, "that you buried paving-stones and earth in that there coffin. Don't go and tell *me* that you buried Cly. It was a take-in. Me and two more knows it."

"How do you know it?"

"What's that to you? Ecod!" growled Mr. Cruncher, "it's you I have got an old grudge agin, is it, with your shameful impositions upon tradesmen! I'd catch hold of your throat and choke you for half a guinea."

Sydney Carton, who, with Mr. Lorry, had been lost in amazement at this turn of the business, here requested Mr. Cruncher to moderate and explain himself.

"At another time, sir," he returned, evasively, "the present time is ill-conwenient for explainin'. What I stand to, is that he knows well wot that there Cly was never in that there coffin. Let him say he was, in so much as a word of one syllable, and I'll either catch hold of his throat and choke him for half a guinea"; Mr. Cruncher dwelt upon this as quite a liberal offer; "or I'll out and announce him."

"Humph! I see one thing," said Carton. "I hold another card, Mr. Barsad. Impossible, here in raging Paris, with Suspicion filling the air, for you to outlive denunciation, when you are in communication with another aristocratic spy of the same antecedents as yourself, who, moreover,

great house of Tellson's as a blind, and that
an unlawful occupation of an infamous
you have, don't expect me to befriend you
back to England. If you have, don't expect me
secret. Tellson's shall not be imposed upon."

sir," pleaded the abashed Mr. Cruncher, "that a
like yourself wot I've had the honour of odd job-
grey at it, would think twice about harming of
if it wos so—I don't say it is, but even if it wos.
h it is to be took into account that if it wos, it
, even then, be all o' one side. There'd be two
it. There might be medical doctors at the present
picking up their guineas where a honest tradesman
ick up his fardens—fardens! no, nor yet his half far-
half fardens! no, nor yet his quarter—a banking
like smoke at Tellson's, and a cocking their medical
at that tradesman on the sly, going in and out to their
carriages—ah! equally like smoke, if not more so.
l, that 'ud be imposing too, on Tellson's. For you cannot
se the goose and not the gander. And here's Mrs.
uncher, or leastways wos in the Old England times, and
ould be to-morrow, if cause given, a floppin agin the busi-
ess to that degree as is ruinating—stark ruinating!
Whereas them medical doctors' wives don't flop—catch
'em at it! Or, if they flop, their floppin goes in favour of
more patients, and how can you rightly have one without
the t'other? Then, wot with undertakers, and wot with
parish clerks, and wot with sextons, and wot with private
watchmen (all awaricious and all in it), a man wouldn't get
much by it, even if it wos so. And wot little man did get,
would never prosper with him, Mr. Lorry. He'd never have
no good of it; he'd want all along to be out of the line, if he
could see his way out, being once in—even if it wos so."

"Ugh!" cried Mr. Lorry, rather relenting, nevertheless. "I
am shocked at the sight of you."

"Now, what I would humbly offer to you, sir," pursued
Mr. Cruncher, "even if it wos so, which I don't say it is—"

has the mystery about him of having feigned death and
come to life again! A plot in the prisons, of the foreigner
against the Republic. A strong card—a certain Guillotine
card! Do you play?"

"No!" returned the spy. "I throw up. I confess that we
were so unpopular with the outrageous mob, that I only got
away from England at the risk of being ducked to death, and
that Cly was so ferreted up and down, that he never would
have got away at all but for that sham. Though how this man
knows it was a sham, is a wonder of wonders to me."

"Never you trouble your head about this man," retorted
the contentious Mr. Cruncher; "you'll have trouble
enough with giving your attention to that gentleman. And
look here! Once more!"—Mr. Cruncher could not be
restrained from making rather an ostentatious parade of
his liberality—"I'd catch hold of your throat and choke
you for half a guinea."

The Sheep of the prisons turned from him to Sydney
Carton, and said, with more decision, "It has come to a
point. I go on duty soon, and can't overstay my time. You told
me you had a proposal; what is it? Now, it is of no use asking
too much of me. Ask me to do anything in my office, putting
my head in great extra danger, and I had better trust my life
to the chances of a refusal than the chances of consent. In
short, I should make that choice. You talk of desperation. We
are all desperate here. Remember! I may denounce you if I
think proper, and I can swear my way through stone walls,
and so can others. Now, what do you want with me?"

"Not very much. You are a turnkey at the Conciergerie?"

"I tell you once for all, there is no such thing as an escape
possible," said the spy firmly.

"Why need you tell me what I have not asked? You are a
turnkey at the Conciergerie?"

"I am sometimes."

"You can be when you choose?"

"I can pass in and out when I choose."

Sydney Carton filled another glass with brandy, poured it

slowly out upon the hearth, and watched it as it dropped. It being all spent, he said, rising:

"So far, we have spoken before these two, because it was as well that the merits of the cards should not rest solely between you and me. Come into the dark room here, and let us have one final word alone."

THE GA

WHILE Sydney Carton and the Shee   away were in the adjoining dark room,   eyes that not a sound was heard, Mr. Lorry look   own considerable doubt and mistrust. That honest   We manner of receiving the look, did not inspire con   san changed the leg on which he rested, as often as   C fifty of those limbs, and were trying them all; he e.   w his finger-nails with a very questionable closeness o   tion; and whenever Mr. Lorry's eye caught his, he was with that peculiar kind of short cough requiring the ho of a hand before it, which is seldom, if ever, known to be infirmity attendant on perfect openness of character.

"Jerry," said Mr. Lorry. "Come here."

Mr. Cruncher came forward sideways, with one of his shoulders in advance of him.

"What have you been, besides a messenger?"

After some cogitation, accompanied with an intent look at his patron, Mr. Cruncher conceived the luminous idea of replying, "Agricultooral character."

"My mind misgives me much," said Mr. Lorry, angrily shaking a forefinger at him, "that you have used the

respectable an
you have ha
description. I
when you ge
to keep your
"I hope,
gentleman
bing till I'
me, even
And whi
wouldn't
sides to
hour, a
don't p
dens—

"Don't prevaricate," said Mr. Lorry.

"No, I will *not*, sir," returned Mr. Cruncher, as if nothing were further from his thoughts or practice—"which I don't say it is—wot I would humbly offer to you, sir, would be this. Upon that there stool, at that there Bar, sets that there boy of mine, brought up and growed up to be a man, wot will errand you, message you, general-light-job you, till your heels is where your head is, if such should be your wishes. If it was so, which I still don't say it is (for I will not prewaricate to you, sir) let that there boy keep his father's place, and take care of his mother; don't blow upon that boy's father—do not do it, sir—and let that father go into the line of the reg'lar diggin', and make amends for what he would have undug—if it wos so—by diggin' of 'em in with a will, and with conwictions respectin' the futur' keepin' of 'em safe. That, Mr. Lorry," said Mr. Cruncher, wiping his forehead with his arm, as an announcement that he had arrived at the peroration of his discourse, "is wot I would respectfully offer to you, sir. A man don't see all this here a goin' on dreadful round him, in the way of Subjects without heads, dear me, plentiful enough fur to bring the price down to porterage and hardly that, without havin' his serious thoughts of things. And these here would be mine, if it wos so, entreatin' of you fur to bear in mind that wot I said just now, I up and said in the good cause when I might have kep' it back.".

"That at least is true," said Mr. Lorry. "Say no more now. It may be that I shall yet stand your friend, if you deserve it, and repent in action—not in words. I want no more words."

Mr. Cruncher knuckled his forehead, as Sydney Carton and the spy returned from the dark room. "Adieu, Mr. Barsad," said the former; "our arrangement thus made, you have nothing to fear from me."

He sat down in a chair on the hearth, over against Mr. Lorry. When they were alone, Mr. Lorry asked him what he had done?

"Not much. If it should go ill with the prisoner, I have ensured access to him, once."

Mr. Lorry's countenance fell.

"It is all I could do," said Carton. "To propose too much would be to put this man's head under the axe, and, as he himself said, nothing worse could happen to him if he were denounced. It was obviously the weakness of the position. There is no help for it."

"But access to him," said Mr. Lorry, "if it should go ill before the Tribunal, will not save him."

"I never said it would."

Mr. Lorry's eyes gradually sought the fire; his sympathy with his darling, and the heavy disappointment of this second arrest, gradually weakened them; he was an old man now, overborne with anxiety of late, and his tears fell.

"You are a good man and a true friend," said Carton, in an altered voice. "Forgive me if I notice that you are affected. I could not see my father weep, and sit by, careless. And I could not respect your sorrow more, if you were my father. You are free from that misfortune, however."

Though he said the last words, with a slip into his usual manner, there was a true feeling and respect both in his tone and in his touch, that Mr. Lorry, who had never seen the better side of him, was wholly unprepared for. He gave him his hand, and Carton gently pressed it.

"To return to poor Darnay," said Carton. "Don't tell Her of this interview, or this arrangement. It would not enable Her to go to see him. She might think it was contrived, in case of the worst, to convey to him the means of anticipating the sentence."

Mr. Lorry had not thought of that, and he looked quickly at Carton to see if it were in his mind. It seemed to be; he returned the look, and evidently understood it.

"She might think a thousand things," Carton said, "and any of them would only add to her trouble. Don't speak of me to her. As I said to you when I first came, I had better not see her. I can put my hand out, to do any little helpful work for her that my hand can find to do, without that. You are going to her, I hope? She must be very desolate to-night."

"I am going now, directly."

"I am glad of that. She has such a strong attachment to you and reliance on you. How does she look?"

"Anxious and unhappy, but very beautiful."

"Ah!"

It was a long, grieving sound, like a sigh—almost like a sob. It attracted Mr. Lorry's eyes to Carton's face, which was turned to the fire. A light, or a shade (the old gentleman could not have said which), passed from it as swiftly as a change will sweep over a hillside on a wild bright day, and he lifted his foot to put back one of the little flaming logs, which was tumbling forward. He wore the white riding-coat and top-boots, then in vogue, and the light of the fire touching their light surfaces made him look very pale, with his long brown hair, all untrimmed, hanging loose about him. His indifference to fire was sufficiently remarkable to elicit a word of remonstrance from Mr. Lorry: his boot was still upon the hot embers of the flaming log, when it had broken under the weight of his foot.

"I forgot it," he said.

Mr. Lorry's eyes were again attracted to his face. Taking note of the wasted air which clouded the naturally handsome features, and having the expression of prisoners' faces fresh in his mind, he was strongly reminded of that expression.

"And your duties here have drawn to an end, sir?" said Carton, turning to him.

"Yes. As I was telling you last night when Lucie came in so unexpectedly, I have at length done all that I can do here. I hoped to have left them in perfect safety, and then to have quitted Paris. I have my Leave to Pass. I was ready to go."

They were both silent.

"Yours is a long life to look back upon, sir?" said Carton, wistfully.

"I am in my seventy-eighth year."

"You have been useful all your life; steadily and constantly occupied; trusted, respected, and looked up to?"

"I have been a man of business, ever since I have been a man. Indeed, I may say that I was a man of business when a boy."

"See what a place you fill at seventy-eight. How many people will miss you when you leave it empty!"

"A solitary old bachelor," answered Mr. Lorry, shaking his head. "There is nobody to weep for me."

"How can you say that! Wouldn't She weep for you? Wouldn't her child?"

"Yes, yes, thank God. I didn't quite mean what I said."

"It *is* a thing to thank God for; is it not?"

"Surely, surely."

"If you could say, with truth, to your own solitary heart, to-night, 'I have secured to myself the love and attachment, the gratitude or respect, of no human creature; I have won myself a tender place in no regard; I have done nothing good or serviceable to be remembered by!' your seventy-eight years would be seventy-eight heavy curses; would they not?"

"You say truly, Mr. Carton; I think they would be."

Sydney turned his eyes again upon the fire, and, after a silence of a few moments, said:

"I should like to ask you:—Does your childhood seem far off? Do the days when you sat at your mother's knee, seem days of very long ago?"

Responding to his softened manner, Mr. Lorry answered:

"Twenty years back, yes; at this time of my life, no. For, as I draw closer and closer to the end, I travel in the circle, nearer and nearer to the beginning. It seems to be one of the kind smoothings and preparings of the way. My heart is touched now, by many remembrances that had long fallen asleep, of my pretty young mother (and I so old!), and by many associations of the days when what we call the World was not so real with me, and my faults were not confirmed in me."

"I understand the feeling!" exclaimed Carton, with a bright flush. "And you are the better for it?"

"I hope so."

Carton terminated the conversation here, by rising to help him on with his outer coat. "But you," said Mr. Lorry, reverting to the theme, "you are young."

"Yes," said Carton. "I am not old, but my young way was never the way to age. Enough of me."

"And of me, I am sure," said Mr. Lorry. "Are you going out?"

"I'll walk with you to her gate. You know my vagabond and restless habits. If I should prowl about the streets a long time, don't be uneasy; I shall reappear in the morning. You go to the Court to-morrow?"

"Yes, unhappily."

"I shall be there, but only as one of the crowd. My Spy will find a place for me. Take my arm, sir."

Mr. Lorry did so, and they went down-stairs and out in the streets. A few minutes brought them to Mr. Lorry's destination. Carton left him there; but lingered at a little distance, and turned back to the gate again when it was shut, and touched it. He had heard of her going to the prison every day. "She came out here," he said, looking about him, "turned this way, must have trod on these stones often. Let me follow in her steps."

It was ten o'clock at night when he stood before the prison of La Force, where she had stood hundreds of times. A little wood-sawyer, having closed his shop, was smoking his pipe at his shop-door.

"Good night, citizen," said Sydney Carton, pausing in going by; for the man eyed him inquisitively.

"Good night, citizen."

"How goes the Republic?"

"You mean the Guillotine. Not ill. Sixty-three to-day. We shall mount to a hundred soon. Samson and his men complain sometimes, of being exhausted. Ha, ha, ha! He is so droll, that Samson. Such a barber!"

"Do you often go to see him——"

"Shave? Always. Every day. What a barber! You have seen him at work?"

"Never."

"Go and see him when he has a good batch. Figure this to yourself, citizen; he shaved the sixty-three today, in less than two pipes. Less than two pipes. Word of honour!"

As the grinning little man held out the pipe he was smoking to explain how he timed the execution, Carton was so sensible of a rising desire to strike the life out of him, that he turned away.

"But you are not English," said the wood-sawyer, "though you wear English dress?"

"Yes," said Carton, pausing again, and answering over his shoulder.

"You speak like a Frenchman."

"I am an old student here."

"Aha, a perfect Frenchman! Good night, Englishman."

"Good night, citizen."

"But go and see that droll dog," the little man persisted, calling after him. "And take a pipe with you!"

Sydney had not gone far out of sight, when he stopped in the middle of the street under a glimmering lamp, and wrote with his pencil on a scrap, of paper. Then, traversing with the decided step of one who remembered the way well, several dark and dirty streets—much dirtier than usual, for the best public thoroughfares remained uncleansed in those times of terror—he stopped at a chemist's shop, which the owner was closing with his own hands. A small, dim, crooked shop, kept in a tortuous, uphill thoroughfare, by a small, dim, crooked man.

Giving this citizen, too, good night, as he confronted him at his counter, he laid the scrap of paper before him. "Whew"; the chemist whistled softly, as he read it. "Hi! hi, hi!"

Sydney Carton took no heed, and the chemist said:

"For you, citizen?"

"For me."

"You will be careful to keep them separate, citizen. You know the consequences of mixing them?"

"Perfectly."

Certain small packets were made and given to him. He put them, one by one, in the breast of his inner coat, counted out the money for them, and deliberately left the shop. "There is nothing more to do," said he, glancing upward at the moon, "until to-morrow. I can't sleep."

It was a reckless manner, the manner in which he said these words aloud under the fast-sailing clouds, nor was it more expressive of negligence than defiance. It was the settled manner of a tired man, who had wandered and struggled and got lost, but who at length struck into his road and saw its end.

Long ago, when he had been famous among his earliest competitors as a youth of great promise, he had followed his father to the grave. His mother had died, years before. These solemn words, which had been read at his father's grave, arose in his mind as he went down the dark streets, among the heavy shadows, with the moon and the clouds sailing on high above him. "I am the resurrection and the life, saith the Lord: he that believeth in me, though he were dead, yet shall he live: and whosoever liveth and believeth in me, shall never die."[7]

In a city dominated by the axe, alone at night, with natural sorrow rising in him for the sixty-three who had been that day put to death, and for to-morrow's victims then awaiting their doom in the prisons, and still of to-morrow's and to-morrow's, the chain of association that brought the words home, like a rusty old ship's anchor from the deep, might have been easily found. He did not seek it, but repeated them and went on.

With a solemn interest in the lighted windows where the people were going to rest, forgetful through a few calm hours of the horrors surrounding them; in the towers of the churches, where no prayers were said, for the popular revulsion had even travelled that length of self-destruction from years of priestly impostors, plunderers, and profligates; in the distant burial-places reserved, as they wrote upon the gates, for Eternal Sleep; in the abounding gaols; and in the streets along which the sixties rolled to a death which had become so common and material, that no sorrowful story of a haunting Spirit ever arose among the people out of all the working of the Guillotine; with a solemn interest in the whole life and death of the city settling down to its short nightly pause in fury; Sydney Carton crossed the Seine again for the lighter streets.

Few coaches were abroad, for riders in coaches were liable to be suspected, and gentility hid his head in red nightcaps, and put on heavy shoes, and trudged. But, the theatres were all well filled, and the people poured cheerfully out as he passed, and went chatting home. At one of the theatre doors, there was a little girl with a mother, looking for a way across the street through the mud. He carried the child over, and before the timid arm was loosed from his neck asked her for a kiss.

"I am the resurrection and the life, saith the Lord: he that believeth in me, though he were dead, yet shall he live: and whosoever liveth and believeth in me, shall never die."

Now, that the streets were quiet and the night wore on, the words were in the echoes of his feet, and were in the air. Perfectly calm and steady, he sometimes repeated them to himself as he walked; but, he heard them always.

The night wore out, and, as he stood upon the bridge listening to the water as it splashed the river-walls of the Island of Paris, where the picturesque confusion of houses and cathedral shone bright in the light of the moon, the day came coldly, looking like a dead face out of the sky. Then, the night, with the moon and the stars, turned pale and died, and for a little while it seemed as if Creation were delivered over to Death's dominion.

But the glorious sun, rising, seemed to strike those words, that burden of the night, straight and warm to his heart in its long bright rays. And looking along them, with reverently shaded eyes, a bridge of light appeared to span the air between him and the sun, while the river sparkled under it.

The strong tide, so swift, so deep, and certain, was like a congenial friend, in the morning stillness. He walked by the stream, far from the houses, and in the light and warmth of the sun fell asleep on the bank. When he awoke and was afoot again, he lingered there yet a little longer, watching an eddy that turned and turned purposeless, until the stream absorbed it, and carried it on to the sea.—"Like me!"

A trading-boat, with a sail of the softened colour of a dead leaf, then glided into his view, floated by him, and died away. As its silent track in the water disappeared, the prayer that had broken up out of his heart for a merciful consideration of all his poor blindness and errors, ended in the words, "I am the resurrection and the life."

Mr. Lorry was already out when he got back, and it was easy to surmise where the good old man was gone. Sydney Carton drank nothing but a little coffee, ate some bread, and, having washed and changed to refresh himself, went out to the place of trial.

The court was all astir and a-buzz, when the black sheep—whom many fell away from in dread—pressed him into an obscure corner among the crowd. Mr. Lorry was there, and Doctor Manette was there. She was there, sitting beside her father.

When her husband was brought in, she turned a look upon him, so sustaining, so encouraging, so full of admiring love, and pitying tenderness, yet so courageous for his sake, that it called the healthy blood into his face, brightened his glance, and animated his heart. If there had been any eyes to notice the influence of her look, on Sydney Carton, it would have been seen to be the same influence exactly.

Before that unjust Tribunal, there was little or no order of procedure, ensuring to any accused person any reasonable hearing. There could have been no such Revolution, if all laws, forms, and ceremonies, had not first been so monstrously abused, that the suicidal vengeance of the Revolution was to scatter them all to the winds.

Every eye was turned to the jury. The same determined patriots and good republicans as yesterday and the day before, and to-morrow and the day after. Eager and prominent among them, one man with a craving face, and his fingers perpetually hovering about his lips, whose appearance gave great satisfaction to the spectators. A life-thirsting, cannibal-looking, bloody-minded juryman, the Jacques Three of Saint Antoine. The whole jury, as a jury of dogs empanelled to try the deer.

Every eye then turned to the five judges and the public prosecutor. No favourable leaning in that quarter to-day. A fell, uncompromising, murderous business-meaning there. Every eye then sought some other eye in the crowd, and gleamed at it approvingly; and heads nodded at one another before bending forward with a strained attention.

Charles Evrémonde, called Darnay. Released yesterday. Reaccused and retaken yesterday. Indictment delivered to him last night. Suspected and Denounced enemy of the Republic, Aristocrat, one of a family of tyrants, one of a race proscribed, for that they had used their abolished privileges to the infamous oppression of the people. Charles Evrémonde, called Darnay, in right of such proscription, absolutely Dead in Law.

To this effect, in as few or fewer words, the Public Prosecutor.

The President asked, was the Accused openly denounced, or secretly?

"Openly, President."

"By whom?"

"Three voices. Ernest Defarge, wine vendor of Saint Antoine."

"Good."

"Thérèse Defarge, his wife."

"Good."

"Alexandre Manette, physician."

A great uproar took place in the court, and in the midst of it, Doctor Manette was seen, pale and trembling, standing where he had been seated.

"President, I indignantly protest to you that this is a forgery and a fraud. You know the accused to be the husband of my daughter. My daughter, and those dear to her, are far dearer to me than my life. Who and where is the false conspirator who says that I denounce the husband of my child?"

"Citizen Manette, be tranquil. To fail in submission of the authority of the Tribunal would be to put yourself out of Law. As to what is dearer to you than life, nothing can be so dear to a good citizen as the Republic."

Loud acclamations hailed this rebuke. The President rang his bell, and with warmth resumed.

"If the Republic should demand of you the sacrifice of your child herself, you would have no duty but to sacrifice her. Listen to what is to follow. In the meanwhile, be silent!"

Frantic acclamations were again raised. Doctor Manette sat down, with his eyes looking around, and his lips trembling; his daughter drew closer to him. The craving man on the jury rubbed his hands together, and restored the usual hand to his mouth.

Defarge was produced, when the court was quiet enough to admit of his being heard, and rapidly expounded the story of the imprisonment, and of his having been a mere boy in the Doctor's service, and of the release, and of the state of the prisoner when released and delivered to him. This short examination followed, for the court was quick with its work.

"You did good service at the taking of the Bastille, citizen?"

"I believe so."

Here an excited woman screeched from the crowd: "You were one of the best patriots there. Why not say so? You were a cannonier that day there, and you were among the first to enter the accursed fortress when it fell. Patriots, I speak the truth!"

It was The Vengeance who, amidst the warm commendations of the audience, thus assisted the proceedings. The President rang his bell; but, The Vengeance, warming with encouragement, shrieked, "I defy that bell!" wherein she was likewise much commended.

"Inform the Tribunal of what you did that day, within the Bastille, citizen."

"I knew," said Defarge, looking down at his wife, who stood at the bottom of the steps on which he was raised, looking steadily up at him; "I knew that this prisoner, of whom I speak, had been confined in a cell known as One Hundred and Five, North Tower. I knew it from himself. He knew himself by no other name than One Hundred and Five, North Tower, when he made shoes under my care. As I serve my gun that day, I resolve, when the place shall fall, to examine that cell. It falls. I mount to the cell, with a fellow-citizen who is one of the Jury, directed by a gaoler. I examine it, very closely. In a hole in the chimney, where a stone has been worked out and replaced, I find a written paper. That is that written paper. I have made it my business to examine some specimens of the writing of Doctor Manette. This is the writing of Doctor Manette. I confide this paper, in the writing of Doctor Manette, to the hands of the President."

"Let it be read."

In the dead silence and stillness—the prisoner under trial looking lovingly at his wife, his wife only looking from him to look with solicitude at her father, Doctor Manette keeping his eyes fixed on the reader, Madame Defarge never taking hers from the prisoner, Defarge never taking his from his feasting wife, and all the other eyes there intent upon the Doctor, who saw none of them—the paper was read as follows.

10

THE SUBSTANCE OF THE SHADOW

———✦———

"I—ALEXANDRE MANETTE,[8] unfortunate physician, native of Beauvais, and afterwards resident in Paris—write this melancholy paper in my doleful cell in the Bastille, during the last month of the year 1767. I write it at stolen intervals, under every difficulty. I design to secrete it in the wall of the chimney, where I have slowly and laboriously made a place of concealment for it. Some pitying hand may find it there, when I and my sorrows are dust.

"These words are formed by the rusty iron point with which I write with difficulty in scrapings of soot and charcoal from the chimney, mixed with blood, in the last month of the tenth year of my captivity. Hope has quite departed from my breast. I know from terrible warnings I have noted in myself that my reason will not long remain unimpaired, but I solemnly declare that I am at this time in the possession of my right mind—that my memory is exact and circumstantial—and that I write the truth as I shall answer for these my last recorded words, whether they be ever read by men or not, at the Eternal Judgment-seat.

"One cloudy moonlight night, in the third week of December (I think the twenty-second of the month) in the year 1757, I was walking on a retired part of the quay by the Seine for the refreshment of the frosty air, at an hour's distance from my place of residence in the Street of the School of Medicine, when a carriage came along behind me, driven very fast. As I stood aside to let that carriage pass, apprehensive that it might otherwise run me down, a head was put out at the window, and a voice called to the driver to stop.

"The carriage stopped as soon as the driver could rein in his horses, and the same voice called to me by my name. I answered. The carriage was then so far in advance of me that two gentlemen had time to open the door and alight before I came up with it. I observed that they were both wrapped in cloaks, and appeared to conceal themselves. As they stood side by side near the carriage door, I also observed that they both looked of about my own age, or rather younger, and that they were greatly alike, in stature, manner, voice, and (as far as I could see) face too.

" 'You are Doctor Manette?' said one.

" 'I am.'

" 'Doctor Manette, formerly of Beauvais,' said the other; 'the young physician, originally an expert surgeon, who within the last year or two has made a rising reputation in Paris?'

" 'Gentlemen,' I returned, 'I am that Doctor Manette of whom you speak so graciously.'

" 'We have been to your residence,' said the first, 'and not being so fortunate as to find you there, and being informed that you were probably walking in this direction, we followed, in the hope of overtaking you. Will you please to enter the carriage?'

"The manner of both was imperious, and they both moved, as these words were spoken, so as to place me between themselves and the carriage door. They were armed. I was not.

" 'Gentlemen,' said I, 'pardon me; but I usually inquire who does me the honour to seek my assistance, and what is the nature of the case to which I am summoned.'

"The reply to this was made by him who had spoken second. 'Doctor, your clients are people of condition. As to the nature of the case, our confidence in your skill assures us that you will ascertain it for yourself better than we can describe it. Enough. Will you please enter the carriage?'

"I could do nothing but comply, and I entered it in silence. They both entered after me—the last springing in, after putting up the steps. The carriage turned about, and drove on at its former speed.

"I repeat this conversation exactly as it occurred. I have no doubt that it is, word for word, the same. I describe everything exactly as it took place, constraining my mind not to wander from the task. When I make the broken marks that follow here, I leave off for the time, and put my paper in its hiding place. . . .

"The carriage left the streets behind, passed the North Barrier, and emerged upon the country road. At two-thirds of a league from the Barrier—I did not estimate the distance at that time, but afterwards when I traversed it—it struck out of the main avenue, and presently stopped at a solitary house. We all three alighted, and walked, by a damp soft footpath in a garden where a neglected fountain had overflowed, to the door of the house. It was not opened immediately, in answer to the ringing of the bell, and one of my two conductors struck the man who opened it, with his heavy riding-glove, across the face.

"There was nothing in this action to attract my particular attention, for I had seen common people struck more commonly than dogs. But, the other of the two, being angry likewise, struck the man in like manner with his arm; the look and bearing of the brothers were then so exactly alike, that I then first perceived them to be twin brothers.

"From the time of our alighting at the outer gate (which we found locked, and which one of the brothers had opened to admit us, and had relocked), I had heard cries proceeding from an upper chamber. I was conducted to this chamber straight, the cries growing louder as we ascended the stairs, and I found a patient in a high fever of the brain, lying on a bed.

"The patient was a woman of great beauty, and young; assuredly not much past twenty. Her hair was torn and ragged, and her arms were bound to her sides with sashes and handkerchiefs. I noticed that these bonds were all portions of a gentleman's dress. On one of them, which was a fringed scarf for a dress ceremony, I saw the armorial bearings of a Noble, and the letter E.

"I saw this, within the first minute of my contemplation of the patient; for, in her restless strivings she had turned over on her face on the edge of the bed, had drawn the end of the scarf into her mouth, and was in danger of suffocation. My first act was to put out my hand to relieve her breathing; and in moving the scarf aside, the embroidery in the corner caught my sight.

"I turned her gently over, placed my hands upon her breast to calm her and keep her down, and looked into her face. Her eyes were dilated and wild, and she constantly uttered piercing shrieks, and repeated the words, 'My husband, my father, and my brother!' and then counted up to twelve, and said, 'Hush!' For an instant, and no more, she would pause to listen, and then the piercing shrieks would begin again, and she would repeat the cry, 'My husband, my father, and my brother!' and would count up to twelve, and say 'Hush!' There was no variation in the order, or the manner. There was no cessation, but the regular moment's pause, in the utterance of these sounds.

" 'How long,' I asked, 'has this lasted?'

"To distinguish the brothers, I will call them the elder and the younger; by the elder, I mean, him who exercised the most authority. It was the elder who replied, 'Since about this hour last night.'

" 'She has a husband, a father, and a brother?'

" 'A brother.'

" 'I do not address her brother?'

"He answered with great contempt, 'No.'

" 'She has some recent association with the number twelve?'

"The younger brother impatiently rejoined, 'With twelve o'clock.'

" 'See, gentlemen,' said I, still keeping my hands upon her breast, 'how useless I am, as you have brought me! If I had known what I was coming to see, I could have come provided. As it is, time must be lost. There are no medicines to be obtained in this lonely place.'

"The elder brother looked to the younger, who said haughtily, 'There is a case of medicines here'; and brought it from a closet, and put it on the table. . . .

"I opened some of the bottles, smelt them, and put the stoppers to my lips. If I had wanted to use anything save narcotic medicines that were poisons in themselves, I would not have administered any of those.

" 'Do you doubt them?' asked the younger brother.

" 'You see, monsieur, I am going to use them,' I replied, and said no more.

"I made the patient swallow, with great difficulty, and after many efforts, the dose that I desired to give. As I intended to repeat it after a while, and as it was necessary to watch its influence, I then sat down by the side of the bed. There was a timid and suppressed woman in attendance (wife of the man down-stairs), who had retreated into a corner. The house was damp and decayed, indifferently furnished—evidently, recently occupied and temporarily used. Some thick old hangings had been nailed up before the windows, to deaden the sound of the shrieks. They continued to be uttered in their regular succession, with the cry, 'My husband, my father, and my brother!' the counting up to twelve, and 'Hush!' The frenzy was so violent, that I had not unfastened the bandages restraining the arms; but I had looked to them, to see that they were not painful. The only spark of encouragement in the case, was, that my hand upon the sufferer's breast had this much soothing influence, that for minutes at a time it tranquilised the figure. It had no effect upon the cries; no pendulum could be more regular.

"For the reason that my hand had this effect (I assume), I had sat by the side of the bed for half an hour, with the two brothers looking on, before the elder said:

" 'There is another patient.'

"I was startled, and asked, 'Is it a pressing case?'

" 'You had better see,' he carelessly answered; and took up a light. . . .

"The other patient lay in a back room across a second staircase, which was a species of loft over a stable. There was a low plastered ceiling to a part of it; the rest was open, to the ridge of the tiled roof, and there were beams across. Hay and straw were stored in that portion of the place, faggots for firing, and a heap of apples in sand. I had to pass through that part, to get at the other. My memory is circumstantial and unshaken. I try it with these details, and I see them all, in this my cell in the Bastille, near the close of the tenth year of my captivity, as I saw them all that night.

"On some hay on the ground, with a cushion thrown under his head, lay a handsome peasant boy—a boy of not more than seventeen at the most. He lay on his back, with his teeth set, his right hand clenched on his breast, and his glaring eyes looking straight upward. I could not see where his wound was, as I kneeled on one knee over him; but, I could see that he was dying of a wound from a sharp point.

" 'I am a doctor, my poor fellow,' said I. 'Let me examine it.'

" 'I do not want it examined,' he answered; 'let it be.'

"It was under his hand, and I soothed him to let me move his hand away. The wound was a sword-thrust, received from twenty to twenty-four hours before, but no skill could have saved him if it had been looked to without delay. He was then dying fast. As I turned my eyes to the elder brother, I saw him looking down at this handsome boy whose life was ebbing out, as if he were a wounded bird, or hare, or rabbit; not at all as if he were a fellow-creature.

" 'How has this been done, monsieur?' said I.

" 'A crazed young common dog! A serf! Forced my brother to draw upon him, and has fallen by my brother's sword—like a gentleman.'

"There was no touch of pity, sorrow, or kindred humanity in this answer. The speaker seemed to acknowledge that it was inconvenient to have that different order of creature dying there, and that it would have been better if he had died in the usual obscure routine of his vermin kind. He was quite incapable of any compassionate feeling about the boy, or about his fate.

"The boy's eyes had slowly moved to him as he had spoken, and they now slowly moved to me.

" 'Doctor, they are very proud, these Nobles; but we common dogs are proud too, sometimes. They plunder us, outrage us, beat us, kill us; but we have a little pride left, sometimes. She—have you seen her, Doctor?'

"The shrieks and the cries were audible there, though subdued by the distance. He referred to them, as if she were lying in our presence.

"I said, 'I have seen her.'

" 'She is my sister, Doctor. They have had their shameful rights, these Nobles, in the modesty and virtue of our sisters, many years, but we have had good girls among us. I know it, and have heard my father say so. She was a good girl. She was betrothed to a good young man, too: a tenant of his. We were all tenants of his—that man's who stands there. The other is his brother, the worst of of a bad race.'

"It was with the greatest difficulty that the boy gathered bodily force to speak; but, his spirit spoke with a dreadful emphasis.

" 'We were so robbed by that man who stands there, as all we common dogs are by those superior Beings—taxed by him without mercy, obliged to work for him without pay, obliged to grind our corn at his mill, obliged to feed scores of his tame birds on our wretched crops, and forbidden for our lives to keep a single tame bird of our own, pillaged and plundered to that degree that when we chanced to have a bit of meat, we ate it in fear, with the door barred and the shutters closed, that his people should not see it and take it from us—I say, we were so robbed, and hunted, and were made so poor, that our father told us it was a dreadful thing to bring a child into the world, and that what we should most pray for, was, that our women might be barren and our miserable race die out!'

"I had never before seen the sense of being oppressed, bursting forth like a fire. I had supposed that it must be latent in the people somewhere; but, I had never seen it break out, until I saw it in the dying boy.

" 'Nevertheless, Doctor, my sister married. He was ailing at that time, poor fellow, and she married her lover, that she might tend and comfort him in our cottage—our dog-hut, as that man would call it. She had not been married many weeks, when that man's brother saw her and admired her, and asked that man to lend her to him—for what are husbands among us! He was willing enough, but my sister was good and virtuous, and hated his brother with a hatred as strong as mine. What did the two then, to persuade her husband to use his influence with her, to make her willing?'

"The boy's eyes, which had been fixed on mine, slowly turned to the looker-on, and I saw in the two faces that all he said was true. The two opposing kinds of pride confronting one another, I can see, even in this Bastille; the gentleman's all negligent indifference; the peasant's, all trodden-down sentiment, and passionate revenge.

" 'You know, Doctor, that it is among the Rights of these Nobles to harness us common dogs to carts, and drive us. They so harnessed him and drove him. You know that it is among their Rights to keep us in their grounds all night, quieting the frogs, in order that their noble sleep may not be disturbed. They kept him out in the unwholesome mists at night, and ordered him back into his harness in the day. But he was not persuaded. No! Taken out of harness one day at noon, to feed—if he could find food—he sobbed twelve times, once for every stroke of the bell, and died on her bosom.'

"Nothing human could have held life in the boy but his determination to tell all his wrong. He forced back the gathering shadows of death, as he forced his clenched right hand to remain clenched, and to cover his wound.

" 'Then, with that man's permission and even with his aid, his brother took her away; in spite of what I know she must have told his brother—and what that is, will not be long unknown to you, Doctor, if it is now—his brother took her away—for his pleasure and diversion, for a little while. I saw her pass me on the road. When I took the tidings home, our father's heart burst; he never spoke one of the words that filled it. I took my young sister (for I have another) to a place beyond the reach of this man, and where, at least, she will never be *his* vassal. Then, I tracked the brother here, and last night climbed in—a common dog, but sword in hand.—Where is the loft window? It was somewhere here?'

"The room was darkening to his sight; the world was narrowing around him. I glanced about me, and saw that the hay and straw were trampled over the floor, as if there had been a struggle.

" 'She heard me, and ran in. I told her not to come near us till he was dead. He came in and first tossed me some pieces of money; then struck at me with a whip. But I, though a common dog, so struck at him as to make him draw. Let him break into as many pieces as he will, the sword that he stained with my common blood; he drew to defend himself—thrust at me with all his skill for his life.'

"My glance had fallen, but a few moments before, on the fragments of a broken sword, lying among the hay. That weapon was a gentleman's. In another place, lay an old sword that seemed to have been a soldier's.

" 'Now, lift me up, Doctor; lift me up. Where is he?'

" 'He is not here,' I said, supporting the boy, and thinking that he referred to the brother.

" 'He! Proud as these Nobles are, he is afraid to see me. Where is the man who was here? Turn my face to him.'

"I did so, raising the boy's head against my knee. But, invested for the moment with extraordinary power, he raised himself completely: obliging me to rise too, or I could not have still supported him.

" 'Marquis,' said the boy, turned to him with his eyes opened wide, and his right hand raised, 'in the days when all these things are to be answered for, I summon you and yours, the last of your bad race, to answer for them. I mark this cross of blood upon you, as a sign that I do it. In the days when all these things are to be answered for, I summon your brother, the worst of the bad race, to answer for them separately. I mark this cross of blood upon him, as a sign that I do it.'

"Twice, he put his hand to the wound in his breast, and with his forefinger drew a cross in the air. He stood for an instant with the finger yet raised, and, as it dropped, he dropped with it, and I laid him down dead. . . .

"When I returned to the bedside of the young woman, I found her raving in precisely the same order and continuity. I knew that this might last for many hours, and that it would probably end in the silence of the grave.

"I repeated the medicines I had given her, and I sat at the side of the bed until the night was far advanced. She never abated the piercing quality of her shrieks, never stumbled in the distinctness or the order of her words. They were always 'My husband, my father, and my brother! One, two, three, four, five, six, seven, eight, nine, ten, eleven, twelve! Hush!'

"This lasted twenty-six hours from the time when I first saw her. I had come and gone twice and was again sitting by her, when she began to falter. I did what little could be done to assist that opportunity, and by-and-by she sank into a lethargy, and lay like the dead.

"It was as if the wind and rain had lulled at last, after a long and fearful storm. I released her arms, and called the woman to assist me to compose her figure and the dress she had torn. It was then that I knew her condition to be that of one in whom the first expectations of being a mother have arisen; and it was then that I lost the little hope I had had of her.

" 'Is she dead?' asked the Marquis, whom I will still describe as the elder brother, coming booted into the room from his horse.

" 'Not dead,' said I; 'but like to die.'

" 'What strength there is in these common bodies!' he said, looking down at her with some curiosity.

" 'There is prodigious strength,' I answered him, 'in sorrow and despair.'

"He first laughed at my words, and then frowned at them. He moved a chair with his foot near to mine, ordered the woman away, and said in a subdued voice,

" 'Doctor, finding my brother in this difficulty with these hinds, I recommended that your aid should be invited. Your reputation is high, and, as a young man with your fortune to make, you are probably mindful of your interest. The things that you see here, are things to be seen, and not spoken of.'

"I listened to the patient's breathing, and avoided answering.

" 'Do you honour me with your attention, Doctor?'

" 'Monsieur,' said I, 'in my profession, the communications of patients are always received in confidence.' I was guarded in my answer, for I was troubled in my mind with what I had heard and seen.

"Her breathing was so difficult to trace, that I carefully tried the pulse and the heart. There was life, and no more. Looking round as I resumed my seat, I found both the brothers intent upon me. . . .

"I write with so much difficulty, the cold is so severe, I am so fearful of being detected and consigned to an underground cell and total darkness, that I must abridge this narrative. There is no confusion or failure in my memory; it can recall, and could detail, every word that was ever spoken between me and those brothers.

"She lingered for a week. Towards the last, I could understand some few syllables that she said to me, by placing my ear close to her lips. She asked me where she was, and I told her; who I was, and I told her. It was in vain that I asked her for her family name. She faintly shook her head upon the pillow, and kept her secret, as the boy had done.

"I had no opportunity of asking her any questions, until I had told the brothers she was sinking fast, and could not live another day. Until then, though no one was ever presented to her consciousness save the woman and myself, one or other of them had always jealously sat behind the curtain at the head of the bed when I was there. But when it came to that, they seemed careless what communication I might hold with her; as if—the thought passed through my mind—I were dying too.

"I always observed that their pride bitterly resented the younger brother's (as I call him) having crossed swords with a peasant and that peasant a boy. The only consideration that appeared to affect the mind of either of them was the consideration that this was highly degrading to the family, and was ridiculous. As often as I caught the younger brother's eyes, their expression reminded me that he disliked me deeply, for knowing what I knew from the boy. He was smoother and more polite to me than the elder; but I saw this. I also saw that I was an incumbrance in the mind of the elder, too.

"My patient died, two hours before midnight—at a time, by my watch, answering almost to the minute when I had first seen her. I was alone with her, when her forlorn young head dropped gently on one side, and all her earthly wrongs and sorrows ended.

"The brothers were waiting in a room down-stairs, impatient to ride away. I had heard them, alone at the bedside, striking their boots with their riding-whips, and loitering up and down.

" 'At last she is dead?' said the elder, when I went in.

" 'She is dead,' said I.

" 'I congratulate you, my brother,' were his words as he turned round.

"He had before offered me money, which I had postponed taking. He now gave me a rouleau of gold.[9] I took it from his hand, but laid it on the table. I had considered the question, and had resolved to accept nothing.

" 'Pray excuse me,' said I. 'Under the circumstances, no.'

"They exchanged looks, but bent their heads to me as I bent mine to them, and we parted without another word on either side.

"I am weary, weary, weary—worn down by misery; I cannot read what I have written with this gaunt hand.

"Early in the morning, the rouleau of gold was left at my door in a little box, with my name on the outside. From the first, I had anxiously considered what I ought to do. I decided, that day, to write privately to the Minister, stating the nature of the two cases to which I had been summoned, and the place to which I had gone: in effect, stating all the circumstances. I knew what Court influence was, and what the immunities of the Nobles were, and I expected that the matter would never be heard of; but, I wished to relieve my own mind. I had kept the matter a profound secret, even from my wife; and this, too, I resolved to state in my letter. I had no apprehension whatever of my real danger; but I was conscious that there might be danger for others, if others were compromised by possessing the knowledge that I possessed.

"I was much engaged that day, and could not complete my letter that night. I rose long before my usual time next morning to finish it. It was the last day of the year. The letter was lying before me just completed, when I was told that a lady waited, who wished to see me. . . .

"I am growing more and more unequal to the task I have set myself. It is so cold, so dark, my senses are so benumbed, and the gloom upon me is so dreadful.

"The lady was young, engaging, and handsome, but not marked for long life. She was in great agitation. She presented herself to me as the wife of the Marquis St. Evrémonde. I connected the title by which the boy had addressed the elder brother, with the initial letter embroidered on the scarf, and had no difficulty in arriving at the conclusion that I had seen that nobleman very lately.

"My memory is still accurate, but I cannot write the words of our conversation. I suspect that I am watched more closely than I was, and I know not at what times I may be watched. She had in part suspected, and in part discovered, the main facts of the cruel story, of her husband's share in it, and my being resorted to. She did not know that the girl was dead. Her hope had been, she said in great distress, to show her, in secret, a woman's sympathy. Her hope had been to avert the wrath of Heaven from a House that had long been hateful to the suffering many.

"She had reasons for believing that there was a young sister living, and her greatest desire was, to help that sister. I could tell her nothing but that there was such a sister; beyond that, I knew nothing. Her inducement to come to me, relying on my confidence, had been the hope that I could tell her the name and place of abode. Whereas, to this wretched hour I am ignorant of both. . . .

"These scraps of paper fail me. One was taken from me, with a warning yesterday. I must finish my record to-day.

"She was a good, compassionate lady, and not happy in her marriage. How could she be! The brother distrusted and disliked her, and his influence was all opposed to her; she stood in dread of him, and in dread of her husband too. When I handed her down to the door, there was a child, a pretty boy from two to three years old, in her carriage.

" 'For his sake, Doctor,' she said, pointing to him in tears, 'I would do all I can to make what poor amends I can. He will never prosper in his inheritance otherwise. I have a presentiment that if no other innocent atonement is made for this, it will one day be required of him. What I have left to call my own—it is little beyond the worth of a few jewels—

I will make it the first charge of his life to bestow, with the compassion and lamenting of his dead mother, on this injured family, if the sister can be discovered.'

"She kissed the boy, and said, caressing him, 'It is for thine own dear sake. Thou wilt be faithful, little Charles?' The child answered her bravely, 'Yes!' I kissed her hand, and she took him in her arms, and went away caressing him. I never saw her more.

"As she had mentioned her husband's name in the faith that I knew it, I added no mention of it to my letter. I sealed my letter, and, not trusting it out of my own hands, delivered it myself that day.

"That night, the last night of the year, towards nine o'clock, a man in a black dress rang at my gate, demanded to see me, and softly followed my servant, Ernest Defarge, a youth, up-stairs. When my servant came into the room where I sat with my wife—O my wife, beloved of my heart! My fair young English wife!—we saw the man, who was supposed to be at the gate, standing silent behind him.

"An urgent case in the Rue St. Honoré, he said. It would not detain me, he had a coach in waiting.

"It brought me here, it brought me to my grave. When I was clear of the house, a black muffler was drawn tightly over my mouth from behind, and my arms were pinioned. The two brothers crossed the road from a dark corner, and identified me with a single gesture. The Marquis took from his pocket the letter I had written, showed it to me, burnt it in the light of a lantern that was held, and extinguished the ashes with his foot. Not a word was spoken. I was brought here, I was brought to my living grave.

"If it had pleased God to put it in the hard heart of either of the brothers, in all these frightful years, to grant me any tidings of my dearest wife—so much as to let me know by a word whether alive or dead—I might have thought that He had not quite abandoned them. But, now I believe that the mark of the red cross is fatal to them, and that they have no part in His mercies. And them and their descendants, to the last of their race, I, Alexandre Manette, unhappy prisoner, do this last night of the year 1767, in my unbearable agony, denounce to the times when all these things shall be answered for. I denounce them to Heaven and to earth."

A terrible sound arose when the reading of this document was done. A sound of craving and eagerness that had nothing articulate in it but blood. The narrative called up the most revengeful passions of the time, and there was not a head in the nation but must have dropped before it.

Little need, in the presence of that tribunal and that auditory, to show how the Defarges had not made the paper public, with the other captured Bastille memorials borne in procession, and had kept it, biding their time. Little need to show that this detested family name had long been anathematised by Saint Antoine, and was wrought into the fatal register. The man never trod ground whose virtues and services would have sustained him in that place that day, against such denunciation.

And all the worse for the doomed man, that the denouncer was a well-known citizen, his own attached friend, the father of his wife. One of the frenzied aspirations of the populace was, for imitations of the questionable public virtues of antiquity, and for sacrifices and self-immolations on the people's altar. Therefore when the President said (else had his own head quivered on his shoulders), that the good physician of the Republic would deserve better still of the Republic by rooting out an obnoxious family of Aristocrats, and would doubtless feel a sacred glow and joy in making his daughter a widow and her child an orphan, there was wild excitement, patriotic fervour, not a touch of human sympathy.

"Much influence around him, has that Doctor?" murmured Madame Defarge, smiling to The Vengeance. "Save him now, my Doctor, save him!"

At every juryman's vote, there was a roar. Another and another. Roar and roar.

Unanimously voted. At heart and by descent an Aristocrat, an enemy of the Republic, a notorious oppressor of the People. Back to the Conciergerie, and Death within four-and-twenty hours!

11

DUSK

THE wretched wife of the innocent man thus doomed to die, fell under the sentence, as if she had been mortally stricken. But, she uttered no sound; and so strong was the voice within her, representing that it was she of all the world who must uphold him in his misery and not augment it, that it quickly raised her, even from that shock.

The judges having to take part in a public demonstration out of doors, the tribunal adjourned. The quick noise and movement of the court's emptying itself by many passages had not ceased, when Lucie stood stretching out her arms towards her husband, with nothing in her face but love and consolation.

"If I might touch him! If I might embrace him once! O, good citizens, if you would have so much compassion for us!"

There was but a gaoler left, along with two of the four men who had taken him last night, and Barsad. The people had all poured out to the show in the streets. Barsad proposed to the rest, "Let her embrace him then; it is but a moment." It was silently acquiesced in, and they passed her over the seats in the hall to a raised place, where he, by leaning over the dock, could fold her in his arms.

"Farewell, dear darling of my soul. My parting blessing on my love. We shall meet again, where the weary are at rest!"

They were her husband's words, as he held her to his bosom.

"I can bear it, dear Charles. I am supported from above: don't suffer for me. A parting blessing for our child."

"I send it to her by you. I kiss her by you. I say farewell to her by you."

"My husband. No! A moment!" He was tearing himself apart from her. "We shall not be separated long. I feel that this will break my heart by-and-by; but I will do my duty while I can, and when I leave her, GOD will raise up friends for her, as He did for me."

Her father had followed her, and would have fallen on his knees to both of them, but that Darnay put out a hand and seized him, crying:

"No, no! What have you done, what have you done, that you should kneel to us! We know now, what a struggle you made of old. We know now, what you underwent when you suspected my descent, and when you knew it. We know now, the natural antipathy you strove against, and conquered, for her dear sake. We thank you with all our hearts, and all our love and duty. Heaven be with you!"

Her father's only answer was to draw his hands through his white hair, and wring them with a shriek of anguish.

"It could not be otherwise," said the prisoner. "All things have worked together as they have fallen out. It was the always-vain endeavour to discharge my poor mother's trust that first brought my fatal presence near you. Good could never come of such evil, a happier end was not in nature to so unhappy a beginning. Be comforted, and forgive me. Heaven bless you!"

As he was drawn away, his wife released him, and stood looking after him with her hands touching one another in the attitude of prayer, and with a radiant look upon her face, in which there was even a comforting smile. As he went out at the prisoners' door, she turned, laid her head lovingly on her father's breast, tried to speak to him, and fell at his feet.

Then, issuing from the obscure corner from which he had never moved, Sydney Carton came and took her up. Only her father and Mr. Lorry were with her. His arm trembled as it raised her, and supported her head. Yet, there was an air about him that was not all of pity—that had a flush of pride in it.

"Shall I take her to a coach? I shall never feel her weight."

He carried her lightly to the door, and laid her tenderly down in a coach. Her father and their old friend got into it, and he took his seat beside the driver.

When they arrived at the gateway where he had paused in the dark not many hours before, to picture to himself on which of the rough stones of the street her feet had trodden, he lifted her again, and carried her up the staircase to their rooms. There, he laid her down on a couch, where her child and Miss Pross wept over her.

"Don't recall her to herself," he said, softly, to the latter, "she is better so. Don't revive her to consciousness, while she only faints."

"Oh, Carton, Carton, dear Carton!" cried little Lucie, springing up and throwing her arms passionately round him, in a burst of grief. "Now that you have come, I think you will do something to help mamma, something to save papa! O, look at her, dear Carton! Can you, of all the people who love her, bear to see her so?"

He bent over the child, and laid her blooming cheek against his face. He put her gently from him, and looked at her unconscious mother.

"Before I go," he said, and paused—"I may kiss her?"

It was remembered afterwards that when he bent down and touched her face with his lips, he murmured some words. The child, who was nearest to him, told them afterwards, and told her grandchildren when she was a handsome old lady, that she heard him say, "A life you love."

When he had gone out into the next room, he turned suddenly on Mr. Lorry and her father, who were following, and said to the latter:

"You had great influence but yesterday, Doctor Manette; let it at least be tried. These judges, and all the men in power are very friendly to you, and very recognisant of your services; are they not?"

"Nothing connected with Charles was concealed from me. I had the strongest assurances that I should save him; and I did." He returned the answer in great trouble, and very slowly.

"Try them again. The hours between this and to-morrow afternoon are few and short, but try."

"I intend to try. I will not rest a moment."

"That's well. I have known such energy as yours do great things before now—though never," he added, with a smile and a sigh together, "such great things as this. But try! Of little worth as life is when we misuse it, it is worth that effort. It would cost nothing to lay down if it were not."

"I will go," said Doctor Manette, "to the Prosecutor and the President straight, and I will go to others whom it is better not to name. I will write too, and—But stay! There is a celebration in the streets, and no one will be accessible until dark."

"That's true. Well! It is a forlorn hope at the best, and not much the forlorner for being delayed till dark. I should like to know how you speed; though mind! I expect nothing! When are you likely to have seen these dread powers, Doctor Manette?"

"Immediately after dark, I should hope. Within an hour or two from this?"

"It will be dark soon after four. Let us stretch the hour or two. If I go to Mr. Lorry's at nine, shall I hear what you have done, either from our friend or from yourself?"

"Yes."

"May you prosper!"

Mr. Lorry followed Sydney to the outer door, and, touching him on the shoulder as he was going away, caused him to turn.

"I have no hope," said Mr. Lorry, in a low and sorrowful whisper.

"Nor have I."

"If any one of these men, or all of these men, were disposed to spare him—which is a large supposition; for what is his life, or any man's to them!—I doubt if they durst spare him after the demonstration in the court."

"And so do I. I heard the fall of the axe in that sound."

Mr. Lorry leaned his arm upon the door-post and bowed his face upon it.

"Don't despond," said Carton, very gently; "don't grieve. I encouraged Doctor Manette in this idea, because I felt that it might one day be consolatory to her. Otherwise, she might think 'his life was wantonly thrown away or wasted,' and that might trouble her."

"Yes, yes, yes," returned Mr. Lorry, drying his eyes, "you are right. But he will perish; there is no real hope."

"Yes. He will perish: there is no real hope," echoed Carton. And he walked with a settled step, down-stairs.

12

DARKNESS

❦

SYDNEY CARTON paused in the street, not quite decided where to go. "At Tellson's banking-house at nine," he said, with a musing face. "Shall I do well, in the meantime, to show myself? I think so. It is best that these people should know there is such a man as I here; it is a sound precaution, and may be a necessary preparation. But care, care, care! Let me think it out!"

Checking his steps which had begun to tend towards an object, he took a turn or two in the already darkening street, and traced the thought in his mind to its possible consequences. His first impression was confirmed. "It is best," he said, finally resolved, "that these people should know there is such a man as I here." And he turned his face towards Saint Antoine.

Defarge had described himself, that day, as the keeper of a wine-shop in the Saint Antoine suburb. It was not difficult for one who knew the city well, to find his house without asking any question. Having ascertained its situation, Carton came out of those closer streets again, and dined at a place of refreshment and fell sound asleep after dinner. For the first time in many years, he had no strong drink. Since last night he had taken nothing but a little light thin wine, and last night he had dropped the brandy slowly down on Mr. Lorry's hearth like a man who had done with it.

It was as late as seven o'clock when he awoke refreshed, and went out into the streets again. As he passed along towards Saint Antoine, he stopped at a shop-window where there was a mirror, and slightly altered the disordered arrangement of his loose cravat, and his coat-collar, and his wild hair. This done, he went on direct to Defarge's, and went in.

There happened to be no customers in the shop but Jacques Three, of the restless fingers and the croaking voice. This man, whom he had seen upon the Jury, stood drinking at the little counter, in conversation with the Defarges, man and wife. The Vengeance assisted in the conversation, like a regular member of the establishment.

As Carton walked in, took his seat and asked (in very indifferent French) for a small measure of wine, Madame Defarge cast a careless glance at him, and then a keener, and then a keener, and then advanced to him herself, and asked him what it was he had ordered.

He repeated what he had already said.

"English?" asked Madame Defarge, inquisitively raising her dark eyebrows.

After looking at her, as if the sound of even a single French word were slow to express itself to him, he answered, in his former strong foreign accent. "Yes, madame, yes. I am English!"

Madame Defarge returned to her counter to get the wine, and, as he took up a Jacobin journal[10] and feigned to pore over it puzzling out its meaning, he heard her say, "I swear to you, like Evrémonde!"

Defarge brought him the wine, and gave him Good Evening.

"How?"

"Good evening."

"Oh! Good evening, citizen," filling his glass. "Ah! and good wine. I drink to the Republic."

Defarge went back to the counter, and said, "Certainly, a little like." Madame sternly retorted, "I tell you a good deal like." Jacques Three pacifically remarked, "He is so much in your mind, see you, madame." The amiable Vengeance added, with a laugh. "Yes, my faith! And you are looking forward with so much pleasure to seeing him once more to-morrow!"

Carton followed the lines and words of his paper, with a slow forefinger, and with a studious and absorbed face. They were all leaning their arms on the counter close together, speaking low. After a silence of a few moments, during which they all looked towards him without disturbing his outward attention from the Jacobin editor, they resumed their conversation.

"It is true what madame says," observed Jacques Three. "Why stop? There is great force in that. Why stop?"

"Well, well," reasoned Defarge, "but one must stop somewhere. After all, the question is still where?"

"At extermination," said madame.

"Magnificent!" croaked Jacques Three. The Vengeance, also, highly approved.

"Extermination is good doctrine, my wife," said Defarge, rather troubled; "in general, I say nothing against it. But this Doctor has suffered much; you have seen him to-day; you have observed his face when the paper was read."

"I have observed his face!" repeated madame, contemptuously and angrily. "Yes. I have observed his face. I have observed his face to be not the face of a true friend of the Republic. Let him take care of his face!"

"And you have observed, my wife," said Defarge, in a deprecatory manner, "the anguish of his daughter, which must be a dreadful anguish to him!"

"I have observed his daughter," repeated madame; "yes, I have observed his daughter, more times than one. I have observed her to-day, and I have observed her other days. I have observed her in the court, and I have observed her in the street by the prison. Let me but lift my finger——!" She seemed to raise it (the listener's eyes were always on his paper), and to let it fall with a rattle on the ledge before her, as if the axe had dropped.

"The citizeness is superb!" croaked the Juryman.

"She is an Angel!" said The Vengeance, and embraced her.

"As to thee," pursued madame, implacably, addressing her husband, "if it depended on thee—which, happily, it does not—thou wouldst rescue this man even now."

"No!" protested Defarge. "Not if to lift this glass would do it! But I would leave the matter there. I say, stop there."

"See you then, Jacques," said Madame Defarge, wrathfully; "and see you, too, my little Vengeance: see you both! Listen! For other crimes as tyrants and oppressors, I have this race a long time on my register, doomed to destruction and extermination. Ask my husband, is that so."

"It is so," assented Defarge, without being asked.

"In the beginning of the great days, when the Bastille falls, he finds this paper of to-day, and he brings it home, and in the middle of the night when this place is clear and shut, we read it, here on this spot, by the light of this lamp. Ask him, is that so."

"It is so," assented Defarge.

"That night, I tell him, when the paper is read through, and the lamp is burnt out, and the day is gleaming in above those shutters and between those iron bars, that I have now a secret to communicate. Ask him, is that so."

"It is so," assented Defarge again.

"I communicate to him that secret. I smite this bosom with these two hands as I smite it now, and I tell him, 'Defarge, I was brought up among the fishermen of the seashore, and that peasant family so injured by the two Evrémonde brothers, as that Bastille paper describes, is my family. Defarge, that sister of the mortally wounded boy upon the ground was my sister, that husband was my sister's husband, that unborn child was their child, that brother was my brother, that father was my father, those dead are my dead, and that summons to answer for those things descends to me!' Ask him, is that so."

"It is so," assented Defarge once more.

"Then tell Wind and Fire where to stop," returned madame; "but don't tell me."

Both her hearers derived a horrible enjoyment from the deadly nature of her wrath—the listener could feel how white she was, without seeing her—and both highly commended it. Defarge, a weak minority, interposed a few words of the memory of the compassionate wife of the Marquis; but only elicited from his own wife a repetition of her last reply. "Tell the Wind and the Fire where to stop; not me!"

Customers entered, and the group was broken up. The English customer paid for what he had had, perplexedly counted his change, and asked, as a stranger, to be directed towards the National Palace. Madame Defarge took him to the door, and put her arm on his, in pointing out the road. The English customer was not without his reflections then, that it might be a good deed to seize that arm, lift it, and strike under it sharp and deep.

But, he went his way, and was soon swallowed up in the shadow of the prison wall. At the appointed hour, he emerged from it to present himself in Mr. Lorry's room again, where he found the old gentleman walking to and fro in restless anxiety. He said he had been with Lucie until just now, and had only left her for a few minutes, to come and keep his appointment. Her father had not been seen, since he quitted the banking-house towards four o'clock. She had some faint hopes that his mediation might save Charles, but they were very slight. He had been more than five hours gone: where could he be?

Mr. Lorry waited until ten; but, Doctor Manette not returning, and he being unwilling to leave Lucie any longer, it was arranged that he should go back to her, and come to the banking-house again at midnight. In the meanwhile, Carton would wait alone by the fire for the Doctor.

He waited and waited, and the clock struck twelve; but Doctor Manette did not come back. Mr. Lorry returned, and found no tidings of him, and brought none. Where could he be?

They were discussing this question, and were almost building up some weak structure of hope on his prolonged absence, when they heard him on the stairs. The instant he entered the room, it was plain that all was lost.

Whether he had really been to any one, or whether he had been all that time traversing the streets, was never known. As he stood staring at them, they asked him no questions, for his face told them everything.

"I cannot find it," said he, "and I must have it. Where is it?"

His head and throat were bare, and, as he spoke with a helpless look straying all around, he took his coat off, and let it drop on the floor.

"Where is my bench? I have been looking everywhere for my bench, and I can't find it. What have they done with my work? Time presses: I must finish those shoes."

They looked at one another, and their hearts died within them.

"Come, come!" said he, in a whimpering miserable way; "let me get to work. Give me my work."

Receiving no answer, he tore his hair, and beat his feet upon the ground, like a distracted child.

"Don't torture a poor forlorn wretch," he implored them, with a dreadful cry; "but give me my work! What is to become of us, if those shoes are not done to-night?"

Lost, utterly lost!

It was so clearly beyond hope to reason with him, or try to restore him, that—as if by agreement—they each put a hand upon his shoulder, and soothed him to sit down before the fire, with a promise that he should have his work presently. He sank into the chair, and brooded over the embers, and shed tears. As if all that had happened since the garret time were a momentary fancy, or a dream, Mr. Lorry saw him shrink into the exact figure that Defarge had had in keeping.

Affected, and impressed with terror as they both were, by this spectacle of ruin, it was not a time to yield to such emotions. His lonely daughter, bereft of her final hope and reliance, appealed to them both too strongly. Again, as if by agreement, they looked at one another with one meaning in their faces. Carton was the first to speak:

"The last chance is gone: it was not much. Yes; he had better be taken to her. But, before you go, will you, for a moment, steadily attend to me? Don't ask me why I make the stipulations I am going to make, and exact the promise I am going to exact; I have a reason—a good one."

"I do not doubt it," answered Mr. Lorry. "Say on."

The figure in the chair between them, was all the time monotonously rocking itself to and fro, and moaning. They spoke in such a tone as they would have used if they had been watching by a sickbed in the night.

Carton stooped to pick up the coat, which lay almost entangling his feet. As he did so, a small case in which the Doctor was accustomed to carry the list of his day's duties, fell lightly on the floor. Carton took it up, and there was a folded paper in it. "We should look at this!" he said. Mr. Lorry nodded his consent. He opened it, and exclaimed, "Thank GOD!"

"What is it?" asked Mr. Lorry, eagerly.

"A moment! Let me speak of it in its place. First," he put his hand in his coat, and took another paper from it, "that is the certificate which enables me to pass out of this city. Look at it. You see—Sydney Carton, an Englishman?"

Mr. Lorry held it open in his hand, gazing in his earnest face.

"Keep it for me until to-morrow. I shall see him to-morrow, you remember, and I had better not take it into the prison."

"Why not?"

"I don't know; I prefer not to do so. Now, take this paper that Doctor Manette has carried about him. It is a similar certificate, enabling him and his daughter and her child, at any time, to pass the barrier and the frontier. You see?"

"Yes!"

"Perhaps he obtained it as his last and utmost precaution against evil, yesterday. When is it dated? But no matter; don't stay to look; put it up carefully with mine and your own. Now, observe! I never doubted until within this hour or two, that he had, or could have such a paper. It is good, until recalled. But it may be soon recalled, and I have reason to think, will be."

"They are not in danger?"

"They are in great danger. They are in danger of denunciation by Madame Defarge. I know it from her own lips. I have overheard words of that woman's, to-night, which have presented their danger to me in strong colours. I have lost no time, and since then, I have seen the spy. He confirms me. He knows that a wood-sawyer living by the prison-wall, is under the control of the Defarges, and has been rehearsed by Madame Defarge as to his having seen Her"—he never mentioned Lucie's name—"making signs and signals to prisoners. It is easy to foresee that the pretence will be the common one, a prison plot, and that it will involve her life—and perhaps her child's—and perhaps her father's—for both have been seen with her at that place. Don't look so horrified. You will save them all."

"Heaven grant I may, Carton! But how?"

"I am going to tell you how. It will depend on you, and it could depend on no better man. This new denunciation will certainly not take place until after to-morrow; probably not until two or three days afterwards; more probably a week afterwards. You know it is a capital crime to mourn for, or sympathise with, a victim of the Guillotine. She and her father would unquestionably be guilty of this crime, and this woman (the inveteracy of whose pursuit cannot be described) would wait to add that strength to her case, and make herself doubly sure. You follow me?"

"So attentively, and with so much confidence in what you say, that for the moment I lose sight," touching the back of the Doctor's chair, "even of this distress."

"You have money, and can buy the means of travelling to the seacoast as quickly as the journey can be made. Your preparations have been completed for some days, to return to England. Early to-morrow have your horses ready, so that they may be in starting trim at two o'clock in the afternoon."

"It shall be done!"

His manner was so fervent and inspiring, that Mr. Lorry caught the flame, and was quick as youth.

"You are a noble heart. Did I say we could depend upon no better man? Tell her, to-night, what you know of her danger as involving her child and her father. Dwell upon that, for she would lay her own fair head beside her husband's cheerfully." He faltered for an instant; then went on as before. "For the sake of her child and her father, press upon her the necessity of leaving Paris, with them and you at that hour. Tell her that it was her husband's last arrangement. Tell her that more depends upon it than she dare believe, or hope. You think that her father, even in this sad state, will submit himself to her; do you not?"

"I am sure of it."

"I thought so. Quietly and steadily have all these arrangements made in the court-yard here, even to the taking of your own seat in the carriage. The moment I come to you, take me in, and drive away."

"I understand that I wait for you under all circumstances?"

"You have my certificate in your hand with the rest, you know, and will reserve my place. Wait for nothing but to have my place occupied, and then for England!"

"Why, then," said Mr. Lorry, grasping his eager but so firm and steady hand, "it does not all depend on one old man, but I shall have a young and ardent man at my side."

"By the help of Heaven you shall! Promise me solemnly that nothing will influence you to alter the course on which we now stand pledged to one another."

"Nothing, Carton."

"Remember these words to-morrow: change the course,

or delay in it—for any reason—and no life can possibly be saved, and many lives must inevitably be sacrificed."

"I will remember them. I hope to do my part faithfully."

"And I hope to do mine. Now, good-bye!"

Though he said it with a grave smile of earnestness, and though he even put the old man's hand to his lips, he did not part from him then. He helped him so far to arouse the rocking figure before the dying embers, as to get a cloak and hat put upon it, and to tempt it forth to find where the bench and work were hidden that it still meaningly besought to have. He walked on the other side of it and protected it to the court-yard of the house where the afflicted heart—so happy in the memorable time when he had revealed his own desolate heart to it—outwatched the awful night. He entered the court-yard and remained there for a few moments alone, looking up at the light in the window of her room. Before he went away, he breathed a blessing towards it and a Farewell.

13

FIFTY-TWO

$$\blacktriangledown$$

IN THE black prison of the Conciergerie, the doomed of the day awaited their fate. They were in number as the weeks of the year. Fifty-two were to roll that afternoon on the lifetide of the city to the boundless everlasting sea. Before their cells were quit of them, new occupants were appointed; before their blood ran into the blood spilled yesterday, the blood that was to mingle with theirs to-morrow was already set apart.

Two score and twelve were told off. From the farmer-general of seventy, whose riches could not buy his life, to the seamstress of twenty, whose poverty and obscurity could not save her. Physical diseases, engendered in the vices and neglects of men, will seize on victims of all degrees; and the frightful moral disorder, born of unspeakable suffering, intolerable oppression, and heartless indifference, smote equally without distinction.

Charles Darnay, alone in a cell, had sustained himself with no flattering delusion since he came to it from the Tribunal. In every line of the narrative he had heard, he had heard his condemnation. He had fully comprehended that no personal influence could possibly save him, that he was virtually sentenced by the millions, and that units could avail him nothing.

Nevertheless, it was not easy, with the face of his beloved wife fresh before him, to compose his mind to what it must bear. His hold on life was strong, and it was very, very hard, to loosen; by gradual efforts and degrees unclosed a little here, it clenched the tighter there; and when he brought his strength to bear on that hand and it yielded, this was closed again. There was a hurry, too, in all his thoughts, a turbulent and heated working of his heart, that contended against resignation. If, for a moment, he did feel resigned, then his wife and child who had to live after him, seemed to protest and to make it a selfish thing.

But, all this was at first. Before long, the consideration that there was no disgrace in the fate he must meet, and that numbers went the same road wrongfully, and trod it firmly every day, sprang up to stimulate him. Next followed the thought that much of the future peace of mind enjoyable by the dear ones, depended on his quiet fortitude. So, by degrees he calmed into the better state, when he could raise his thoughts much higher, and draw comfort down.

Before it had set in dark on the night of his condemnation, he had travelled thus far on his last way. Being allowed to purchase the means of writing, and a light, he sat down to write until such time as the prison lamps should be extinguished.

He wrote a long letter to Lucie,[11] showing her that he had known nothing of her father's imprisonment, until he had heard of it from herself, and that he had been as ignorant as she of his father's and uncle's responsibility for that misery, until the paper had been read. He had already explained to her that his concealment from herself of the name he had relinquished, was the one condition—fully intelligible now—that her father had attached to their betrothal, and was the one promise he had still exacted on the morning of their marriage. He entreated her, for her father's sake, never to seek to know whether her father had become oblivious of the existence of the paper, or had had it recalled to him (for the moment or, for good), by the story of the Tower, on that old Sunday under the dear old plane-tree in the garden. If he had preserved any definite remembrance of it, there could be no doubt that he had supposed it destroyed with the Bastille, when he had found no mention of it among the relics of prisoners which the populace had discovered there, and which had been described to all the world. He besought her—though he added that he knew it was needless—to console her father, by impressing him through every tender means she could think of, with the truth that he had done nothing for which he could justly reproach himself, but had uniformly forgotten himself for their joint sakes. Next to her preservation of his own last grateful love and blessing, and her overcoming of her sorrow, to devote herself to their dear child, he adjured her, as they would meet in Heaven, to comfort her father.

To her father himself, he wrote in the same strain; but, he told her father that he expressly confided his wife and child to his care. And he told him this, very strongly, with the hope of rousing him from any despondency or dangerous retrospect towards which he foresaw he might be tending.

To Mr. Lorry, he commended them all, and explained his worldly affairs. That done, with many added sentences of grateful friendship and warm attachment, all was done. He never thought of Carton. His mind was so full of the others, that he never once thought of him.

He had time to finish these letters before the lights were put out. When he lay down on his straw bed, he thought he had done with this world.

But, it beckoned him back in his sleep, and showed itself in shining forms. Free and happy, back in the old house in Soho (though it had nothing in it like the real house), unaccountably released and light of heart, he was with Lucie again, and she told him it was all a dream, and he had never gone away. A pause of forgetfulness, and then he had even suffered, and had come back to her, dead and at peace, and yet there was no difference in him. Another pause of oblivion, and he awoke in the sombre morning, unconscious where he was or what had happened, until it flashed upon his mind, "this is the day of my death!"

Thus, had he come through the hours, to the day when the fifty-two heads were to fall. And now, while he was composed, and hoped that he could meet the end with quiet heroism, a new action began in his waking thoughts, which was very difficult to master.

He had never seen the instrument that was to terminate his life. How high it was from the ground, how many steps it had, where he would be stood, how he would be touched, whether the touching hands would be dyed red, which way his face would be turned, whether he would be the first, or might be the last: these and many similar questions, in no wise directed by his will, obtruded themselves over and over again, countless times. Neither were they connected with fear: he was conscious of no fear. Rather, they originated in a strange besetting desire to know what to do when the time came; a desire gigantically disproportionate to the few swift moments to which it referred; a wondering that was more like the wondering of some other spirit within his, than his own.

The hours went on as he walked to and fro, and the clocks struck the numbers he would never hear again. Nine gone for ever, ten gone for ever, eleven gone for ever, twelve coming on to pass away. After a hard contest with the eccentric action of thought which had last perplexed him, he had got the better of it. He walked up and down softly repeating their names to himself. The worst of the strife was over. He could walk up and down, free from distracting fancies, praying for himself and for them.

Twelve gone for ever.

He had been apprised that the final hour was Three, and he knew he would be summoned some time earlier, inasmuch as the tumbrils jolted heavily and slowly through the streets. Therefore, he resolved to keep Two before his mind, as the hour, and so to strengthen himself in the interval that he might be able, after that time, to strengthen others.

Walking regularly to and fro with his arms folded on his breast, a very different man from the prisoner, who had walked to and fro at La Force, he heard One struck away from him, without surprise. The hour had measured like most other hours. Devoutly thankful to Heaven for his recovered self-possession, he thought, "There is but another now," and turned to walk again.

Footsteps in the stone passage outside the door. He stopped.

The key was put in the lock, and turned. Before the door was opened, or as it opened, a man said in a low voice, in English: "He has never seen me here; I have kept out of his way. Go you in alone; I wait near. Lose no time!"

The door was quickly opened and closed, and there stood before him face to face, quiet, intent upon him, with the light of a smile on his features, and a cautionary finger on his lip, Sydney Carton.

There was something so bright and remarkable in his look, that, for the moment, the prisoner misdoubted him to be an apparition of his own imagining. But, he spoke, and it was his voice; he took the prisoner's hand, and it was his real grasp.

"Of all the people upon earth, you least expected to see me?" he said.

"I could not believe it to be you. I can scarcely believe it now. You are not"—the apprehension came suddenly into his mind—"a prisoner?"

"No. I am accidentally possessed of a power over one of the keepers here, and in virtue of it I stand before you. I come from her—your wife, dear Darnay."

The prisoner wrung his hand.

"I bring you a request from her."

"What is it?"

"A most earnest, pressing, and emphatic entreaty,

addressed to you in the most pathetic tones of the voice so dear to you, that you well remember."

The prisoner turned his face partly aside.

"You have no time to ask me why I bring it, or what it means; I have no time to tell you. You must comply with it—take off those boots you wear, and draw on these of mine."

There was a chair against the wall of the cell, behind the prisoner. Carton, pressing forward, had already, with the speed of lightning, got him down into it, and stood over him, barefoot.

"Draw on these boots of mine. Put your hands to them; put your will to them. Quick!"

"Carton, there is no escaping from this place; it never can be done. You will only die with me. It is madness."

"It would be madness if I asked you to escape; but do I? When I ask you to pass out at that door, tell me it is madness and remain here. Change that cravat for this of mine, that coat for this of mine. While you do it, let me take this ribbon from your hair, and shake out your hair like this of mine!"

With wonderful quickness, and with a strength both of will and action, that appeared quite supernatural, he forced all these changes upon him. The prisoner was like a young child in his hands.

"Carton! Dear Carton! It is madness. It cannot be accomplished, it never can be done, it has been attempted, and has always failed. I implore you not to add your death to the bitterness of mine."

"Do I ask you, my dear Darnay, to pass the door? When I ask that, refuse. There are pen and ink and paper on this table. Is your hand steady enough to write?"

"It was when you came in."

"Steady it again, and write what I shall dictate. Quick, friend, quick!"

Pressing his hand to his bewildered head, Darnay sat down at the table. Carton, with his right hand in his breast, stood close beside him.

"Write exactly as I speak."

"To whom do I address it?"

"To no one." Carton still had his hand in his breast.

"Do I date it?"

"No."

The prisoner looked up, at each question. Carton standing over him with his hand in his breast, looked down.

" 'If you remember,' " said Carton, dictating, " 'the words that passed between us, long ago, you will readily comprehend this when you see it. You do remember them, I know. It is not in your nature to forget them.' "

He was drawing his hand from his breast; the prisoner chancing to look up in his hurried wonder as he wrote, the hand stopped, closing upon something.

"Have you written 'forget them'?" Carton asked.

"I have. Is that a weapon in your hand?"

"No; I am not armed."

"What is it in your hand?"

"You shall know directly. Write on; there are but a few words more." He dictated again. " 'I am thankful that the time has come, when I can prove them. That I do so is no subject for regret or grief.' " As he said these words with his eyes fixed on the writer, his hand slowly and softly moved down close to the writer's face.

The pen dropped from Darnay's fingers on the table, and he looked about him vacantly.

"What vapour is that?" he asked.

"Vapour?"

"Something that crossed me?"

"I am conscious of nothing; there can be nothing here. Take up the pen and finish. Hurry, hurry!"

As if his memory were impaired, or his faculties disordered, the prisoner made an effort to rally his attention. As he looked at Carton with clouded eyes and with an altered manner of breathing, Carton—his hand again in his breast—looked steadily at him.

"Hurry, hurry!"

The prisoner bent over the paper, once more.

" 'If it had been otherwise' "; Carton's hand was again watchfully and softly stealing down; " 'I never should have used the longer opportunity. If it had been otherwise' "; the hand was at the prisoner's face; " 'I should but have had so much the more to answer for. If it had been otherwise———,' " Carton looked at the pen and saw it was trailing off into unintelligible signs.

Carton's hand moved back to his breast no more. The prisoner sprang up with a reproachful look, but Carton's hand was close and firm to his nostrils, and Carton's left arm caught him round the waist. For a few seconds he faintly struggled with the man who had come to lay down his life for him; but, within a minute or so, he was stretched insensible on the ground.

Quickly, but with his hands as true to the purpose as his heart was, Carton dressed himself in the clothes the prisoner had laid aside, combed back his hair, and tied it with the ribbon the prisoner had worn. Then, he softly called, "Enter there! Come in!" and the Spy presented himself.

"You see?" said Carton, looking up, as he kneeled on one knee beside the insensible figure, putting the paper in the breast; "is your hazard very great?"

"M. Carton," the Spy answered, with a timid snap of his fingers, "my hazard is not *that*, in the thick of business here, if you are true to the whole of your bargain."

"Don't fear me. I will be true to the death."

"You must be, Mr. Carton, if the tale of fifty-two is to be right. Being made right by you in that dress, I shall have no fear."

"Have no fear! I shall soon be out of the way of harming you, and the rest will soon be far from here, please God! Now, get assistance and take me to the coach."

"You?" said the Spy nervously.

"Him, man, with whom I have exchanged. You go out at the gate by which you brought me in?"

"Of course."

"I was weak and faint when you brought me in, and I am fainter now you take me out. The parting interview has overpowered me. Such a thing has happened here, often, and too often. Your life is in your own hands. Quick! Call assistance!"

"You swear not to betray me?" said the trembling Spy, as he paused for a last moment.

"Man, man!" returned Carton, stamping his foot; "have I sworn by no solemn vow already, to go through with this, that you waste the precious moments now? Take him yourself to the court-yard you know of, place him yourself in the carriage, show him yourself to Mr. Lorry, tell him yourself to give him no restorative but air, and to remember my words of last night, and his promise of last night, and drive away!"

The Spy withdrew, and Carton seated himself at the table, resting his forehead on his hands. The Spy returned immediately, with two men.

"How then?" said one of them, contemplating the fallen figure. "So afflicted to find that his friend has drawn a prize in the lottery of Sainte Guillotine?"

"A good patriot," said the other, "could hardly have been more afflicted if the Aristocrat had drawn a blank."

They raised the unconscious figure, placed it on a litter they had brought to the door, and bent to carry it away.

"The time is short, Evrémonde," said the Spy, in a warning voice.

"I know it well," answered Carton. "Be careful of my friend, I entreat you, and leave me."

"Come, then, my children," said Barsad. "Lift him, and come away!"

The door closed, and Carton was left alone. Straining his powers of listening to the utmost, he listened for any sound that might denote suspicion or alarm. There was none. Keys turned, doors clashed, footsteps passed along distant passages: no cry was raised, or hurry made, that seemed unusual. Breathing more freely in a little while, he sat down at the table, and listened again until the clock struck Two.

Sounds that he was not afraid of, for he divined their meaning, then began to be audible. Several doors were opened in succession, and finally his own. A gaoler, with a list in his hand, looked in, merely saying, "Follow me, Evrémonde!" and he followed him into a large dark room, at a distance. It was a dark winter day, and what with the shadows within, and what with the shadows without, he could but dimly discern the others who were brought there to have their arms bound. Some were standing; some seated. Some were lamenting, and in restless motion; but, these were few. The great majority were silent and still, looking fixedly at the ground.

As he stood by the wall in a dim corner, while some of the fifty-two were brought in after him, one man stopped in passing, to embrace him, as having a knowledge of him. It thrilled him with a great dread of discovery; but the man went on. A very few moments after that, a young woman, with a slight girlish form, a sweet spare face in which there was no vestige of colour, and large widely opened patient eyes, rose from the seat where he had observed her sitting, and came to speak to him.

"Citizen Evrémonde," she said, touching him with her cold hand. "I am a poor little seamstress, who was with you in La Force."

He murmured for answer: "True. I forget what you were accused of?"

"Plots. Though the just Heaven knows I am innocent of any. Is it likely? Who would think of plotting with a poor little weak creature like me?"

The forlorn smile with which she said it, so touched him, that tears started from his eyes.

"I am not afraid to die, Citizen Evrémonde, but I have done nothing. I am not unwilling to die, if the Republic which is to do so much good to us poor, will profit by my death; but I do not know how that can be, Citizen Evrémonde. Such a poor weak little creature!"

As the last thing on earth that his heart was to warm and soften to, it warmed and softened to this pitiable girl.

"I heard you were released, Citizen Evrémonde. I hoped it was true?"

"It was. But, I was again taken and condemned."

"If I may ride with you, Citizen Evrémonde, will you let me hold your hand? I am not afraid, but I am little and weak, and it will give me more courage."

As the patient eyes were lifted to his face, he saw a sudden doubt in them, and then astonishment. He pressed the work-worn hunger-worn young fingers, and touched his lips.

"Are you dying for him?" she whispered.

"And his wife and child. Hush! Yes."

"O you will let me hold your brave hand, stranger?"

"Hush! Yes, my poor sister; to the last."

The same shadows that are falling on the prison, are falling in that same hour of the early afternoon, on the Barrier with the crowd about it, when a coach going out of Paris drives up to be examined.

"Who goes here? Whom have we within? Papers!"

The papers are handed out, and read.

"Alexandra Manette. Physician. French. Which is he?"

This is he; this helpless, inarticulately murmuring, wandering old man pointed out.

"Apparently the Citizen-Doctor is not in his right mind? The Revolution-fever will have been too much for him?"

Greatly too much for him.

"Hah! Many suffer with it. Lucie. His daughter. French. Which is she?"

This is she.

"Apparently it must be. Lucie, the wife of Evrémonde; is it not?"

It is.

"Hah! Evrémonde has an assignation elsewhere. Lucie, her child. English. This is she?"

She and no other.

"Kiss me, child of Evrémonde. Now, thou hast kissed a

good Republican; something new in thy family; remember
it? Sydney Carton. Advocate. English. Which is he?"

He lies here in this corner of the carriage. He, too, is
pointed out.

"Apparently the English advocate is in a swoon?"

It is hoped he will recover in the fresher air. It is represented that he is not in strong health, and has separated
sadly from a friend who is under the displeasure of the
Republic.

"Is that all? It is not a great deal that! Many are under
the displeasure of the Republic, and must look out at the little window. Jarvis Lorry. Banker. English. Which is he?"

"I am he. Necessarily, being the last."

It is Jarvis Lorry who has replied to all the previous questions. It is Jarvis Lorry who has alighted and stands with his
hand on the coach door, replying to a group of officials.
They leisurely walk round the carriage and leisurely mount
the box, to look at what little luggage it carries on the roof;
the country-people hanging about, press nearer to the
coach doors and greedily stare in; a little child, carried by its
mother, has its short arm held out for it, that it may touch
the wife of an aristocrat who has gone to the Guillotine.

"Behold your papers, Jarvis Lorry, counter-signed."

"One can depart, citizen?"

"One can depart. Forward, my postilions! A good journey!"

"I salute you, citizens.—And the first danger passed!"

These are again the words of Jarvis Lorry, as he clasps his
hands, and looks upward. There is terror in the carriage,
there is weeping, there is the heavy breathing of the insensible traveller.

"Are we not going too slowly? Can they not be induced
to go faster?" asks Lucie, clinging to the old man.

"It would seem like flight, my darling. I must not urge
them too much; it would rouse suspicion."

"Look back, look back, and see if we are pursued!"

"The road is clear my dearest. So far, we are not pursued."

Houses in twos and threes pass by us, solitary farms,

ruinous buildings, dye-works, tanneries, and the like, open country, avenues of leafless trees. The hard uneven pavement is under us, the soft deep mud is on either side. Sometimes, we strike into the skirting mud, to avoid the stones that clatter us and shake us; sometimes we stick in ruts and sloughs there. The agony of our impatience is then so great, that in our wild alarm and hurry we are for getting out and running—hiding—doing anything but stopping.

Out of the open country, in again among ruinous buildings, solitary farms, dye-works, tanneries, and the like, cottages in twos and threes, avenues of leafless trees. Have these men deceived us, and taken us back by another road? Is not this the same place twice over? Thank Heaven, no. A village. Look back, look back, and see if we are pursued! Hush! the posting-house.

Leisurely, our four horses are taken out; leisurely, the coach stands in the little street, bereft of horses, and with no likelihood upon it of ever moving again; leisurely, the new horses come into visible existence, one by one; leisurely, the new postilions follow, sucking and plaiting the lashes of their whips; leisurely, the old postilions count their money, make wrong additions, and arrive at dissatisfied results. All the time, our overfraught hearts are beating at a rate that would far outstrip the fastest gallop of the fastest horses ever foaled.

At length the new postilions are in their saddles, and the old are left behind. We are through the village, up the hill, and down the hill, and on the low watery grounds. Suddenly the postilions exchange speech with animated gesticulations, and the horses are pulled up, almost on their haunches. We are pursued?

"Ho! Within the carriage there. Speak then!"

"What is it?" asks Mr. Lorry, looking out at window.

"How many did they say?"

"I do not understand you."

"—At the last post. How many to the Guillotine today?"

"Fifty-two."

"I said so! A brave number! My fellow-citizen here would have it forty-two; ten more heads are worth having. The Guillotine goes handsomely. I love it. Hi forward. Whoop!"

The night comes on dark. He moves more; he is beginning to revive, and to speak intelligibly; he thinks they are still together; he asks him, by his name, what he has in his hand. O pity us, kind Heaven, and help us! Look out, look out, and see if we are pursued.

The wind is rushing after us, and the clouds are flying after us, and the moon is plunging after us, and the whole wild night is in pursuit of us, but, so far, we are pursued by nothing else.

14

THE KNITTING DONE

❦

IN THAT same juncture of time when the Fifty-Two
awaited their fate, Madame Defarge held darkly ominous
council with The Vengeance and Jacques Three of the
Revolutionary Jury. Not in the wine-shop did Madame
Defarge confer with these ministers, but in the shed of the
wood-sawyer, erst a mender of roads. The sawyer himself
did not participate in the conference, but abided at a little
distance, like an outer satellite who was not to speak until
required, or to offer an opinion until invited.

"But our Defarge," said Jacques Three, "is undoubtedly
a good Republican? Eh?"

"There is no better," the voluble Vengeance protested in
her shrill notes, "in France."

"Peace, little Vengeance," said Madame Defarge, laying
her hand with a slight frown on her lieutenant's lips, "hear
me speak. My husband, fellow-citizen, is a good
Republican and a bold man; he has deserved well of the
Republic, and possesses its confidence. But my husband
has his weaknesses, and he is so weak as to relent towards
this Doctor."

"It is a great pity," croaked Jacques Three, dubiously

shaking his head, with his cruel fingers at his hungry mouth; "it is not quite like a good citizen; it is a thing to regret."

"See you," said madame, "I care nothing for this Doctor, I. He may wear his head or lose it, for any interest I have in him; it is all one to me. But, the Evrémonde people are to be exterminated, and the wife and child must follow the husband and father."

"She has a fine head for it," croaked Jacques Three. "I have seen blue eyes and golden hair there, and they looked charming when Samson held them up." Ogre that he was, he spoke like an epicure.

Madame Defarge cast down her eyes, and reflected a little.

"The child also," observed Jacques Three, with a meditative enjoyment of his words, "has golden hair and blue eyes. And we seldom have a child there. It is a pretty sight!"

"In a word," said Madame Defarge, coming out of her short abstraction, "I cannot trust my husband in this matter. Not only do I feel, since last night, that I dare not confide to him the details of my projects; but also I feel that if I delay, there is danger of his giving warning; and then they might escape."

"That must never be," croaked Jacques Three; "no one must escape. We have not half enough as it is. We ought to have six score a day."

"In a word," Madame Defarge went on, "my husband has not my reason for pursuing this family to annihilation, and I have not his reason for regarding this Doctor with any sensibility. I must act for myself, therefore. Come hither, little citizen."

The wood-sawyer, who held her in the respect, and himself in the submission, of mortal fear, advanced with his hand to his red cap.

"Touching those signals, little citizen," said Madame Defarge, sternly, "that she made to the prisoners; you are ready to bear witness to them this very day?"

"Ay, ay, why not!" cried the sawyer. "Every day, in all

weathers, from two to four, always signalling, sometimes with the little one, sometimes without. I know what I know. I have seen with my eyes."

He made all manner of gestures while he spoke, as if in incidental imitation of some few of the great diversity of signals that he had never seen.

"Clearly plots," said Jacques Three. "Transparently!"

"There is no doubt of the Jury?" inquired Madame Defarge, letting her eyes turn to him with a gloomy smile.

"Rely upon the patriotic Jury, dear citizeness. I answer for my fellow-Jurymen."

"Now, let me see," said Madame Defarge, pondering again. "Yet once more! Can I spare this Doctor to my husband? I have no feeling either way. Can I spare him?"

"He would count as one head," observed Jacques Three, in a low voice. "We really have not heads enough; it would be a pity, I think."

"He was signalling with her when I saw her," argued Madame Defarge; "I cannot speak of one without the other; and I must not be silent, and trust the case wholly to him, this little citizen here. For I am not a bad witness."

The Vengeance and Jacques Three vied with each other in their fervent protestations that she was the most admirable and marvellous of witnesses. The little citizen, not to be outdone, declared her to be a celestial witness.

"He must take his chance," said Madame Defarge. "No, I cannot spare him! You are engaged at three o'clock; you are going to see the batch of to-day executed.—You?"

The question was addressed to the wood-sawyer, who hurriedly replied in the affirmative: seizing the occasion to add that he was the most ardent of Republicans, and that he would be in effect the most desolate of Republicans, if anything prevented him from enjoying the pleasure of smoking his afternoon pipe in the contemplation of the droll national barber. He was so very demonstrative herein, that he might have been suspected (perhaps was, by the dark eyes that looked contemptuously at him out of Madame Defarge's head) of having his small individual fears for his own personal safety, every hour in the day.

"I," said madame, "am equally engaged at the same place. After it is over—say at eight to-night—come you to me, in Saint Antoine, and we will give information against these people at my Section."

The wood-sawyer said he would be proud and flattered to attend the citizeness. The citizeness looking at him, he became embarrassed, evaded her glance as a small dog would have done, retreated among his wood, and hid his confusion over the handle of his saw.

Madame Defarge beckoned the Juryman and The Vengeance a little nearer to the door, and there expounded her further views to them thus:

"She will now be at home, awaiting the moment of his death. She will be mourning and grieving. She will be in a state of mind to impeach the justice of the Republic. She will be full of sympathy with its enemies. I will go to her."

"What an admirable woman; what an adorable woman!" exclaimed Jacques Three, rapturously. "Ah, my cherished!" cried The Vengeance; and embraced her.

"Take you my knitting," said Madame Defarge, placing it in her lieutenant's hands, "and have it ready for me in my usual seat. Keep me my usual chair. Go you there, straight, for there will probably be a greater concourse than usual, to-day."

"I willingly obey the orders of my Chief," said The Vengeance with alacrity, and kissing her cheek. "You will not be late?"

"I shall be there before the commencement."

"And before the tumbrils arrive. Be sure you are there, my soul," said The Vengeance, calling after her, for she had already turned into the street, "before the tumbrils arrive!"

Madame Defarge slightly waved her hand, to imply that she heard, and might be relied upon to arrive in good time, and so went through the mud, and round the corner of the prison wall. The Vengeance and the Juryman, looking after her as she walked away, were highly appreciative of her fine figure, and her superb moral endowments.

There were many women at that time upon whom the time laid a dreadfully disfiguring hand; but there was not one among them more to be dreaded than this ruthless woman, now taking her way along the streets. Of a strong and fearless character, of shrewd sense and readiness, of great determination, of that kind of beauty which not only seems to impart to its possessor firmness and animosity, but seems to strike into others an instinctive recognition of those qualities; the troubled time would have heaved her up, under any circumstances. But, imbued from her childhood with a brooding sense of wrong, and an inveterate hatred of a class, opportunity had developed her into a tigress. She was absolutely without pity. If she had ever had the virtue in her, it had quite gone out of her.

It was nothing to her that an innocent man was to die for the sins of his forefathers; she saw, not him, but them. It was nothing to her, that his wife was to be made a widow and his daughter an orphan; that was insufficient punishment, because they were her natural enemies and her prey, and as such had no right to live. To appeal to her, was made hopeless by her having no sense of pity, even for herself. If she had been laid low in the streets, in any of the many encounters in which she had been engaged, she would not have pitied herself; nor, if she had been ordered to the axe to-morrow, would she have gone to it with any softer feeling than a fierce desire to change places with the man who sent her there.

Such a heart Madame Defarge carried under her rough robe. Carelessly worn, it was a becoming robe enough, in a certain weird way, and her dark hair looked rich under her coarse red cap. Lying hidden in her bosom, was a loaded pistol. Lying hidden at her waist, was a sharpened dagger. Thus accoutred, and walking with the confident tread of such a character, and with the supple freedom of a woman who had habitually walked in her girlhood, bare-foot and bare-legged, on the brown sea sand, Madame Defarge took her way along the streets.

Now, when the journey of the travelling coach, at that very moment waiting for the completion of its load, had been planned out last night, the difficulty of taking Miss Pross in it had much engaged Mr. Lorry's attention. It was not merely desirable to avoid overloading the coach, but it was of the highest importance that the time occupied in examining it and its passengers, should be reduced to the utmost; since their escape might depend on the saving of only a few seconds here and there. Finally, he had proposed, after anxious consideration, that Miss Pross and Jerry, who were at liberty to leave the city, should leave it at three o'clock in the lightest-wheeled conveyance known to that period. Unencumbered with luggage, they would soon overtake the coach, and, passing it and preceding it on the road, would order its horses in advance, and greatly facilitate its progress during the precious hours of the night, when delay was the most to be dreaded.

Seeing in this arrangement the hope of rendering real service in that pressing emergency, Miss Pross hailed it with joy. She and Jerry had beheld the coach start, had known who it was that Solomon brought, had passed some ten minutes in tortures of suspense, and were now concluding their arrangements to follow the coach, even as Madame Defarge, taking her way through the streets, now drew nearer and nearer to the else-deserted lodging in which they held their consultation.

"Now what do you think, Mr. Cruncher," said Miss Pross, whose agitation was so great that she could hardly speak, or stand, or move, or live: "what do you think of our not starting from this court-yard? Another carriage having already gone from here to-day, it might awaken suspicion."

"My opinion, miss," returned Mr. Cruncher, "is as you're right. Likewise wot I'll stand by you, right or wrong."

"I am so distracted with fear and hope for our precious creatures," said Miss Pross, wildly crying, "that I am incapable of forming any plan. Are *you* capable of forming any plan, my dear good Mr. Cruncher?"

"Respectin' a future spear o' life, miss," returned Mr. Cruncher, "I hope so. Respectin' any present use o' this here blessed old head o' mine, I think not. Would you do me the favour, miss, to take notice o' two promises and wows wot it is my wishes fur to record in this here crisis?"

"Oh, for gracious sake!" cried Miss Pross, still wildly crying, "record them at once, and get them out of the way, like an excellent man."

"First," said Mr. Cruncher, who was all in a tremble, and who spoke with an ashy and solemn visage, "them poor things well out o' this, never no more will I do it, never no more!"

"I am quite sure, Mr. Cruncher," returned Miss Pross, "that you never will do it again, whatever it is, and I beg you not to think it necessary to mention more particularly what it is."

"No, miss," returned Jerry, "it shall not be named to you. Second: them poor things well out o' this, and never no more will I interfere with Mrs. Cruncher's floppin', never no more!"

"Whatever housekeeping arrangement that may be," said Miss Pross, striving to dry her eyes and compose herself, "I have no doubt it is best that Mrs. Cruncher should have it entirely under her own superintendence. O my poor darlings!"

"I go so far as to say, miss, moreover," proceeded Mr. Cruncher, with a most alarming tendency to hold forth as from a pulpit—"and let my words be took down and took to Mrs. Cruncher through yourself—that wot my opinions respectin' floppin' has undergone a change, and that wot I only hope with all my heart as Mrs. Cruncher may be a-floppin' at the present time."

"There, there, there! I hope she is, my dear man," cried the distracted Miss Pross, "and I hope she finds it answering her expectations."

"Forbid it," proceeded Mr. Cruncher, with additional

solemnity, additional slowness, and additional tendency to hold forth and hold out, "as anything wot I have ever said or done should be wished on my earnest wishes for them poor creeturs now! Forbid it as we shouldn't all flop (if it was anyways conwenient) to get 'em out o' this here dismal risk! Forbid it, miss! Wot I say, for-BID it!" This was Mr. Cruncher's conclusion after a protracted but vain endeavour to find a better one.

And still Madame Defarge, pursuing her way along the streets, came nearer and nearer.

"If we ever get back to our native land," said Miss Pross, "you may rely upon my telling Mrs. Cruncher as much as I may be able to remember and understand of what you have so impressively said; and at all events you may be sure that I shall bear witness to your being thoroughly in earnest at this dreadful time. Now, pray let us think! My esteemed Mr. Cruncher, let us think!"

Still, Madame Defarge, pursuing her way along the streets, came nearer and nearer.

"If you were to go before," said Miss Pross, "and stop the vehicle and horses from coming here, and were to wait somewhere for me; wouldn't that be best?"

Mr. Cruncher thought it might be best.

"Where could you wait for me?" asked Miss Pross.

Mr. Cruncher was so bewildered that he could think of no locality but Temple Bar. Alas Temple Bar was hundreds of miles away, and Madame Defarge was drawing very near indeed.

"By the cathedral door," said Miss Pross. "Would it be much out of the way, to take me in near the great cathedral door between the two towers?"

"No, miss," answered Mr. Cruncher.

"Then, like the best of men," said Miss Pross, "go to the posting-house straight, and make that change."

"I am doubtful," said Mr. Cruncher, hesitating and shaking his head, "about leaving of you, you see. We don't know what may happen."

"Heaven knows we don't," returned Miss Pross, "but have no fear for me. Take me in at the cathedral, at three o'clock, or as near it as you can, and I am sure it will be better than our going from here. I feel certain of it. There! Bless you, Mr. Cruncher! Think—not of me, but of the lives that may depend on both of us!"

This exordium, and Miss Pross's two hands in quite agonised entreaty clasping his, decided Mr. Cruncher. With an encouraging nod or two, he immediately went out to alter the arrangements, and left her by herself to follow as she had proposed.

The having originated a precaution which was already in course of execution, was a great relief to Miss Pross. The necessity of composing her appearance so that it should attract no special notice in the streets, was another relief. She looked at her watch, and it was twenty minutes past two. She had no time to lose, but must get ready at once.

Afraid, in her extreme perturbation, of the loneliness of the deserted rooms, and of half-imagined faces peeping from behind every open door in them, Miss Pross got a basin of cold water and began laving her eyes, which were swollen and red. Haunted by her feverish apprehensions, she could not bear to have her sight obscured for a minute at a time by the dripping water, but constantly paused and looked round to see that there was no one watching her. In one of those pauses she recoiled and cried out, for she saw a figure standing in the room.

The basin fell to the ground broken, and the water flowed to the feet of Madame Defarge. By strange stern ways, and through much staining blood, those feet had come to meet that water.

Madame Defarge looked coldly at her, and said, "The wife of Evrémonde; where is she?"

It flashed upon Miss Pross's mind that the doors were all standing open, and would suggest the flight. Her first act was to shut them. There were four in the room, and she shut them all. She then placed herself before the door of the chamber which Lucie had occupied.

Madame Defarge's dark eyes followed her through this rapid movement, and rested on her when it was finished. Miss Pross had nothing beautiful about her; years had not tamed the wildness, or softened the grimness, of her appearance; but, she too was a determined woman in her different way, and she measured Madame Defarge with her eyes, every inch.

"You might, from your appearance, be the wife of Lucifer," said Miss Pross, in her breathing. "Nevertheless, you shall not get the better of me. I am an Englishwoman."

Madame Defarge looked at her scornfully, but still with something of Miss Pross's own perception that they two were at bay. She saw a tight, hard, wiry woman before her, as Mr. Lorry had seen in the same figure a woman with a strong hand, in the years gone by. She knew full well that Miss Pross was the family's devoted friend; Miss Pross knew full well that Madame Defarge was the family's malevolent enemy.

"On my way yonder," said Madame Defarge, with a slight movement of her hand towards the fatal spot, "where they reserve my chair and my knitting for me, I am come to make my compliments to her in passing. I wish to see her."

"I know that your intentions are evil," said Miss Pross, "and you may depend upon it, I'll hold my own against them."

Each spoke in her own language; neither understood the other's words; both were very watchful, and intent to deduce from look and manner, what the unintelligible words meant.

"It will do her no good to keep herself concealed from me at this moment," said Madame Defarge. "Good patriots will know what that means. Let me see her. Go tell her that I wish to see her. Do you hear?"

"If those eyes of yours were bed-winches," returned Miss Pross, "and I was an English four-poster, they shouldn't loose a splinter of me. No, you wicked foreign woman; I am your match."

Madame Defarge was not likely to follow these idiomatic remarks in detail; but, she so far understood them as to perceive that she was set at naught.

"Woman imbecile and pig-like!" said Madame Defarge, frowning. "I take no answer from you. I demand to see her. Either tell her that I demand to see her, or stand out of the way of the door and let me go to her!" This, with an angry explanatory wave of her right arm.

"I little thought," said Miss Pross, "that I should ever want to understand your nonsensical language; but I would give all I have, except the clothes I wear, to know whether you suspect the truth, or any part of it."

Neither of them for a single moment released the other's eyes. Madame Defarge had not moved from the spot where she stood when Miss Pross first became aware of her; but, she now advanced one step.

"I am a Briton," said Miss Pross. "I am desperate. I don't care an English Twopence for myself. I know that the longer I keep you here, the greater hope there is for my Ladybird. I'll not leave a handful of that dark hair upon your head, if you lay a finger on me!"

Thus Miss Pross, with a shake of her head and a flash of her eyes between every rapid sentence, and every rapid sentence a whole breath. Thus Miss Pross, who had never struck a blow in her life.

But, her courage was of that emotional nature that it brought the irrepressible tears into her eyes. This was a courage that Madame Defarge so little comprehended as to mistake for weakness. "Ha, ha!" she laughed, "you poor wretch! What are you worth! I address myself to that Doctor." Then she raised her voice and called out, "Citizen Doctor! Wife of Evrémonde! Child of Evrémonde! Any person but this miserable fool, answer the Citizeness Defarge?"

Perhaps the following silence, perhaps some latent disclosure in the expression on Miss Pross's face, perhaps a sudden misgiving apart from either suggestion, whispered to Madame Defarge that they were gone. Three of the doors she opened swiftly, and looked in.

"Those rooms are all in disorder, there has been hurried packing, there are odds and ends upon the ground. There is no one in that room behind you! Let me look."

"Never!" said Miss Pross, who understood the request as perfectly as Madame Defarge understood the answer.

"If they are not in that room, they are gone, and can be pursued and brought back," said Madame Defarge to herself.

"As long as you don't know whether they are in that room or not, you are uncertain what to do," said Miss Pross to herself; "and you shall not know that, if I can prevent your knowing it; and know that, or not know that, you shall not leave here while I can hold you."

"I have been in the streets from the first, nothing has stopped me, I will tear you to pieces, but I will have you from that door," said Madame Defarge.

"We are alone at the top of a high house in a solitary court-yard, we are not likely to be heard, and I pray for bodily strength to keep you here, while every minute you are here is worth a hundred thousand guineas to my darling," said Miss Pross.

Madame Defarge made at the door. Miss Pross, on the instinct of the moment, seized her round the waist in both her arms, and held her tight. It was in vain for Madame Defarge to struggle and to strike; Miss Pross, with the vigorous tenacity of love, always so much stronger than hate, clasped her tight, and even lifted her from the floor in the struggle that they had. The two hands of Madame Defarge buffeted and tore her face; but, Miss Pross, with her head down, held her round the waist, and clung to her with more than the hold of a drowning woman.

Soon, Madame Defarge's hands ceased to strike, and felt at her encircled waist. "It is under my arm," said Miss Pross, in smothered tones, "you shall not draw it. I am stronger than you, I bless Heaven for it. I'll hold you till one or other of us faints or dies!"

Madame Defarge's hands were at her bosom. Miss Pross looked up, saw what it was, struck at it, struck out a flash and a crash, and stood alone—blinded with smoke.

All this was in a second. As the smoke cleared, leaving an awful stillness, it passed out on the air, like the soul of the furious woman whose body lay lifeless on the ground.

In the first fright and horror of her situation, Miss Pross passed the body as far from it as she could, and ran down the stairs to call for fruitless help. Happily, she bethought herself of the consequences of what she did, in time to check herself and go back. It was dreadful to go in at the door again; but she did go in, and even went near it, to get the bonnet and other things that she must wear. These she put on, out on the staircase, first shutting and locking the door and taking away the key. She then sat down on the stairs a few moments to breathe and to cry, and then got up and hurried away.

By good fortune she had a veil on her bonnet, or she could hardly have gone along the streets without being stopped. By good fortune, too, she was naturally so peculiar in appearance as not to show disfigurement like any other woman. She needed both advantages, for the marks of gripping fingers were deep in her face, and her hair was torn, and her dress (hastily composed with unsteady hands) was clutched and dragged a hundred ways.

In crossing the bridge, she dropped the door key in the river. Arriving at the cathedral some few minutes before her escort, and waiting there, she thought, what if the key were already taken in a net, and if it were identified, what if the door were opened and the remains discovered, what if she were stopped at the gate, sent to prison, and charged with murder! In the midst of these fluttering thoughts, the escort appeared, took her in, and took her away.

"Is there any noise in the streets?" she asked him.

"The usual noises," Mr. Cruncher replied; and looked surprised by the question and by her aspect.

"I don't hear you," said Miss Pross. "What do you say?"

It was in vain for Mr. Cruncher to repeat what he said; Miss Pross could not hear him. "So I'll nod my head," thought Mr. Cruncher, amazed, "at all events she'll see that." And she did.

"Is there any noise in the streets now?" asked Miss Pross again, presently.

Again Mr. Cruncher nodded his head.

"I don't hear it."

"Gone deaf in a hour?" said Mr. Cruncher, ruminating, with his mind much disturbed; "wot's come to her?"

"I feel," said Miss Pross, "as if there had been a flash and a crash, and that crash was the last thing I should ever hear in this life."

"Blest if she ain't in a queer condition!" said Mr. Cruncher, more and more disturbed. "Wot can she have been a takin', to keep her courage up? Hark! There's the roll of them dreadful carts! You can hear that, Miss?"

"I can hear," said Miss Pross, seeing that he spoke to her, "nothing. O, my good man, there was first a great crash, and then a great stillness, and that stillness seems to be fixed and unchangeable, never to be broken any more as long as my life lasts."

"If she don't hear the roll of those dreadful carts, now very nigh their journey's end," said Mr. Cruncher, glancing over his shoulder, "it's my opinion that indeed she never will hear anything else in this world."

And indeed she never did.

15

THE FOOTSTEPS DIE OUT FOR EVER

A LONG THE Paris streets, the death-carts rumble, hollow and harsh. Six tumbrils carry the day's wine to La Guillotine. All the devouring and insatiate Monsters imagined since imagination could record itself, are fused in the one realisation, Guillotine. And yet there is not in France, with its rich variety of soil and climate, a blade, a leaf, a root, a sprig, a peppercorn, which will grow to maturity under conditions more certain than those that have produced this horror. Crush humanity out of shape once more, under similar hammers, and it will twist itself into the same tortured forms. Sow the same seed of rapacious license and oppression over again, and it will surely yield the same fruit according to its kind.

Six tumbrils roll along the streets. Change these back again to what they were, thou powerful enchanter, Time, and they shall be seen to be the carriages of absolute monarchs, the equipages of feudal nobles, the toilettes of flaring Jezebels,[12] the churches that are not my Father's house but dens of thieves, the huts of millions of starving peasants! No; the great magician who majestically works out the appointed order of the Creator, never reverses his transformations. "If thou be changed into this shape by the will of God," say the seers to the enchanted, in the wise Arabian stories, "then remain so! But, if thou wear this form through mere passing conjuration, then resume thy former aspect!" Changeless and hopeless, the tumbrils roll along.

As the sombre wheels of the six carts go round, they seem to plough up a long crooked furrow among the populace in the streets. Ridges of faces are thrown to this side and to that, the ploughs go steadily onward. So used are the regular inhabitants of the houses to the spectacle, that in many windows there are no people, and in some occupation of the hands is not so much as suspended, while the eyes survey the faces in the tumbrils. Here and there, the inmate has visitors to see the sight; then he points his finger, with something of the complacency of a curator or authorised exponent, to this cart and to this, and seems to tell who sat here yesterday, and who there the day before.

Of the riders in the tumbrils, some observe these things, and all things on their last roadside, with an impassive stare; others, with a lingering interest in the ways of life and men. Some, seated with drooping heads, are sunk in silent despair; again, there are some so heedful of their looks that they cast upon the multitude such glances as they have seen in theatres, and in pictures. Several close their eyes, and think, or try to get their straying thoughts together. Only one, and he a miserable creature, of a crazed aspect, is so shattered and made drunk by horror, that he sings, and tries to dance. Not one of the whole number appeals by look or gesture, to the pity of the people.

There is a guard of sundry horsemen riding abreast of the tumbrils, and faces are often turned up to some of them, and they are asked some question. It would seem to be always the same question, for it is always followed by a press of people towards the third cart. The horsemen abreast of that cart, frequently point out one man in it with their swords. The leading curiosity is, to know which is he; he stands at the back of the tumbril with his head bent down, to converse with a mere girl who sits on the side of the cart, and holds his hand. He has no curiosity or care for the scene about him, and always speaks to the girl. Here and there in the long street of St. Honoré, cries are raised against him. If they move him at all, it is only to a quiet smile, as he shakes his hair a little more loosely about his face. He cannot easily touch his face, his arms being bound.

On the steps of a church, awaiting the coming-up of the tumbrils, stands the Spy and prison-sheep. He looks into the first of them: not there. He looks into the second: not there. He already asks himself, "Has he sacrificed me?" when his face clears, as he looks into the third.

"Which is Evrémonde?" says a man behind him.

"That. At the back there."

"With his hand in the girl's?"

"Yes."

The man cries, "Down, Evrémonde! To the Guillotine all aristocrats! Down, Evrémonde!"

"Hush, hush!" the Spy entreats him, timidly.

"And why not, citizen?"

"He is going to pay the forfeit: it will be paid in five minutes more. Let him be at peace."

But the man continuing to exclaim, "Down, Evrémonde!" the face of Evrémonde is for a moment turned towards him. Evrémonde then sees the Spy, and looks attentively at him, and goes his way.

The clocks are on the stroke of three, and the furrow ploughed among the populace is turning round, to come on into the place of execution, and end. The ridges thrown to this side and to that, now crumble in and close behind the last plough as it passes on, for all are following to the Guillotine. In front of it, seated in chairs, as in a garden of public diversion, are a number of women, busily knitting. On one of the foremost chairs, stands The Vengeance, looking about for her friend.

"Thérèse!" she cries, in her shrill tones. "Who has seen her? Thérèse Defarge!"

"She never missed before," says a knitting-woman of the sisterhood.

"No; nor will she miss now," cries The Vengeance petulantly. "Thérèse."

"Louder," the woman recommends.

Ay! Louder, Vengeance, much louder, and still she will scarcely hear thee. Louder yet, Vengeance, with a little oath or so added, and yet it will hardly bring her. Send other women up and down to seek her, lingering somewhere; and yet, although the messengers have done dread deeds, it is questionable whether of their own wills they will go far enough to find her!

"Bad Fortune!" cries The Vengeance, stamping her foot in the chair, "and here are the tumbrils! And Evrémonde will be despatched in a wink, and she not here! See her knitting in my hand, and her empty chair ready for her. I cry with vexation and disappointment!"

As The Vengeance descends from her elevation to do it, the tumbrils begin to discharge their loads. The ministers of Sainte Guillotine are robed and ready. Crash!—a head is held up, and the knitting-women, who scarcely lifted their eyes to look at it a moment ago when it could think and speak, count One.

The second tumbril empties and moves on; the third comes up. Crash!—And the knitting-women, never faltering or pausing in their work, count Two.

The supposed Evrémonde descends, and the seamstress is lifted out next after him. He has not relinquished her patient hand in getting out, but still holds it as he promised. He gently places her with her back to the crashing engine that constantly whirs up and falls, and she looks into his face and thanks him.

"But for you, dear stranger, I should not be so composed, for I am naturally a poor little thing, faint of heart; nor should I have been able to raise my thoughts to Him who was put to death, that we might have hope and comfort here to-day. I think you were sent to me by Heaven."

"Or you to me," says Sydney Carton. "Keep your eyes upon me, dear child, and mind no other object."

"I mind nothing while I hold your hand. I shall mind nothing when I let it go, if they are rapid."

"They will be rapid. Fear not!"

The two stand in the fast-thinning throng of victims, but they speak as if they were alone. Eye to eye, voice to voice, hand to hand, heart to heart, these two children of the Universal Mother, else so wide apart and differing, have come together on the dark highway, to repair home together, and to rest in her bosom.

"Brave and generous friend, will you let me ask you one last question? I am very ignorant, and it troubles me—just a little."

"Tell me what it is."

"I have a cousin, an only relative and an orphan, like myself, whom I love very dearly. She is five years younger than I, and she lives in a farmer's house in the south country. Poverty parted us, and she knows nothing of my fate—for I cannot write—and if I could, how should I tell her! It is better as it is."

"Yes, yes, better as it is."

"What I have been thinking as we came along, and what I am still thinking now, as I look into your kind strong face which gives me so much support, is this:—If the Republic really does good to the poor, and they come to be less hungry, and in all ways to suffer less, she may live a long time: she may even live to be old."

"What then, my gentle sister?"

"Do you think"; the uncomplaining eyes in which there is so much endurance, fill with tears, and the lips part a little more and tremble: "that it will seem long to me, while I wait for her in the better land where I trust both you and I will be mercifully sheltered?"

"It cannot be, my child; there is no Time there, and no trouble there."

"You comfort me so much! I am so ignorant. Am I to kiss you now? Is the moment come?"

"Yes."

She kisses his lips; he kisses hers; they solemnly bless each other. The spare hand does not tremble as he releases it; nothing worse than a sweet, bright constancy is in the patient face. She goes next before him—is gone; the knitting-women count Twenty-Two.

"I am the resurrection and the life, saith the Lord: he that believeth in me, though he were dead, yet shall he live: and whosoever liveth and believeth in me, shall never die!"

The murmuring of many voices, the upturning of many faces, the pressing on of many footsteps in the outskirts of the crowd, so that it swells forward in a mass, like one great heave of water, all flashes away. Twenty-Three.

They said of him, about the city that night, that it was the peacefullest man's face ever beheld there. Many added that he looked sublime and prophetic.

One of the most remarkable sufferers by the same axe— a woman—had asked at the foot of the same scaffold, not long before, to be allowed to write down the thoughts that were inspiring her. If he had given any utterance to his, and they were prophetic, they would have been these:

"I see Barsad, and Cly, Defarge, The Vengeance, the Jurymen, the Judge, long ranks of the new oppressors who have risen on the destruction of the old, perishing by this retributive instrument, before it shall cease out of its present use. I see a beautiful city and a brilliant people rising from this abyss, and, in their struggles to be truly free, in their triumphs and defeats, through long, long years to come, I see the evil of this time and of the previous time of which this is the natural birth, gradually making expiation for itself and wearing out.

"I see the lives for which I lay down my life, peaceful, useful, prosperous and happy, in that England which I shall see no more. I see Her with a child upon her bosom, who bears my name. I see her father, aged and bent, but otherwise restored, and faithful to all men in his healing office, and at peace; I see the good old man, so long their friend, in ten years' time enriching them with all he has, and passing tranquilly to his reward.

"I see that I hold a sanctuary in their hearts, and in the hearts of their descendants, generations hence. I see her, an old woman, weeping for me on the anniversary of this day. I see her and her husband, their course done, lying side by side in their last earthly bed, and I know that each was not more honoured and held sacred in the other's soul, than I was in the souls of both.

"I see that child who lay upon her bosom and who bore my name, a man winning his way up in that path of life which once was mine. I see him winning it so well, that my name is made illustrious there by the light of his. I see the blots I threw upon it, faded away. I see him, foremost of just judges and honoured men, bringing a boy of my name, with a forehead that I know and golden hair, to this place—then fair to look upon, with not a trace of this day's disfigurement—and I hear him tell the child my story, with a tender and a faltering voice.

"It is a far, far better thing that I do, than I have ever done; it is a far, far better rest that I go to, than I have ever known."

NOTES

Book the First: Recalled to Life

1. **one thousand seven hundred and seventy-five:** In 1775, the thrones of England and France were occupied by George III and Louis XVI, respectively. The American Revolution was imminent as unrest was spreading in the American colonies.

2. **paper money:** In the years before the Revolution, France experienced a serious financial crisis during which the crown printed paper money.

3. **Temple Bar:** A stone gate that marked the entrance to the city of London.

4. **pecuniary Mangle:** After clothing was washed, particularly in public laundries, it was run through a machine called a mangle that pressed clothing between heated rollers. Mr. Lorry suggests that he operates a mangle that flattens money instead of clothes.

5. **filling up blank forms of the consignment:** The reference is to lettres de cachet, blank warrants that allowed the holder to write in any name and so have whomever they wished arrested and imprisoned without trial. Influential people were able to procure these, and their use and abuse went unchecked.

6. **lee-dyed:** Lee is the sediment deposited by wine it its cask. Figuratively, the word *lee* means dregs or refuse. Perhaps Dickens intends the literal meaning to apply to the actual dregs of the wine and the figuratively to apply to the residents of Saint Antoine.

7. **Saint Antoine:** An eastern suburb of Paris, containing the Bastille.

Book the Second: The Golden Thread

1. **Barmecide:** One of the tales of the *Arabian Nights* concerns a prince of the Barmecide family who was asked by a beggar for food. The prince put a succession of empty dishes before the beggar, declaring each to contain some sumptuous morsel. Thus, here the Barmecide room is a place where Tellson's puts things it is pretending to take care of but is really ignoring.

2. **heads exposed on Temple Bar:** Until 1780 the heads and limbs of executed criminals were publicly displayed on spikes at Temple Bar.

3. **the Old Bailey:** Nickname for the criminal court building on the street of the same name.

4. **Bedlam:** The Hospital of St. Mary of Bethlehem, an insane asylum, established in 1402. During Dickens's time, people paid to see the insane as a form of entertainment. *Bedlam*, a contraction of *Bethlehem*, is in common usage today for a place or state of chaos and confusion.

5. **State Trials:** Published collections of reports of the trials involving crimes against the state. Dickens likely used details from these published reports in describing Darnay's trial. Of course, Dickens, as a former court reporter, would have been familiar with the procedures of English criminal courts of his day, but he would not have been as familiar with the court customs of nearly seventy years prior.

6. **Sydney Carton:** Dickens began writing the manuscript with Carton's first name as Dick. Thus his initials would

have been the reverse of Charles Darnay's, which would have strongly implied the notion of Darnay and Carton as mirror images. Midway through the book Dickens changed the character's name to Sydney instead.

7. **Hilary term and Michaelmas:** The dates from the thirteenth of January to the twenty-ninth of September. Both of these dates mark the beginning of terms of the High Court of Justice in England.

8. **Soho-square:** A parish of London which was known for its population of European immigrants, most notably a large number of French Protestants (known as Huguenots) who came seeking religious asylum after the Edict of Nantes was revoked in 1685. It is thought that the Carlisle House, a former hotel in the parish, was the building that Dickens had in mind as the Manette residence.

9. **merry Stuart:** Charles II, known as the "merry monarch," ruled from 1660 to 1685. He was called "merry" both because of his own pleasure-seeking lifestyle and because he lifted restrictions on entertainment that had been put into place during the rule of Oliver Cromwell, a Puritan, who governed England as Lord Protector from 1649 to 1658. Charles was secretly a Catholic, and in 1670 signed the Treaty of Dover with Louis XIV of France in which he promised to make England a Catholic nation once again in exchange for a stipend from France.

10. **Unbelieving Chemists who had an eye on the transmutation of metals:** Alchemists, who sought the chemical processes by which a base metal could be turned into gold. They are termed unbelieving, as are the philosophers, because belief in Christian doctrine was fading among the intellectual elite in France during this time.

11. **Convulsionists:** Fanatic religious sect that arose in France in the eighteenth century whose members went to the tombs of saints, where they fell into fits and convulsions, hoping for miraculous cures.

12. **Palace of Tuileries:** The former royal palace of Paris, used as the primary royal residence until Louis XIV moved his court to Versailles. After an attempt to flee the country in October 1789, Louis XVI was sequestered at Tuileries until his execution.

13. **shaken the dust from his feet:** An ironic reference to Matthew 10:14: "And whosoever shall not receive you, nor hear your words, when ye depart out of that house or city, shake off the dust of your feet."

14. **fagged:** Worked exceedingly hard.

15. **Furies:** In Greek mythology, dreaded goddesses with snakes either instead of or twined in their hair or whose function was to punish murderers, particularly those who had slain blood relatives.

16. **rain falls impartially:** From Matthew 5:45: ". . . he maketh his sun to rise on the evil and the good, and sendeth rain on the just and the unjust."

17. **poniarded:** Stabbed; from poniard, a type of dagger.

18. **German ballad of Leonora:** An extremely popular poem "Lenore" by Gottfred August Bürger (1747–1794) which tells of Lenore, who is awaiting the return of her fiancé, William, who has been away at war. He returns and takes her with him on the back of his horse, stating that they are riding to their wedding bed. After an hour's ride, they come to a cemetery where William suddenly turns into the figure of Death. Lenore tries to escape but cannot. Thus Dickens is suggesting that Gabelle and his servant might be riding to their deaths.

19. **King's Bench bar:** One of the three superior courts of common law in England. King's Bench had exclusive jurisdiction over criminal cases.

20. **Versailles:** Louis XIV's palace, eleven miles outside Paris. On Sundays, the King and Queen dined in view of the public.

21. **bells . . . melted into thundering cannon:** Thomas Carlyle notes that during the Revolution iron church bells were melted to make cannons.

22. **as old as Adam:** That is, from the beginning of time when, according to the book of Genesis in the Bible, God created Adam.

23. **Bastille:** A prison in Paris that housed many political prisoners. The storming of the Bastille, which marked the start of the Revolution, is depicted here by Dickens.

24. **seven faces of prisoners:** When the Bastille was stormed it was found to contain only seven prisoners: four forgers, two insane men, and a follower of the Marquis de Sade.

25. **The Vengeance:** It was common during the revolutionary period for people to adopt political or moral concepts as names.

26. **tocsin:** An alarm sounded by the ringing of a bell or bells, used as much as a siren is today.

27. **reading the Lord's Prayer backwards:** It was a common superstitious belief that one could summon the Devil by reading the Lord's Prayer backward.

28. **Lucifer's pride, Sardanapalus's luxury:** Lucifer was the angel who, because of his pride, rebelled against God, was thrown out of heaven, and subsequently set up his own kingdom, Hell. Sardanapalus was the last king of Assyria who, according to legend, loved luxurious things and was effeminate. When he was overthrown, rather than be captured by the enemy, he burned his sumptuous palace with his family and himself inside.

Book the Third: The Track of a Storm

1. **red caps . . . tricoloured cockades:** Red caps were worn by those sympathetic to the Revolution. The tricolor is the blue, white, and red French flag still used today. It was adopted in 1794 as a contrast to the white cockades and banners of the Bourbon kings. A cockade is a ribbon rosette.

2. **the Bastille that is no more:** After the Bastille was stormed it was pulled down.

3. **strong man of Old Scripture:** Samson, whose story can be found in Judges 13–16. Samson was given incredible strength by God, and so he was able to perform astounding feats that staved off the Philistine rule over the Israelites.

4. **popular Revolution song:** Dickens is probably referring to "La Carmagnole," considered the most popular song of the French Revolution. A dance, also called the Carmagnole, accompanined the song.

5. **Conciergerie:** The prison attached to the Palace of Justice in Paris.

6. **the Goddess of Liberty:** a popular figure in the imagery of the Revolution. A statue to her was erected in the place de la Révolution in August 1793.

7. **"I am the resurrection . . . shall never die":** Sydney Carton is quoting, from John 11:25, the words of Jesus to Martha just before he raised her brother, Lazarus, from the dead.

8. **I—Alexandre Manette:** The testament of Dr. Manette is probably based on reports of similar such testaments found in the walls of the Bastille before it was destroyed.

9. **rouleau of gold:** A stack of gold coins rolled in paper.

10. **Jacobin journal:** There were many magazines published by the various radical parties in Paris at the time of the revolution, this being just one. The Jacobin club by this time had become the dominant faction among the Revolutionaries.

11. **He wrote a long letter to Lucie:** Condemned prisoners were allowed to write such letters. However, few of these "last words" ever reached their intended destination.

12. **Jezebels:** Loose and immoral women; from the wife of the evil King Ahab in Kings, which portrayed Jezebel as a wicked woman. Also see Revelation 2:20–21, which descibes Jezebel as a seducer.

INTERPRETIVE NOTES

✦

The Plot

The novel begins in 1775 with Mr. Lorry, an agent of Tellson's Bank, making the dangerous trek from London to Paris on business for the bank. At an inn on the English coast Mr. Lorry has an appointment with Lucie Manette, a French-born woman who, unbeknownst to her, has important business with Tellson's. The business, as Mr. Lorry relates, is that her father, Dr. Manette, who she long thought dead, has been imprisoned for the last eighteen years in the Bastille. Dr. Manette has been released and is in Paris under the supervision of the Defarges, wine-shop keepers in the Saint Antoine district. In Dr. Manette's release we have the first instance of resurrection, an important theme in the novel. Dr. Manette, dead in his daughter's mind, has arisen from the dark depths of the Bastille. But what has he arisen to? Dr. Manette, at least at first, does not achieve new life but rather suffers from the mental instability that his imprisonment has wrought. In this way, Dickens introduces the notion of resurrection but also poses the question of whether resurrection is really possible.

After father and daughter are reunited in Paris, they begin the journey back to London. While crossing the English Channel, Lucie meets Charles Darnay, who shows compassion and consideration for the pathetic father and daughter pair.

Five years later Charles Darnay is on trial in London accused of spying for the French government. Darnay's fate appears sealed when a witness testifies that he recovered incriminating documents from Darnay's possession. The momentum of the trial shifts, though, when Sydney Carton, part of Darnay's legal team, suggests a line of argument that ultimately convinces the jury that Darnay is innocent. This line of argument centers on the physical resemblance of Darnay and Carton, a fact first noted during the trial and returned to repeatedly throughout the novel. Here again Dickens plays with the alternation of death and life. Darnay appears as good as dead before Carton, Darnay's strange physical double, steps in and saves him from the clutches of the English gallows. Darnay is granted life when death seemed inescapable. Darnay, the "good" man, is saved by Carton, a wretched drunk.

By this time, the Manettes have settled in London, and Dr. Manette is almost fully recovered (or fully resurrected) from his mental instability. He resumes practicing medicine and Mr. Lorry, Carton, and Darnay become regular fixtures at the Manette residence. Carton, a man of great talents wasted both professionally and personally, falls in love with Lucie, but he determines that a man of his poor character should never demand her affections. In this Dickens shows us the despondency of a man who believes regeneration (or resurrection) of his character is not possible. In this despondency, Carton goes to Lucie in secret, reveals his love, but does not seek her hand in marriage, pledging that if ever given the chance he will make any sacrifice for her happiness.

During this time, Darnay also falls in love with Lucie. Darnay, Carton's double, does not suffer Carton's character flaws, and so without shame he marries Lucie. Tranquil years of familial happiness follow for the Manette and Darnay household in London as revolutionary fervor increases in France. Darnay's uncle, a French aristocrat, is murdered as the French Revolution gets underway. Darnay is in England because he renounced his French titles out of disgust for the injustices of the French aristocracy system. But he returns to France after receiving a letter imploring him to come to the aid of a manager of his family's estate, who has been unjustly imprisoned. Before even arriving in Paris, Darnay is arrested for being a French aristocrat. Upon hearing this dreadful news, Dr. Manette and Lucie, with Lucie and Charles's young daughter in tow, travel to Paris in the hopes of being able to aid the imprisoned Darnay.

Dr. Manette and Lucie's long struggle with the French revolutionaries comprises the final third of the novel. Surprising revelations and sudden reversals throw the family's fate into jeopardy repeatedly. As in many Dickens novels, amazing coincidences play a hand in the plot, as each character seems to have a secret in his or her past that has a direct impact on the present action. In the end, Darnay is suddenly and unexpectedly freed by an unlikely savior, and Dickens gives readers one of the most famous, stirring, and satisfying conclusions ever written.

Characters

Doctor Manette. Father of Lucie. Caring and humane physician unjustly imprisoned in the Bastille. As the message telling of his release from prison indicates, Manette is "recalled to life" from a dark period of mental illness during which time he literally forgets his identity. His continuing struggle with mental illness highlights the fact that being "recalled to life" during such a troubled time might not be desirable.

Lucie Manette. Daughter of Doctor Manette. French born, she is raised as an orphan in England. As a young woman she is told that her father actually lives, and upon being reunited with him, she devotes herself to restoring him to health. Throughout the book, those who see her remark upon her beauty. She marries Charles Darnay and they have a child, Lucie.

Charles Darnay. The nephew of the Marquis St. Evrémonde. As a young man Darnay renounces his future claim to the title of Marquis, and so ignites enmity between him and his uncle, the Marquis. Fleeing the family heritage, Darnay moves to London, where he earns a living tutoring students in French. He marries Lucie Manette.

Jarvis Lorry. Agent of Tellson's Bank. Mr. Lorry, an inveterate businessman, becomes involved with the Manette family through his handling of the Manette account at Tellson's. Through the years he becomes a close family friend and plays an important role as the family navigates the perils of revolutionary Paris.

Ernest Defarge. A wine-shop keeper in Paris, he is a central figure in the revolutionary tides that foment before and during the French Revolution. He also happens to have been the servant of Doctor Manette before his imprisonment in the Bastille, and after Doctor Manette's imprisonment he continues to cross paths with the Manette family.

Thérèse Defarge, Madame Defarge. The wife of Ernest Defarge, she knits the record of those who have been unjustly killed before the revolution, and she also knits the names of those upon whom the revolution exacts its vengeance. She is a key player among the peasant revolutionaries and strikes fear in the hearts of many, at times including her husband. A dark secret ties her to Charles Darnay's family, and this secret motivates her fierce desire for Darnay's head. Critics liken her to Shakespeare's Lady Macbeth.

Sydney Carton. As part of the legal counsel for Darnay, Carton's legal acumen helps save his client from the gallows. Though of great talent, Carton lives the life of a wastrel and so remains only the assistant to Mr. Stryver, an inferior though more ambitious lawyer. Carton is the novel's Christ figure.

Miss Pross. Companion and friend of the Manette family. Rather opportunely, she is enlisted by Mr. Lorry to travel with him and Lucie as they go to meet Doctor Manette after his imprisonment. Through this connection she becomes a family friend and takes up residence with the Manettes in London. In the final chapters she plays a crucial role as she shows her mettle in a deadly confrontation with Madame Defarge. In a sense, she is the stalwart British counterpart of the ruthless, imposing Madame Defarge. By having the two women confront each other in the end, Dickens gave British readers the chance to cheer for the victory of their own values and country.

Jerry Cruncher. Porter at Tellson's Bank. Jerry is an unrefined and uneducated porter who perches daily at the door of Tellson's. By night he plies a darker trade; as a resurrectionist he robs graves to supply doctors with fresh bodies to study. He travels with Mr. Lorry to Paris to assist him in closing out the Paris branch and in so doing plays an important role in the final stages of the novel.

Mr. Stryver. Lead counsel in Darnay's spy trial, he is as loud and garrulous as he is large. A social climber (as his name suggests), unencumbered by his lack of social and mental deftness, he barrels through every scene in which he appears with a large ego and an ambitious grin in tow.

Marquis St. Evrémonde. Uncle of Charles Darnay. A ruthless French aristocrat who wages a bitter family battle with his nephew. His cruel and contemptuous attitude toward the death of a boy who his carriage crushes to death ultimately leads to his death. The avenger accomplishes his task as the Marquis sleeps in his own bed.

John Barsad. Brother of Miss Pross. His given name is Solomon Pross. He first appears as a witness against Darnay in Darnay's trial. Later in the novel Barsad is discovered to be Miss Pross's brother and also a French spy in the streets of Paris. He plays an important part in getting Carton his final "interview" with Darnay.

Symbols and Themes

Fury of the French Peasantry. Dickens first introduces the reader to the French commoner with a disturbing image: at Defarge's wine shop a cask breaks open as it is unloaded from a cart. The people in the street in an almost bestial way lap up all the wine until there is not a drop left. The symbolic import is explicitly spelled out when a peasant dips his finger in the wine and scrawls the word *blood* on a nearby wall (p. 35). Here, in compact, we have Dickens's view of the role of the French peasantry in the French Revolution. Just as the people in the street rabidly drank down the spilled wine, so the French revolutionaries rabidly split and drank down the blood of the nobility. It is a savage image, but one that Dickens consistently portrays throughout *A Tale of Two Cities*. Though Dickens is in no way sympathetic to the unjust French aristocracy, he is shocked by the bloodlust of the French peasantry. There is not a single positive portrayal of the French peasantry once the revolution begins. Dickens clearly sees the many tides within the revolution as the vicissitudes of a mobocracy. The result is a ghastly rule by an ungainly and explosive mob.

Resurrection. The notion of resurrection has multiple manifestations and inversions in *A Tale of Two Cities*. Dr. Manette's resurrection from the dark of the Bastille, and in the mind of his daughter since she thought him dead, is the most straightforward incidence of resurrection in the novel. His full resurrection is not immediate but gradual as he slowly regains his mental health. Jerry Cruncher, on the other hand, inverts the religious notion of resurrection. As a resurrectionist, he desecrates graves by stealing their sacrosanct cargo and selling their contents to the highest bidder. Thus, he makes the dead live again in the laboratories of London. The classic Christian meaning of resurrection is invoked explicitly at the end of the novel as Carton contemplates his own death and recalls the prayer said over his father's grave: "I am the resurrection and the life, saith the Lord: he that believeth in me, though he were dead, yet shall he live: and whosoever liveth and believeth in me, shall never die" (Book Three, Chapter 9). This quote sounds like a tolling bell throughout the final chapters.

Duality and Doubleness. From the first line of the novel, it is clear that Dickens is asking readers to explore the ideas of similarity and dissimilarity, of "twinship" and "oppositeness." London and Paris—the two cities of the title—are like twin sisters in a period of duality. Dickens also uses twins and doubles as characters to further the theme. The physical resemblance of Darnay and Carton implies some sort of deeper metaphysical connection between the two. The connection is first established at Darnay's spy trial. As he sits in the dock, his image is reflected in a mirror positioned above him (Book Two, Chapter 3). As the trial ends, Carton approaches Darnay and Carton's image fills the mirror. Here their images overlap and are interchanged. As they bear a physical resemblance, they appear to bear a metaphysical difference. Darnay is the honorable and justice-seeking man while Carton is the irresolute wastrel. Their connection though is more than skin deep, because both men love Lucie. And ultimately it takes both of them to secure Lucie's happiness. Charles's father and uncle are also twins. His father, while corrupt and often cruel, seems to have the potential to improve, when his uncle, the marquis, is entirely irredeemable. Dickens's use of doubling raises interesting questions about the absolute nature of good and evil and the possibility of reform and redemption.

CRITICAL EXCERPTS

◆

Biographical Studies

Forster, John. *The Life of Charles Dickens*. London: Cecil Palmer, 1872–74.

Forster was Dickens's closest friend and constant correspondent with the author. This biography was written just a few years after Dickens's death, a time when his popularity was enormous.

Charles Dickens, the most popular novelist of the century, and one of the greatest humourists that England has produced, was born at Landport in Portsea on Friday, the seventh of February, 1812. . . . The excitement and sorrow at his death are within the memory of all. Before the news of it even reached the remoter parts of England, it had been flashed across Europe; was known in the distant continents of India, Australia, and America; and not in English-speaking communities only, but in every country of the civilised earth, had awakened grief and sympathy. In his own land it was as

if a personal bereavement had befallen every one. Her
Majesty the Queen telegraphed from Balmoral "her
deepest regret at the sad news of Charles Dickens's
death"; and this was the sentiment alike of all classes of
her people. There was not an English journal that did
not give it touching and noble utterance; and the *Times*
took the lead in suggesting that the only fit resting-
place for the remains of a man so dear to England was
the Abbey in which the most illustrious Englishmen are
laid.

Johnson, Edgar. *Charles Dickens: His Tragedy and
Triumph*. New York: Simon & Schuster, 1952.
  Johnson's work was the first major modern biography of
Dickens.

Dr. Manette's imprisonment symbolizes this supreme
isolation. *Recalled to Life* Dickens once thought of
calling the tale: but though Dr. Manette is recalled to
life by love, he emerges from the Bastille frightfully
mutilated in spirit and but slowly capable of achieving
an unstable regeneration. He has been even more cru-
elly changed by a more dreadful incarceration than
Mr. Dorrit by his confinement in the Marshalsea. If all
of modern society, as *Little Dorrit*, implied, is a
prison, it is more terrible for the man of ability, of
inspiration, of genius, like Charles Dickens, who beats
against its bars more fiercely and understands it more
clearly, though only he, perhaps, can painfully burst
through its doors.

Ackroyd, Peter. *The Life and Times of Charles Dickens*.
London: Hydra Publishing, 2002.
  Ackroyd, a writer of fiction and nonfiction, provides a
contemporary perspective on the life of one of the nine-
teenth century's literary giants.

Dickens was a mercurial character, with enormous vitality, wit and humor, yet he also lived with a sense of loss and longing that constantly reiterated itself in his work. He died having achieved the success and riches he had aspired to, while still harboring the deep sadness he had experienced all his life.

Early Reviews and Interpretations

Stephen, Sir James Fitzjames. "A Tale of Two Cities." *Saturday Review*, December 17, 1859.
    This is a scathing early review from an aristocratic critic.

The broken-backed way in which the story maunders along from 1775 to 1792 and back again to 1760 or thereabouts, is an excellent instance of the complete disregard of the rules of literary composition which have marked the whole of Mr. Dickens's career as an author. No portion of his popularity is due to intellectual excellence.

Shannon, Edgar F. "The Dramatic Element in Dickens." *The Sewanee Review*, July 1913.
    This article, in contrast to Stephen's review, argues that *A Tale of Two Cities* is a mature work by a mature artist.

A Tale of Two Cities occupies, according to all critics, a unique place in Dickens's work. Though it is one of his best novels, it is least like the Dickens who is so much loved for his comic fun and pathetic sentiment. Lacking in humor it is, to be sure, but in it that dramatic power, for which Dickens so early showed a taste, is developed to a very high degree. Writing twenty-two years after he wrote *Oliver Twist*, with much experience in portraying character and inventing situations, he naturally gives us in *A Tale of Two Cities* a far more artistic piece of work.

In this novel we have the plot developed according to the requirements of the drama.

Chesterton, G. K. *Charles Dickens*. London: Methuen & Co., 1949 (22nd edition).

A well-known British author, Chesterton, with his characteristic confidence, tells of the greatness of Dickens. This is a master of the English language describing a giant of English literature.

In everyday talk, or in any of our journals, we may find the loose but important phrase, "Why have we no great men to-day? Why have we no great men like Thackeray, or Carlyle, or Dickens?" Do not let us dismiss this expression, because it appears loose or arbitrary. "Great" does mean something, and the test of its actuality is to be found by noting how instinctively and decisively we do apply it to some men and not to others; above all, how instinctively and decisively we do apply it to four or five men in the Victorian era, four or five men of whom Dickens was not the least. The term is found to fit a definite thing. Whatever the word "great" means, Dickens was what it means. Even the fastidious and unhappy who cannot read his books without a continuous critical exasperation, would use the word of him without stopping to think. They feel that Dickens is a great writer even if he is not a good writer. He is treated as a classic; that is, as a king who may now be deserted, but who cannot now be dethroned. The atmosphere of this word clings to him; and the curious thing is that we cannot get it to cling to any of the men of our own generation. "Great" is the first adjective which the most supercilious modern critic would apply to Dickens. And "great" is the last adjective that the most supercilious modern critic would apply to himself. We dare not claim to be great men, even when we claim to be superior to them.

Critical Interpretations: 1940s and 1950s

House, Humphry. *Dickens World*. Oxford: Oxford University Press, 1941.

A scholarly study of the world of Dickens, from religion to reformism to the relationship of Dickens's work to history. Here is an interesting comment upon the title of the work:

> The word "Dickens" in the title of this book is used as an adjective, as when somebody says he has had a Dickens Christmas. What that conveys varies very widely according to the taste and reading of those who hear it: but popularly it suggests a frosty morning; coaches; delightful inn at the end of the stage; portly landlord; smiling barmaid; brandy by the fireside; smoking joints; good time for all. Hard upon these *Pickwick* items follow mixed impressions of poverty and good cheer and tears of happiness from the *Christmas Books*. To call a man a Dickens person would popularly mean that he was of the Pickwick-Fezziwig-Cheeryble type.

Orwell, George. *Dickens, Dali, and Others*. London: Reynal & Hitchcock, 1946.

In the forties, Orwell's interest in Dickens, and that of a few other literary lights, reawakened a critical interest in Dickens.

> The apologists of any revolution generally try to minimize its horrors; Dickens's impulse is to exaggerate them—and from a historical point he has certainly exaggerated. Even the Reign of Terror was a much smaller thing than he makes it appear. Though he quotes no figures, he gives impressions of a frenzied massacre lasting for years, whereas in reality the whole of the Terror, so far as the number of deaths goes, was a joke compared with one of Napoleon's battles. But the bloody knives

and the tumbrils rolling to and fro create in his mind a special, sinister vision which he has succeeded in passing on to generations of readers. Thanks to Dickens, the very word "tumbril" has a murderous sound; one forgets that a tumbril is only a sort of farm-cart. To this day, to the average Englishman, the French Revolution means no more than a pyramid of severed heads. It is a strange thing that Dickens, much more in sympathy with the ideas of the Revolution than most Englishmen of his time, would have played a part in creating this impression.

Lindsay, Jack. "*A Tale of Two Cities*." *Life and Letters*. July-Sept., 1949.

Contrary to many critics' interpretations of *A Tale of Two Cities*, Lindsay argues that Dickens ultimately saw the French Revolution as a necessary process of progress.

Throughout the book there runs this ambivalent attitude towards the Revolution, shuddering, yet inclining to a deep and thorough acceptance. Not a blank-cheque acceptance, but one based on the subtle dialectics of conflict revealed by the story of Manette. For that story, symbolizing the whole crisis and defining its tensions in the depths of the spirit, makes a serious effort to work out the process of change, the rhythms of give-and-take, the involved struggles with their many inversions and opposed refractions, the ultimate resolution in death and love, in the renewal of life.

Fielding, K. J. *Charles Dickens: A Critical Introduction*. London: Longmanns, Green & Co., Ltd., 1958.

A collection of essays, each focusing on a different major work of Dickens's, this book is a helpful introduction to a number of Dickens's novels.

Even in the darkest scenes there is the steady suggestion of a brighter future in which "the evil of this time" will be "gradually making expiation for itself and wearing out." It is to be found not only in Carton's final version. Each of the three men grouped about Lucie Manette is "recalled to life." Her father regains his, on release from the Bastille; her husband's life is restored by his deliverance from La Force; and Carton finds his by seeking to lose it. As before he gives himself up in place of Darnay, the words of the service at his father's graveside persistently arise in his mind. . . . As he faces death beneath the guillotine they recur again: not simply as seemly pious ending, but as a vital expression of the Christian ethic, which all along has been contrasted with the savagery of the Revolution.

Critical Interpretations: 1960s and 1970s

Marshall, William H. "The Method of *A Tale of Two Cities*." *The Dickensian*. September 1961.

In this article, Marshall explores the religious imagery and import of *A Tale of Two Cities*.

The Christ-like image of Carton is now, though faint and uncertain, inescapable, and—aware of the significance of the blood and wine imagery—we look backward and forward seeking signs. The guilt of Darnay is not really his own but, like Original Sin, that inherited which he himself cannot remove and from the effects of which he must be saved by one who, closely resembling him in his physical being, will take upon himself through his own death the burden of guilt. The guillotine has become for the people what the Cross was formerly: "It was the sign of regeneration of the human race. It superseded the Cross. Models of it were worn on the breasts from which the Cross was discarded, and it was bowed down to and believed in where the Cross was denied." But by his death Sydney Carton makes the guillotine in reality what the people imagine it to be. Carton is clearly the agent through whom good destroys evil.

Cockshut, A. O. J. *The Imagination of Charles Dickens*. New York: New York University Press, 1962.

Cockshut introduces psychological categories into the critical analysis of Dickens and so adds a layer of depth to the discussion of Dickens's work.

Dickens used the imagery of the prison for a steady gaze, without self-pity or hysteria, at the general miseries of life. For although Manette can recover his wits and his human dignity, the prison is lurking within him, ready to regain control, when a new emotional crisis occurs. At the time of his daughter's marriage he goes back to his unconscious shoemaking. Perhaps this incident has a somewhat unreal and contrived air. But its importance in the author's development is nevertheless considerable. Dickens . . . was exceptionally aware of external objects; his imagination was extraordinarily literal: his psychological grasp, which was eventually to become formidable, was slow to develop. His natural tendency, therefore, was to blame all the misery he observed on circumstances, on tyrants, on social conditions. So it was bound to take time for him to comprehend that the prison he was endlessly seeking to describe and understand was, in part, the mental creation of the prisoner, that to strike away the chains and fetters could not solve all the prisoner's problems.

Welsh, Alexander. *The City of Dickens*. Oxford: Oxford University Press, 1971.

Welsh traces commonplace entities within Dickens's works, such as city or home, and places them in a context in order to understand their larger metaphorical import.

The means of expressing value and purpose in fiction vary, and are especially difficult to isolate in the case of

Dickens, whose positive values were vague compared
with the sharpness of his attack on things he disliked.
The means include statement and dialogue, the manipu-
lation of settings and outcome of actions, the endow-
ment of certain characters with special virtues, and often
strained uses of metaphor. Nor are such positive expressions rightly interpreted by the reader except against
what is condemned or repudiated in the novel. The most
obvious expressions of value in Dickens are devoted to
the celebration of home, and are delivered in almost religious tones. But to remark that Dickens and other
Victorians were officially or even spontaneously in love
with home life does not explain very much; and a reason
for taking novels seriously is presumably that they will
help explain as well as illustrate love affairs. My dictio-
nary gives the first definition of *home* as one's dwelling
place or that of one's family; but the second, as one's
abode after death.

Beckwith, Charles E. (editor). *Twentieth Century
Interpretations of* A Tale of Two Cities. Englewood Cliffs,
N.J.: Prentice-Hall, 1972.

This collection of essays provides a number of view-
points and approaches to *A Tale of Two Cities*. It includes
pieces written by George Orwell and George Bernard
Shaw.

More than most works of Dickens's, this book needs at
the present time to be approached thematically. Its special moments and descriptions stand out so unforgettably
for most of us—the implacable grimness of Madame
Defarge; the sudden upsurge of the mob (a kind of pre-
view of their later quest for blood) when the wine is
spilled; the calm of heroism, above life and death alike,
of Sydney Carton—that they tend to obscure some of
the larger and deeper of Dickens's themes—larger and
deeper than, for example, social injustice, revolutionary

violence, or even individual self-sacrifice. These last, of
course, are what the book is "about" in an important
sense that we must not slight. But they are obvious
themes, themes of statement, themes which lend themselves easily to the merely visual apprehension of its
events, hence to the stage and movie career the novel
has enjoyed to the detriment of its appreciation as a work
of literary art—though, as Dickens's comments make it
clear, it was as art he wanted it appreciated. The larger
and deeper themes, on the other hand, lead us in more
profitable directions. First of all backward—to a view of
Dickens's childhood and early life. Then forward—
toward a more modern judgement of this strangely
"modern" book.

Critical Interpretations: 1980s and Beyond

Stone, Henry. *The Night Side of Darkness: Cannibalism,
Passion, Necessity*. Columbus, Ohio: Ohio State University
Press, 1994.

This work explores the darker and more gruesome
aspects of Dickens's writings.

In boyhood, in the *Terrific Register*, in "The Furies of
the Guillotine," Dickens had read about wild cannibalistic female revolutionaries, fierce and depraved, who
paraded with their grisly trophies through the bloody
streets of Paris. These frenzied women, violent and dangerous, "headed processions where the bleeding heads
of butchered innocence were carried in triumph; they
assisted at the savage feasts where the hearts of victims
of loyalty and honour were served up roasted, and were
devoured as the most delicious morsels" (TR 1: 772).
Given obsession with cannibalism, given his cannibalistic
fantasies concerning fierce, empowered women (especially fierce, empowered mothers), given the way the
Terrific Register purveyed to these and similar sensitivi-

ties (conflicted sensitivities) over and over again—it is no wonder that Dickens bought and avidly read each weekly issue of the magazine, and this despite the fact that it made him unspeakably miserable, "frightening" his "very wits out of [his] head." Finally, it is no wonder that the *Terrific Register* creeps into his writings so often, so darkly, and so powerfully.

Schlicke, Paul, (editor). *Oxford Reader's Companion to Dickens*, Oxford: Oxford University Press, 2000.

This is a vast compendium of knowledge about Dickens, his times, and his influences. Here, for instance, is a passage about the advertising and marketing schemes often associated with Dickens's works.

Dickens lived in an era of brash and relentless advertising. Walls, fences, and hoardings in city and village were plastered with urgent bills and posters for all kinds of products and placebos. In "Bill-sticking" (*HW* 22 March 1851; *RP*) Dickens describes the fights between rival groups of bill-stickers covering "the hoarding of Trafalgar Square" with their offerings. . . . Most of Dickens's novels were issued in monthly shilling parts in green paper wrappers, with Dickens's text sandwiched between sections of copious and varied advertisements.

Questions for Discussion

In contemporary literature it is often the case that characters are not clearly cast as "villains" or "heroes." Victorian literature, in contrast, is typified by more straightforward categorizations of characters as good or evil. In *A Tale of Two Cities*, is Dickens more modern or Victorian in the way in which he paints his characters?

Madame Defarge is a well-remembered character for the terror that she inspires. Can you think of any female characters from contemporary movies or books of today that similarly inspire such fear?

Dickens uses the callousness and cruelty of the marquis to represent the injustice of the French aristocracy system. Are there any contemporary political or business figures that you think compare with the marquis?

In *A Tale of Two Cities* Dickens repeatedly uses the "business" of a character to describe that character to the reader. Dickens's description of Mr. Lorry is a good example of this. Dickens appears to see the "business" of many of the characters as central to who the characters are. Does this connecting of person with profession fit with how you think about the relationship between who a person is and what he or she does professionally?

Dickens has been criticized for employing improbable plot twists to motivate his stories (for example, Charles Darnay happens to be the son of the man who imprisoned Dr. Manette, and Charles's uncle is responsible for the deaths of Madame Defarge's brother, father, and sister). Are such plot developments believable to you? Does it matter? In general, what is it about a plot development that makes it believable or unbelievable?

Some modern critics have charged that Sydney Carton's sacrifice does not amount to much of a sacrifice since his life, as Carton readily and repeatedly admits, has not been worth much. Do you agree with these critics' estimation of the value of Sydney Carton's sacrifice?

A Tale of Two Cities has been adapted for the screen more than a dozen times. If you were the casting director for a new movie adaptation of A Tale of Two Cities, who would you cast in the major roles and why?

SUGGESTIONS FOR THE INTERESTED READER

If you liked *A Tale of Two Cities*, you might also be interested in the following:

A Tale of Two Cities; 1991 (DVD and VHS). This widely acclaimed *Masterpiece Theatre* production of the novel is faithful to the book and wonderfully acted.

Hibbert, Christopher. *The Days of the French Revolution*. New York: Perennial, 1999. An excellent introduction for general readers interested in the French Revolution.

Morris Jan. *Heaven's Command: An Imperial Progress*. New York: Harvest Books, 2002. The first volume in a trilogy about the British Empire, this book covers the Victorian era using fascinating stories and anecdotes.

Baroness Orczy. *The Scarlet Pimpernel*. An exciting adventure novel set during the Reign of Terror.